ALSO AVAILABLE FR
ON AMAZON.COM

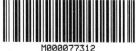

Set deep in the heart of 1980's Texas, *Cast No Shadow* tells the harrowing tale of Vietnam veteran, husband, and father, Beau Moreland. By day he helps his elderly neighbors and watches his son's baseball practice; by night he hunts drug gangs.

In his quest for justice and a more peaceful life for his family, Beau inadvertently sets off an un-stoppable chain of events which will hurtle his family toward a startling and breath-taking conclusion.

"A really powerful piece by someone clearly in control of their craft."

CHAD GRACIA
WINNER SUNDANCE FILM FESTIVAL, 2015

Santi attends his father's funeral out of obligation, only to learn that the man who abandoned him as a child has left a trail of debt, both monetary and spiritual, for him to repay.

Camino Real is an enthralling fable that follows the pilgrimage of Santi as he encounters thieves, priests, magic potions, brutality, and more to discover if he can not only save his father's soul, but perhaps his own.

"Shockingly good... My God, so beautiful."

BRAD JERSAK
AUTHOR AND PATRISTIC SCHOLAR

1st Edition

Cover design and layout by Rafael Polendo (polendo.net)

Cover illustration by Derik Hobbs (derikhobbsillustration.com) and Kevin Catalan (kevincatalan.com)

Interior illustrations by Derik Hobbs (derikhobbsillustration.com)

ISBN 978-1-938480-71-3

This volume is printed on acid free paper and meets ANSI Z39.48 standards.

Printed in the United States of America

QUOIR

Published by Quoir
Oak Glen, California

www.quoir.com

THE WAGES OF GRACE

A NOVEL BY

BRANDON DRAGAN

DEDICATION

For Jami Nicole, Natalie Grace, and Brooklyn Hope.

Dedicated to the memory of Eugene and Lydia Bascharow, Peter and Lydia Dragan, Chris Mastalia, and Brian Busch.

ACKNOWLEDGMENTS

Thanks to Don and Lydia Dragan, Irene Mastalia, Jamie Jean, Derik Hobbs, Dr. Olsen, Dr. Hutchins, Kevin Catalan, Matthew Distefano, Rafael Polendo, Elliott Davis, Savannah Cottrell, my extended family, and everyone else who helped make this possible.

ONE

Forgiveness is the fragrance that the violet sheds
on the heel that has crushed it.

MARK TWAIN

He could taste salt on his tongue as the waves broke around him; whether the gentle flavor lingered because of the misty spray, or the tender touch of her lips, he could not be sure. He sat wrapped in a wool blanket, the sun bright through hazy clouds, the ocean pulsing in perfect rhythm. His feet planted in the cold, wet sand, he had never been more happy. She floated effortlessly over the waves—as far as the moon and as close as his heartbeat. Her soft, rosy lips nearly touched his ear as he gently bit his bottom lip. She softly whispered his name. Her beauty was ravishing, and she didn't even know it. Delicate strands of perfect ash brown hair fell smoothly on her bare, freckled shoulders. He would have tied a millstone around his neck and plunged himself into the sea for just one more kiss.

In the next instant, there were rocks below, jagged and sharp. He stood forty feet above on the edge of the precipice, while the rough sea crashed spectacularly against the boulders below. Birds picked ruthlessly at the carcasses of dead fish, unwilling to leave them mercifully to their eternal rest. The tips of the rocks gleamed in the gray sunlight—the raging sea roaring against them deafeningly. He closed his eyes and imagined flinging himself toward them, but he knew from previous experience that he would only wake again in his bed, dejected but unharmed.

He recoiled in surprise when he heard his name again. He looked up and saw her in the distance, flowing white dress whipping in the wind. She stood erect at sea, his very own Venus, beckoning him. Tears streamed down his wind beaten face as he stretched his arms toward her, but the distance between them was impassable. His old muscles cramped with longing—longing for just one more touch, one more embrace, one more tender word. The rain began to fall heavily as it always did, and the wind began to howl as he was certain it would, and he knew that once more he had to say goodbye. Too great, however, was the disquiet of his soul to utter mere words.

Slowly, silently, she began to sink. He watched for the thousandth time in horror, unable to intervene. He also knew that she would return the following night, and that the aching in his soul would never dissipate, would never relent. It has been said that time heals all wounds, but this is untrue—some wounds only turn gangrenous with time.

There was unremitting sorrow in this subconscious nightly ritual, but there was also the numbing consolation that, at least he had seen her again, in all her glory.

His eyelids fluttered rapidly in the dark as his mind's eye watched her calmly submerge in the black, foaming sea. He told her that he loved her, and that was all. She sank to her waist, her breasts, her neck, her nose, and her eyes without panic, without struggle or fear. Then, he could see her no more.

Her name was Hope.

September 3, 1990

The sun rose gently through the clearing that our wise sage knew as his home. The trees stood tall and strong, full of foliage and confidence in their old age. The woods were already alive, an endless array of creatures stirring, some waking from a warm night's slumber, some seeking repose after a warm night's hunt. After all, there is nothing quite as comforting as going to bed with a full stomach.

A long, slender cat nimbly abandoned the woods and entered the clearing. He was mostly black, but had white markings on his underside and some patches of white on his chin and face. He had already eaten. His name was Duke.

Having already eaten, however, would not dissuade him from walking through the tall grass near the tree line, then the freshly mowed grass near the long, winding gravel driveway, up the wooden steps and through the hole in the screen that the old man had cut for him. Duke did this for several reasons. First, the old man would be waking soon and would naturally come to feed the cat on the back porch, as he had done every morning since the cat could remember. His second reason was simply the weather. It was going to be hot and sunny—yet again—and he knew that, aside from the creek down by the old barn, the back porch was the best place to catch a breeze and a nap.

Inside the century-old farm house, on the second floor, a right turn and a brief walk up the hall from the stairway, Thierry Laroque laid awake in bed, mesmerized by the rhythmic pulse of the ceiling fan. If he stared at the white paint on the ceiling through the blades as they silently whirled, it almost appeared that they changed direction. He knew this was an optical illusion, but would try it several times each summer morning, almost as if to reassure himself that the laws of physics and nature were still in effect after another night.

He turned to the analog clock radio on the worn nightstand beside the bed: it was 6:04am. He had slept in.

Retirement, however, affords such simple luxuries as this to those lucky enough to see it. He didn't have anywhere to go, or anything particularly pressing to do that day, aside from lunch with the judge and a quick run to the supermarket, but nevertheless, after all those years of waking up at 5:30 sharp, he couldn't help but feel a pang of guilt for wasting part of the daylight in sleep. He rose quietly and sat on the edge of the bed, stretching his arms towards the sky. He stood up and checked on his old friend who slept quietly behind the clock radio, next to an antique copy of *The Count of Monte Cristo*, and thanked God that still another night had passed without cause to use it. He put on his jeans from the night before, holstered that very handgun to his belt, and simultaneously prayed that this day would too pass without cause to use it.

He walked slowly and wearily to the bathroom at the end of the hall, brushed his teeth, and sprayed his deodorant on. He then got about the business of shaving. Thierry and shaving had never quite had an amicable relationship, but he still did it every morning. He couldn't help but think, that in some ways, the act of shaving his face was a lot like the act of life itself. Every morning, new opportunities would arise, new passions and energies would spring to life, and every morning, for one reason or another, he would shave them back to the skin. And there they were, covered in lather, clinging to the sides of the white porcelain sink as if begging not to be rinsed down and forgotten. They knew as well as the man did that there would be more of them to deal with tomorrow morning, and that the only thing truly gained by the process was sore skin.

Back to the bedroom he went to select a clean shirt from the closet, and down the stairs to start coffee and breakfast. The eggs would be fried in butter, the sausage would be spicy, the berries would be fresh, and the coffee would be black. That was the way it was every morning, and while there were endless other possibilities for breakfast, Thierry preferred this combination to any other.

The man's border collie, shepherd mix, could still be heard snoring contently under the big oak desk in the library, but as soon as the cast iron skillet hit the stove, Useless, who was actually quite the contrary despite his name, sprung to life. He raced into the living room, through the eat-in portion of the kitchen, and slid across the tiled floor until he bumped clumsily into the back of the man's legs as he stood over the stove.

"Well, good morning, there," Thierry laughed, as he regained his balance. "I see you're up and ready to go."

The canine sneezed.

"Bless you," the man replied. "You were in quite a heavy sleep when I came downstairs, weren't you?"

The dog tilted his head, his large pink tongue dangling from one corner of his mouth.

"What were you dreaming about so contently, huh?"

Useless straightened his face and snorted. The man chuckled and threw the dog a chunk of sausage which was caught mid-air and consumed in one motion.

Thierry then made his way with his plate and coffee mug to the back door and out onto the porch. Useless was hardly a step behind him. Once they reached the porch, however, the dog immediately began his search for the cat, who, as previously mentioned, was also on the porch at this time every day. The two creatures got along as best they could, and by way of greeting every morning, Useless would quickly and clumsily sniff the cat's underbelly. It could be counted on that Duke would tolerate this behavior for precisely four seconds, and would then let out a guttural growl that would end up as a low, elongated hiss. Such a simple warning was always good enough for Useless, who would then back off and collapse at the man's feet.

Thierry rocked back and forth, sipping his coffee and taking in another brilliant sunrise. The rays of the sun were already quite warm. It had been a sweltering summer and there was almost nothing that the old man disliked more than heat and humidity. How, he asked himself, did he end up, then, in Middle Tennessee? It must have been the music.

He loved the area, however. It was, after all, a wonderful place to live. Nashville, a growing and friendly city, was a mere twenty miles to his west, as the crow flies, and the town where he had made a living for many years was also pleasant and rapidly expanding. He lived another five miles or so to the northwest of the town. Thierry was fortunate enough to own a couple hundred acres of woods, streams, and raw, untouched land, some of which gently hugged the Cumberland

River to his north. In the middle of all of this natural beauty and ruggedness, there was the small clearing described earlier, where Thierry's humble home sat. The clearing was no bigger than three or four acres, and housed not only the main farm house, but also a large mechanic's garage, a couple storehouses, an underground storm shelter, and an old, Civil War-era barn, which sat dilapidated, and in much the same condition as it had been when Thierry came into possession of the estate some time earlier. Aside from the weather, he felt that Tennessee offered everything a man could hope for—low taxes, cheap land, and friendly people—and he happened to be a proponent of all three.

He ate breakfast slowly and enjoyed the weather as long as he could. Duke and Useless were both asleep by the time he finished.

After a couple hours of tinkering with his truck and moving some tools around in the garage, Thierry returned to the old farm house, showered in the bathroom on the second floor, and dressed again for his trip to town. He climbed in his old, steady Ford truck and began the slow, winding journey through the woods that surrounded his property. His driveway was almost a half mile long, curling tightly around trees and through the dense summer brush. The gravel was, in some places, completely overtaken by grass and weeds, and in some places closer to the creek, by Spanish moss. After a few moments, he was at the exit of his property, a small opening in the forest that would hardly be recognized as a driveway by someone passing by. Thierry preferred it this way.

In hardly no time, he was in the center of town, past the old brick courthouse with the granite steps and marble columns, and parked conveniently on the street outside of Warren's Restaurant on the town square. The air conditioning in his Ford always ran efficiently and freezing cold, and the old man regretted having to leave the truck at all.

Inside Warren's, he was greeted by the effervescent Nicole Burns, the seventeen year-old daughter of Warren Burns, the restaurant's proprietor. She practically ran to Thierry and embraced him like a child would her grandfather. Being fifteen minutes before twelve, the restaurant had only a couple other patrons, neither of which Thierry recognized, but he did feel them glance over at him as he was trapped in Nicole's death-grip of a hug. She finally let go.

"Where have you been?" she asked, as if he had at some point suddenly and without warning disappeared.

"Retired, darling," he replied tenderly.

"That's no excuse!" she said loudly, in her perfectly charming Tennessee drawl. She slapped his shoulder playfully.

"I know, I know—But shouldn't you be in school?"

"I was. I'm a senior now, and my last class ends at eleven," she answered proudly.

"I see—" he began to reply, but was cut short by the emergence of her father from the kitchen.

"Hey rascal!" he shouted excitedly. "I thought I heard your voice! It's been forever!"

The two men warmly shook hands and embraced quickly and with strong pats on the back, as men do.

"I know, your sweet waitress was just reminding me that it's been all of, what, three weeks since I've been in for a good meal?"

"Has it only been three weeks?" Warren replied in his own thick accent. "It feels like it's been a lifetime! After all, you were in here practically every day for ten years! I guess when you're used to seeing someone every day, it feels like forever when all of a sudden they're not around as much anymore!"

"Yes, I apologize," Thierry sincerely replied, placing his right hand over his heart for dramatic embellishment. "I promise to visit more often than I have."

"You better," Nicole replied in a good-humored, yet serious tone while pointing her slender finger at him like a mother warning a child of the consequences of his behavior.

"Yes, ma'am," Thierry quickly replied as his eyebrows shot up. He glanced over at her father who shook his head in a mixture of pride and fascination.

"So what'll it be?" she asked, reverting back to waitress mode.

"Well, I'm meeting the judge, but drinks would be lovely—sweet tea for the judge; un-sweet for me."

She rolled her eyes sarcastically.

"You're such a Yankee," she muttered playfully as she turned back towards the kitchen. On the way, she stopped by the table of their other guests to check in. The patron and the owner sat at a table for two by the front window, which overlooked the quietly bustling square.

"You did a great job," Thierry commented.

"Thank you," he answered with a quick glance toward the heavens, "By the grace of God…"

"Yes, and I must say, having been a hermit for a few months now, it's refreshing to see her again."

Warren smiled warmly.

"Welp, I've got to get back to the kitchen, but it was so good to see you. Please stop in more often—if not for me, then for Nicole. She misses you a lot."

"I'll make certain I do that."

"Yours is on the house today, by the way."

"You don't have to do that."

"Just come by and see us more often, ok?"

"Thank you. I sure will."

At that moment, Nicole returned from the kitchen with the tea. She walked almost silently with innate and inadvertent elegance. The two men looked up at her and smiled.

"What are you two talkin' about?" she asked accusingly as she put the drinks on the table.

"You," her father said playfully.

She stuck her tongue out at him.

"You're on the clock, get back to work," she ordered teasingly.

Warren stood up quickly and saluted. He shook Thierry's hand firmly and walked off to the kitchen chuckling.

"So, darling, what have you been up to these last few months?"

"Well," Nicole said slowly and blushed a little, "I'm seeing a boy."

"You are, are you?"

"Yes, his name's Kevin."

She slipped into the seat across from Thierry that her father had recently vacated.

"Kevin, hmm," Thierry pondered. "Do I know him?"

"Probably not," she replied slowly.

"Well? Tell me about him."

The pace of her words picked up eagerly.

"Well, he's really cute, and really tall, and really strong."

"Strong in what way, my dear? Strength has a lot of different applications."

"Well, he's the star quarterback for the Tigers, and there's lot of talk about him playing college ball for the Vols, too—he's that good."

"Ok, so strong in the athletic sense. That's wonderful. What's he like?"

"He's popular, really funny and outgoing, and he's really cute," her sparkling brown eyes beamed with girlish excitement as she raved about her new beau.

"Yes, you mentioned the cute part earlier," Thierry quipped. "How long have you been seeing this boy?"

"About a month."

"And how has he treated you so far?"

"Very well, he's taken me out a few times and I've had a lot of fun. He really makes me laugh a lot."

"And are you being a good girl with this new boy?"

She clicked her tongue against her top row of teeth in censure.

"I can't believe you would even ask that, Mr. Terry!" she reproached him while mispronouncing his name, as many Southerners did. Thierry was used to it by this point, although he wasn't particularly fond of the name *Terry*.

"Well, sweetheart, you're growing up, and I thought it would be unacceptable for me not to ask, given our relationship over these many years."

"I know, and I appreciate it. And yes, we are very close, and always will be," she said, taking his hand in hers gently. "And I've been very proud of him because he hasn't tried anything aside from just a peck on the cheek, so far. And believe me, being a star athlete and so cute and all, he's done a lot of things with a lot of girls. But he knows where I stand, and like I said, he's been a perfect gentleman so far."

"Well, good, my dear, I'm glad to hear it," he said as he placed his other hand on top of hers gently. "You're very mature."

"Oh, I know," she said seriously, and then stuck her tongue out at him.

At that moment, the bell rang as the door opened and the judge walked in suddenly. He was a short, pudgy man, and on this day he wore a short-sleeved white dress shirt with a red tie and black slacks. He was sweating profusely, wiping his nearly bald head with his handkerchief as he entered.

"Hey Judge!" Nicole stood from the table and waved casually.

"Hi, Nicole!" he replied with boisterous robustness.

"And where have you been?" she said accusingly in much the same way she had to Thierry upon his entrance earlier.

"Sweetie, I was here for lunch yesterday!"

"But no breakfast today!"

"Sweetheart, I love your *deddy's* cooking and all, but do I have to eat here three times-a-day?"

"No!" she half-yelled back, then looked down at Thierry with a quick smile and then replied to the judge in a lower tone of voice, "Just two times… we're closed for dinner."

After a quick laugh, the judge greeted Thierry warmly and plopped down heavily in his chair at the table. Nicole greeted another set of patrons entering and seated them in the far corner.

"She's a piece of work, huh?" the judge joked in his thick Georgia accent.

"Yes, yes she is. And how are you my friend?"

"Oh, I'm great, me and Mabel are busy, busy, but doing great."

"Busy, that's good, right?"

"It's better than bein' *dey-ed*," the judge joked loudly.

The newest patrons glanced over quickly from the far corner.

"So what's been keeping you so busy?"

"The grandkids were in from Atlanta a couple weeks ago, and Mabel's been keeping me running with helpin' her *peck* out wallpaper and stain for refinishing the floors, and oh, God, I love her to death, but that woman takes forever to make a decision!"

Just then, Nicole came back to their table and took their lunch orders.

"And how was court this morning?" Thierry inquired of his friend.

"Oh, *Gawd*, don't get me started," the judge replied in an exasperated tone. "The old man kicks the bucket, his will been sealed up in a safe behind an old Gifford painting or somethin' like it. The new wife—the twenty-five year old—wants all of it. The old wife—the sixty-five year old he left for the young one two years ago—wants all of it, too. His four kids want it all, too. So the will gets unsealed and the creditors start pouring in and instead of a couple mil' sitting in the bank, there's a hundred grand in some life insurance policy that was taken out by one of his other wives who's been dead for ten years, and there's no living beneficiary listed. And so now everyone that's still alive is clamoring over that. Awful! It's just awful how kin can treat each other in such a way! And all over money! Nobody even cares to remember the old man... Well, after all, it's probably for the best—what a pompous asshole he was."

Thierry laughed at the sheer ridiculousness of it all, and even though he didn't know the family involved, he had known enough human beings to get the picture.

"If I could find a way, I'd make sure nobody got a damned cent, and I wouldn't care if it hair-lipped every one of 'em."

"I can't say I blame you," Thierry said quietly. "Who was he anyway?"

"Nobody. A total nobody," the judge replied seriously. "Just a brat that come from old money. His *deddy* owned a half million acres of farm land that'd been passed down from his great, great *granddeddy* or something like it, I reckon. And his son sold most of it off, for pennies on the dollar just to get rid of it. Lived in that big house on Carter Avenue off Division, you know the one, sat up real high and overlooked the river?"

Thierry nodded in affirmation. "Yeah, I know it."

"Well, he let it go to hell in a hand-basket. Place looks like shit now."

"What a shame," Thierry said in genuine sorrow.

"It's a *damn* shame… But hey, come to think of it, the land you got from old JC, well, he bought from this old man. There's still probably another couple hundred acres that touch your property, if you're interested. You can probably get it cheap from whoever ends up with it if you make 'em a cash offer. It ain't nothin' but fields and woods, but it's awful pretty land."

"Well, I appreciate the notice, but I don't know if I'm in a position to buy more acreage right now."

"Well, I understand, completely. Hell, who is now-a-days? I just wanted to make sure you knew about it, that's all."

"Certainly appreciated, my friend," Thierry replied sincerely.

"Change your mind and you let me know, okay?"

Thierry nodded thoughtfully.

The two old friends ate, talked about the weather and Mabel's plans for the renovation of several of the judge's rooms, and ended their lunch with a warm handshake and the mutual promise to get together again soon. They left Nicole a nice tip and headed out—Thierry to the grocery store, the judge back to the courthouse.

Thierry cruised the aisles of what was still, at that point, a mom and pop grocery store, and ran into several people he knew. There were polite exchanges, smiles and nods, and even several affectionate hugs and handshakes.

At the checkout counter, he ran into Adam Buford, a young man of about thirty with Down syndrome. He had worked at the grocery store for more than ten years as a bag-boy and was also well-liked, well-respected, and well-known by those who habitually shopped there. Adam's father, Chester Buford, operated a machine shop that Thierry, in his auto repair business, had patronized for more than a decade. The two men had built quite the business relationship over the years and had also developed quite the friendship. Chester and his wife Abigail adopted Adam when he was a toddler, knowing full-well the challenges they would face as a family, and as a result, Thierry had always thought very highly of them.

Thierry paid with cash for his groceries, as people did back in those days, and began to load the last of his bags into his cart with Adam's help.

"Hi, Mr. Terry!" Adam said excitedly.

"Well, hello, my old friend," Thierry replied warmly. "How have you been?"

"Good, Mr. Terry—real good!"

"Well that's good to hear, Adam. Anything in particular that has you in such a good mood? Maybe a new girlfriend?"

Adam laughed nervously and waved his hand at Thierry to dismiss such a silly accusation.

"My dad said he was gonna take me camping next weekend! He said we were gonna go fishing and sleep outside!"

"That's great, Adam! Have you ever been camping before?"

"Oh, lots, Mr. Terry! But not in a real long time! I think I'm gonna catch the biggest fish I ever caught before!"

"Oh, really! What makes you think that?"

"My dad said he was gonna get me some new lures that were gonna work better than the old ones I got."

"That's great Adam," Thierry replied while quietly reaching in his pocket. "Well, it was good seeing you, and I've got to get these home before they rot, but please say hi to your dad for me, okay?"

"I sure will, Mr. Terry!"

With that, Thierry shook the young man's hand, leaving in it a folded twenty dollar bill.

Adam stared down at the money at first as if he'd had no idea how it got there, but then looked up quickly as Thierry walked away, pushing his grocery cart through the automatic doors at the exit. Adam suddenly ran after him and took him by the arm.

"Is this for me, Mr. Terry?" he asked bewilderedly.

"It sure is, my friend."

Adam swallowed hard while looking from the money in his hand to Thierry and back quickly. "But… what for?"

"For some extra lures—if you're gonna catch the biggest fish you've ever caught, you're going to need plenty of good lures."

"Thanks, Mr. Terry! I promise I'll bring you a picture of the fish I catch!"

"Do that, Adam—I'll be excited to see it!"

With that, Adam abruptly hugged Thierry in what can only be described as a bear hug, and didn't release him for a full ten seconds. The two men said goodbye, again, thanked each other again, shook hands again, and then parted ways... again—Thierry back to his truck in the parking lot, and Adam back inside to his work. The young man would spend the rest of the day thinking about the lures he would buy with the money Thierry gave him, and needless to say there would be a smile plastered on his face until he went to bed that night.

September 4, 1990

Adam had inspired him. Thierry was up before the night ended. He poured some coffee into a thermos and left food on the porch for Duke, who had not yet emerged from his hunt. Thierry ate a handful of berries, woke Useless with a quick whistle, grabbed his fishing gear, and began walking through the dense woods which surrounded his home toward the river. The loyal dog followed after him sleepily.

He passed the old barn on his right and followed his usual path toward his favorite fishing spot. The path itself could hardly be considered a path, as it had only been roughly worn through his years of following the same steps through the brush. It was not uncommon for him to come across a herd of deer who would quickly scamper off. Useless had learned not to make a fuss after them. In fact, he hardly ever barked. This was in part because his owner disliked incessant barking. It was also due to the fact that the first few times the dog tried to chase the deer, he returned, panting, to Thierry's heel after about thirty seconds, wearing a look on his face that said, "Wow, they're really fast."

Cracks of low sunlight began to stream through tree limbs as he approached his spot along the river bank. The water, crystal clear, was low for the time of year, but still sparkled. The man poured some coffee and then breathed in the isolation and the beauty around him.

After an hour or so and no luck, a branch snapped close by. Useless shot up at the same time Thierry instinctively put his hand on his pistol. Steps, coming closer and closer from the east. Rhythmic, steady, heavy—definitely not deer. Thierry squinted in the distance and Useless began to silently bare his upper teeth. The man was able to make out the lower half of a human, which made him half-relieved, half-anxious at the approach. It was not often Thierry ran into another soul in this place. Not willing to give up the element of surprise in the unlikely event that this person wanted trouble, Thierry waited silently, peering intently as the person moved closer. When the person finally cleared through the bush where Thierry could see his face, he instantly recognized Nate Hendricks, the son of Wilson Hendricks, who had purchased Thierry's business upon his retirement.

"Nate!" he called out.

The young man grabbed his chest in surprise, and then squinted to see who had called him.

"Oh, hey, Mr. Terry! You scared the devil outta me," the young man panted as he approached.

"The same could just about be said here," Thierry laughed.

"I know this is kinda close to your place, but I didn't ever expect to see someone out here this early."

"Neither did I," Thierry said, extending his hand as Nate walked toward him. "What are you doing out here?"

The young man paused for a moment. "Just walking, I guess."

Thierry looked at him with slight bewilderment. "Nate, you've got to be six miles from home. How long have you been walking?"

"What time is it now?"

Thierry glanced at his watch. "About six-thirty."

Nate wiped his glistening forehead with the palm of his hand. "'Bout four hours, then."

"Four hours? Nate, were you lost?"

"No, sir."

"I didn't think so," Thierry replied with a smile. "So why are you all the way out here at such a time?"

"Just thinkin', I guess."

"Anything in particular?"

"Well," he hesitated. "I've got a girl on my mind."

The old man nodded and smiled. "That's a reason to be walking in the woods all night. I've done it myself." Nate smiled, a bit nervously. "Who is she, if you don't mind me asking?"

The young man stayed silent for a minute, thinking through his words before he said them. "You know her."

"I do?"

"It's Nicole Burns."

Thierry subconsciously ran his tongue over the scar on his lower lip when he heard her name.

"I see."

"Well, Mr. Terry... I know this sounds crazy, 'cos I'm only nineteen n' all... but I think I love her."

Thierry thought quickly back to his conversation with Nicole the day before and felt slightly saddened for Nate. Did he have a clue about Kevin?

"Why is that crazy?" Thierry asked.

The young man shrugged. "'Cos I've heard people say you can't really fall in love so young, but... truth is, I've loved her for years now."

Thierry was a bit surprised to hear such a confident declaration from a young man who wouldn't normally display such emotion.

"Why are you walking in the woods just now, then?"

"'Cos I think she might be in trouble."

"Trouble?" he asked nervously, "What kind of trouble?"

"She's started seeing this guy named Kevin—"

So he did have a clue about Kevin.

"—And, he's just no good for her," Nate continued on. "Sure, he's a jock, and he's popular and all, and I just... I'm..."

Thierry thought he might probe Nate's motives: "Jealous?"

Nate looked up sharply and shook his head firmly.

"No, I'm not jealous," he said with certainty. "I'm worried about her."

After a moment of silence, Thierry pressed, "Are you going to tell me why you're worried?"

"You see, Kevin... well, he has a certain reputation around school, but—it's hard to put into words—it's more than that. I don't think he means any good by her. In fact, I'm sure of it." Thierry watched as the look of concern on Nate's face morphed into anger. "He's really only after one thing, and he'll do anything to get it—lie, cheat, break her heart—"

"Now hold on a minute," Thierry interrupted with a wave of his hand. "Just how well do you know this Kevin fellow?"

"Not very well," Nate shrugged. "I've watched him play ball a few times—"

"And was there anything in his play on the football field that would indicate that he's a vile person?"

Nate shook his head. "But I have run into him a few times over the weekends."

Thierry raised his eyebrows quizzically. "Same question," he said.

Nate hesitated and was starting to get upset. "No, nothing in particular, but Mr. Terry—I know that kind of guy. Deep down in my gut, there's just something not right about him."

Thierry put up both hands to let Nate know that he was backing off that line of interrogation.

"Is he a violent person?"

"He might of been in a fight or two, but nothing more than what jocks get into here and there."

"Then, your concern is not with Kevin." Nate gave a quizzical glance; Thierry shrugged his shoulders. "Your concern is with Nicole."

"Wait a second, what do you mean by that?" Nate blurted in a halfway accusatory tone.

"Logic, my boy, logic," Thierry answered. "If you're worried about Nicole, but have no reason to believe Kevin to be the cause of harm, then you must believe that she is capable of harming herself." The young man shook his head as if the words were echoing around inside it. "Let me ask you this," Thierry continued, "Is she a virtuous girl?"

"Of course she is," he answered defensively. "She's an angel."

"From what I know of her, I would tend to agree with you."

After processing for a moment, Nate quickly asked: "So what's your point?"

"The point is, that if Nicole is virtuous and Kevin is no fiend, you have nothing to fret about." The young man nodded silently—he looked pitifully unconvinced. "Nate," Thierry began in a comforting tone, "I know what you're going through. May I give you a couple pieces of advice, from a friend to a friend? First, don't worry about her—she's a big girl with a good head on her shoulders and a good upbringing. Second, and I know this will be hard to hear, but there are other fish in the sea."

Nate rolled his eyes in despair upon hearing those words. Thierry put his hand on the young man's shoulder. "It's true," he said gently. "You're a young man with a lot going for you, and there are plenty of other young fish with big hair and silly makeup in the sea."

The young man looked back down at his shoes and laughed under his breath. "And one more thing," Thierry said as Nate lifted his eyes again, "If you really love her—"

"I do," Nate interjected passionately. "I really do—"

"Ok, ok," Thierry said. "If you really love her, you'll be there for her when she needs a friend—and for no other reason but that she needs a friend."

Nate sighed loudly and nodded in agreement.

"You're a pretty good person to know, Mr. Terry. I'm glad I ran into you like this," he said genuinely, extending his hand, which Thierry warmly shook.

"Well, thank you. And you're a good kid. Keep your head up, ok?"

Nate nodded and then started to walk home.

Thierry sat and thought for a while. At one point, Useless got up and moved to the bank of the river. He lapped the cool, clean water for what must have been five whole minutes. *It is getting warm*, the man thought to himself.

"Well, my friend," he said to the dog, "what do you say we pack it up and get something to eat?"

Thierry gathered his fishing gear and thought for a moment how disappointing it was to have not caught anything, but was also thankful for running into Nate in such a way. He thought about how hard it would be to take his own advice. He couldn't help but feel worried about Nicole and he didn't even know why. Perhaps it was because he had had such a special bond with her since she was a small girl, but now that he was retired and not in town six days per week, felt like that had faded. Maybe it was because she was growing up and he was nervous about letting her go.

Letting her go... he laughed to himself. What control had he ever had over her? He had always tried to be a mentor, tried to be someone she could count on, and he had done well on that account, but she wasn't his child to raise, nor was she his daughter to set free. She was her own woman and would make her own choices. There was nothing he could do but be there if she ever needed him. Oddly enough, Nate's inner monologue followed much the same stream of thought.

He tossed his keys down on the kitchen table covered in the checkerboard tablecloth, and poured some water in one bowl and dog food in the other for Useless. The man patted his canine friend gently on the head and said, "Good boy." The dog was patient enough to briefly show that he appreciated the affection, but not patient enough to let it keep him from eating. Thierry glanced up and noticed the light flashing on his answering machine on the counter. He poured himself a glass of cold water and then strolled over to listen to the message.

At first, the static was so bad that Thierry thought the person calling must have had a bad connection. He was about to erase the message when he heard a distinct voice cursing in the background. Every muscle in his body froze. He hadn't heard that voice in at least fifteen years. Static continued, then the sound of a whistle, then people talking in the background. Then there was that voice again:

"Hello... Hello?" it shouted angrily. "Thierry? Thierry? Pick up the damn phone!"

More static, more commotion. Thierry suddenly felt sick.

"It's your brother, Marty," said the old voice in a thick New York accent. "Listen, I'm gonna be down in your neck of the woods and was hoping—Damn it! Hey, leave that right there! Don't you touch it!"

Feeling as if his knees were about to give out, Thierry collapsed into his chair.

"Sorry," the voice on the answering machine continued, "But look, I'd like to see if," {*inaudible*}, "and that's about it. I'll try to ring you again when I get in—"

More static, more commotion, then the long dial tone.

Finally, there was silence.

Thierry sat stunned, as if he had been punched in the gut. He covered his mouth with both hands and his eyes watered. He then stood up quickly and erased the message. He didn't want to hear that voice again. In fact, he didn't even want to hear the phone ring knowing that Marty would try to call again. He calmly took it off the hook and placed the headset on the counter.

He sat in his library for hours, gently swiveling back and forth behind the desk. He tried to figure out why his brother would want to see him now, after all these years. He couldn't bear the thought of laying eyes on him.

As if snapping out of a trance, he suddenly realized that he was sitting in the dark. He flipped the desk lamp on and checked his watch. 9:22pm. He turned the light back off and went into the kitchen. The old man was hungry, as he hadn't really eaten at all that day, but was more nervous about eating something and immediately throwing it back up. He double checked the locks on the doors and headed up to bed.

The dream that haunted him every night returned, but this time, with a twist. He was not standing on the precipice this time. He was cautiously balanced on jagged rocks. He strained his eyes to the sea to catch a glimpse of his love, but she was not there. He strained his ears for her gentle voice, but only heard the waves savagely crashing against the rocks. He turned to his right to find her, but she was not there. He turned to his left, and far off in the distance, he could see a white dress billowing in the violent wind. He couldn't run to her because of the waves and the rocks, but he began a steady, frantic dash along the slippery surfaces. Several times, he slipped and felt his ribs burn with pain as he crashed down on the hard rocks. He lifted himself up despite the pain—he could not abandon his love in the hour of her need. He trudged on, only to slip again. After what seemed like an eternity, out of breath and staggering from the intense pain, he came upon her.

She was lying across several large boulders, on her back as angry waves crashed all around. He slid across the platform of one rock on his knees and took her hand in his. He kissed it rapturously over and over, her fingers, her palm, her wrist, her forearm. And then, in a moment of clarity, he realized she was cold. He held her beautiful arm, limp and stiff in his hands, and stared at it in shock for a moment. He then turned his eyes to her face and to his horror, saw it badly bruised, blood pooled behind her glassy eyes. His senses racing back to him, he for the first time noticed the unnatural position of her body upon the rocks. He slid his hand under her head to caress it, only to feel the contents of her skull leaking out in a steady stream.

He recoiled in horror and slipped off the wet surface of the crag. He fell to a rock four feet below and saw stars for a moment, then felt in full force the dull pain where the back of his head hit the surface below. He simply laid there, staring up at the cliffs above—some forty or fifty feet up—his usual vantage point during this dream.

He found himself asking—*Why is this dream so different, so violent?*

As his vision slowly came back into focus, he noticed the figure of a young man, standing on the cliff, peering down below. At first, he thought he might be looking at an apparition of himself. He sat up and strained his eyes. A huge wave suddenly roared over his head, and he awoke, sitting straight up in bed and covered in sweat, but in the split second before the dream was over, he recognized the young man atop the cliff, staring down at the broken, beaten love of his life.

It was his brother Marty.

September 6, 1990

Thierry sipped his coffee and stared out over the field that dissolved into black woods to the north. The air was stifling and not a star could be seen above. Crickets and tree frogs chirred their monotonously relentless songs. Even in the oppressive humidity, Thierry shivered under his blanket. He thought he might be getting the flu. He watched Duke trot from the woods blissfully, the success of his hunt obvious in the felicity of his step. The dexterous cat ducked inside the screen and leapt gracefully on the empty chair beside him. Thierry mindlessly stroked his head. Duke's raucous purring nearly drowned out the song of the insects and amphibians.

The man dreaded the idea of speaking with Marty, but as the sun came up, he started to realize that he was under no obligation to speak to his brother. After all, it had already been more than a decade since he'd heard from him. In fact, if it wasn't for the occasional newspaper article featuring a quote or a photo of his Wall Street super-broker brother, he wouldn't have even known if he was dead or alive. Beams of light began to peek through the dense trees and Thierry began to feel better. He, after all, didn't care if Marty wanted to speak to him; he did not want to speak to Marty.

His spirit revived, Thierry realized how hungry he was—he hadn't eaten in nearly twenty-four hours. He had breakfast, and then walked his beaten driveway to get the daily newspaper. The cracks of sunlight earlier visible were again overtaken by clouds and the sky turned various shades of gray without raining. Once back inside, he grabbed another cup of coffee and sat again on the back porch, newspaper in hand.

Sports first, as usual. *The Yankees won!* A narrow 2–1 victory over the mediocre California Angels would not, however, salvage their dismal season. He shook his head, remembering the glory days and wondering if, in the modern era of free agency, expansion, and financial considerations, his team would ever dominate as they once had. With a disappointed sigh, he flipped back to the front page.

"Saddam Hussein urges Arabs to rise up against Western powers."

I don't think that will end well for him, thought the old man as he continued skimming from article to article.

"Bob Newhart turns 61..."

This brought a smile to his face. It also made him feel old.

"Wall Street firm executive declares bankruptcy… page C5." Thierry licked his pointer finger and flipped to C5 to begin reading. "Investment firm Graham, Bates, and Leiberman CFO Martin Laroque has been relieved of his position at the firm just one day after filing for bankruptcy in federal court…"

Thierry put the paper down in shock. This was impossible! His brother Marty had an enormous fortune and was lauded as one of the top financial and investment minds in the world. *How did this happen?*

The article went on without much detail at all, simply stating that Mr. Laroque took a leave of absence back in July for undisclosed "personal reasons." It went on with a long statement from Collin Graham, Chairman of the Board, that Mr. Laroque's personal financial instability in no way effected the company's wellbeing, nor did it effect the security of the company's many investors. Graham continued, "Our clients and the general public should have no apprehensions about this situation, as it has been appropriately handled internally, and is completely contained to Mr. Laroque's personal circumstances. We wish Mr. Laroque the best success in all of his future endeavors…"

He put the paper down again and gazed at the tips of gray clouds as they floated by, the low roll of thunder humming in the distance. He couldn't believe what he had read and was certain that this had something to do with the phone call he'd received out of the blue the previous day. He was selfishly interested to learn what had happened to his brother, but had never been more disinterested to get involved in the situation. He did, however, decide that it was pointless to leave the phone off the hook indefinitely. He walked to the kitchen and picked the handset up. He could hear the dull, "beep beep beep," tone that was meant to alert him that the phone was off the hook. He gently placed the handset back on the holder, hanging on the wall beside him. At that moment, Thierry was startled by frenzied barking in the front room.

"Useless!" This usually hushed the dog immediately, but he continued barking ferociously. "Useless!" he yelled again as he walked into the living room.

At that moment, he saw a shadow pass over the glass, covered by a sheer white curtain, on the front door. He stood frozen there for a minute as the dog kept barking. The shadow reappeared and grew larger and larger in the window. Then it stopped growing, and a loud knock make Thierry's heart skip a beat. His innate reaction was to put his hand on his pistol again, but then he calmed himself and barked at Useless to be quiet. The dog listened this time.

As he approached the door, the man outside knocked again loudly and impatiently. Thierry's worst fear was confirmed when he peeled the curtain back to see his brother Marty, much older and weaker than he remembered him, standing outside. He closed his eyes for a moment and then unlocked and opened the door. Useless grew impatient and stood up. He growled ever so slightly and his top teeth became visible again.

"Library!" With a stern snap and point of the man's finger the dog obeyed, albeit only begrudgingly. He would keep a watchful eye on his owner from the library door.

"Well, aren't you going to let me in?" asked Marty impatiently. A screen door, which was also locked, was all that stood between the two men.

"Why should I?" asked Thierry quietly.

"Why should you?" Marty replied incredulously. "Because I'm your brother for God's sake, and I've come all the way to this God-forsaken wilderness to see you," he said in an agitated tone, looking quickly to his left and his right as if to illustrate his point.

Thierry stood stoically.

"And I'm soaking wet," Marty added. "And for the love of God, how long does your driveway have to be? It took my driver almost an hour to even find it and by the time he did, that stinky kebab was too frustrated to even drive me down it, so I walked. I walked, in my condition, in the pouring rain. Look at me," he held up his foot so Thierry could see his shoes, "these are six-hundred dollar shoes—Italian leather—covered in mud! My socks are soaked through. I swear to God I'm gonna catch pneumonia in the middle of the goddamn summer coming to a place like this."

"I didn't ask you to come here," Thierry curtly replied.

"For God's sake, Thierry, I'm your older brother—you haven't spoken to me in at least fifteen years!"

"You're right—and with good reason."

"With good reason? With what reason?" Marty asked, his tone become more incredulous as he spoke. "You're gonna let something that happened forty-five years ago—you're gonna let that invented offense from a bygone era—keep you from inviting your own flesh and blood into your home?"

"You're right, I don't want you in my home. In fact, I don't even want you on my land."

"Oh, sure, right," Marty carried on in his thick Manhattan accent, waving his arms around sarcastically, "your precious land. It's a back-country swamp, Thierry! The only good it'd do would be if you logged it, and I doubt you've even thought about your ROI on that."

Thierry stood silently, his eyes red with malice.

"But, no, of course you hadn't thought of that," Marty continued condescendingly. "You were never one for business, you know that? You had a sharp mind, but instead of doing something useful with it, you filled it with delusions of God-knows-what and revenge for an offense that never happened. Daydreams and nightmares about a life gone by. You could have done something for yourself, you know. You could have made some real money and actually accomplished something if you'd just gotten control over your own emotions. You're not Edmond Dantès for gods sake—whatever Château d'If you've been living in is of your own making."

The two stood in deafening silence for a moment, rain pounding the roof over the front porch, until Thierry flatly said: "Is that all?"

"What do you mean is that all? Aren't you gonna let me in?"

Thierry laughed out of disbelief and slowly closed the door in his face.

"Oh, come on, Thierry!" Marty yelled from behind the door. "Your own flesh and blood! You're gonna let your own brother die out here in the elements?"

In the elements, thought Thierry, walking back to the kitchen. *He always had a flair for the dramatic.*

Upon seeing Thierry leave the room, Useless returned to his post by the front door and began growling again. Thierry let him be.

"I'm not leaving, Thierry!" hollered Marty, "You can either let me in or carry my stiff corpse off in a body bag!"

The low temperature that night was 76 degrees, cloudy and humid.

Marty slept on the rocker on the porch, stripped out of his wet clothes to his undershirt and shorts. For the first night in years, Thierry didn't dream.

September 7, 1990

He stared up at his ceiling fan, whirling round and round. He went through his usual ritual—brushing his teeth, shaving, and dressing—and then walked slowly downstairs, the bottom landing putting him just two feet from the front door. He thought to himself that if Marty was still out there, he would have to let him in. The old man bit the inside of his cheek at the thought.

He looked down and noticed Useless still standing guard by the door. It was then that he was sure his brother was still on the porch. Thierry calmly ordered the dog to the library with a click of his tongue and then unlocked and opened the wood door and the screen door behind it. Marty was sleeping, halfway hanging out of the wood rocker. It was then that Thierry saw how bad his brother looked. He had always remembered him so strong, fit, and young. Thierry noticed the sun spots all over Marty's hands, the thin hairs on his wrinkled arms, and the dark, heavy bags beneath his eyes. Marty's hair was white and thin; his collar bone poked through his gaunt skin.

His breathing was labored and hard. It had been at least a few days since he had shaved.

Thierry made the sound of clearing his throat. When Marty didn't respond, he did it louder. Marty stirred this time and opened one eye. When he saw his younger brother, he sat up and with some effort straightened himself in the chair. He then coughed loudly, and then coughed again from deep in his chest. His whole fragile body shook.

"Jesus, Thierry," Marty said, looking back up at his brother. "Was this some kind of sick joke? Was that some kind of punishment?"

"Do you want some breakfast?" he asked with a degree of kindness he had not hitherto been able to muster.

"Hell yes. It's been a day and half since I've eaten anything at all."

He got to his feet with some effort, a hard cough racking his body as he did.

"Well then, come in," Thierry said, holding the screen door open with his back. Marty collected his coat, pants, shoes, and socks. He grabbed his suitcase and walked toward the door.

"You're not gonna let that dog attack me, are you?"

Thierry shook his head.

"Yeah, well, I gotta take a piss and get a shower," he said as soon as he'd entered in the house.

"Upstairs, hang a right. Soap and a fresh towel in the closet."

"Yeah, thank you," Marty said gruffly. "Can I get a shave, too?"

"Razor and shaving cream in the medicine cabinet."

Marty nodded his head and trudged up the stairs. Thierry heard him cough again when he reached the landing.

A few minutes later, Marty came back downstairs, his hair still damp from the shower, but combed, and found his way into the kitchen. Thierry motioned him to sit at the table, and then brought out a plate of piping hot eggs, sausage, and fresh berries.

"Coffee?" Thierry asked.

"Uh, yeah, thank you."

"Cream? Sugar?"

"Both," Marty replied, grabbing his fork and plunging right in.

Thierry sat down across the table and watched his brother eat ravenously. He felt complete and total disdain for him, but at the same time, felt sorry for him—for his age, for how bad he looked, and for what was in the paper yesterday.

"So, what happened to the money?" Thierry asked after a couple minutes.

"What kind of sausage is this?"

"Country sausage."

"Are you trying to kill me or something? It's hot as hell."

"Water?" Thierry asked, somewhat sarcastically.

Marty just shook his head quickly.

"You wanna know about the money, huh?" he asked, wiping his lips quickly with his napkin. "You read about it in the paper?"

Thierry nodded.

"Humph," grunted Marty. "Then that should be all you need to know."

"That's not the first time you've told me that."

Marty locked eyes with his younger brother, then quickly glanced away.

"So you don't want to talk about it?"

"Talk about it? What is there to talk about? It's gone. It's all gone—along with the place on the Upper West Side, the yacht, and Carmen."

"Who is Carmen?"

"Who is Carmen? She was my wife."

"Your wife? What happened to Susan?"

"Oh, that bitch is long gone."

"When did that happen?"

Marty closed one eye and looked toward the ceiling with the other, as if doing some sort of mathematical calculation.

"We've been divorced about fourteen years."

"Well I'm sorry to hear that," replied Thierry.

"Eh, don't be," Marty said with a wave of his hand. "She'd been on my nerves for a while. It all worked out, though— she got her money, and I got Mary."

"Mary?"

"Yeah," answered Marty. "My third wife."

Thierry laughed in disbelief.

"How long did she stick around?"

"About eight months."

"And then came Carmen," Thierry said dryly.

"Oh, no, there was Monica in between."

"Monica? My God, Marty, how many times have you been married?"

He leaned towards his plate to shovel some eggs in his mouth.

"Just six," he answered through his food.

"Oh, just six," Thierry repeated.

"Yeah, but I tell you what," Marty continued while swallowing, "losing Carmen's the one that's hurt the most—by far."

"Why, because she got the rest of your money?"

"Money? No, stupid," Marty replied condescendingly, "That little bitch was dumb enough to sign a pre-nup. Plus, as you read, it's all gone anyway. Nah, I'm upset about losing her 'cos she's only nineteen."

"Nineteen?"

"Yeah," said Marty with a loud laugh, "and it's always been my dream to die in the arms of a nineteen year old."

He then coughed so hard that some bits of egg flew back out onto the table.

"God, Thierry," he said, "you should see her—she's about five-eleven, a buck-twenty-five—"

"I don't care," interrupted the younger brother.

"That's only cause you haven't seen her!"

"And what about Vivian?"

"What about her?"

"Do you ever hear from her?" Thierry asked.

"No, do you?"

Thierry shook his head. "Are you finished eating?"

"Yeah, I'm done."

"Then get your things together," Thierry said abruptly, picking the dishes up off the table and placing them in the sink.

"What do you mean?" asked Marty.

"I said get your things together—we're going to the airport."

"Just like that?" he asked scoffingly.

"Yeah," Thierry answered. "You said you wanted to see me, you wanted to be in my house, well you've done both, and now it's time for you to leave."

"I don't have anywhere to be."

"Well, you can't be here, that's for sure. Let's get you on the first flight back to New York, and then at least I can pretend this never happened."

"No, Thierry," said Marty meekly, "I mean I don't have anywhere to go."

Thierry turned and looked his older brother in the eyes. Marty's eyes were weak and almost moist, but Thierry's hurt and anger were brimming over.

"I don't care," he said harshly.

"Your own brother? And you don't care," Marty said with a shrug of his shoulders.

"I'm not responsible for you, your wives, your money, or your well-being. I said I'd take you to the airport, and believe me, with the way I feel about you, that's awfully generous of me."

"Well then, how do you feel about me?" Marty asked, getting slightly riled up.

"I hate you," answered Thierry without any hesitation. "I hate you for being the cause of the vast majority of all the pain in my life.

You destroyed whatever chance of happiness there was for me in the world."

"Oh sure, it's still my fault? It wasn't not having a father, or mom dying, it wasn't the Depression, or the War, or being homeless and poor, or anything *you* might have done, huh? It was all my fault?"

"Don't change the subject, you know exactly what I'm talking about," Thierry said, raising his voice for the first time. Useless came trotting into the room upon hearing it.

"Yeah, I do, Thierry—and I wish you could let it go!" yelled Marty, slamming his fist on the table.

Useless barked loudly.

"Out!" Thierry yelled at the dog who quickly turned tail.

"It's been forty-five years, Thierry," Marty continued desperately.

"And those have been the worst forty-five years of my life!"

"How many times do I have to tell you that I had nothing to do with it? How many times did you read the police reports? How many hours did you spend combing through the newspapers? Not only was there no evidence of any kind against me, but on top of it, you won't take your own brother's word because you've got some kind of a sick hunch!"

"The reason there is no evidence," Thierry replied accusingly, "is that your people—who would cheat, rob, and murder to keep one of their own out of trouble—did *just* that!"

"Damn it, Thierry! You're accusing people you've never even met—good people!—of a serious crime that you have no proof of! How many people would you implicate in your insane conspiracy theory? And for that sick hunch you're gonna forsake your own brother, who loves you?"

"You're damn right I will, Marty," answered Thierry coldly. "And that's some sick brand of love you pedal."

Marty shrugged. "There's no way that I can prove to you that it was an accident, is there, Thierry?" he asked softly.

Thierry bit both his lips and shook his head.

"How are you gonna stand before God one day, with brazen hatred in your heart?"

The two men locked eyes and then looked away—Marty to the floor and Thierry to the ceiling.

"You lost Hope, Thierry," Marty said softly. "And you made a choice in your heart that you wanted to lose me, too." After a couple moments of silence and heavy breath, Marty said: "I'm sick, little brother."

"What do you mean?"

"I've got cancer. Lungs, liver, pancreas—you name it. Doc says I've only got a few weeks to live."

"I'm, sorry to hear that," said Thierry with as much sympathy as he could muster.

"What-a-you gonna do?" he said with a forced laugh.

"Is that why Carmen left you?" Asked Thierry.

"Isn't that sensitive? But no—she didn't even know about the cancer. She left 'cos of the money. She's Collin Graham's side job at present, among others."

"Well, again, I'm sorry about your problems."

"*Problems*? Losing everything, having the woman of your dreams walk out on you, and cancer—those are just, 'problems' to you—kind of like, your car won't start or you got gum on your shoe? How about, your only brother hates you—does that qualify as a problem?"

Thierry remained silent.

"Well—what are we gonna do? In light of my present condition, are we gonna let bygones be bygones and patch things up?"

The younger one tried to hold back another rush of moisture in his eyes.

"We're the only family we've got, kid. You're the only person I've got to turn to. What do you say?"

Thierry watched his older brother's eyes for a long moment.

"I said get your things. We're going to the airport."

TWO

We are all born for love. It is the principle of existence, and its only end.

BENJAMIN DISRAELI

December 1927

By this point in her life, Nina Laroque (maiden name unknown) had spectacularly low expectations. She was twenty years old—a daughter, a wife, a mother of two, and a Catholic, although not a particularly observant one. She had been raised in rural France, some fifty miles from Paris, and left home for the city at the tender age of fifteen to find work and a better life for herself. Being free from her father's farm was a bonus. At sixteen, she married the notorious Jacques Laroque, while being three months shy of the delivery of their first child: a boy named Martin. Jacques was a terribly handsome man of twenty-two, of medium build with long, dark hair, and a fiery temperament. Their story began in early 1923, when they met at a small café on Rue des Martyrs: Nina was working as a waitress and Jacques was carousing with several women, which was his usual practice. The young man was immediately thunderstruck by the beauty and charming country manners of the young lady. The next phase of their relationship was a short and rather common history that requires no further exposition.

Four months after their meeting, however, Nina was forced to tell her parents, who were still attempting to support her with what meager means they had, of her condition. One month after that, the couple was at the altar. It may be added here, that Jacques's appearance and commitment to the young Nina were certainly helped along with the stern guidance and a bit of arm-twisting by the young lady's good father and older brothers, as the young groom was not seen by many in his society as the type of man that would settle down before his fifties, and it was widely assumed that he would most certainly be dead long before then. It may also be assumed that his behavior over the next several years, may in part be attributed, in addition to his utter lack of character, to the fact that his forced marriage to a sixteen year old, however beautiful she might have been, ruined his reputation as one of the premier womanizers in all of Paris, and that over this ruined reputation he was exceedingly bitter. Nina, for her part, spent many nights alone, rocking her young infant and wondering where her husband was and who he was with, although she was certainly not blind to the fact that he was most certainly sharing another woman's bed. Nina was terribly hurt, but unable to curb her husband's "adventurous spirit," as he liked to call it. Being with Jacques was still the pinnacle of happiness for Nina; it just so happened that more often than not, he was utterly absent.

One morning, after another night of loneliness for her and another night of quite the opposite for him, he walked in and asked for his breakfast as usual. She brought over a small plate of freshly cut fruit and two hardboiled eggs. Jacques took her hand tenderly and unexpectedly, and looked in her eyes for the first time in months. Nina was actually startled. A sweet smile dawned on his lips.

"Darling," he said lowly and affectionately, "How would you like to be done with this?"

"Done with what?"

"With this," he motioned with one hand at the room around them, still holding her small hand with the other. "Done with this room, this city? Done with this life, how would you like that?"

"I don't know what you mean," she stuttered. He hadn't been this tender to her since the first day they met, or maybe it was the first night they slept together. "Done with this city? Are you talking about leaving Paris?"

He laughed gently, his grin growing wider with every bewildered word she spoke. "Yes, to be done with this city, but not just leave Paris. I'm asking you if you want to move somewhere far away from here, and start over with everything, including you and me," he suddenly got quiet and rather serious. "Darling… I'm asking you to forgive me."

She almost fainted.

He lifted her hand to his lips and kissed it earnestly, never looking away from her eyes. She had dreamt of her husband saying these words, kissing her hand like that, and looking into her eyes, but she almost couldn't believe it was actually happening. It was an answer to prayer, a signal from the heavens that, indeed there must be a just and loving God.

Nina burst into tears and crumpled to the floor. Jacques immediately got down from his chair and onto his knees beside his sobbing wife. He wrapped her in his strong arms tightly and held her head against his chest.

"I've been a terrible man, Nina. I know this now. I've neglected you and our child. I've wasted your love and taken advantage of your kindness. Forgive me, my darling."

She sobbed even more loudly in his arms and nodded her head.

"Let's leave this city," he said quietly. "Let's leave this all behind us."

She looked up and into his eyes and nodded again.

She asked timidly, "Where should we go? To Spain… or London?" The more she thought of the possibilities, the more excited she got. "Or Rome? Oh, I've heard so many wonderful things about Rome!"

He laughed softly while stroking her long, chestnut colored hair.

"I was thinking about somewhere maybe a little farther, where we don't have to be reminded of our Parisian roots, where we don't have to speak French or any one of those damn Latins, and where we certainly don't have to put up with the British!"

She laughed through her tears and her lips broke into an excited smile. "Tell me where, and I'll follow you—straight to the ends of the earth if that's where you lead me."

"Will you follow me to America?"

She burst out laughing. She could have conceived living somewhere in Europe, but didn't even think he could be remotely serious about going to somewhere as far and as foreign as the United States.

"Of course I will! Of course I will go with you!"

"Ah, my darling," he said joyfully, squeezing her tightly to his chest again, "Then to America, to New York it is! We will start afresh! Just you, me, and little Martin! We will make the world our own, we will conquer it and prosper! We will be like the Vanderbilts or the Rockefellers!"

The truth was that although Jacques at this moment truly did desire a fresh start with Nina, he had more practical reasons for suggesting such a dramatic upheaval. He had been in the habit of gambling and had been rather successful at it over the last several years—successful enough to keep food on the table and the rent paid without working. However, as of late, he had slid into a long losing streak that had suddenly become a rather desperate situation when several of his gambling colleagues called in his debts at once. Upon hearing of his utter inability to pay his debts, and then upon hearing of the sheer largess of those amounts and to whom else it was owed, his debtors turned to threats of violence and even preemptory demonstrations thereof. The young husband owed more than he could possibly hope to repay in a lifetime and was firmly convinced that the violence threatened to him would soon become a reality if he stayed in Paris, or anywhere in Europe for that matter.

So in the early spring of 1926, Jacques, the newly pregnant Nina, and their infant son Martin departed France on a steamer boat and docked at Ellis Island, America. By late April they were settled in a cozy one room apartment in Brooklyn. Jacques managed to find a job on the docks, loading and unloading cargo ships.

On 6 September of that same year, Nina gave birth to their second child, a son they named Thierry.

As time progressed, Nina began to notice that Jacques was picking up night shifts, but didn't seem to be bringing in more pay. Typically, there was also the smell of liquor on his breath when he arrived home in the mornings. When asked about this, he simply stated that the bosses felt so bad about not being able to pay him in cash that they offered him a few shots of good American whisky at the end of his shift as a good-will gesture. This, however, did not explain the smell of ladies' perfume on his neck.

Eventually he not only stopped working altogether, but also stopped keeping up any appearances that he did. His familiar habits took hold of him again, and he again began disappearing for days and nights at a time. When pressed on the subject, he explained that pretty American girls simply could not resist a handsome Frenchman, and that concordantly a handsome Frenchman simply could not resist pretty American girls. Jacques also formed a new habit: beating Nina after such confrontations.

At some point in early 1927, Mr. Clifton Weebles knocked on the young family's door. Mr. Weebles was the landlord of the building in which the Laroques lived, although he might be more appropriately be described as a slumlord. He was a short, greasy man in his late forties—portly, bald, and altogether unappealing. Jacques was away on one of his "adventures" and had not been home for several days. Nina answered the door, and timidly looked towards the floor when Mr. Weebles's stern gaze caught her eyes.

"Do you know why I am here?" he asked condescendingly.

"Yes, sir, I know," she answered in broken English.

"Well then, why am I here?"

"Because this month's rent is late, monsieur," she answered sheepishly.

"Is that what you think?"

"I don't know monsieur," she answered, shaking her head and avoiding contact with his eyes. "Why else would you come?"

"Well, either you don't understand English at all, or you must be flat dumb," he retorted harshly. "I'm not only here for this month's rent; I am here for last month's rent and the rent from the month before that! I am not running a charity house here! I am in business to make a profit, and I cannot make a profit when my tenants do not pay me rent!"

"Monsieur—"

"Stop speaking French, bitch! Don't know where you are?"

"I'm sorry mon—Mr. Weebles," she corrected herself before she made him truly angry. "But please, I have two young children, my husband is out of work—"

"Oh I know all about your husband. He's a whore monger and a gambler!"

"Sir, please, my children—"

"If you can't pay me what you owe me, you will be out by next week! Do you understand me? Out!"

Upon hearing those words, a desperate thought struck young Nina which had never occurred to her in her entire life.

"Sir," she said quietly, lifting her head to look into his eyes for the first time, "would it be possible to work out another arrangement between us to settle accounts?"

He got the hint but was apparently intent on torturing her.

"Well, what did you have in mind?"

She glanced down the hallway to make sure it was empty, and then cast a quick look over her shoulder to make sure her children were still sleeping. She unbuttoned the top few buttons of her blouse and checked Mr. Weebles's face for his reaction.

"Well," he spoke quietly and slowly, "you are a rather pretty young thing. I've always thought your looks were being wasted by that drunkard of a husband."

The fat man touched her cheek gently with the back of his plump, hairy hand, and slowly ran it down her neck and across her chest. She felt like she would vomit.

"Yes… I think we might be able to work out another arrangement, but first, let me preview the goods before I make a purchase," he said, pushing her inside and closing the door behind him. Needless to say, Mr. Weebles made the purchase.

For the first time in her life, Nina Laroque slept with a man other than Jacques. She prayed desperately that her husband would never find out. The arrangement she and Mr. Weebles agreed to included the use of her body over the course of several weeks in order to repay back rent that was still owed. The landlord was painstaking in making sure that his wife, the equally grotesque Mrs. Weebles, was unaware of this particular transaction. Over the course of a few weeks, he actually grew quite fond of Nina, her charm being something truly extraordinary, and over the next several months, even began recommending her services to other professionals to which she was indebted, most of whom were happy to enter into such alternative methods of payment with the pretty young girl from the French countryside. Eventually, Mr. Weebles was running quite a lucrative side business out of the Laroque's apartment, allowing Nina a certain percentage of the profits, although she was never aware of quite how low her percentage was, in goods and services and sometimes in cash.

By this time, Jacques had nearly disappeared completely, and would emerge from New York's rotting underbelly only once a week or so. Even when he was home he was terribly neglectful of his children, the state of the apartment, and even of Nina, although he did make her fully cognizant that despite his absence she still had wifely duties to perform. She was by this point completely accustomed to being used, and for the sake of maintaining what had become a rather lush lifestyle by not upsetting him, she submitted without a word of protest. Jacques did not notice the new china, he did not notice the new mattress, or the new bed for the boys; he did not notice the new paintings on the walls, nor did he notice the new and brightly patterned dresses she wore. He did not notice that the rent was always paid, the lights were always on, the boys always had fresh milk, and that there always seemed to be meat on the table. The drunkard simply assumed that American landlords, electric companies, milkmen, and butchers were much more generous and accommodating than their European counterparts. He did, however, notice that her English had improved dramatically, but did not stop to wonder where she might have had the opportunity to practice it much.

He was fairly sober by the time he got home on this particular day, due to the fact that he had woken up in a woman's bed roughly seventy blocks from his family's apartment. He walked all of those blocks in the early morning, mid-December frost—a light dusting of snow crunching under his feet as he went. He began his walk in possession of a terrible headache, but it gradually faded the more he trudged on. The cold air in his lungs in combination with the vigorous exercise was ultimately quite refreshing, and by the time he entered the building owned by Mr. Weebles, he actually felt reasonably alert.

Jacques bounced up the stairs lightly, all ten flights, to his young family's apartment. He fumbled around in his pocket for the key, standing outside the door for a long moment. Suddenly, his ears perked to something inside that he had never heard before in that apartment. There was the sound of what might have been several men and women talking, and then he distinctly picked out the sound of Nina laughing heartily, and then his two young boys giggling along simultaneously. He finally found his key and opened the door slowly. Inside, Jacques saw Nina, Martin, and Thierry, a toddler by this time, sitting on the floor together on a lush Persian (*is that a Persian?*) rug, crowded around a brand new and fairly expensive looking piece of furniture—a radio in a deep cherry wood finish. He blinked twice just to make sure that what his eyes were taking in was indeed reality. He had never dreamt of being able to afford such an expensive luxury item, and was flabbergasted by its appearance in his humble home.

Nina stood gracefully, although she was a little surprised by his entrance, and approached him, throwing her arms around his neck and kissing him gently. Jacques did not kiss back. In fact, he stood completely frozen, eyes staring past her straight at the radio. She continued by greeting him warmly, as if everything in the world was completely at peace.

"Where…" he gulped as if he was having trouble formulating the words, "did you get that radio?"

"Oh darling!" she responded cheerfully. "Do you know that radio shop over on Delancey Street that we always used to pass on the way to Monsieur Philippe's café? You know the one where we used to get that wonderful coffee?"

"Mhmm," he murmured slowly.

"Well, Mr. Weebles knows the owner of that shop, in fact, they're good friends from what I hear—in some sort of business club together or something," she spoke rapidly and excitedly. "Well, Mr. Weebles knows how difficult it is for me to entertain these two young boys all day by myself… with you working most of the time."

Jacques lowered his eyes and glared at her suspiciously as he heard her emphasize that he had been out working. He sensed she had something up her sleeve but had no idea what it could possibly be.

"And so, he asked Mr. Hermann to keep us in mind if—"

"Who is Mr. Hermann?" he snapped.

"The radio store owner, darling!" she replied, as if he should have known all along. "Mr. Hermann couldn't sell this radio because of the damage to the finish on the side, so he gave it to Mr. Weebles to give to us! Out of the goodness of his heart! It was delivered a couple days ago—right after you left! I was so disappointed that you didn't get to see it when it arrived!"

Jacques glanced over at the radio. He could see no signs of damage.

"It looks fine to me. What is wrong with it?" he asked accusingly.

"Oh," she responded, for the first time rather nervously. She wished more than anything else that his questions would cease. He was prying for the first time and she desperately wished that he would stop. She had taken his lack of interest for granted and hadn't really prepared a story for everything in the apartment that she had acquired, nor had she prepared a general explanation for the status of their newly found material success. "Darling," she continued quickly, "it's all scratched on the side. You or I might not notice, but you know how picky Americans are about everything—especially rich ones! There's not a chance that this beaten-up old thing would sell to an American family!"

"I see," he drawled slowly.

"Well, how about some breakfast? You must be famished!"

"Um, sure," he responded, his eyes locked again on the beautiful radio.

There was an uncomfortable silence while she spun toward the stove and began slicing some bread. He was now completely aware that something had been going on behind his back, and his mind was working a mile a minute to try to figure it out. Maybe she had gotten a job; maybe a rich relative that he didn't know about had kicked the can and the estate had sent money. Every possibility he could concoct sounded highly unlikely, but he knew that something just wasn't right. She was wearing a beautiful dress; she almost looked as if she was dressed up. She even appeared to be wearing makeup. He had never seen her in makeup before. Simply put, she looked stunning. However, he recognized her dress—he had seen it in an expensive department store window on his trudge home that very morning.

He sat down at what appeared to be a new kitchen table. He propped his elbows on his knees and leaned forward in her direction.

"Nina?"

"Yes, darling?" she called back over her shoulder, still facing the stove, also wracking her brain as to how to explain all of this to Jacques, because she felt sure that he would continue asking.

"Where did you get that dress?"

She spun quickly toward him, but remained silent for a moment, her mind racing for an explanation.

"It's funny that you should ask about that, too," she said anxiously. "You see, Mr. Weebles introduced me to a wonderful and kind old woman who lives just several blocks from here. We've become fast friends. Well, it just so happened… that her daughter's husband took a job in Boston! He's a banker or something and makes a lot of money. Anyway, this kind old woman's daughter simply couldn't pack all of her wonderful dresses and shoes—and makeup, too!—for their trip (she had such a large wardrobe, you should have seen it yourself!), and so being that we share the exact same size, she was generous enough to give them to me! Isn't that incredible?"

Nina searched his face eagerly for a response, hoping and praying with all the spiritual fervor she possessed that he would believe her and simply let the argument rest at that. In the past, he may have let such questions settle, but today, he was in rare form and had decided that he would not be satisfied until he had uncovered the truth.

"Yes, darling… It is absolutely unbelievable," he said slowly.

She thought she sensed sarcasm in his voice, but chose to believe that he believed her, and once again tried to change the subject, and also, perhaps, tried to shift some of the discomfort of this situation onto him: "So have you found much work, darling?"

Jacques ignored her question completely. His body position remained fixedly accusatory. He looked from the radio towards her faced, searched it for a minute and then looked her up and down.

"Nina, that dress does not look worn at all. In fact, it looks like it might have just come from the shop today."

She laughed nervously. "Well dear, like I said, this young lady—Mrs. Brewer, as I recall—had so many things that she never touched simply because she had so many things! It would have taken her a lifetime to wear all of the things she had, even if she wore two a day!"

"I see…"

His gaze searched her eyes again; she looked quickly back to the stove to avoid his eyes.

"Nina," he began a new line of questioning, noticing the fresh provisions near the stove. "Where did you get all that food? Is that salami? Where did you get salami?"

She was beginning to get quite irritated with his questioning and was unsure how to shake him off her trail. She just knew that whatever story she invented had to sound believable. "One of Mr. Weebles's tenants is the butcher, Khohklakov, a Russian or a Jew, I think, or maybe both. Anyway, he rents his shop space from Mr. Weebles and is greatly indebted to him for the generous rate he receives—I believe. So, Mr. Weebles simply asked him to spare some extra meat for us whenever he could, knowing that we have two growing boys—"

"Monsieur Weebles?"

"Yes, dear… our landlord," she answered timidly.

"Every answer to any question I ask seems to begin with Mr. Weebles. Mr. Weebles knows this person; Mr. Weebles knows that person. May I ask, to what do we owe all of this kindness from Mr. Weebles?"

Her minded raced again.

"Why, it's just that, well… he is an exceedingly generous man."

Jacques looked out from under his brow in utter disbelief. He knew that Weebles was a conceited, money-hungry lowlife, and that taking care of a young, foreign family was the last thing he would have on his mind. He felt a primeval rage bubbling to the surface of his countenance.

"Gen-er-ous?" he asked, enunciated each syllable and giving his best effort at keeping his building anger in check.

"Yes, darling, he knows how hard you are working and how hard it is to provide for a family these days, and he is simply using his connections to benefit us and our children. He is a very charitable man, Jacques."

She swallowed hard as she realized how absurd her statement had been and how unlikely her husband was to believe it.

"Char-it-a-ble?" he said quietly, shaking his head.

"Yes, he is very charitable," she said softly, attempting to reassure him that this was indeed the truth.

Suddenly, Jacques flew into a rage, standing up promptly and pounding his fist on the table.

"I will not be another man's charity!" he screamed.

Nina recoiled suddenly in fear, and both of their children suddenly looked up from the floor at their father. Nina quickly ran and took them in her arms.

"Jacques, please don't yell," she pleaded sweetly. "You will scare the children."

"I will not allow you to disgrace me, woman, by taking handouts from other men and their wives!"

"It's not like that!" she responded, becoming somewhat agitated herself. "We all must rely on the goodwill of our friends and neighbors from time to time."

"No, no, no!" he thundered, continually banging his fist on the table for effect. "Not me! Not my family! I am Jacques Laroque! I am not a pauper, I am not a beggar, and I am not a charity case! I am a husband, a father, and I am the provider for this family!"

There was a moment of silence when suddenly Nina let go of the children and stood up. She and Jacques were face to face.

"Then provide for us, damn it!" she yelled at him. He was a bit taken aback by her boldness. "If you are the provider for this family, then provide! All you do is take handouts from your women—clothes, liquor, and god-knows what else! But you do not provide for your own family at home!"

He stared at her, the fire behind his eyes building again. He felt as if the room had suddenly gotten hot, and reached up to feel the sweat building on his brow.

"You insolent woman—you ungrateful bitch!"

"Ungrateful? What am I supposed to be grateful to you for?" her tone had shifted to one of utter disbelief at his audacity. She had lost the will to protect him, and had lost the will to pretend that she loved him. "Am I ungrateful to you for seducing and getting me pregnant at sixteen? For sleeping with other women from the very first weeks of our marriage? For being dragged halfway around the world to live in misery, far away from everything I know? For being left with your sons to be turned out into the street, while you waste your days drinking and fornicating?"

He was too shocked to respond, and simply let his jaw hang open while she berated him. There was another moment of silence between them before Nina continued, growing quieter after being suddenly aware of the children again, although the anger in her tone did not subside.

"Jacques, you are a pauper. You are a beggar, and on top of that, you are the worst man I have ever known—"

At hearing this, his heart actually broke. However, he responded in the only way he knew how—he hit her.

Her nose and mouth went numb and her eyes watered from the force of the blow. She did not fall to the ground; she kept her balance out of pride, although she did feel the room spinning around her. She put her hand to her face and felt warm blood running down. She looked down toward her hands and saw it dripping down onto her new dress, down onto the new table, and down onto the new Persian rug. He had hit her before, but she had never been hit that hard in her life.

Little Thierry began to cry behind her. His older brother Martin took him in his arms and began to rock him slowly, avoiding his parents with his eyes. Jacques walked over to the radio slowly, and suddenly kicked it down onto its face, the force of the shock shaking the room. He then turned it over roughly onto its side, and then again onto its back—rolling it towards the door.

Nina began to protest, pleading with him not to break it, not to destroy it because the children loved it. Jacques simply rolled it from side to side, broken shards of glass and splinters of rich cherry wood flying off in all directions.

"Jacques, please!" she cried.

When he reached the door he shoved it roughly out into the narrow hallway. Nina grabbed him by the arm; she was almost hysterical.

"Jacques, please, do you know what that cost?" she shrieked.

"It was free, you stupid woman! And I will not tolerate another man's charity in my home!"

He quickly pulled his arm loose from her grasp and then froze. He stared into her eyes, soaked with tears, and her face, running with blood, and for the first time he understood. There was indeed something running much deeper under the surface than what she presented. A silence of just a few seconds ensued, which felt more like an eternity to her.

"You whore," he said, looking her up and down with utter distain. She weakly stared back at him, with growing horror in her eyes. "You're not a charity case after all… you're a slut. How long, eh? How long has my wife been the village harlot?"

"What does it matter to you?" she yelled back.

"Well, I'd like to know how far this goes back. How long have you been making a fool out of me?"

"A fool out of you? Do you think I wanted this? I would have traded a pauper's existence for this hell a thousand times, as long as it would have meant being poor with you!"

He hit her again, and this time, her brightly-colored blood spattered on the wall just inside the apartment, on the stacks of china just inside the door, and, worst of all, across the face of little Martin. Nina screamed when she saw her little boy's face spotted in her warm blood. She feverishly tried to wipe the splotches off her child's frozen face with the folds of her dress, but succeeded only in smearing the red fluid over his cheeks and forehead. The boy stood there as if in a state of shock. She wept hysterically, blood still dripping from her nose and mouth. There was a terrible pounding in her head.

Suddenly, she heard a series of thunderous crashes outside the door, and she immediately climbed to her feet. At the threshold, she saw Jacques returning from the landing. He grabbed her roughly by the hair and pulled her toward the stairs.

"Look!" he commanded, pointing down the staircase.

Her radio lay smashed into a thousand pieces at the bottom. Her husband strengthened his grip on her hair and said slowly and quietly, "You're going to look something like that when I'm through with you, slut."

Just then, a door creaked open down the hall, and for a moment, Nina thought she might be saved, but it was only the old Italian lady who lived by herself, peering out to see what all the commotion was. Once she saw the blood on Nina's face and Jacques standing over her, she quickly closed the door and went back in to the safety of her small abode.

Nina prepared herself for death. She had always feared that Jacques would kill her if he found out about her new occupation. She had been torn between her Christian faith, her vows to her husband, however unfaithful he might have been, and her duty to provide for her children above all else. So now she prayed. She prayed that God might have mercy on her soul. She prayed that he would accept her into heaven because, although her sins were many, they were committed selflessly.

Jacques pulled up on her hair, and she knew that he was about to send her down the stairs as hard as he could. She may have still had the will to resist him, but simply did not have the strength. Then suddenly, she was saved—her prayers answered from on high.

A small voice cried out behind the couple. Jacques immediately turned, yanking Nina's throbbing head around with him. Little Martin stood on the threshold, his small face still smeared in his mother's blood.

"Monsieur," he called softly. "Monsieur please… my mama… please… it's my mama…"

Jacques stared at his son who did not even recognize his own father and clenched his teeth. He did not feel mercy; he did not feel a tinge of remorse. In actuality, he felt quite the opposite—he felt repulsion and utter disgust towards the woman he had married and his small son. He released his grip on Nina's blood-soaked hair and she crumpled down to the floor, but not down the stairs. The boy just stood there with long, streaky tears flowing down his red stained face.

Jacques approached him slowly and calmly. Martin stood his ground.

"Go to your mama," he commanded softly, pointing to the woman lying in the heap on the floor. Martin ran to her and embraced her. She began to weep and gently hugged back.

Jacques disappeared into the apartment momentarily, and then emerged with Thierry, carrying the toddler gently. The young boy was calm and curiously stared at his father's sweaty face. His father did not look back at his. Jacques knelt beside Nina and Martin, and placed Thierry down gently next to them. He lifted Nina's head gently so that their eyes met.

"Woman, if I ever see you again," he drew up a breath, "I swear on everything holy…"

Jacques did not finish his sentence. He simply stood upright, brushed off his pants, and walked nonchalantly back into the apartment. The door then slammed behind him.

That was the last time either Martin or Thierry ever saw their father.

After several minutes, Nina regained the strength to stand and in that moment she made a conscious decision to carry on. She wiped her lip on her sleeve, picked up Thierry, and took Martin by the hand. They walked down each flight of stairs, step by step. When they got down to the bottom, she gently stepped over the shattered remains of her cherished radio and helped little Martin navigate his way through the splintered mess without tripping.

Nina and her two boys stepped out of the apartment building and into the bright sunlight, and this young woman again began an endeavor to leave her past behind.

January 1928

Christmas came and went that year, all without Nina's notice. The boys received no gifts.

The young lady moved her two children across two rivers into New Jersey, where the friend of a distant relative back in France had agreed to loan her a small room in an apartment building for a couple months, until she could find work. Nina knew that this arrangement could not possibly be permanent, and felt that she owed the new landlord, whom she had never actually met before, to find work as soon as she felt capable of getting out in the weather, and as soon as her bruises went in completely.

The mother and her children had a small wooden stove in one corner of the room, a table with one stool adjacent to it, and five ragged, but warm blankets for both a mattress and covering. There was a communal toilet on the first floor of the six-story building. Nina's new landlords were also kind enough to give her a half-carton of eggs, two loaves of bread, and a few thin pieces of bologna. This, in addition to the clothes on their backs, was all that they could claim as their own.

She laid on the blankets with the boys for long periods of the day and night, although she rarely slept. She tried desperately to regain her strength, knowing that their food supply would soon run out, and that she must get up and find some kind of work. She had made up her mind that no matter what the cost, she would not allow herself to be used like she had in New York. She would find some other kind of legitimate and humane line of work.

Then, a terrifying thought struck her for the first time: how would she take care of the children while she worked? This thought came to her in the middle of the night and she sat up in her makeshift bed in a cold sweat. Certainly no employer would allow her to watch two young children, prone to getting into things, while she worked.

She noticed Thierry was stirring a bit, and gently reached down to touch his face. The small boy's nose felt frozen stiff, so she got up and stoked her last log on the stove. She knew that before the night was over she would need more wood for the fire, so she tucked the two boys in under the blankets, except for the one on the top layer which she wrapped around her fragile frame.

Outside the apartment building, and around the corner in the alley, there was a small wood pile kept under lock for the tenants of the building. A portion of their rent each month would go to provide fuel for the stoves that kept each small apartment warm. The cold was bitter, and a cruel wind blew steadily from the North. Nina trudged through a few inches of snow and into the dark alley that always made her feel uncomfortable. She usually tried to load up on wood before dark, but the temperatures dipped so low that extra was required.

When she reached the metal crate that held the wood, she searched her pocket for the small key that would open the padlock. The realization that she had left it upstairs made her curse under her breath. She noticed two decent sized pieces of timber sticking precariously out of the crate, and thought that she might simply be able to tug them out without having to unlock the top. She struggled mightily, yanked and pulled, but to no avail. The wood wouldn't budge.

Tears began to stream down her face and she became angry. She was almost ready to give up, not just on pulling the wood out of the crate, but on life itself. It seemed to her that all she knew was hardship, and that she could not catch a break—one piece of good luck. Her life had been on a continual spiral out of control for as long as she could remember, and the only things keeping her going at all were the two sleeping boys on the sixth floor.

She pathetically yanked at the two pieces of fire food, and just when the thought crossed her mind that her life could not possibly get any worse, she heard a loud voice behind her in the dark:

"Hey! What are you doing?"

She startled, and realized that it looked like she was trying to steal from the pile. She prayed that the strong voice wasn't that of a police officer. Nina turned and saw a tall, thin black man in a heavy, but tattered coat.

"I was just… trying to get some wood."

"Well I can see that!" he said accusingly, his tone raised, although he kept his volume down as if to keep from disturbing the otherwise peaceful night.

"Sir, please," she replied, "I live in this building, I just forgot my key upstairs."

She shivered, a fresh gust of frigid air blowing raw against her face.

"I know you live here!" he said as he looked quickly over his shoulder. "I've passed you on the stairs. You have those two little boys."

She nodded.

"I'm just trying to get some wood for the fire."

"I didn't mean what are you doing getting wood—I meant what are you doing out here in this weather, wearing practically nothing!"

Nina felt a sharp sting in her heart—she hadn't expected kindness.

"Get inside!" he ordered.

"But sir, I need this wood for my fire—"

"Get inside!" he commanded again, this time pointing towards the front door.

She was frustrated, but didn't quite know what to do, so she obeyed. As she passed him, he said gently, "Now you just wait in the foyer."

Inside the foyer the building wasn't much warmer, but at least she was out of the wind. She shook her hair and stamped her feet to knock the snow loose. The air inside the building had a smoky quality from all of the stoves and cigarettes lit up constantly during the course of the day. She wondered if she should just go get her key to the wood box.

At that moment the man entered through the door carrying more wood than she could have grabbed in five trips. He stomped his feet as well.

"Ok, what floor?"

"Me?"

"Well, of course you! I know what floor I live on!" he retorted cheerfully.

Nina thought that his smile was genuine and pure. He was middle aged, with half of his hair turned white, the other half still youthfully black. There were lines on his face—laugh lines—and for as cold as he may have been at the moment, he radiated warmth.

"Six," she said with a responsive smile.

"Ok, well, up we go."

As he leaned towards her he asked her to grab the log on top of his pile and said, "You didn't think I was gonna do this by myself, did you?"

He carried the rest of the wood all the way up all six flights of stairs, Nina following behind, feeling guilty that she wasn't doing more to help him help her.

"Are you sure I can't carry another? I can at least grab two or three more!"

"Don't you worry about it, child; I may look old, but I'm strong as an ox."

"You don't look old," she replied, afraid that she may have offended him.

Then, under his breath, she heard him say with confidence, "I know."

Eventually, they reached her door. She opened it and asked him to come in. The man gently placed the pile of wood down next to the stove. As he stood up straight, Nina heard his back crack loudly.

"Oh, well that was a good one," he said, arching backward to stretch his muscles.

"Are you okay?" she asked quietly.

"Oh yeah, I'm fine."

He looked down at her two sleeping boys under the blankets, then at the small table and over at the stove. He glanced at the bare walls and the one small window that was practically draftier closed than it would have been open. He motioned her out into the hallway.

Nina walked out and closed the door gently behind her. She wasn't sure what to expect. The man leaned in seriously, but didn't say a word. He simply watched her face, as if searching for something. Nina was a bit uncomfortable, but wasn't sure what to say, if anything at all. After a few seconds, which felt more like an eternity to her, the man's serious expression quickly changed and he backed up a step, helping her to feel more at ease.

"Honey, is that all you got?"

"I beg your pardon?"

"Inside," he pointed behind her towards her door, "is that all you've got?"

She nodded.

"Oh, honey…" he shook his head in sympathy and disbelief that she could be that poor. "Are you doing anything tomorrow morning?"

"What time?" she asked, even though she knew that she had no plans—what could she possibly do?

"Seven."

"Nothing, it's open." After the words escaped her lips she suddenly realized that there was an outside chance that he was asking her to do precisely what she swore she would never do again, but in that moment, the thought of having some cash in her hands and some food in her stomach convinced her to take him up on the offer.

"Well, why don't you come down to number 306?" he said slowly.

She thought for a moment about this choice and its potential to crush her dreams of starting over. She closed her eyes and swallowed hard. She nodded her head.

"Great! And bring the boys!" he exclaimed, suddenly cheerful again.

Nina's mind went blank.

"The boys?" she asked quietly, not sure what else to say.

"Yeah, the boys!" he said excitedly. "I'll have my wife Henrietta cook up some good breakfast! You like eggs right?"

She began to sob in relief. No tears would come to her eyes, but she struggled to control her breath. She had given herself to the worst kind of existence imaginable, again, but this kind stranger's intentions had been as pure and noble as his smile.

"Hey, are you alright?" he asked, putting his hand on her shoulder to steady her.

"Your wife?" she asked, as soon as she was able to compose herself.

"Yes, Henrietta. And my name's Henry. What do you think of that?"

She didn't know what she thought.

"About breakfast?" he asked reassuringly.

"Oh," she was calming down, and a smile came back to her face, "that would be lovely!"

"Great! Well, we'll see you tomorrow then! Seven o'clock, number 306!"

With that Henry tipped his hat, turned and bounced down the stairs like a man in his twenties. Nina went over to the railing and thanked him. She could see him hold his hand up and point upwards towards her as he lightly jogged down.

Back inside the apartment the boys were still sleeping, so she stoked a couple more logs into the stove, and stood near it for a few moments so that she wouldn't be cold when she got back under the blankets. She thanked God for her new friend, for the unlikely angel that he had sent into her life at such a bleak moment. The feeling of hopelessness had suddenly vanished and, with a content smile on her face, she was able to sleep peacefully for the first time that she could remember.

At seven A.M. sharp, Nina knocked on door number 306. There was a bustle inside the door, the sound of raucous laughter (the type you might hear at midnight rather than early in the morning), and then a cheery and high pitched, "Coming!"

Henrietta opened the door quickly and smiled immediately when she saw Nina, holding little Martin's hand and Thierry in her arms. Nina smiled back instinctively, and said, "Hello."

"Well, hi, honey!" Henrietta exclaimed, immediately hugging Nina around the shoulder. She then said hello to Martin in a serious, but playful tone, and then cooed at the silent Thierry. "Please, come in!"

The apartment was warm and smelled like butter and fresh bacon. There was a wood stove, similar to Nina's, although slightly newer, a wooden table set with chipped porcelain plates and chairs, and most magnificent of all, a cherry colored radio that stood in the corner. Nina put Thierry down and the two boys immediately ran towards the music machine, spun the dial to a familiar setting, and plopped down in front of it as if mesmerized. Nina glanced at Henrietta nervously and began to apologize for her children's harmless, but impolite behavior.

"Honey," Henrietta cut in, "please don't apologize. Your children are lovely! I know we only just met a minute ago, but please, please, make yourself at home here. We're gonna get to know you and your children just fine, and you're gonna get to know us, so in the meantime, why act like strangers, huh?"

"Thank you," she replied with a naturally charming smile.

"Don't mention it," Henrietta replied warmly. "After all, life is too short to and this world is too cruel to go around pretending like everybody's out to get us, like we're just wandering around and can't see nothin' 'cause of the dark."

Nina could sense that Henrietta had suffered a great deal in her lifetime, and was amazed at the poise, the subtle grace, and the deep joy of this woman. There was something about this couple that Nina had never experienced before, and for a minute, she wondered if it had something to do with race, being as she had never really spoken with a black person before.

"Sometimes, the world is very dark," Nina replied.

Henrietta smiled sweetly. "Well, honey, that's what I mean. That's why we're here—and I'm not talking about you and me, I'm talking about all of us." She waved her hand around the room. Then she spoke slowly, enunciating each word for emphasis: "Humankind. We *make* the light." Henrietta raised her eyebrows and leaned backwards slightly, a smile crawling across her lips.

At that moment, there was more commotion at the door, and Henry entered, dressed in the thick coat he had worn last night as well as a navy blue wool cap, and carrying a large bundle wrapped in brown paper. He was whistling happily. When he looked up, he saw Nina and a bright smile shot onto his face.

"Hey, young lady—glad to see you could make it!" He placed the bundle down on the kitchen table and hugged her tightly. "Make yourself at home," he said cordially.

Henry then wrapped his wife in his arms and squeezed. She let out a quick squeal. He did not let her go and rocked her back and forth, saying "Wow, did I miss you! You're even more beautiful than I remember!"

When he finally did let go, Henrietta took a moment to catch her breath, shaking her head and smiling.

"Well, you've only been gone twenty minutes, you old fool!" she teased. "What did you think I looked like?"

Henry shot a playful glance at Nina, and then shouted playfully toward the boys, who turned suddenly from the radio to see the large man. Within minutes, the three boys were wrestling on the floor. Nina sat at the table drinking hot coffee—real coffee—and staring in amazement at the playful scene taking place on the floor. She had never actually seen her boys with an authentic father figure, and she practically had to choke back tears at how happy they seemed.

"How's the coffee?" Henrietta asked. "Do you need milk?"

Nina took a sip and shook her head. "I drink it just black. And it's marvelous, thank you."

"Good—I'm glad to hear it!"

Henrietta turned back to the stove, and after about a minute of scraping some pots and pans, announced that breakfast was served. She then removed the large bundle from the table and placed it gently in the corner.

The meal was fantastic. Fried eggs, bacon, toast, and more coffee. Henrietta even served buttered grits, which Nina had never eaten before, but thoroughly enjoyed. She learned that grits were a Southern thing, and that both Henry and Henrietta were from Georgia.

"The weather down there is great. At least the winters are," laughed Henry.

"How did you end up all the way up here?"

"Work," Henry replied. "Couldn't find nothin' down there."

"You see," Henrietta chimed in to help explain her husband, "both sets of our parents were born slaves."

Nina nodded in understanding, although all she knew about the American Civil War was that it ended slavery and that it itself ended some time ago.

"We were both born free, though, after the war," Henrietta continued. "But things are tough down there. Our parents were from the same plantation and the master told them to beat it once things calmed down. He wasn't gonna pay no Negroes to work for him—he was one of the principled ones. So, our folks picked up work on farms here and there, and a lot of us stayed together wherever we went. The two of us," she pointed to herself and her husband, "grew up together."

Nina smiled at the thought of that.

"And I knew I was gonna marry that woman from the time I was twelve years old!" Henry exclaimed, pointing to Henrietta quickly and then slamming his fist on the table for effect. "And good God was she beautiful! I mean, she still is—look at her. But every boy I ever met wanted to marry that woman, and I—"

"You're an old fool!" Henrietta piped in playfully. "Now shut up and let me tell the story!"

Henry waved at her and pretended to be upset. She continued:

"So we ended up all over the South—Tennessee, the Carolinas, even Texas for a minute—but it was hard to put your feet down anywhere. No colored person could get a break, and although there were some good white folk who would'a helped, most of them had enough trouble putting food on their own plates, so what could they do?"

"Then we got married!" Henry chimed in again. "And that woman made me the happiest man there ever was! Oh, Lord, we had nothin'!

Not even a dime to our name, but that woman made me the happiest man the Good Lord ever blessed."

Nina couldn't fathom such genuine devotion. She had always known that her marriage was one of necessity, at least on her husband's part, and in addition, due to the fact that most of her former johns had been married, she had begun to believe that such honor and fidelity did not exist among men. Her beauty had always made her the focus of admiration and adulation, but never genuine fondness and respect.

"How long have you been married?" Nina inquired.

"Thirty-eight years of wedded bliss!" Henry replied happily.

"Thirty-eight years! Whew!" Nina exclaimed.

"Yes, honey," said Henrietta with a sigh, "I was sixteen and Henry over there was seventeen, and we didn't have a damn clue what we were doin'."

"Hmm, I sure did," Henry coyly responded.

Henrietta laughed gently and shook her head. "You old fool... Anyway, we were young, but having each other's been the only thing that's kept us alive."

"Do you have children?" Nina asked.

Henrietta nodded and sighed again, this time quite solemnly.

"We did, but they passed on to a better place."

"I'm so sorry," Nina gasped at the thought.

"Some things just weren't meant to be," Henry answered. "We had two who were stillborn, one drowned when she was eleven, and one was lynched in Aiken, South Carolina."

"Lynched?" Nina wasn't quite sure what the word meant, but imagined it must be something horrible.

Henry nodded soberly. "That was Junior, our first son."

"I'm so sorry," was the only thing Nina could think to say.

"Well, that's life, ain't it?" Henry asked rhetorically. "The good Lord giveth, and sometimes man taketh away."

"That's so horrible," Nina said as she took another sip from her mug.

"There's nothing we can do but look back with fond memories and be thankful. Our children, for the short time they were here, made the world a brighter place."

"Well how about you, sweetie?" Henrietta asked. "We've been talking about us for so long, tell us about yourself—I mean, other than the fact that you're European. We'd figured that out all by ourselves," she joked.

"Well, where to begin?" Nina thought out loud. She did not want to burden them with the details of her relationship with Jacques, so she told the story's abridged version.

"I moved here, to New York, with my husband several years ago. These are our two boys. We had a bit of a falling out and separated. So I'm here."

She shrugged her shoulders as if to imply that this was all there really was to the story.

"So you're here…" Henrietta repeated with a tinge of sadness in her voice.

"Yes, and now I suppose my biggest worry is looking for work. I can't imagine what I can do with two boys to watch. Martin will be old enough for school next year, but in the meantime, I don't know what to do. And then even when he goes, what to do about little Thierry?"

"Well, what did you do before you separated from your husband?" Henry asked innocently.

Nina blushed and was afraid that her guests could see it.

"Um, I was just a housewife," she replied nervously. "Although I have done some sewing and worked in cafes and such."

"Well, I know there are still plenty of places like that in business," Henrietta replied. "Whether they're offering jobs or not—I don't know what to tell you. I'd expect that they're trying to protect their own, and no offense, but you ain't their own."

"What do you mean?" Nina asked naively.

"Well, honey, you're an immigrant," Henry replied.

Nina glanced quizzically back and forth between them.

"What Henry means, is that you're not from here. People are trying to protect American jobs first and foremost, and you're gonna be hard pressed to find somebody that wants to give a new job, if they have one, to someone with an accent."

A look of hurt crossed Nina's face. She had never considered that anyone would consider her to be anything but American at this point.

"Hell, you might as well be a Negro like us!" Henry blurted out jokingly.

"But what have we done to deserve this kind of treatment?" Nina asked after a moment of stern consideration. "Aside from the color of our skin, or the way ours words sound, what is so different about us that we are outcast?"

Henry chuckled warmly.

"Look," he responded in his typically assuring charm, "it's the way of the world, what can I say? There will always be rich folk, and there will always be poor folk. There will always be people who let power get to their heads and there will always be some that never lose their sense of humility. Don't let us get you down, though—that's the last thing we're trying to do."

"You're right, Henry," his wife chimed in. "I'm sorry if you thought I was trying to discourage you. Like I said earlier, we have to make a way for ourselves to survive, and more than to just survive, to thrive—wherever we find ourselves."

"And there are plenty of good people out there," Henry continued. "They're sometimes a little bit harder to find, though. The good ones are usually the ones that stay quiet—they don't make as much noise. So, we just gotta know where to look for 'em sometimes."

"Do you work?" Nina asked the couple.

Henry nodded.

"We both work at night—I fix the big presses at a printer, and my wife cleans offices. That's why we're in such a good mood this morning, you see? We just got off work an hour before you came over, and we make a habit of eating a good breakfast every morning to celebrate!"

Nina smiled. She looked over at the small clock that stood on a shelf in the corner. It was almost 11am.

"Oh my, we've stayed so long, and you both must be tired," she started.

"Don't worry a thing about it," Henrietta said reassuringly. "We don't sleep till later in the afternoon anyway."

"And we sure ain't got nothin' to do now, except enjoy your company and your boys," Henry said, pointing over to the two lads who had dozed on the floor in front of the radio.

Henrietta got up and moved toward the bundle that Henry had brought in earlier.

"This is for you, honey," she said, placing the package in Nina's lap. "I didn't want to forget to give it to you before you left."

Nina looked at it in wonder and disbelief. She opened the package slowly, and saw inside it three gently used winter coats. They were thick and would be quite warm. The two boys' coats were a little bit oversized, and Henry explained that they would grow into them and could be of use the next couple years as well. Her coat was marvelous—it looked like it had been quite expensive at one point, and was sized perfectly for her. She looked back and forth between the couple and the coats in her lap, not sure quite what to think.

"You have both been so kind to me," Nina said softly, and with those words she burst into overwhelmed tears of gratitude mixed with disbelief.

"Oh, honey!" Henrietta exclaimed, as she got up from the table and moved around towards Nina. The two women embraced as Nina bawled uncontrollably.

After about a minute, Nina calmed down a bit and composed herself the best she could.

"I'm sorry," she said, wiping her face dry with her sleeves. "Things have been so hard lately, and I can't tell you the last time I found kindness like yours. I can't believe that you've only just met me, and have taken me into your home and your hearts like you have."

Henrietta smiled widely.

"It's what we do, honey," she said in such a nonchalant way that Nina just shook her head in disbelief.

"But why? Things aren't easy for you either. The food, the coffee, the coats—the way you treat my boys—what have I done to deserve this?"

"If it's dark in your room at night and you want to be able to see in order to read or eat or whatever, what do you have to do? You can't just think and make it bright, you have to flip a switch or light a match or *something*."

Nina shook her head, not sure where the old woman was headed.

"There was only one time somebody spoke and the lights came on, and that was a long, long time ago. It's the same in your room as it is in the big world out there. If we want to see more clear, if we want to chase that darkness, we're the ones who gotta make it happen."

Henry just smiled calmly and added, "*We* gotta strike the match."

His wife nodded affectionately. "And if we can get enough of them matches lit," she paused, closed her eyes, and breathed deeply, as if the words were emanating from her very soul, "then this world ain't gonna be such a dark place no more."

With those words, the spark within Nina began to glow.

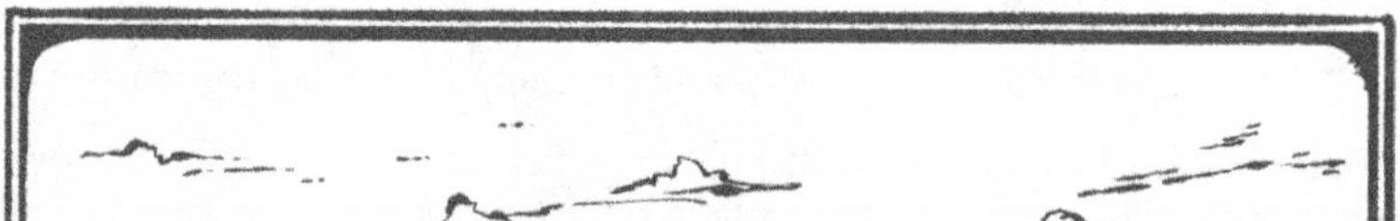

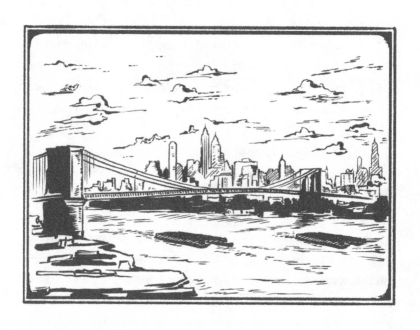

THREE

Where Mercy, Love, and Pity dwell
There God is dwelling too.

WILLIAM BLAKE

MAY 1928

Life was changing drastically for Nina, and for once, changing for the better. Her relationship with Henry and Henrietta grew deeply, and as a result, she felt herself bounding into life like she hadn't since she was an eight-year-old farm girl in the French countryside. The couple agreed, rather happily, to watch her children during the day while she sought work, and she was able to pick up odd jobs here and there. She was putting food on the table and keeping her boys warm, and that was all she cared about at this time. She was meeting lots of people, some nice and some nasty, and was learning slowly to let her inside seep onto her outside. Her existence was still not easy by any means, but once in a while, she was stopped in her tracks by the thought that she might actually be happy. She considered this thought seriously for an instant, and after a short moment, a large and genuine smile would force itself onto her face, which would be followed by a burst of laughter.

One warm Sunday afternoon, Nina took the boys for a walk. They walked for several miles, window shopping, telling jokes, and laughing. Nina even had enough spare change to buy the boys an ice cream cone. She had never seen anything as truly precious as those chocolate smeared smiles.

As the trio was entering their apartment building, Henry came bursting upon them, smiling excitedly like a little boy, himself. He grabbed Nina by the shoulders and then hugged her so tightly that he squeezed the air from her lungs momentarily. When he relaxed his grip he took her by the shoulders again.

"Great news! Great news!" he exclaimed.

"What? What is it?" Nina replied anxiously.

"We found you a job!"

Nina's jaw dropped in disbelief. The old man picked up the two boys and swung them around happily. Squeals of laughter spun round the foyer.

"A job? Where? Doing what?" Nina asked impatiently.

"Come on up and we'll tell you!"

Henry flung Thierry over his shoulder and all of them bounded up the stairs to the third floor. Once inside the couple's apartment Henrietta squealed and threw her own bear hug around Nina.

"Oh, honey, this is great!" Henrietta exclaimed. "Did Henry tell you?"

Nina shook her head, "Just barely!"

Henrietta calmed herself for a moment, adding to the anticipation Nina was feeling.

"There's a rich older white lady in our church—and I don't mean old like me, honey, I mean older—whose husband passed away a couple years ago and she told me this morning that she's looking for a companion!"

Nina quizzically looked back and forth between the large smiles of her friends.

"What does this mean—companion?"

"It's a job! And it's easy!" Henry replied hastily. By this time, he and the boys were wrestling on the floor, as was their custom.

"Yes, and Mrs. Carrington is a sweet, kind woman!" Henrietta added.

"That's good… right?" Nina asked, still a bit perplexed.

"Yes of course that's good!" Henry called out.

"But again, what is it? What do I do?"

"It's gonna be wonderful for you!" Henrietta practically shouted. "All she needs is someone, five days a week, to go over the house, do some cleaning, some cooking, and sit around and talk! That's all there is to it!"

"That's it?"

"That's it, honey!"

"And she wants me?"

The older woman nodded emphatically. Nina threw her arms around Henrietta.

"I don't know how I'll ever thank you."

"All she wants is for you to stop over in the morning and get acquainted. She wants to make sure she likes you before she hires you full time."

Nina suddenly got frantically worried. "Will she like me? I mean, does she know I'm not from here? Does she know I'm unmarried—"

"Slow down, slow down, honey," Henrietta insisted. "She's gonna like you just fine. And it doesn't matter to her where you're from or anything like that. She's gonna love you just like we love you—you ain't got nothin' to worry about."

As much as Nina trusted Henrietta by this time, she didn't quite agree with her on this point—she felt like she had a lot to worry about. What if Mrs. Carrington didn't like the way she cleaned or cooked? She had never cooked for an American before and was worried that the old woman would be particular and cranky. Nina swallowed hard and Henrietta could see that she was still nervous.

"I'll tell you two things, honey," she said reassuringly. "The first thing is this—give it a shot. What have you got to lose? If, for some bizarre, crazy reason, it doesn't work out, then so what? You move on to somethin' else."

Nina quickly nodded her understanding. She was trying desperately to calm her nerves.

"And second," Henrietta continued, "be yourself."

Henrietta let that thought sink in for a moment. Nina bit her lip, feeling the tension rising in her again.

"Believe me," Henrietta said with emphasis. "Don't doubt now. This is your chance! And I'm telling you, this lady will love you and you will love her."

Nina seemed a bit more at ease after those confident words.

"Rest, child," Henrietta said gently. "It's all gonna work itself out and you ain't gonna help it one bit by worrying."

The young mother smiled and nodded.

Nina had trouble sleeping that night. She couldn't stop thinking about this new opportunity. She desperately didn't want to make a fool of herself. Although her English had continued to improve, she was still having language issues from time to time—uncomfortable moments where she wasn't sure she understood the native speaker and was positive they did not understand her. Nina, however, did seem to have enough charm to avoid ugly scenes, as most of the time, she was able to laugh off any misunderstandings, whether it be with a merchant at the market or an employer. She was sure she could do the job, but the nagging monologue in her head tried to tell her otherwise. This was a church-going woman she'd be working for. What if she found out about Nina's past transgressions? What if she found out Nina was pregnant before wedlock or the fact that she worked as a prostitute? What if Nina didn't live up to her moral standards for someone working in her home? She felt like Henrietta's advice to rest was the last thing she possibly could do, but just when the night seemed like it would never end, she fell asleep.

The morning was glorious. Warm rays of sunshine filled her spirit and the soft spring breeze kissed her face as she walked. She was already familiar with the neighborhood where Mrs. Carrington lived, as she had done some odd work for a couple families on adjacent streets.

Nina was wearing a soft blue dress with a delicate floral print that she had been given by Henry and Henrietta when the weather turned warmer. She thought it was a beautiful dress, though gently worn, and made her feel elegant and confident again. During this time, it was not uncommon for people to sell off used items for almost nothing, although many times, they were in near perfect condition, because of other demands. Would a young lady part with a dress that she's only worn once to keep the electric running for her children? The key to finding a great bargain on such things was knowing where to look, and it so happened that Henry knew where to look. He found great buys on everything from the radio they had sitting in their home, to pots and pans, tools, and clothing. And on top of it all, he was a legendary haggler.

300 block, Essex Avenue. Here she was.

The house was gorgeous—and massive. It had been built in the late 1800's and then updated, added to, and redecorated through the years. Most of the homes in this neighborhood were large, luxurious, and dignified, but Nina had never seen a house as beautiful as Mrs. Carrington's. It was inviting, no pretension in its design. Painted a light blue—it almost matched her dress—with white trim on the windows and doors, and a white porch that stretched across the front, turned onto the sides, and meandered back as far as she could see. The front door was large and solid—also painted white.

Nina walked slowly up the cement slab leading to the front door. She was surrounded on both sides by budding flowers, lush green grass, and delicately positioned shrubs. The yard was immaculate. She took the four steps onto the porch and paused to collect herself before knocking confidently. After about a minute of silence she knocked again—still no reply. She tried to look in the front windows on either side of the door, but the drapes were pulled. For a moment she wondered if she was at the right house. She checked the sheet of paper she had with the address and then checked the numbers on the door. This was it.

Glancing down the porch again, she decided to try walking around it to see if someone would answer the back door. She followed the porch all the way around to the back yard—the house was actually bigger than it looked from the street. The back yard was even more exquisite than the front—filled with exotic plants and delicate flowers. It was exactly how she pictured the elegant serenity of an English garden. The aroma was fantastic. The back door of the house was an exact duplicate of the front, and so again, she paused for a moment and then knocked. Nothing. She was beginning to get anxious and thought about walking away altogether. She raised her hand to knock one last time when she heard a strong female voice call out behind her:

"She won't hear you in there!"

Nina spun around quickly, her heart practically leaping into her throat.

"The old bat is deaf as a tree trunk," said the woman dressed in white. She was wearing an outdoor jacket, smeared with mud and dirt, a gardening hat and gloves, and was moving swiftly towards Nina with a small spade and a plant of some kind, roots and all, in her hands. Nina thought she might have been in her fifties.

"I'm sorry, you startled me," Nina replied.

"Well, I'm sorry, I didn't mean to," the woman replied. Due to the sarcastic tone of her words, Nina wasn't sure if she was apologizing.

"I… I'm here for an interview with Mrs. Carrington. My name is Nina Laroque."

"I know who you are," the woman said, brushing briskly past Nina and towards a table holding an array of planters and bowls. "I heard you were coming by."

"Oh… you did?"

"Yeah—although I don't know why you'd want to work for this old crab."

"Well, it's work isn't it? And I've heard that she's lovely."

"Ha!" the woman exclaimed. She then started to giggle as she placed the plant into the pot.

"Well… what is she like?" Nina asked innocently.

"Old. Crotchety. Mean. I suppose that'd be a good place to start describing her."

Nina could hardly believe her ears. Surely a friend of Henry and Henrietta's couldn't fit that description.

"She can't be that bad," Nina replied.

"Hmm," the woman mumbled something under her breath. "You just wait and see."

"I was told she is looking for a companion," Nina replied.

"Ha! A companion! Or should I say another companion?"

"What do you mean?" Nina asked timidly.

"Oh, that crazy old witch runs them off almost as soon she hires 'em," the woman replied harshly. "The one before you lasted two hours, and that was nearly a record."

Nina was stunned. "Then why do you work for her—if she's such a terrible person?"

"First of all," the woman replied, "I know how to handle her—been around her long enough. And secondly, I'm a gardener, so I'm outside most of the time. God knows I'd go crazy, too, if I was cooped up in that house all day."

Nina's frustration began to boil over.

"Well, that's fine that you don't like her. You probably won't like me either, but can you take me in to see her? I need to meet her and I need to start work."

The woman turned around suddenly.

"Now who do you think you're talking to?" she snapped. "Am I your servant or something?"

"Of course not, but you work here, and I am not going to barge into someone's home without permission."

There was a moment of silence between the two women on the porch.

"You're a bit feisty aren't you?" the woman asked.

Nina rolled her eyes, hands on her hips. "Only when I have to be."

The woman smiled.

"You're European?"

"Yes, but what does that have to do with anything?"

"Do you cook?"

"Of course I cook," Nina replied flatly.

"Is your food any good?"

"That depends on the person's taste," Nina said harshly, becoming more and more irritated by the inane conversation.

The woman simply nodded and began to take off her gloves.

"Well, I'm not very picky," she said quietly.

"What does it matter what your taste is?" Nina replied hotly. "Now, will you please show me inside so I can speak with the lady of the house?"

"Oh, you don't need to go in there."

"Madame, please," Nina pleaded. "I need to see if I can get this job. I have children to feed and I will put up with anything—a crotchety old woman or even you."

The gardener laughed kindly, grabbing her side with one hand.

"Like I said, you don't need to go in there. You've already got the job."

The look of perplexity that shot on Nina's face made the woman laugh again.

"I'm Mrs. Carrington," she said warmly, extending her delicate, blue veined hand.

Nina swallowed hard and almost fainted. She took the woman's pale hand and shook it.

"I… I'm sorry… I thought you were the gardener," she said nervously.

The woman looked around at the cultivated Eden surrounding them and casually said:

"I am the gardener."

Nina couldn't believe her ears.

"It just so happens that I'm also the lady of the house," Mrs. Carrington said. "And I'd like to apologize for that little game I played. Most girls don't even make it to the back door, and you're only the second that's made it through to the end."

"Please don't apologize," Nina responded sincerely, still catching her breath. "But may I ask why you do this?"

Mrs. Carrington shrugged.

"I need to know who is going to be in my home with me," she answered. "I want a companion who wants to work, who is honest and respectable. And above all, I need someone with a little personality. And you've got all of those things. So, if you would like to be my friend and help me with a thing or two around this old place, I'd love to pay you more than it's worth."

Nina smiled broadly and took the woman's hand again.

"Yes, yes, Mrs. Carrington. I will do anything you ask of me."

"Well that's great! But rule number one is this: please call me Beth," the lady said amiably.

"Ok, I will," Nina answered. "And you can call me Nina."

Thus, a friendship was born.

Working for Beth was an uncommon pleasure. It turned out that despite her youthful face and considerably good health, she was already in her mid-seventies. She was sincere, kind, and not at all hard to please. She had a passion for horticulture and for watching things blossom to life. She enjoyed coffee in the mornings and tea in the afternoons. Most of Nina's day was spent outdoors, which she relished. The air at that time of year was growing warmer and rain was keeping the ladies indoors less often. They planted, they watered, they transplanted, they trimmed, they weeded, and they pruned. While working, the two women also laughed quite a bit, as Beth had an extraordinary sense of humor. She was a refined lady in many ways—it was obvious that she had become accustomed to money and living well—but she was also incredibly earthy, and Nina began to suspect that she had suffered her fair share of hardships, as well. The two ladies got to know each other quickly, although Nina did not include much detail about her rocky relationship with Jacques and her previous form of "employment."

One balmy afternoon, while the two ladies sat on the porch with tea, Nina realized that Beth had not said much at all about her own family life. Nina didn't think it was because she had something to hide or wished to forget, but genuinely believed that she hadn't brought it up because she was too interested in learning about Nina's life.

"Beth, do you have children?"

"Yes, I do," she answered. "I have three—two boys and a girl. I lost one boy to diphtheria in 1899, but my other two are alive and in good health."

"How old was he?"

"He was twenty-one," she replied sorrowfully. "He was traveling the Pacific and came down with it somewhere in the Philippines. His name was Jack."

"I'm so sorry to hear that," Nina empathized. "I couldn't imagine losing a child at any age—may God forbid it."

"It is the hardest thing that a mother can ever endure," Beth replied. "But he is in a better place that I may get to see one day, along with my dear husband."

"What was his name?"

"Charles," the old woman replied, a warm smile spreading on her lips as she said the name. "He passed in twenty-four. He was eighty-five years old and the love of my life."

"That is very sweet. How long were you married?"

"Fifty-four beautiful years," Beth responded. "I married him when I was eighteen. I would have married him earlier if it hadn't been for my father."

"What do you mean?" Nina asked inquisitively.

"Well, we had already been in love for a couple years, but Charles was almost fourteen years older than me, and worked for my father to boot. My father simply wouldn't allow us to marry until I was eighteen."

"Were you angry with him?"

"At the time, I suppose I was. But after having children of my own, especially a daughter, I understood his reason. I was still a child and would be for many years. He wanted to make sure that I wasn't rushing into something that would inevitably alter my life forever. So, he kept strict rules on where and when and in whose company we were allowed to meet, and when I turned eighteen, he gave us his blessing."

Nina reflected on her own youthful marriage and how rushing into something like love had certainly altered the course of her life. She couldn't say that it was all negative—she had two beautiful children whom she lived for—but Jacques had stolen her innocence and caused her unimaginable anguish. She wished that she had had a father like Beth's—a father who would have looked out for her wellbeing rather than simply wishing her out of his hair. How different her life might have been. She might have married a nice French boy and still been on a farm in Europe. She might have had security and even wealth by now. The thought of her two boys, however, kept her from daydreaming about what might have been, and she actually felt a pang of guilt for thinking such things.

"If he was so much older, how did you meet and fall in love? You said he worked for your father. What did your father do?"

"Did you know that before all these towns and cities started springing up around here, this area was mainly just farmland?"

"No I didn't. It is hard to imagine."

"Well sure, and it was some of the most fertile land in the whole country. I know it's hard to believe now, but years ago this was a regular old bread basket. And all those farmers needed supplies—feed, seeds, tools—so many years ago, my father, James William Beckett, opened a small shop to try to provide some of those things. It was a tough business at first—very competitive—but the one thing my father was best at was, was finding new ways to do things. So he started selling consumer goods as well as farming products. He started selling little shaving kits for gents and magazines and dime novels for the ladies. He even stocked little trinkets and toys for their children. At first, everybody thought he was out of his mind—especially his competition. But over time, people started to realize that instead of having to run to four different stores on every corner in town, they could just stop at Beckett's and get everything they needed."

"That's amazing," Nina said in true admiration. "It was almost like a modern department store?"

"Exactly!" Beth replied. "My father was successful, but it wasn't until he met Charles that the business really came to life."

It was 1871, and I was fifteen years old. I had been working in my father's shop, when not in school, for several years already. All four of my siblings worked for Father, too. We all had different jobs and different talents, and Father tried to get as much out of us as he could. My job was arranging things on the shelves, sweeping, cleaning, and helping customers as was needed.

One very ordinary day, the most extraordinary gentleman I would ever meet walked into the store and changed my life forever. He was wearing a brown suit and his clever mustache was groomed for business. He was dapper and handsome, and as clumsy as a bat is blind. Lord knows how he made it all the way to eighty-five years old without getting himself killed. So, in walked Charles with his stiff leather briefcase. He was so handsome that I blushed and hid behind a stack of big burlap bags filled with chicken feed.

He stood there and looked around the store, clearing his throat several times as he saw no one to help him. Father must have heard him and came out from the back room.

"Beth? Beth?" he called. I was too embarrassed to reply.

"I'm sorry, sir," Father said to Charles. "How can I help you?"

"Hello, sir," Charles replied cordially. "I must admit that I am here to ask you the very same question."

"I don't understand," Father replied.

"My name is Charles Carrington, and I have come to offer my services."

"Well, young man, I certainly appreciate your offer, but am fully staffed at the moment and don't require any further assistance."

"That's perfectly fine, sir. I will work for free," Charles replied confidently.

"I do not understand you. Is the goal of employment not to make a living?"

"Most certainly, sir."

"Then how can you work for free? Are you bored and independently wealthy?" Father asked with a laugh. Charles smiled as well.

"Quite the contrary, I assure you."

"Well, what then? Is this some kind of joke?"

"Not at all, sir. I assure you I am quite serious."

"Well, come with it then," Father replied sternly. "I am a very busy man—either get to your point, buy something, or leave."

"That's just it, sir," Charles countered. "You're very busy, and I imagine that much of the work that consumes your time is work you would rather not do."

"This is my business and I do the work that is required to run it efficiently."

"Exactly, sir!" Charles answered, pointing his finger quickly at my father. He then just stood for a moment and smiled.

"So, again, what is your point?" Father asked, this time on the verge of anger.

"What would you say if I offered you an opportunity to spend more time with your customers, with your children, and with your wife? What if you knew beyond a shadow of a doubt that your business was being run exactly as you would run it yourself, like clockwork, and the all while freeing up your time to do more of the things you love?"

"Naturally, that would be wonderful," Father said in a much more calm tone of voice. He spoke with the slightest ring of sarcasm. "And I suppose you're going to tell me how that can happen?"

"Certainly," Charles answered. "I have a small inheritance from an uncle who died in combat—it's just enough for me to live on for six months, or so. I was an officer's steward during the war and have a great mind for minute detail. Planning and organizing and acquiring goods and the like—I've done it all."

Fathered chuckled at the thought that he was actually entertaining this conversation with a man that he'd never met before.

"So," Father continued, "I am to let you take over the duties of managing this store and you are to work free of charge?"

"For six months," Charles added, nodding his head quickly.

"For six months—and then what?"

"And then you are to pay me a percentage of the store's profits—"

"Oh, so I am to take you on as a partner as well?" Father countered. "You must be crazy! I've never seen you in my life and you have the gall to propose that I give my business away?"

Charles took it as an insult and looked quite hurt for a moment, but then bounced back.

"Well, you didn't let me finish, sir," he said calmly. "You will pay me a percentage of the store's profits above what they are today."

"I'm afraid I still do not understand you," Father replied suspiciously.

"Simply put, if after six months of my work—free of charge—you are not making more money than you are today, you will not owe me a penny. If, on the other hand, I have managed to cut costs and raise revenues, then I shall require twenty-five percent of profits, again, over what you are currently making."

Father thought hard. I could see him biting his lower lip, which he always did when concentrating on a problem. It was at that moment that I lost my balance and fell loudly into a rack of pots and pans. I got up awkwardly and ran towards the back of the store.

My eyes did catch Charles's for a moment and I thought I heard a cannon shot. He simply stared at me, wild and wide-eyed.

"What are you doing?" Fathered called to the blur of motion that was his daughter.

I simply ran to the back and closed the door behind me. I was out of breath and felt as if an arrow had pierced my heart. Had that man felt what I had felt in that moment? I put my ear to the door to listen to the rest of the conversation between the two men.

"Do you have references?" Father asked.

"Oh... of course, sir," Charles answered, sounding completely unsure of himself and utterly preoccupied. To this point, he had seemed supremely confident. The change in his demeanor was striking to me, although my father did not seem to notice much. "My aunt lives in town... Mrs. Hensley."

"Mrs. Hensley!" Father almost shouted. "Say no more. Allow me to talk to her and you will have your answer."

"Thank you, sir," Charles said, sounding as if he was trying to catch his breath. "I also have references from officers under whom I served who will vouch for my work ethic and my character."

"Certainly, certainly," Father replied. "But I do not believe them to be necessary. As far as I'm concerned, your connection with Mrs. Hensley is sufficient. I believe we have a deal, Mr. um..?"

"Carrington, sir. Charles Carrington."

"A pleasure, Mr. Carrington," Father replied affably. "And my name is James Beckett."

"A pleasure, as well, Mr. Beckett."

There was a moment of silence in which I assume the two men shook hands.

"One more thing, Mr. Beckett, before I go," Charles blurted out nervously.

"Certainly," Father replied.

"May I presume to ask about that girl who ran through here a moment ago. Does she work here?"

"Yes," Father said slowly and sternly.

"Sir, she may very well be the most beautiful sight I have ever gazed upon. She is breathtaking!"

I was flattered and embarrassed by his high praise. I certainly was pretty—who isn't at fifteen?—but had never thought of myself as a real beauty. I know now that from the first moment he caught a glimpse of me to the very last breath he took, Charles Carrington believed with all his heart that I was the most beautiful woman who had ever lived, and, while it may be foolishness, it is something that I will always cherish.

There was another moment or two of silence before in sheer naivety, Charles asked:

"Does she come from a respectable family?"

"Yes, she does," I heard Father answer in a low, serious tone.

"Who is her father, sir? I must meet him and ask for her hand immediately, if she is not spoken for already."

"Well, I can assure you that she is not spoken for yet," Father said. It sounded as if he was clinching his teeth.

"Oh, wonderful!" Charles exclaimed. "So you know her father?"

"I am her father, you idiot!" he roared. "And she is but fifteen years old, you scoundrel!"

There was such a frantic commotion after this that I thought Father might kill him. The two men were yelling—Father in fury and Charles in apology—and didn't stop for a few minutes. Suddenly, I heard the bell ring at the front door and both men immediately went silent. After a moment, I heard a female voice ask for a bag of oats. My father began conversing with her warmly, as he did with all of our customers. After a few more seconds, I heard the lady leave the store—the bell rang again—and instead of picking up where they left off, there was more silence. I heard Father say something quietly, to which Charles did not respond—at least he didn't respond loud enough for me to hear through the door. I began to wonder if Charles had left along with our customer, but then I heard Father call my name.

I immediately opened the door and rushed through. I knew well enough not to keep Father waiting. Charles glanced at me quickly and turned his attention back to my father.

"Beth, this is Mr. Charles Carrington. He may be working with us starting next week," Father said, pointing towards the young man in the tidy suit. "And this is my precious daughter, Beth," he said, pointing back towards me.

I looked back at Charles and he looked quickly at me. I will always remember how kind his eyes were at that moment. He had no venom in him at all, but simply a forlorn longing, like a traveler who had wandered a great distance and had not yet found his home.

"It's a pleasure to meet you, sir," I replied, trying not to show Father how smitten and embarrassed I was. Charles nodded and bowed like a true gentleman.

"Well, then," Father continued sternly, "now that our introductions have been made, I have one simple rule, and I better not catch either of you crossing it. You are not to communicate with each other during working hours, or even after, for that matter. You may say 'good morning,' in the mornings and 'good evening,' in the evenings, and that is to be the extent of your discourse. Am I understood?"

We both looked at Father and nodded our assent. I was trembling.

"Good," Father pronounced. "Mr. Carrington, allow me to make my inquiry with Mrs. Hensley in the morning, and I will certainly send you word as to my final decision."

"Thank you, sir," Charles replied confidently. "I will look forward to hearing from you."

The two gentlemen firmly shook hands, Charles looking my father unflinchingly in the eyes. He then bowed to me and said, "Good evening," as he left, even though it was only eleven in the morning. I couldn't help but smile.

After Charles walked out, Father turned to me. I was expecting another strict admonition, but instead, he simply put his arm around me and kissed my forehead. When a moment in his embrace passed, he pointed to the door and then, in the most peculiarly melancholy tone, said the most curious thing:

"Marry that man… and you will be happy and well-fed all your days."

My smile must have faded into a look of sheer bewilderment because he began to laugh heartily. He then got playfully serious and said with a slight chuckle and a shake of his head, "But not now." He pointed his long, calloused finger at me and smiled again. "For now, you must obey my rule—understood?"

Needless to say, Father interviewed Mrs. Hensley about her nephew and was thoroughly impressed. Charles had served during every year of the war, most of it under Major General Henry Blackstone Banning, and saw action everywhere from Bull Run to Jackson to Nashville. His service and experience were distinguished. Father learned, quite accurately, from Mrs. Hensley that Charles was gentlemanly, industrious, and most importantly, honest. We would soon thereafter learn that Charles was also undoubtedly brilliant.

By the end of the first six months of his work one of our competitors had shuttered his doors, our store's profits were up almost thirty percent, and Father was spending more time enjoying life and less time worried about keeping the shop open and the children fed. At first we were both very careful about abiding by Father's rule and would only greet each other as we came and went. However, as time went on and Father gained firsthand knowledge of Charles's character he became more comfortable with the young man, and although he never verbalized a change in his rule about the two of us, we did slowly start to talk more and more and he never said a word.

Shortly after I turned sixteen, Charles asked Father for my hand in marriage. It was not terribly uncommon for a girl to be married at sixteen in those days, nor was it terribly uncommon for her to marry a man who was substantially older than she, but still my Father rejected the proposal outright, telling Charles that he would not consent to his daughter's marriage until she was eighteen. I was heartbroken at the time, and in a moment of girlish desperation, even told Charles that we should run away together. He was mortified by the thought, as his honor would not allow him to consider such a rash and improper action. Twenty-two months later, we were married, and twelve months after that, I gave birth to our eldest son who we called Jack.

Father's business continued to profit and soon expanded to two, three, then four locations. This all took place largely under the careful direction of my new husband, although he and Father certainly did work closely together. Eventually, Father took Charles on as a full partner, which allowed us to purchase our first home. Charles insisted that we pay cash, as debt was anathema to him, so it was a small, rickety old house, but it was ours, and we filled it with such happy memories over the years. Our daughter Rachel was born there a couple years later, and our youngest boy Jasper was born there as well.

Eventually, as the business expanded, we were able to buy a larger house on this side of town, though I certainly don't associate that home with as much happiness. In fact, after a while, I hated the sight of it. A few years ago, it was badly damaged in a storm and they had to tear it down completely. I couldn't have been more delighted.

It was in that second house that my life became unraveled. The children were growing up and were getting their educations, while working in the shops. Charles was working more and more, as Father had retired, and a fifth store was in the planning. It was 1898, and in April, the Spanish-American War broke out. We were shocked to learn that shortly thereafter, our eldest boy Jack, by this time in his second year of university studies, enlisted in the army. Charles, knowing full well the terrible nature of war, did everything that he could to talk him out of it, but it was no use. Jack was a strong-headed young man and dreamed of seeing the world. No argument, no form of persuasion was of use, and Jack headed off towards the Pacific.

Charles went out of his mind. He put the plans for the new store on hold and was able to convince some old army comrades from the Civil War to allow him to reenlist as a steward in the company in which Jack would be serving. I hated the idea, but was somewhat comforted by the thought that at least Charles would be with him. So Father came out of retirement and my husband went off to war as well.

With Charles and Jack overseas and my two younger children preoccupied with school, work, and youthful living, I grew terribly lonely and bored. At first I would try to visit lady friends of mine or go to the city and shop or have lunch, but eventually I became increasingly isolated, though I might not have realized it at the moment. I was so accustomed to family and friends and work and suddenly found myself feeling useless. Letters from my boys were few and far between, as the distance was so great. With no husband to love, no children to care for, and no real work to do, I began to lose all sense of purpose in my life.

Then, one cold, snowy day in December of that year, just a few days after Christmas, I learned that our next door neighbor Max had suddenly lost his lovely wife, Louise. He was utterly devastated, as you might expect. They were both a couple years older than I and had no children, and I felt terrible that Max was seemingly all alone in the world. I would bring Rachel and Jasper over at night with meals in an attempt to cheer him up and entertain him a bit. He was very glad of our company, and over the course of the next few months began to slowly reemerge from the abyss of his desolation. The same could not be said for me, however.

It had been almost two months since I had heard from either Jack or Charles, and while the two younger children were away at school, I felt like I would lose my mind completely. I happened to glance out the back window and saw Max pacing around his garden, which was frozen stiff at this point, wearing a large overcoat and looking rather sullen. I quickly heated a kettle of tea, dressed for the weather, and headed out to meet him. He smiled warmly when I greeted him and invited me inside. I hesitated for a moment, but then thought of how foolish it would have been for me to make tea and then force the man to drink it outside on such a fiercely cold day. We spent several hours in his parlor, talking and laughing and forgetting our troubles. He was a genuinely nice man and was very conversational. He shook my hand warmly, thanked me for the tea, and then walked me to my door in a very gentlemanly fashion. I really didn't think anything of our meeting, and a few days later, under much the same circumstances,

I met him with tea again. Over the course of the next few weeks, we met regularly for afternoon tea and each day our time would end with him walking me to my door in all types of weather. He was a salve for my loneliness, and I believe I served something of the same function for him.

At tea on an early spring afternoon—I now had not heard from my husband or my son in close to three months—a terrible thing occurred. Max told a story in his typically poetic style and had me laughing so hard that I spilled my tea all over the rug in front of me. I apologized fervently as I dropped to my knees and began to blot the stain with my handkerchief. He did the same with his handkerchief while telling me adamantly not to apologize. A moment later, with such curious timing, our eyes locked. We had never been that close before. I remember he had a warm smile on his lips. His eyes pleaded to me, not lustfully, but as if he couldn't speak the words in his heart because I was another man's wife. I was yearning for affection and tenderness. I slowly closed my eyes, leaned forward, and pressed my lips against his. At first, he did not kiss back, and I was suddenly afraid that I had offended him or the memory of his wife. I swallowed hard and leaned back.

"I'm so sorry," I whispered.

He sat there for a moment, looking at me again with those tender, lonesome eyes.

"No, it's alright," he whispered in reply.

I do not know what came over me at that moment, but I leaned forward and kissed him again. This time, he returned my kiss. We embraced each other and kissed yet again, more fervently this time. After a while, I was lying nude on my back, staring up at the ceiling in another man's home, in another man's bed, another man pressed warmly against my body. Max lay sleeping, his head propped on my shoulder, his strong arms around my waist. It felt so satisfyingly human to be held, to be warm, to share comfort as well as a bed with another person. I could smell his expensive cologne, which he had more than likely purchased at one of my husband's stores.

Charles.

I suddenly thought of my husband. I cupped my hand to my mouth in horror. This was betrayal of the worst kind. I was Judas Iscariot. I didn't know what to think; I didn't know what to do. I had to get up—I had to get out of there.

"Max," I whispered to no response. "Max!" I said louder, waking him.

He looked at me almost lovingly and smiled. I knew that I was going to break his heart all over again, but I felt that I had to.

"Max, I'm sorry," I said, sitting up in his bed and brushing his arm off of me gently. "This shouldn't have happened."

"I know," he said softly as he traced the contours of my back with his fingers.

"Please, this must never happen again."

"I understand," he replied tenderly, a warm smile again on his lips.

"I am very sorry, but this should not have happened. I should never have—"

"Beth," he cut in, "It's alright. You're married… and I can't expect you to continue this."

He was being truly genuine. I got out of bed and rushed to put my clothes back on. I could feel his stare, watching my skin as I clothed myself.

"Can I walk you to your door?" he asked politely.

"No—please don't," I answered sternly, shaking my head quickly back and forth.

He just watched me, that affectionate smile clinging to his face. Throughout all of this, he conducted himself with a matter of gentility. I could not be angry with him; I was, however, furious with myself.

"One last kiss then?" he asked, those grey eyes again pleading for affection. I kissed him again quickly, perhaps in recognition of my own role in the affair, then grabbed the rest of my things and quickly walked home.

To my utter astonishment my daughter was home when I walked through the back door. She looked at me, jaw dropped open, without saying a word. My hair was disheveled, my dress untidy, and I'm sure I looked as if I had just seen a ghost. Rachel glanced out the window, directly at Max's home, and then turned her piercing blue eyes back to me. It was obvious that she had put two and two together. I tried to apologize quickly, but am not sure if any words came out, as I brushed past her and up the stairs into my bedroom. I locked the door, threw myself on the bed, and wept bitterly, burying my face in my husband's pillow. I did not come out of my room all evening and no one came to disturb me or even check on me. Rachel must have told Jasper what I had done when he arrived and they both decided to let me alone.

It wasn't until very late that night that I was able to sleep at all. I had vivid and horrible dreams about my husband and my son suffering on some God-forsaken tropical island. I saw them in a squalid war camp, bruised and bloody, barely clinging to life. I could hear Jack coughing and wheezing and could see Charles weeping uncontrollably. There were enormous insects buzzing all around the men and filthy rodents picking at their skin. There were some men harshly yelling orders and others crying out in pain. Puddles of blood gathered on the floor and a pile of limbs lay rotting in the corner. I dreamed that there was a very loud explosion that rang in my ears—or was it a dream?

I shot up suddenly.

Silence.

Something, however, was not right. I suddenly heard commotion outside my room and unlocked my door. I looked into the hall and saw Jasper moving quickly towards the stairs, still dressed in his night clothes, the shotgun in his hands.

"Is everything alright?" I asked anxiously.

"I don't know," he answered harshly.

Rachel came running from her room and quickly into mine.

"What was that?" she asked.

"I don't know, I thought it was a dream."

We sat on the bed and held each other closely. We could hear Jasper moving hastily around the house downstairs. We could hear him checking the locks on the doors and windows, and then it got quieter as he moved towards the back of the house. For a moment there was silence. Then we could hear the back door open and close.

A man's scream rang out in the black stillness.

I got up and ran to the top of the steps. The back door opened and closed again.

"Oh God!" the scream came again, this time from inside the house.

"Jasper!" I hollered down the stair case.

"Oooh God…" his scream had turned to a horrified wail.

I cried his name again as I flew down the stairs. He was dreadfully pallid and was clutching his hands to his temples. "Jasper, what it is?" I asked, trying to pry his hands from his head.

"Outside, outside," he replied in a frenzied state of shock, pointing towards the back door.

"Where's your gun?" I asked quickly. "Is it safe?"

He just nodded, tears streaming down his face. In my attention to him I barely notice Rachel whizzing past me. I heard the door open and close again, a moment of silence, and then another blood curdling scream. I ran through the kitchen and flew out the back door. I saw my daughter standing there, turned towards Max's house, clutching her hands over her heart. I spun in the direction of her gaze and remember a scream catching in my throat as I saw Max's limp body, sagging in his lawn chair. He was completely nude in the glacial air; a pistol still dangling from his lifeless hand. In the clear moonlight his blood, which looked terrifyingly black, was sprayed all over the side of his house, chunks of his brain and skull plastered onto the siding. His mouth was open and the top of his head was completely gone. His eyes, and I will never forget his eyes, were open and still had that aching stare, which will haunt me all my days.

It's my fault, was the first thought that entered my mind after the initial shock of the moment. He hadn't even dressed himself after I left him.

Rachel began sobbing wildly and I remember calling for Jasper to come take her inside. He was always a strong child and had been able to compose himself enough to take his sister by the shoulders and lead her back into the house. I remember staring at Max's corpse, until for a brief second, I thought I saw him smile at me. It was at that moment that Jasper came through the door again, telling me that a police officer had arrived.

The police interviewed all of us thoroughly that night and an ambulance wagon arrived to take the body away. Dawn was upon us, and Rachel was back in bed, although I don't believe she slept. Jasper and I sat at the kitchen table, staring blankly at the dying fire in the hearth. A sudden knock on the back door jolted us both. Jasper answered and I heard a police officer identify himself and ask to come in.

"Are you Mrs. Beth Carrington? This was left for you," the policeman said, handing me a folded sheet of paper with my name written on it in delicate, masculine hand. He then told us that the death had been officially ruled a suicide and that their investigation was over. Jasper showed the officer out and then promptly and silently went upstairs.

I turned the paper over in my hands and saw that the seal had been broken, meaning that a police investigator had already read it. I read it several times and then tossed it in the fire, although I will never forget what it said:

My Dearest Beth,

You have been an unimaginable comfort to me in these hard times. I thought that losing my dear Louise would be the end of my life, but I have now found that losing you is the final, unbearable torment that leads me to a desperate act. I know that I cannot, and should not, have you to myself, and this is an agony that I simply cannot live with. Do not blame yourself for my actions or my feelings—you are truly an angel and have made these last months worth living. I feel as if I have sinned against my God and my darling wife, and now throw myself upon their mercy that I may join them soon.

Your dear friend,

—Maximilian

That morning at eight o'clock, I received a telegram that my son Jack was dead.

A few days after that, I received a letter from Charles. He was to be returning home with our son's body and would see us in a matter of a week. I couldn't help but feel that Jack's death was a punishment for my infidelity with Max, although witnessing the aftermath of his violent end would certainly have been punishment enough. I couldn't sleep; I couldn't eat. My two living children would not speak to me. In fact, Jasper had begun to pack his things as though he was moving out.

That next week dragged on painfully, but it couldn't have lasted long enough. I entertained the idea of keeping my affair a secret, but knew that I couldn't live with myself if I did. I also knew that my secret would not be safe with either of my children, for they were far too loyal to their father to allow him to live in ignorance. But how could I tell him? How could I admit that while he was in the midst of the most terrible suffering, watching our little boy die a dreadful death, his most beloved wife was lying in the luxury of another man's embrace?

It was a frosty morning when Charles opened our front door. A friend of his from the army picked him up by carriage and drove him home. I sat in the parlor, sipping tea and anticipating the scene that would unfold. He walked in slowly, put his bags down and turned to look at me. He looked like a different man—he looked old. His eyes sagged in their sockets, much of his hair had fallen out, and his skin was wrinkled and brown, a stark contrast from the whiteness of the frost that blanketed everything outside. He just stared at my tear soaked face with a blank expression, as if somehow he already knew what I had to tell him. Suddenly he nearly ran towards me and picked me up from my seat. He embraced me so tightly that I could hardly breathe and began kissing my face and my neck with such fervor that I thought we might have been on our wedding night all over again. I tried to stop him, the shame of my deeds completely overwhelming me; I did not want him to love me as he once did. As much as I longed to comfort him, I wanted to suffer as he had suffered, and worse. He suddenly cried out and began to sob. I felt his warm tears dripping down my neck. Finally after a moment I was able to pry myself from his arms.

"Charles," I whispered. He simply stared at me. I couldn't bear the look of anguish on his face and knew that I had to tell him immediately. Suddenly his eyes dropped to the floor. His hands were cupped together in front of him; for a moment I thought he might have been praying.

"Yes, my love," he said softly, his glance shifting back to mine.

"Charles, let me first say that I'm sorry—terribly sorry."

He did not respond. His soft, kind eyes penetrated my soul. I collapsed to my knees and clutched at my heart.

"Charles, please!" I wailed. He did not react. His body was simply frozen, but I could tell that his mind raced as it always did.

Then, he slowly extended his hands. He simply said, "Come." I took his worn hands and he lifted me to my feet. I was not sure if for the first time he would hit me. Instead, he didn't do anything. There we stood for what felt like an hour holding hands.

"I heard about Louise," he finally said. "And I heard about Max."

"What did you hear?" I asked sheepishly.

"I heard that they're both gone," he answered solemnly.

I nodded.

"It is good," he pronounced confidently.

I couldn't believe my ears—this coming from such a religious man, from such a kind heart.

"How is it good?" I asked anxiously.

"Because you may have lost me forever," he replied quietly. "For I surely would have killed the man with my bare hands."

I closed my eyes and began to quietly sob.

"Charles, please do not blame him… he was a lonely man, grieving the death of his beloved wife."

"Beth," he said tenderly, as he began to caress my cheek. "I am filled to the brim with hatred. I am angry and I am desperate. But I could never hate you."

I looked questioningly into his eyes.

"It is easy for me to hate the world and almost everything in it," he continued. "I can hate this damn country for which I've sacrificed so much. I can hate the Spanish, I can hate the Pacific, and I can hate the sky, the sun, and the moon. I have had my time stolen from me, my decency, my honor, and my son. So please, at the very least allow me, for a time, to hate the man who wounded me so."

"Oh, Charles…" I whispered, taking his face in my hands. "I'm so sorry."

He kissed my hands.

"My dear Beth, I am as much to blame for this as you are."

"What could you mean by that?"

"I allowed my belief that I could control my own destiny blind me into believing that I could control our son's fate. I believed that being with him would somehow allow me to guide his steps, to keep him from harm. I traipsed around the globe, following blindly while I believed that I led, and where did it get me? I left you behind—my one true love—left you alone and that was supremely selfish. In truth, when I admit what I have concealed deep inside, the only person that I considered when I made the decision to follow him was myself, and for that I have suffered greatly."

He suddenly got nervous and cast his gaze at the floor between us.

"I must ask you one thing, however," he said gently.

"You can ask me anything."

He paused for a moment, as if gathering his strength.

"Do you still love me?"

"Charles, of course!" I answered hastily. "With all of my heart and soul! I love you more now than I have ever loved you!"

"Can I make you a promise, then? Beth, I promise that as long as I have breath in me, I will never leave you like that again."

I smiled warmly, took his strong hands in mine and pressed my lips fervently against his.

From that moment, we were never the same. He never brought up my affair after that day—not once. I would spend the rest of my days trying to show him my gratitude for his kindness and mercy, showering him with affection and attention. He would spend the rest of his days trying to convince me that all was truly forgiven. There we were, two people who had already lived more than half our lives, beginning to get to know each other as if we were courting all over again. And in a sense, I suppose that we were.

Watching her father's response to me over the next few days was certainly helpful for Rachel. Seeing his strength and graciousness towards me gave her a sense of direction in dealing with her now complicated relationship with me. We sat together several times and she allowed me to apologize, and eventually I allowed myself to accept her forgiveness. Rachel had always been a strong girl, both physically and emotionally. She was much more like her father in that respect than she was like me.

Jasper was another story completely. Oh, he was furious at me. Charles did everything that he could to calm him, but he was inconsolable. I cannot say that he was irrational, although some of his behavior might have been. He was intent on seeing his father for a week, attending his brother's funeral, and then moving to Philadelphia with a friend.

We laid Jack to rest on a cold, wet Saturday morning, and that night, I overheard part of a conversation between Jasper and Charles in my husband's study. They had already been at it for a while, and their voices were growing agitated.

"Father, I cannot stay in this house with her!"

"And why not, son? For this is my house as well as it is hers!"

"I am not willing to consent to living in this house, with that woman who has shamed you! It's not Christian!"

"That woman? That woman is your mother!"

"Father, I can forgive her for her transgressions against me, but I cannot simply overlook her sins against such an upstanding man as yourself, not to mention the vows she broke in front of almighty God."

"That is not yours to judge, son. I have forgiven your mother her sins against me, and as such you should forgive her as well."

"I will not," Jasper flatly pronounced. "I cannot err on the side of injustice—everything in my upbringing simply will not allow it!"

There was a pause that lasted a few seconds.

"Son," Charles started softly, "in this family, injustice perpetrated against the weak and the oppressed will never be tolerated—about this you are correct. But if we are to err in our dealings with each other, we will boldly err on the side of grace."

I heard rustling within the room and a second later the doors flew open, almost hitting me square in the face. Jasper flew out of the room, carrying a small bag under his arm. He burst through the front door and out into the cold night. I don't think he even saw me. Charles followed him to the door of the study and called out to him. He then turned as he saw me out of the corner of his eye.

"I'm sorry," he said, placing his hand on the top of his balding head.

"You have nothing to be sorry for," I answered. "Thank you for what you said to him."

"How do you talk nonsense into the head of such a rational being?"

"What do you mean?"

"Nonsense," he replied. "Forgiveness is nonsense. It's not rational; it's not logical. But how else is the world to be reborn?" Charles asked the question honestly, as if he really didn't know the answer.

"He'll come around," I tried to assure him. "We raised him, after all."

But Jasper moved to Philadelphia. Charles received regular letters from him, but I did not. I wrote constantly to no reply. He didn't even inquire about me in writing his father, however, Charles let him know that I was well anyway.

Over the next few years, much took place. Charles and Father opened a fifth store and we moved permanently into this house. I was so glad to be rid of the constant reminder of those times. Rachel was married in this very garden to a fine young Princeton man who would go on to be quite a success himself. They now live in Newark in a fine home with three beautiful daughters of their own.

Jasper went on from Philadelphia to Cleveland in 1907 to work for Packard Motor Cars, then served in the First World War as a mechanic. He spent eighteen months in Europe. So our second son also followed his father's footsteps and went off to war. Charles, however, never left my side this time. Thankfully, Jasper survived unscathed, and returned to Ohio. He went on to work for an independent mechanic shop, married a beautiful young lady named Mary, with whom he has several children. As time went on, our relationship healed, thanks in large part to his father's continual insistence that he forgive me. Jasper truly did mature, and from the letters I regularly receive from Mary, he has grown into the kind of husband and father that Charles was. I couldn't be more proud of him. In his last letter to me, he mentioned opening his own shop in Fort Thomas, Kentucky, just across the river from Cincinnati.

Charles and I were, alas, alone together again. My mother was extremely sick for several years, and finally passed away in 1906. Father's heath immediately deteriorated, and within four months, we lost him as well. By this point, however, Charles was in complete control of all of our stores, and was managing them with astonishing success. We made money hand over fist and my husband managed to give much of it away to those in need. He never retired—he would go to work every day until he was physically unable, and we grew inseparably close over those tender years.

"And that's my story."

"Incredible," Nina replied. "I'm so glad that Jasper has come around. It seems to me like he was too hard on you, and that you were too hard on yourself. Everyone must have closeness to other human beings. But your husband's forgiveness without so much as a second thought is truly remarkable."

"Yes it was. The most difficult part, I'll tell you, was finally forgiving myself."

"Yes, but how do you let go? How do you live with yourself when you are your own worst enemy?"

"The key," Beth answered, leaning back in her chair, "is to understand that what you've done is not who you are. That was the biggest lesson Charles ever taught me, and I wasted a lot of years reliving those horrible days, when I should have been living the days I had."

When she got home after dark, Nina picked up the boys from Henry and Henrietta's. She held her children close that night and told them over and over again how much they were loved. The next morning, the sun rose warmly over the skyline of the city, and in the depth of its shadow, she was being set free.

FOUR

It is difficult to know at what moment love begins;
it is less difficult to know that it has begun

HENRY WADSWORTH LONGFELLOW

October 1938

The cracking sound echoed through the crisp fall air.

Focus. Focus.

A bright flash of light, and then dark again, then back into focus.

Thierry squinted in the late afternoon sun and guided the old leather glove that Henry had given him for his last birthday underneath the small white ball as it rapidly hurled back towards the earth.

Squeeze. Tuck, roll, and don't let go.

His worn blue cap flipped into the grass, exposing a shaggy mop of auburn hair. He proudly held his arm up in the air to show that he hadn't dropped it. The small crowd of children gathered by the fence erupted into cheers. The batter, already halfway around first base, threw his arms up in disgust.

Thierry grabbed his hat and jogged back toward the makeshift dugout. He received innumerable pats on the back and "atta-boy's." It hadn't been much more than a pickup game, but beating those snot-nosed brats from William Howard Taft Elementary meant the world to them.

A distinctive voice cried out above the rest, and Thierry immediately turned to see Henry waving his arms energetically. The boy waved back and trotted over.

"Wow! What a catch!"

"Oh, thanks—it was nothing," the boy replied humbly.

"Nothing? It was spectacular! You're a regular Frankie Crosettie!"

Thierry smiled bashfully as Henry rustled his hair.

"Your mama would have been so proud of you."

The late afternoon sun was fading quickly and the air chilled with every passing moment.

"What's for dinner?" the boy asked as they started towards home.

"Why—you hungry?"

"Famished," the child answered bluntly.

"Famished? That must be a new word you learned in school today," the old man joked.

"Where's Marty?"

"Who knows?" Henry answered. "With all those girls he's been chasin' after, he might as well not even live home anymore."

"He's not getting into trouble, is he?" Thierry asked naively.

"How should I know? The kid hardly talks to me. I figured you'd probably know more about that than anyone."

"He hardly talks to me anymore, too."

"Yeah, well, don't let it get you down, young'un," Henry said, noticing his young accomplice's melancholy. "He's just in a phase. He'll come back around."

"You think so?" Thierry asked earnestly.

"Yeah, I think so."

When they got back to the small apartment, Thierry got a bone crushing hug from Henrietta, who was shortly thereafter filled in on the baseball game, vivid descriptions and exaggerations by Henry included.

"That's nice, and all," she said, waving her hand at her husband, "but I want to hear about the child's day at school. What did you learn today?"

He shrugged.

"Come on, now—out with it."

"History."

"History? What, you learned all of it?" she joked. Thierry laughed bashfully. A loud, sharp noise, something similar to a squeak was heard from Henry as he hung their coats on the rack. His wife turned to see that childish grin on his face. She murmured something about how it was her opinion that he was a silly old fool. She then turned her attention back to Thierry and smiled gently.

"No, not all of it," he replied. "The Spanish-American War."

"Mm, and when was that?"

"1898."

She nodded her approval. Although she had lived through it, she had no actual recollection of that war, its outcome, or its consequences.

"And who fought that war?"

"The Spanish and the Americans," he answered nonchalantly.

"Well, I guess that was an easy one. And why was it fought?"

He squinted for a moment and then shrugged his shoulders.

"Mhm. Well, maybe you'll learn that tomorrow," she said.

The three ate dinner—a Southern style meal including cornbread—and then the old woman looked over the boy's homework and made him take some study time. He sat at the same table his mother had at years earlier when she first met the older couple. At one point, as the air got colder, Henrietta came out from the bedroom and placed a rough wool blanket around Thierry and told him not to catch a cold. Ever since Nina died of pneumonia in 1936, Henrietta was completely fixated on keeping everyone warm. A few minutes later, at her command, Henry went outside to fetch more wood and then stoked the fire.

When he was finished studying, Thierry was allowed to listen to the radio for an hour. He switched back and forth between the New York Rangers broadcast and the current events news. At nine on the dot, in the middle of the third period and the Rangers and the Maple Leafs tied at the Garden, Henrietta asked him kindly to head to bed. He reluctantly, but obediently, flipped the radio off, washed his face, and changed into his bedclothes. He gave Henry a big hug and a kiss on the cheek, and then did the same for Henrietta. The hug between the boy and his adopted mother lingered.

The weight of his circumstance—his mother's passing and his brother's distancing—always caught up to him at bedtime. After climbing in beneath the covers, the couple could hear him sniffling quietly, as he did nearly every night. Henrietta hobbled over and sat on the bed next to him. She patted his hair gently and he turned towards her, streams of warm tears running down his rosy cheeks.

"You miss your mama, huh?" she asked tenderly. "I know you do. I do, too."

She wiped his face dry with her warm hands.

"It's still hard, I know," she said reassuringly. "But I'll tell you what you already know—this is life, darling, and even though things are tough, you're gonna be okay. I promise."

Although this wasn't particularly comforting to him, he nodded as to show her that he appreciated the effort.

After a moment of silence, aside from his occasional sniffles, she asked, "And you miss your brother, too?"

He began to cry heavily and nodded his head before burying it in her shoulder.

"Yeah, I know. Me, too," she said, glancing over at Henry, who was sitting at the table with the newspaper. He looked at her and crumpled his lip.

"But I'm telling you the truth, now, boy," she continued. "He's gonna come around. I promise you. He's just in those years of discovery and—and… well, he's growing up and trying to figure out how to do it."

The boy just sniffled and nodded again, looking up at her with his moist, sky blue eyes.

Eventually he fell asleep and slept soundly. Henry waited up for Martin long after his wife went to bed. He stewed about the undue hardship that the elder was forcing upon his young brother. It seemed that as close as they had been when they were little, Martin would have had some semblance of loyalty to Thierry, but this was not the case. Henry reminded himself, however, that Nina was also Martin's mother, and that all people deal with grief in different ways. On the other hand, he had been charged with looking after these boys, and maybe it was time to start acting like the father they never had. Maybe he would have to give Martin a bit of a wakeup call, as his father had done for him, and try to get him back on the right track.

Martin opened the door quietly at a quarter past two. The fire cracked gently as he entered, folding his gloves in his hands. He nodded towards Henry in recognition of his presence. The older man stood and asked the younger out into the hall, as not to disturb the sleeping boy.

"In fact, put your gloves back on, and let's head downstairs—I don't want to disturb the neighbors, either."

"Sure," came the slightly sarcastic reply from the teen.

Once outside Henry stuffed his hands in his pockets and stiffened his shoulders.

"Marty, we need to talk."

"About what?" he replied, reaching for a cigarette in his pocket.

"You've been drinking again, huh?"

"A little bit."

"What do you like?"

"Whisky mostly, when I can get it."

"Me, too," Henry replied.

The two stood in silence for a moment, Martin calmly puffing his smoke, Henry looking down the street and trying to assemble his thoughts. A police car went by, slowed when the officer saw the black man standing on the corner, and then sped back up when he saw the gentle wave from the white boy.

"Marty, I'm worried about your brother," Henry stated quickly.

"Why's that?"

"Did you know that he cries every night?"

"Yeah, I knew that."

"How? You're never home."

"He told me."

"Thierry told you that he cries every night?"

"Yeah, I don't know why he'd admit that to me, but he did."

"And what do you think about that?"

"Kid misses his mom, what can you say? He'll get over it in time," he stated flatly.

Henry let that sink in for a moment.

"And have you gotten over it?"

"As best as a kid can, I suppose," he said with a flick of ash and a quick glance at Henry's eyes.

"I'm not over it yet," Henry answered.

"Well, I don't think you ever quite get completely over it, do you? The loss of a mother or a friend."

"Certainly not."

The two again stood in silence. Henry watched long clouds, like strokes from a paintbrush, pass slowly over the harvest moon.

"How's school, son?"

"Easy."

"Yeah, I noticed," Henry said, referring to Martin's most recent straight A report card. "It's a shame you don't go more often."

"Why would I? Teachers spend half their time trying to get the dummies caught up on stuff I learned two years ago and got the first time."

"Yeah, that's a shame—for you, I mean."

The boy shrugged and lit another cigarette. He offered one to Henry, who declined.

"Where did you get those, anyway?"

"Pazzone's over in Teaneck. I help him out in the afternoons a lot—cleaning shop and taking out trash—stuff like that. He gives me stuff—smokes, whisky when he's got it—and money here and there."

"So it's a job?"

"I guess you could say that."

"Look Marty, we need to talk about the path that you're on."

"Talk then," Marty replied with a roll of his eyes.

"You're a good kid—a smart kid and a good kid—you've got a good heart beneath all that toughness. I'm worried about you, though, and your brother. I'm worried that you two are going to be the only things that will ever be constant in your lives and that you're growing apart. I'm worried that you're gonna end up as a drunk or worse and that your kid brother ain't gonna know what to do with it. He's a good kid, too, Marty, and he's only twelve years old. He needs his older brother to be there for him."

Marty looked at him, blowing smoke out of the side of his mouth.

"You say you're out late and out with girls and drinking and smoking because you're growing up. Do you think that's what it takes to be a man?"

The teenager shrugged scornfully and looked away.

"Things are tough right now, kid, and they have been for a long time. There's a lot of people a lot worse off than we are and it wouldn't take much for us to be out on the street with nothin' at all. This is the day and age where men have to be men—we have to work and we have to be there for our families because ain't no one else will."

"Maybe you should be having this talk with my brother, huh? I can take care of myself. But what about him? I didn't get the luxury of being a kid and grieving and all that. You live and you lose. Life goes on."

"The boy misses his mother and he misses his brother. He feels like both of you went and died on him."

"Maybe we did. And maybe it's time for him to grow up and start taking care of himself. I'm tired of taking care of him. I'm tired of being his father and his mother and his brother and everything. I've got a life of my own and I'm damn sure gonna live it."

Henry shook his head in disbelief. He looked towards the moon for help but it had been smothered by early winter clouds. The boy flicked his cigarette ash again and let out a brief sigh.

"Look, Henry," he said calmly. "I'm sorry. I understand what you're saying and I appreciate it. In fact, I appreciate everything you and Henrietta have done for us—since we were little kids. So what do you want from me?"

"I want you to be home by eight o'clock every night, and I want you to go to school every day unless you're dying."

"Done."

"And I want you to quit drinking—at least until you're older. It's not good for you at this age."

"I said I'd be home on time and go to school—don't take my juice away, too, old man."

Henry looked at him intently.

"Ok, but never in the house and don't you dare come home drunk again."

"Deal."

The two shook hands and the boy flicked his smoke out into the street.

"Alright, well let's get inside—my southern ass is freezing out here."

The next afternoon Martin, new girlfriend at his side, watched Thierry play baseball. Martin walked home with Thierry despite persistent pleas from Maxine for him to stay out with her. He simply told her he had to be home that afternoon and left her on the doorstep in the cold. It was no skin off his back as he had already decided he would trade her in tomorrow for the blonde with the dimples in the chemistry class he had just rejoined.

No one was home when the boys entered the small apartment. A note from Henrietta was laid on the table to let them know she had picked up a shift on short notice and that Henry would be back from work after ten. She had left a half loaf of bread, a few slices of bologna, and two tall glasses of watered down milk out for dinner.

"Sorry about the loss today, champ," Martin said with a sympathetic glance as the two settled down with their sandwiches.

"Well, it's one game," the young one replied. "And plus, Denny—our first rate pitcher—was sick today, so he wasn't even there."

"Yeah, you'll get them next time."

A few minutes passed as the two chewed feverishly.

"So, Thierry, do you have a girlfriend or something?"

Only a parent would have fully appreciated the look on Thierry's face. It was a childish mix of astonishment and disgust. His older brother laughed.

"Well, I guess that's a no."

Thierry stuck out his tongue and mimicked a gag.

"That'll change soon enough—I promise."

More chewing.

"So Marty, who was that girl you were with today?"

"Maxine?"

"Yeah."

"Oh, she's just a dame I've been seeing a lot of the last week or so."

"Is she your girlfriend?"

"She would say she is."

"But she's not?"

Martin shrugged.

"She's just a girl with a pretty face that I've been seeing a lot of. That's really all you need to know."

As his tone was not unkind, Thierry shrugged and changed the subject.

"Marty, do you think you could help me with my math homework?"

Although he had promised to spend more time with his kid brother, spending the better part of the evening doing long division was not what he had envisioned. He did, however, dutifully acquiesce, and actually felt a mild sense of satisfaction. The little one put his books away and sat back down, looking up at Martin for direction on what they would do next.

"Do you want to listen to the radio?" the older brother asked.

"Sure!"

Martin read, or rather breezed through, *King Lear,* which had been assigned in his English class two months ago. He thought it rather amusing. Thierry sat engrossed by the fictional account of a young boy who fought off a savage Indian tribe during covered wagon days.

"What time do you usually go to bed?" Martin asked after seeing his brother yawn so widely he almost swallowed his tongue.

"I don't know," the boy answered. "Whatever time Henrietta tells me to."

"Well, it's already past nine o'clock, so whattaya say?"

"Sure," Thierry replied respectfully. He started to feel that nagging knot in his stomach that always came with bedtime. "Marty?"

"Yeah kid?"

"Will you tuck me in?"

His eyes were desperate.

"Yeah, of course I will, T."

Thierry felt the urge to cry as he usually did around this time of night, but fought it in an effort to appear somewhat grown up in front of his older brother. Martin tucked him in, said a quick prayer with him, and then gave him a hug and told him to turn towards the wall so that he could sleep without distraction. A couple minutes later, King Lear again in his lap, he heard the quiet sobs of his younger brother, muffled by the blanket he had pulled up over his mouth. Part of him felt bad for Thierry—but he also couldn't resist the feeling that his kid brother was going to have to grow up quick if he was ever going to survive in this world. Times were tough on everyone and coddling a kid was the worst thing you could do. It was time to toughen up.

Through his tears and muted sobs, Thierry heard the latch on the door close. When he turned around Martin was gone. He cried himself to sleep that night, unable to shake the feeling that somehow he was driving his brother away.

November 1938

Martin hadn't been home for three weeks, although Henrietta confirmed with the school truancy officer that he had only missed one day. It seemed terribly odd, but all the signs pointed to the fact that he was alright. Henry walked down to Pazzone's shop one day and met Giovanni Pazzone himself. After being told by the proprietor that he didn't want blacks in his store, Henry was at least able to confirm that Martin was working and was in good health—most likely staying with a girlfriend. Henry and Henrietta decided that he would come around when he was ready, and that they would let him take care of himself if that's what he truly wanted.

Thierry, on the other hand, had somewhat of a renewal after his brother left. The night crying stopped completely, and the boy seemed suddenly rejuvenated and focused. His caregivers wondered what could have caused this sharp change, but didn't want to press him about it, particularly as it related to his grief for his mother. The home was calm for once, and aside from a bad cough that Henrietta could not shake, everyone was in good health, happy, and warm. Little did the sweet couple know that the first case of puppy love had ensnared our young hero.

One particularly ordinary day, Thierry sat engrossed in a conversation with his baseball companions about the merits of chewing tobacco. One group argued that it was far superior for an athlete to chew tobacco rather than smoking cigarettes, while another hypothesized that a certain brand of tobacco gave the New York Yankees nearly superhuman strength. The boys hollered and pointed at each other across the lunch table, and while the argument became more heated, each boy attempting to shout his opposing counterpart down, it remained good-natured in its disposition. Then the lightning bolt struck.

Over Davey Ferarro's shoulder, Thierry caught a glimpse of her walking through the doorway into the cafeteria. His mouth suddenly dried up and he lost track of which side of the "tobacco makes you stronger" argument he was on. Her ash brown hair was cut unfashionably short and quite poorly for that matter, but her face more than made up for that deficiency. He saw her slowly turn and look his way, as if she had sensed that she was being stared at. Her deep eyes, the color of the forest in spring, locked on his for just a moment, then coolly drifted back to her girlfriends.

"Hey, Dumbo!" Davey called.

Thierry shook his head quickly and noticed that his tongue felt swollen in his mouth. He tried to mutter something and was immediately mocked by his mates.

"Come on, or we're gonna be late to science and Mr. Nickel will call us miscreants again!" Davey said with a manufactured shiver.

"Oh no!" cried the chorus, feigning dread.

They all got up, one boy grabbing Thierry roughly by the back of his shirt. He snapped out of his trance, picked up his books, and followed the other boys towards the exit. On his way out, he caught sight of her again and almost stumbled over a wayward chair. She didn't even seem to notice, which did perturb him a bit, but he wasn't sure why.

During Mr. Nickel's fascinating lecture on the flora and fauna commonly found in his childhood hometown of Bethlehem, New Hampshire, Thierry could hardly sit still. He was dealing with a hodgepodge of emotions he had never experienced before and could not figure out what he felt so unnervingly guilty about. After all, he hadn't in so many thoughts diagnosed her high, noble cheek bones, long eyelashes, or those soft, sumptuous pink lips—Hold on! Wait a minute! That was it! A wave of nausea broke violently over him as he forced himself to think the thought that had been sneaking in the back of his mind—he thought she was beautiful. In fact, he thought that she was the most beautiful sight he had ever seen. And he didn't even know her name yet. He quickly excused himself to use the restroom and did not respond to Mr. Nickel's inquiry as to whether he was in good health. Out in the quiet hallway, he breathed heavily, his own heartbeat pulsing feverishly in his ears. He felt a crushing weight on his chest and he couldn't get the silly notion out of his head that he had to know who she was or else his life would be long and meaningless. After a long drink from the water fountain, he was able to calm himself enough to go back to class.

"Mr. Laroque, are you quite well?" Mr. Nickel asked.

The boy nodded quickly and sat back down with a thud.

Several giggles were heard throughout the room.

"Well," the teacher said with a quick snap of his suspenders. "Back to… well, where was I?"

"The muskrat," a bored voice called out.

"Ah, yes! The muskrat!" Mr. Nickel proceeded quickly and with great enthusiasm. "The muskrat is a most fascinating creature! Commonly known in scientific circles as Ondatra zibethicus, the muskrat is a semi-aquatic rodent…"

I have got to learn her name. I have got to learn her name.

Henrietta was relieved once again that Thierry didn't cry that night, but he did seem mightily distracted from his school work and even his dinner. She asked if something had happened at school, and he just shook his head.

The next day in the cafeteria, he saw her again. This time the argument at the boys' table was about whether or not the United States should start a war and fight Germany. It was equally as uninformed as the previous day's debate. Thierry was again completely distracted. Her back was to him and he longed for a glimpse of her face. Then, rather abruptly, the three girls who had been sitting with her got up and walked off. One of them said something that sounded mean, and Thierry saw her shoulders slump. He shot out of his seat, not sure what force had taken hold of him, and, completely ignoring his questioning pals, walked around the table and across the aisle that separated him from the object of his infatuation.

When the girl saw him standing there she looked up quickly and then back down. He noticed tears in her eyes and his heart nearly broke on the spot.

"Can I sit here?" he asked sheepishly.

"Why, so you can make fun of me, too?" she sniffled.

"Make fun of you? Why on earth would I do that?"

"The same reason everyone else does."

"Why would anyone make fun of you?"

She looked up at him as if she couldn't believe he didn't know.

"Funny game you're playing," she said sarcastically. "Well, go on, let me hear it."

He sat there in awe of her—in awe of her beauty, in awe of her mysteriousness, in awe of the fact that he already had no idea what she was talking about. His friends were in awe, too—silently mesmerized by the boy who got up to go sit with a girl.

"I'm Thierry," was the only thing he could think to say.

"I know who you are," she replied.

"You do?"

She knew who he was. He couldn't believe it.

"Of course I do. You're the best ball player at this school."

He turned red.

"Well, maybe not the best, but—"

"No, you're the best. I've watched you play."

"When?"

"After school sometimes—until it got too cold."

"How come I never saw you there?"

"You probably did—just don't recognize me without—" She started to cry softly. "Without my hair!" she half-wailed.

"Oh," he answered.

He didn't want her to feel worse about it than she already did, and he certainly didn't want her to think that he was trying to make fun of her like everyone else, so he said:

"Look, everyone is entitled to a bad cut once in a while. Maybe you just shouldn't go back to that barber again."

Her jaw dropped, and then she burst out laughing. Her smile was almost too much for him to bear.

"You think this is just a bad cut?"

"Well, sure, what else could it be?"

She grabbed her stomach with her right hand to try to keep from laughing even louder.

"No, I burned it," she explained.

Maybe she was crazy—the thought crossed his mind. But she was too beautiful to let that deter him.

"Why would you do that?"

"Why would anyone do that? It was an accident, silly."

"Oh, oh good. I mean, it's not good that your hair burned, but I'm glad you didn't burn it on purpose."

She smiled and his heart froze.

"You're really funny, too," she said.

He just grinned like a fool in love.

Then he was hit in the face with a sandwich.

"Hey, Romeo!" yelled Vernon Massey.

The rest of the chorus chimed in with their own playful taunts and jeers while Thierry let the bread and bologna hit the table. The girl with the short hair picked up the sandwich and flung it back over at the table, practically knocking Massey out of his chair.

"Laroque, your girl's got a better arm than you do!" one of them cried.

"Sorry about that," she said, turning back to Thierry.

"Oh, it's ok," he answered.

"I think you do have some mustard on your face, though."

He rubbed his face with his sleeves and at that moment the bell rang.

"Ok, well, nice talking to you," she said.

"Oh, you, too."

"And thanks for cheering me up," she said with a warm smile.

He was melting.

"Wait, wait," he said as she was getting up.

"What is it?"

"What's your name?" he asked bashfully.

Her name was Hope, and it was the most beautiful sound he'd ever heard.

He floated through the rest of the day, utterly unable to concentrate on anything but her. His friends cracked jokes all afternoon, but he didn't mind. That night, he thought about his mother as he was getting ready for bed, but felt peculiarly at peace with her passing for the first time.

The following morning, he saw Hope in the hallway and waved energetically in her direction. When she didn't wave back, he wasn't sure she saw him. For the two hours before lunch, this was all that he could think about. He was standing in line waiting for his tray of school lunch—which happened to be some of the best food some kids ate at that time—he craned his neck towards the door through which she had entered the previous days. No sign of her.

Wait! There she—no, not her.

"Who are you looking for?" asked a gentle voice behind him.

Neck still extended and eyes still fixed on the door, he answered, "Oh, no one in particular."

He turned back to see who had spoken to him and there she stood, right behind him in line. He almost dropped his tray. She snickered girlishly.

"Oh, hi," he stammered.

"Hi."

"I didn't see you come in."

"That's probably because I was behind you. I guess you don't have eyes in the back of your head."

"Ha, no, I don't," he mumbled, his embarrassment growing. Did she know he had been looking for her?

The two stood awkwardly for a moment, waiting on their food to be served.

"So…" she started, obviously interested in some sort of conversation with him (this was good!), "what do you boys do when it's too cold to play baseball?"

He thought for a moment.

"I don't really know," he answered honestly. "Mostly just talk about it, I guess."

"That's silly."

"Why?"

"Well, it's just a game—although you are very good at it," she quickly added, not wanting to offend him.

"So what if it's just a game?"

"Well, it's just that you spend so much time playing it and talking about it, and it just seems like it doesn't lead anywhere."

"It doesn't have to lead anywhere," he said as a small serving of gooey beans were slapped on his plate. "It's just fun."

She shrugged.

"Why does it have to lead somewhere? Isn't a game supposed to be fun?"

"Well, I guess so—it just seems a little… pointless."

"Pointless?" Thierry cried, completely dumbfounded by such a naïve and rather, well, pointless statement.

"It's just a bunch of people chasing a little white ball around a field and running in circles—"

"How can you say the greatest game in America is pointless?"

"I don't know," she answered defensively.

There was another brief, but uncomfortable silence. He couldn't get genuinely angry at her, even though he couldn't believe that she could be so ignorant of such a noble passion as baseball. She, on the other hand, was keenly aware that she might have crossed the line, however unreasonably silly that line may have been, and wanted nothing more than to walk back and start over.

"So, what is the point?" she asked genuinely.

The boy's brow ruffled and he bit the skin on the inside of his cheeks.

"It's fun, that's the point!" he shot back.

"I understand that."

They instinctively moved towards two empty seats at the end of a table.

Davey Ferraro yelled out, "Hey, Thierry!" several times, but his friend didn't even hear him—like he was lost in a totally different world. Several comments were made about this by the boys of Thierry's company, but no sandwiches were thrown today, mostly because of Hope's arm strength as had been duly exhibited the previous day.

"Well, what do you girls do that's so important?"

"What do you mean?"

"If baseball is so pointless, what do girls do that's so important?"

She thought honestly for a minute.

"I make the food at home," she answered.

"I'm not talking about chores," he replied. "I mean with your girlfriends."

She twirled her fork sadly through the watery mashed potatoes on her plate.

"I don't really have any girlfriends."

"What do you mean? I saw you in a group with a bunch of girls the other day—Mary McFadden and Pearl Humphrey—"

"Those are not my friends," she said sternly.

He looked at her glum face for a moment, trying to understand her.

"Why were you with them, then?"

"I thought they were my friends, but after I burned my hair, they wouldn't stop making fun of me."

His little heart ached as saw the hurt in her eyes.

"Oh, I'm sorry," was all that he could get out.

"It's ok," she replied with a shrug. "I guess it's better to know if someone's not really your friend than it is to be a fool."

"So, who are your friends?"

She looked up from her plate and into his eyes.

"I don't really have any friends—aside from you," she answered.

"That's impossible!" he replied, unable to comprehend why a girl so special, so… *nice*, didn't have any friends.

"No, it's not," she retorted gloomily.

"But you're so nice. Why wouldn't someone want to be your friend?"

"I shouldn't say I don't have any friends. I mean that I don't have any here."

"Where are they?"

"Cape May."

"Cape May? Like the Cape May in Africa?"

"No, the Cape May down the shore. That's where I'm from. And that's where all my friends are."

"You grew up by the ocean?" he asked excitedly.

"Yes," she answered with a smile. "And I miss it very much."

"How did you end up here?"

"My dad lost his job this summer, and I have a great uncle who lives here that we're staying with until he can find some work."

"Oh," he answered and then without thinking blurted out: "Well I'm sure glad you're here."

He caught his breath as he wished to catch his words. He didn't mean to sound so mushy with her. But she just smiled. From ear to ear.

"You always manage to cheer me up," she said sweetly.

He just made a silly face and shrugged his shoulders.

"Can I ask you a question?"

"Sure," he replied.

With some hesitation she asked, "Why is your dad a negro?"

A queer look crossed his countenance and she was again afraid that she might have offended him.

"I mean, the black man that walks you home from the ballpark from time to time—is he your dad?"

"Yes—well—he's not actually my dad," Thierry responded, searching for an easy way to explain his home situation. "You see, my mom died a few years ago, and Henry and his wife Henrietta were there to take care of me and my brother."

"I see," she said, still trying to process this unconventional arrangement. "My mom died, too."

"I'm sorry," he said.

"What about your dad? Don't you have any other family that could have taken care of you?"

He shook his head.

"I don't know where my dad is. I think he might be dead, too. My parents came from France—*in Europe*—all by themselves."

"Oh, I see. Do you… like living with negroes?"

He had never thought of it that way.

"What's the difference between living with negroes and living with whites?" he asked innocently.

She had never thought of it that way, either.

"I don't know. Is there a difference?"

"I don't know, either," he replied honestly. "They're the closest thing I have to family, so it doesn't really matter to me what color they are."

"That's nice," she said with a genuine smile. "I'd like to meet them sometime—I don't know any negroes."

"Sure, any time," he answered. "And, I'd maybe like to meet your dad sometime."

"You probably wouldn't like him very much."

"Why not? I like you a lot."

"Yeah, but," she started slowly. "He just drinks all the time. He's not very nice to be around anymore."

The bell rang and the pair picked up their books, said an awkward goodbye, and went their separate ways. Thierry took some ribbing from his pals when he got into the hallway. He didn't see Hope look back over her shoulder in his direction.

Thanksgiving came and went, and the two youngsters continued to see each other every day at lunch time. It felt like the troubles of the world were falling away into the deep well of their newfound bliss.

On the night preceding the 26th, which happened to be a Saturday, a front moved through, bringing with it warm air from the Deep South, which allowed the boys to hurriedly organize one final baseball outing before spring. They lost themselves in the game, the worries of the Depression nowhere to be found. After hours and hours, the sun slowly giving way to the moon and the stars, the series ended with genuine handshakes between the opponents—too much fun had been had on such short notice to carry the bad blood of rivalry all winter long.

Having been so blinded by the true spirit of sport, it was at this point that Thierry noticed for the first time Henry, leaning over the dilapidated fence out in left field, and next to him, upright and tall, Marty. As he bid farewell to his mates, Thierry jogged towards them, leather glove tucked under his right arm casually. On the way, he looked back towards first base for some reason and noticed Hope, looking like she wanted to call out to him but was afraid to because his relatives were there. He, however, had no such concerns, and with a quick wave and a forefinger up to give the signal to wait for him, he immediately changed course and shot over toward his young lady friend.

"Hi," he said breathlessly. "How long have you been here?"

"All day."

"Is that true?"

She smiled bashfully and nodded.

"I didn't even see you," he said.

"I know. You were too involved in your game."

"I'm sorry," he answered, not sure if she was after an apology. She was not.

"Oh, it's fine. I really enjoyed watching today."

"You did?"

"Yes. I think I can see why you and the other boys love it so much."

"Oh, that's good."

"And you played really well."

"Thank you."

She looked past him into the outfield.

"Is that your dad?"

He spun around behind him to look, having in her presence forgotten all about Henry and Marty waiting for him.

"Yeah, and my brother Marty."

"Marty?"

"Yeah, I haven't seen him in a long time. Do you want to meet them?"

"Sure," she said with nervous hesitation.

She reached out and took his hand as she climbed over the waist high fence between them. He had never felt a hand so soft and silky; it fit perfectly in his. A chill, or perhaps a thrill, racked his spinal column, and he swallowed tensely.

They walked across the field together, hardly saying a word to each other.

"Hey there!" Henry called in his typically boisterous manner.

"Hi!" Thierry called back.

"Great game, again, young man!"

"Thanks, Henry!"

When the boy and the girl reached the fence, Thierry introduced her.

"This is my friend Hope."

"Hello, Hope," the old man replied, extending his large, rough hand. "My name is Henry."

"Nice to meet you," she said while extending her small hand to shake Henry's.

"And this is my big brother, Marty," Thierry said with excitement as he launched himself over the small fence and into his brother's arms.

"Hi," Marty said casually in her direction, focusing on not falling backwards with the momentum of his growing younger brother's embrace.

"Hi," she replied with a brief wave.

"Well it's nice to meet you, Hope," Henry said. "Do you go to school with Thierry?"

She nodded silently.

"That's great! I hope you keep a good eye on him—make sure he's not acting up."

She smiled and said, "He usually does okay."

"That's good," Henry said with a laugh and a point of his thumb in Marty's direction. "I wouldn't want him to turn out like his big brother here."

"Funny," Marty countered sarcastically.

"Where have you been, Marty?" Thierry asked eagerly, finally letting go of his brother's waist.

"Oh, I've been around," came the trite reply.

The brothers were silent for a moment and both felt a certain awkwardness.

"Well, Thierry," said Hope, "I've got to go home and help get dinner ready. Great game today!"

"Ok, I'll see you at school on Monday," he said with a bashful smile.

She told Henry and Marty that it was a pleasure to meet them and then waved politely at Thierry as she started off in the direction of North Washington Avenue. Thierry's eyes followed her until his blissfully distracted concentration was interrupted by Marty:

"So, kid, you wanna stand here all day or you wanna go home?"

Thierry shook his head as if he'd been suddenly woken from a deep sleep.

"Sure, Marty! Let's go home!"

The three walked home, not saying much, aside from the occasional remark by Henry about the quality of Thierry's game. He also threw in a couple "girlfriend" jabs, which the young boy answered by blushing deeply.

When they entered the small apartment, Henrietta practically ignored her husband and the young boy, but ran and threw her arms around Marty, who awkwardly hugged back. She did not release her strong grip on him for what seemed like a lifetime. When she finally did let him go, she held his shoulders in both her hands and looked him straight in the eyes. He didn't waiver or wilt, he stared right back at her with equal intensity.

"It's good you came back," she said softly, after a great while.

Marty nodded. Neither of them broke their start until Henry spoke up.

"Well, Thierry, we've all got something to talk about," Henry said.

Thierry was worried by Henry's tone and it was written on his face.

"Your brother, here," he continued, "is a smart young man—very smart—and there are some people who have taken notice."

Marty looked at his brother and then looked at the floor. Thierry glanced back and forth between Marty and Henry, impatient for an explanation as far as his brother's recent reemergence and the tambour of the current conversation.

"There are some folks we met through Mrs. Carrington, and they heard about how well Marty's doing at school, and want to give him a chance to do even better."

Henry looked at his wife for a moment, as if hoping to glean from her the strength to continue.

"Well, what this means, young man, is that these friends, who have some money to be sure, they want to send Marty to a private school, a prestigious private school where he can learn from the best teachers and study with the best students."

"That's great," said Thierry, hoping that this was the end of the conversation, but fully expecting the coming blow to be dealt.

"The only thing is, Thierry," Henry continued, "the school is all the way in Boston."

The young boy's heart sank, and again, it showed on his face. His older brother glanced up at him quickly, blankly, and then back down at the floor distractedly.

"But don't you worry, young man," Henrietta piped in enthusiastically, trying her best to cheer the young boy's spirits. "You'll get to see him on holidays and during the summer time, and when you get a little older, we might even be able to send you up there for a visit!"

Thierry thought for a moment that she was going to say that he might be able to go to this school, too, and was honestly surprised when no mention was made of it. The young boy might have been bright, but didn't have the natural gifts that Marty did for academic subjects. Thierry's good grades were the result of hard work and concentration; Marty's good grades were the result of showing up.

"I know you're disappointed, Thierry," Henry said reassuringly, "but this is a great opportunity for your brother. You should be happy for him."

"I am," answered Thierry with a strained smile—he was doing his best not to cry.

"It'll be ok, kid," Marty spoke softly. "I promise I'll be around."

Thierry didn't feel very comforted by this.

"When do you have to leave?" he asked.

"Tonight."

Thierry felt as if his heart would burst. It was at that moment he noticed a ragged suitcase sitting behind the door, and a big brown canvas bag perched on top of it. The young boy could no longer hold it in. He clenched his lips together in an attempt to avoid sobbing in front of his big brother, but tears streamed down his red face. Marty glanced up at him again and saw him crying, but the only effect it seemed to have on him was to look away again. Thierry thought he saw him roll his eyes.

"It's gonna be ok, buddy," Henry said gently. He put his arm around the young boy who then threw himself into Henry's chest. The boy's body was racked with silent sobs and he shook violently in the man's embrace.

He wasn't even sure why he was crying. He felt similar emotions, confusing as they were, when his mother died. However, this time, there was also the sting of abandonment, rejection. Nina's last words were to Thierry, and while he was too shaken to remember them, he remembered that she spoke to him, and spoke gently. He remembered knowing without a shadow of a doubt that she didn't want to go—she was fighting so hard to stay. He watched tears drip from her sick, yellowed eyes, fixed solely on him, as she took her last breath. His mother loved him, and he knew it. What was breaking his heart now, however, was that he wasn't sure how his brother felt about him. He got the impression that he was a nuisance to Marty, even though he didn't know why. He felt that his older brother had some great, unspoken expectations for him, and it was obvious that he wasn't living up to them—whatever they were. Worst of all, it seemed like his brother actually wanted to leave.

Then Thierry remembered, as if struck by a bolt of lightning, that Marty hadn't even been around all this time. How long had it been since the two of them had actually talked? Heck, Marty had even missed Thanksgiving!

Shortly, the little multi-colored family was headed to the train station on foot. Marty carried one suitcase and Thierry the big canvas bag. For her part, Henrietta carried a small bag of some treats she had baked for Marty's trip. As popular as Thierry imagined Marty to be, he was surprised when they were the only people at the station to say goodbye. The young boy had been expecting crowds of people—schoolmates, girlfriends, celebrities—maybe even a brass band—but there was no one.

Henry and Henrietta hugged Marty warmly and wished him the best. They told him to be good for the Grahams, who Thierry would later learn were the family taking his brother in, and study hard. Marty just nodded patronizingly. Then, his eyes turned to his little brother. Thierry was unsure, at this point, whether to give him a big hug like he'd wanted to, or simply say goodbye, when Marty waved him over. The brothers embraced and for a moment, Thierry felt like his big brother didn't want to leave him. But leave him he did.

They watched Marty take his seat on the train and waved as it left the station. Thierry wasn't sure if Marty even looked back to see them. Henry placed his hand on the young boy's shoulder, and the three then walked back home.

What was more surprising than anything to Thierry, however, was when his sadness suddenly transformed into a giddy kind of jolly excitement, when the thought popped into his head at random that in just two days, he would see Hope again.

December 22, 1939

The following year she gave him a Christmas present. He wasn't expecting it and felt a rush of exhilaration. It was a box wrapped in newspaper. He fumbled to tear the paper away and then flipped the lid of the box open. A brown, obviously used baseball, sat inside and when he turned it over he saw a signature scrawled between the laces.

"This is Clyde McCullough."

"You know him?"

"Know him?—of course I know him! He's a catcher in the Yankees farm system. How did you get this?"

"Well, I went down to a few Bears games in Newark this summer and waited outside for the players to leave. He was really nice and when I told him that the gift was for you, and that you were gonna play for the Yankees one day, he got one of the game balls and signed it for me."

"You've been waiting to give me this since the summer?"

"Since July."

"I can't believe it."

"Do you like it?"

"I love it!" he answered, childishly throwing his arms around her. Then, a sudden rush of shame came over him. "I'm really sorry I didn't get anything for you."

"That's ok," she said calmly. "I'm just glad you're my friend. That's enough of a present for me."

"Well, Merry Christmas."

"Merry Christmas."

October 15, 1941

Thierry's fifteenth birthday had passed without so much as a phone call from his brother. Hope, on the other hand, had gotten so good at getting baseball autographs from members of the International League's Newark Bears that with every holiday his mounting collection—which now included the likes of Joe Beggs, Norm Branch, and half a dozen others—grew. His birthday present from her was a bat signed by Hank Majesky, twenty-four-year-old second and third baseman from Staten Island. He would go on to play for the Boston Braves, the Philadelphia Athletics, and would start two whole games for Thierry's very own New York Yankees.

The young couple grew more and more inseparable. Many of his boyhood friendships dissipated as he spent increasing amounts of his time with her. Even his performance on the baseball field suffered. Although her father was uncomfortable with the idea of a black couple raising a white child, it became common for Hope to share meals with the small, interracial family, and for Henry or Henrietta or both of them to have to remind her to go home as the night grew to a close.

The first time they held hands was invigorating. The first time they kissed, he could have sworn he had touched bare electrical wires. The first time he saw her without a shirt on, he could have at that moment gone on to the next world with a smile on his face. They were well-behaved kids, but they were kids at that—kids who were realizing slowly that their entire worlds revolved around each other.

Hope was there the night when after dinner, Henrietta, who mentioned that she had felt dizzy during the day, suffered her first heart attack. The ambulance took her to St. Mary's in Hackensack. Henry told the kids to stay home as he walked and took a bus to the hospital. The boy and girl sat silently in each other's arms on Thierry's bed for most of the night. Around eleven, Henry called to let them know that Henrietta was fine and that she would be staying a few nights in the hospital. By the time he got home, Thierry had already taken Hope to her father's apartment and made it back. He was sitting at the kitchen table and had brewed a pot of coffee. The old man's eyes were red with tears shed and worry, but he was relieved that he wouldn't be alone that night.

December 24, 1941

The United States was now at war with the military juggernauts of Germany, Japan, and others, and it weighed heavily on the hearts of all citizens that Christmas. Rubber was the first thing to be rationed, and many were concerned about what might follow—probably butter, coffee, gasoline, and God only knew what else. Thierry's family attended church services to pray for the troops and the war effort. Though the mood was dark that Christmas, one good thing that had come about was extra shifts at Henry's work, due to the ramping up of production for the war effort. Thierry and Hope spent a lot of time with Henrietta, who had recovered nicely, but seemed more frail than usual. After Pearl Harbor, Hope's father took to the bottle less, resolving himself to be sober in the event that his nation called upon him. His good intentions, however, were short-lived, as the holidays presented the perfect opportunity to over-indulge.

That evening, Thierry nearly jumped out of his skin with excitement as Hope presented him with a baseball signed by an actual New York Yankee—and future Cooperstown inductee—pitcher, Lefty Gomez. He hugged her so tight that she thought for a moment he might snap her neck.

They took a long stroll that night through the quiet streets and the park by her apartment building. He made some keys jingle in his pocket in imitation of Santa's sleigh and then presented her with a sterling silver necklace and a heart-shaped locket with his photo tucked inside. They kissed on a bench in the snow beside a grove of spruce trees, their branches dusted in white powder.

August 10, 1943

"You don't have the foggiest idea how beautiful you are, do you?"

"I have a good idea how silly you are."

"No, I mean it."

"I mean it, too."

"Kiss me."

"Again?"

"Yes, again."

Her lips tasted like saltwater. His fingertips ran along the top of her silky thigh.

"Thierry," she whispered, her mouth just inches from his. "Not in public."

"There's nobody here."

"Yes, there is," she answered, looking over her shoulder. "And even if there wasn't, I'm in a bathing suit, and it's not proper for you to touch my leg like that."

"Now you're being silly."

"I know," she whispered as she kissed him quickly. "Come on, let's go into the water."

He popped off the blanket and raced down to the edge of the beach and plunged into the Atlantic. He came up out of the surf and with a flick of his head, waved her on. She walked so daintily, and he couldn't take his eyes off of her. She suddenly broke into a run and dove into the waves, letting out a shriek as her body hit the chilly water.

"Why is it still so cold in August?"

"It's not Florida," he quipped, taking her shivering frame in his arms.

"I know, but I don't remember it being this cold when I was a kid."

"Maybe it wasn't."

She shrugged and kissed his cheek.

"I'm glad you're here with me."

"I'm glad to be here with you."

"There was a long time I never thought I would come here again. Things were so bad, you know? My dad was just getting worse and worse, and then the war starting, and all. I guess I'm just trying to say that I never thought I would be this happy ever again."

"I'm really happy, too."

"I am so glad Julianne invited us down with her this week. It's been really nice seeing her, too, after all these years."

"She's really nice. I just wish we could say the same about her aunt."

"Well, she's nice enough to let us stay in her home, so she's not all bad, but she is rather crotchety, huh?"

"That's putting it mildly."

"What do you think about the war?"

"What do you mean?"

"How long do you think it will last?"

"Who knows."

She got quiet and pensive, as was her habit.

"Are you still worried that I'll get drafted?"

"You're only a year and a couple months from being eighteen."

"So? What of it?"

"Surely the war won't be over by then."

"It might be."

"But if it is over this soon, it can't be a good thing for us and our allies, can it?"

"The tide of war can turn rather quickly, I think."

"You sound like a teacher."

"I guess I'm just not that afraid of it."

"You wouldn't be scared of being killed or hurt, which might be even worse?"

"If my country calls… It's a noble fight, after all—"

"And now you sound like a recruiter."

"Listen, all I know is that I won't shrink from service to my country, whatever that may be. Would you want to be with a man that shirks his duty?"

"Of course not, but I wouldn't want to lose you either."

"You won't lose me."

"How can you say that? Eugene McCormack turned eighteen last summer and he was already killed. We went to school with Eugene. We *knew* him."

"And that's terrible—"

"So how can you say it won't happen to you?"

"Look, Hope, nothing in life is guaranteed. How can you be sure a giant shark or a whale won't swallow me up right now?"

"Because I'm not stupid. Your chances of being killed in a world war are much higher than they are swimming twenty feet off the shoreline."

He chuckled.

"And plus," she continued. "I don't think I could bear to be away from you for that long."

"Are you saying you couldn't stay faithful to me?"

"Of course I would be faithful to you. But I don't know how I could live without hearing your voice or being held in your arms or just knowing that you're alright. I don't think my heart could survive that."

He was going to say something patronizingly reassuring, but thought the better of it. He calmed himself and said, "Then let's just enjoy every moment together and not worry about the future."

She smiled and laid back in his arms. Their bodies had adjusted to the water temperature and they were floating gently with the tide.

"What about your brother?"

"Marty?"

"Yeah. What if he gets drafted?"

"I don't think we have to worry about that."

"But he's almost twenty. Don't you think it's just a matter of time before his number comes up?"

"No, I don't. Apparently the program he's in at Yale has some sort of protection on it. As long as he's in that program, I don't think they can draft him."

Her eyes lit up with optimism.

"Maybe you could get into that program!"

"I don't think so," he chuckled.

"Well, why not? You're smart!"

"I'm not as smart as Marty—not nearly. And plus, I'm pretty sure you have to have a private school education and sponsors of some sort."

"Well, what about baseball? What if you made it to the major leagues?"

"Baseball players aren't exempt from the draft."

She rolled over and let out a squeal and a laugh as a crab pinched her toe.

"You ok?"

"Yeah," she chuckled.

"Wasn't one of those man eating whales, was it?"

"I think we should pack a picnic tonight and watch the sun go down by the lighthouse," she said.

"With Julianne?"

"If you want, but I was thinking just the two of us."

"That sounds great to me."

They waited until four in the afternoon and then went back to the duplex where Julianne's aunt lived, and showered. Thierry couldn't believe how much sand collected in the tub. They got dressed, and she packed sandwiches and cold soda bottles. She told him they had to make a stop before they got to the lighthouse.

They walked through the sleepy town until they reached a hole in the wall with a dark green sign and the word "Murphy's" in gold embossed letters.

"Wait here," she said with a smile.

Thierry watched her go in and approach the counter through the window. A moment later, she came bouncing back out with a white sack.

"Ok, now we're ready."

"What did you get?"

"Fried clam strips!"

"Clam strips?"

"Have you ever had fried clam strips?"

He just shook his head.

"Oh, then you haven't lived!"

"Doesn't sound like something I'd normally eat, but… I'll trust you."

They walked down to the light house arm in arm, soaking in the last warm rays of sun. He perspired under his white linen shirt, and in her white floral patterned dress she looked as if the gentlest breeze might just carry her off. They spread a blanket on the warm sand in the shade of the lighthouse. It turned out that Thierry really liked fried clam strips. They watched the sun set over the bay and made love in the splendor of a thousand colors.

"Do you feel guilty?" she asked when it was over, her head pressed against his warm chest.

"Not particularly. Why—do you?"

"Well, it isn't really very Christian, is it?"

"I didn't really think God gets hung up on men and women being men and women."

"But we're not married."

"It feels like we are."

"I know, but we haven't had a church wedding or anything."

"Did Adam and Eve have a church wedding?"

"I guess not."

"Hell, they weren't even baptists."

"That's not funny," she said in jest.

"Do you know why baptists are against premarital relations?"

"No, I don't."

"Because it might lead to dancing."

She laughed and pulled herself closer to him.

"I love you with all my heart."

"I love you with all my heart, too."

"Thierry, look!" she said excitedly.

He sat up and followed the trajectory of her finger pointed toward the ocean. About thirty feet offshore, a group of dolphins danced between the surf and the moonlight. The young couple watched the marvelous creatures spring from the swell with utmost grace and utter power. After a long time, they disappeared, and the giddy young lovers gathered their belongings and walked back through the dark, sleepy town.

SEPTEMBER 15, 1943

He paced her bedroom anxiously, wringing his hands in front of him.

"How do you know for sure?"

"I don't."

"That's good, right? I mean, there's a chance it's nothing."

"Except that I missed my time by almost three full weeks, and I've been throwing up day and night for the past two."

"Yeah… that's not a good sign, is it?"

"What are you so worried about?"

He stopped pacing and stared her down.

"How can you not be worried?"

She just shrugged.

"I mean, how are we going to care for a baby? We're not even out of high school yet."

"They could send you to war in a year's time—I think if you're old enough to sacrifice your life for your country, you're old enough to care for a child."

"That's not what I meant," he answered while resuming his caged stride.

"Then what do you mean?"

"How do I tell Henry and Henrietta? How do you tell your dad?"

"With words, how else?"

"But what will people think?"

"For someone who's not very religious, you do carry an awfully heavy load of shame."

"Isn't there anything," he hesitated as he searched for sensitive words. "Something that… a doctor can do?"

"Yes, Thierry, there is."

"So, why don't we just do that?"

"Because I don't believe in it."

"Well, it's just science, isn't it? What is there not to believe in?"

"I believe there are some questions that science shouldn't try to answer."

"I'm really scared," he said with difficulty.

"Don't you think I am, too?"

"I guess so."

"But this is your baby, and if I'm supposed to have your baby, then I will, and I don't care what anyone thinks about it."

He sighed and sat on the bed beside her.

"The only thing that matters to me, Thierry, is you. I'd be prepared to walk through the valley of the shadow of death if I knew you'd be with me."

He stared at the clenched hands in his lap. She put her delicate hand on top of them.

"You would stay with me, right?"

He lifted his head so his teary gaze could meet her eternal eyes.

"Of course, Hope."

She smiled and felt tears welling. "You're my whole world, Thierry."

"I can't believe how lucky I am to have you."

He put his arm around her and she nestled her head under his neck.

"You are going to be the best daddy a little child could ever wish for."

"Whew," he uttered. "I think it's going to take some time for me to get used to that idea."

"You will," she answered with a smile.

She kissed him with her heart at peace and then excused herself to use the restroom.

He laid back on her bed with his hands under his head and breathed in the magnitude of the situation. He was going to be a father—and a husband. He was nervous about the idea of taking care of a family. He wasn't sure he could pick up any more hours at the grocery store. Should he drop out of school? What if her dad sent her away? He wouldn't. Not if they got married, anyway. But if they got married, where would they live? They couldn't afford rent anywhere. He heard her father shuffle some pots in the kitchen. Thierry wondered if he had any clue what was going on—if he had any clue that his sixteen-year-old daughter and her barely seventeen-year-old beau were about to make him a grandfather. He thought about what his mother would have thought. He imagined that after she got over the initial shock, she would have been happy. He wondered what his brother would think. He couldn't help but think that Marty would be disappointed in him. Marty was going somewhere, his life was destined for something great. Would he think Thierry had just put the kibosh on any hopes for an important life?

He sat up and flipped through her school books on the desk. They were so young, he couldn't believe it. They were still studying Shakespeare. But the idea of a baby had sparked in him a feeling that all would be right—one way or another. He would be a family man, and she would be his faithful rock, and his children would be a crown of glory on his head.

At that moment, she walked back into the room and put her hand on the door frame. He looked up and the ashen look on her face nearly knocked the wind out of him.

"Thierry," she said breathlessly.

"What is it?"

"I'm bleeding—a lot."

September 19, 1943

She miscarried early that morning. After giving Thierry a stern talking-to about the dangers of premarital intimacy, some of which he was obviously already aware, Henrietta left the little apartment and stayed with Hope and her father, taking care of the girl like she would her own daughter. Hope was embarrassed and a little ashamed, but she was more than happy to have someone like Henrietta there with her. The pain was intense and her emotions were raw. Thierry came by after school on several days to check in on her, but Henrietta was insistent that he go home. Hope's father would have flown into a violent rage when he heard the news, if not for Henry being there to keep him calm. Instead, he just poured himself another whisky and downed it in one take. He sat there silently for a long time, and then told Hope how disappointed he was in her. He didn't say a single word to Thierry.

"Are you ashamed of me, Henrietta?"

"No, I ain't ashamed of you. Farthest thing from it."

"Really?"

"You ain't the first young girl to make a bad choice and you won't be the last neither."

"But, am I ruined?"

"What you mean, ruined?"

"Well… down there?"

"Of course not, honey. Our bodies heal and make new and move on, and that's what you'll do, too."

"I don't mean that… exactly."

"Then what you mean?"

"Well, I guess morally. Thierry and I want to get married—did you know that?"

"Yeah, I knew that."

"Do you think it's a good idea?"

"I think when you're both old enough, it's the perfect idea."

"So, won't I be… tainted?… as a bride?"

"Honey, you're puttin' too much pressure on yourself. You're a human being, and human beings make mistakes. Don't mean you're not a good person. Don't mean you ain't got a heart a' gold—and you do—and in my book, that's all that counts."

"Thank you."

The young girl wiped her eyes with her sleeves.

"You get some rest now, honey. I'm gonna go and get some more warm water."

"Are you ashamed of me, Henry?"

"Farthest thing from it, my boy."

"Are you tellin' the truth?"

"You done a dumb thing—but it ain't hard to see why you did it. Believe me, you ain't the first to do it, and you sure won't be the last."

"I still feel really bad about myself. Like I should have been stronger or something."

"You're a human, Thierry, and a teenaged one at that. Take your licking from this and move on, and try not to make the same mistakes over and over—it's all you can do."

"Did you know that we want to get married?"

"I figured as much."

"What do you think?"

"I don't think you're old enough. But when you are, Hope is a keeper, that's for sure."

Thierry smiled as Henry patted his hands from across the table.

"I would have never imagined being in love—really in love—so young."

"You can't predict these kinds of things, T. And the more you try, the wronger you'll end up."

"You know, even when I thought she was going to have the baby—I was scared, yeah—but it just felt so right. I know it wasn't the perfect situation, but the thought of her being mine and having a family together… it just felt like that was my calling in life, the whole reason I'm here."

"I understand that. A good woman can make you feel that way."

"Do you really think she's a good woman, pop? Even after knowing what we did?"

"I do, Thierry. I have no doubt in my mind that she has a heart of gold, and so do you for that matter. Listen, people are people, and you can't put so much pressure on yourself that you gotta be perfect—cos ain't nobody perfect. No matter how good they might look on the outside, everybody is a little bit of a mess on the inside."

Within the week, Hope was back in school after recovering from her "illness." Some rumors were spread that she had been pregnant the whole time and had given a baby up for adoption, but they died out pretty soon after the news hit that former student and baseball team captain Michael Gaskey was killed when his ship was struck by a kamikaze pilot in the South Pacific.

July 4, 1944

"How could you do this to me?" she asked, not with malice but with fear in her voice and tears on her cheeks.

"I had to, Hope."

"You didn't have to and you know it."

Her face contorted into unnatural poses as she fought to push her emotions aside enough to speak.

"Robbie wrote me a letter—"

"Who is Robbie?"

"Robbie Fontaine—from Bloomfield?"

"I don't know him," she said with exasperation in her voice.

"We played ball together—well, he said he spoke to his NCO, and he was going to see what he could do about getting me into the unit."

"But why, Thierry?"

"Because it's an elite unit, Hope. If I get drafted in three months, who knows where I could end up—probably in some meat grinder cannon fodder group of kids who don't know their ass from their rifle."

"But you don't even know that you would get drafted."

"Hope," he said, looking at her sternly. "*Everyone* is getting drafted."

She brushed the sand from the underside of her slender calf and pulled her sweater around her shoulders.

"I don't know what I'm going to do."

He shrugged with frustration.

"We all have to do our duty for our country."

"My dad is getting worse, you know. He's drinking around the clock and hasn't been able to hold a job down for months now."

"I know, but—"

"The only way we're surviving is on what I'm making at the diner and you know that isn't much."

"How does me staying here help that?"

"And you know how sick Henrietta has been. Henry needs you right now, too."

"Henry can take care of himself. My country is calling, and the freedom of the free world is at stake. Am I just supposed to crawl under a rock and hide?

"You could start by not throwing yourself into the middle of it!"

"That's not what I'm doing."

"You're doing everything you can to join a unit that parachutes in behind enemy lines—if that's not throwing yourself headlong into the middle, then I don't know what is."

"Hope, again—they are the best trained and most elite soldiers out there."

"The Germans have elite soldiers, too."

He shifted the basket of clam strips from between them, and slid close to her. When she nearly resisted his reach to put his arm around her shoulder, he realized how upset she really was.

"A year ago, when you were… with child—I was a nervous wreck. And you calmed me down. Somehow, you knew everything was going to be alright—that everything would work out."

She turned her head from the ebbing tide and looked him in the eyes.

"Let me be the one—tonight—to make sure you know that everything will be alright. I've got a good feeling about it."

She nearly rolled her eyes. "You're not even eighteen."

"I fudged the application. They're not exactly scrutinizing them as closely as they once did. Plus, I'm only a couple months away."

"But the point is you didn't even talk to me about it. You just went and enlisted and then kept it a secret so you could surprise me? You waited to tell me until two days before you're supposed to leave for bootcamp?"

"I didn't want you to worry."

"What do you think I'll be doing for the next—what?—four or five years?"

"I'm telling you, I have a good feeling about all of this—"

"Well, I don't."

"Look—it's been almost a month since we landed at Normandy, and look at the progress we've made."

"At what cost, Thierry?"

"What I'm trying to say is that at the rate we're going, the war can't possibly last much longer—there's no way the Germans can fight a two front war."

"I don't care about any of that. I don't care about the predictions, I don't care about the overwhelming victories, I don't even care about the outcome, for God's sake."

"How can you say that?"

"Thierry Laroque—all that I care about in this life is you—that's it. You're my best friend. You have been ever since I can remember, and you always will be. You're my one and only sweetheart, my future husband, and my heart's home. All I care about is that you come back to me. And it makes me feel horribly helpless and frightened that I don't have any control over whether or not that happens."

"No one has control. I could get eaten by a shark or a whale in that water tomorrow."

She smiled, thinking back to more carefree times.

"I will come home to you, Hope. We will have a long, happy life together and lots of children and a dog and maybe even some land somewhere. We'll live out our days in quiet and peace. I'll be yours, and you'll be mine until my dying day."

"You promise?" she asked, her radiant eyes sparkling under the starlight.

"I promise."

He dipped her back and kissed her. She clutched onto this shoulders as if she'd never let him go. Her ash brown hair fell delicately on the blanket as she laid her head down. They kissed with youthful passion and the tender love of old age simultaneously. Their bodies pressed together as he ran his hand down her neck and onto her breast. Her small frame heaved with the avidity of a bride on her wedding night as she struggled to unbutton his shirt.

When their passion had receded, they laid across the blanket, his arms tightly around her body, her arms tightly around his. They breathed contentedly and even chuckled a few times. She turned her face to kiss his lips just as the fireworks down the beach in Wildwood erupted.

"Well, that's awfully patriotic, don't you think?"

"What is, laying a soldier before he heads off to war?"

"That, too," he answered with a laugh.

They watched the show for a while and soaked in the moment.

"I could lay here with you for the rest of my life."

"Come home to me and you will."

"Those are the finest words I think I will ever hear."

"Come home to me, Thierry."

"I will, Hope."

By the end of September, he was shipped directly from Camp Edwards, Massachusetts to Camp Toccoa, Georgia for his Army paratrooper training. By the beginning of December, he was in Duxford, England, readying to be launched headlong into the fray.

FIVE

War is cruelty. There is no use trying to reform it.
The crueler it is, the sooner it will be over.

WILLIAM TECUMSEH SHERMAN

JANUARY 1945

When he opened his eyes, the earth was covered in ash colored snow, the ground underneath him frozen solid. His ears hurt, but he heard no sound. He was startled by how labored his breathing was. He held his breath for a moment, then let it out slowly, a plume of white smoke escaping his mouth. He was lying on his back, he surmised, the trunk of an enormous tree very nearly pinned to his chest. *Off course,* he thought, *I was way off course.* He slowly and carefully lifted his head, eyes straining to get a glimpse of the situation. To his right, charred trees, twisted metal, and corpses all strewn about, covered in a fresh coat of snow. To his left, much of the same, although he could see in the distance what looked to be a single fire still burning, the orange licks of flame the only color to grace the desolately monochromatic landscape. For several seconds, he watched his right hand twitch violently and couldn't tell if he was shivering or shaking still from nerves, but he decided to force himself to his feet and have a cautious look around.

He arched his back and, with some effort, pulled himself out of the earth. He slowly labored to his hands and knees, the dry, frigid air burning his lungs. He spit quietly and watched his saliva freeze in an instant. He quieted his breathing and listened to the perpetual silence. He couldn't remember ever experiencing quiet like this before—it was deafening.

Forcing himself to his feet, he collected his rifle, instinctively slid behind a tree for cover, and looked around again. Not ten feet from him, a corpse lay still, limbs twisted in unnerving positions, face devoid of skin altogether. As he approached it, he noticed a panzer beret a foot to the left, completely untouched, though its owner had been mutilated.

His ears perked as in the distance, a slow, creaking sound commenced. It seemed like it went on for an hour before he heard the tree snap in two, the whoosh of its needled limbs brushing the trees around it, and then finally the dull thud as it crashed to the earth. Then silence again.

His back was throbbing. His hips felt like they were rusted. His hands—his bloodstained hands—ached.

He made his way toward the fire in the distance, keeping his ears and eyes open for any disturbance in the atmosphere.

The Ardennes.

He had no trouble remembering roughly where he was supposed to be; all the trouble came in trying to determine where he was.

The wind was bitter and biting, carrying drifts of snow, ash, and the smell of burnt flesh on its harsh cusp.

All Quiet on the Western Front.

He couldn't help but chuckle at the irony of it.

He approached the fire and was surprised to see a neat pile of brush, obviously abandoned recently. He knelt down by it and reached his hands towards the warmth. After a moment, he pressed his open palms to his face, savoring the feeling of pins and needles on his frozen cheeks. He stood quickly and clutched his rifle.

Someone must be close.

He didn't know who. He listened again for several minutes and heard nothing.

Alertly, cautiously, he knelt back by the fire, its warmth too inviting to ignore. The feeling gradually returned to his hands, accompanied by a burning sensation, but they would not stop shaking. He tried desperately to remember what his last orders had been, what direction he'd been headed, when was the last time he ate.

Who's fire is this?

He figured by the hazy light filtering through the dim that it was some time after noon. That really was only a guess, though. He checked his pack for food—one day's ration, plus one can of beef and potato hash, plus one D-ration. A fork, a spoon, a flashlight, a half-used box of matches, and a carton with 3 cigarettes in it.

He used his knife to puncture the top of the can with the odd portion of beef and potato hash and placed the whole can in the fire. He ate his warm meal slowly, keeping his eyes on the horizon around him. He gathered a few more branches, snapped them to size, and stoked the fire with them.

Do I just wait here?

He listened carefully, straining his ears as if he would hear an audible reply.

Somebody has to know I'm out here... Or maybe they don't.

He sat with his arms around his knees, rocking slowly towards the fire, then away from it.

How the hell did this happen?

His mind began to race.

Who made this fire? And what happens if they come back to it? If they're Krauts, I'm FUBAR. I can't just stay here.

He thought back to the moment he left the plane and then the moment he opened his chute. The anti-aircraft fire had put them off course initially and the howling wind had simply finished the job. He didn't remember being hit by anything but he remembered snapping back to consciousness ten or twelve feet off the frozen ground. Then that was it. And here he was.

Thierry decided he couldn't risk staying there, exposed to the eyes of any passerby. Through the mental fog, he remembered hearing some time ago, he wasn't sure when, that the Germans were withdrawing to the east and that several companies were to pursue them. But that was before the mishap in the air.

Ok, I gotta head east. If I head east, I'll run into my company sooner or later. But what if it didn't work? What if they pushed us back? If I head east, I'll be walking right into an ambush. So, west… right? If I head west, I'll run into our lines sooner or later. Unless the Krauts pincered us and cut us off again. But if we did push them east, our lines might be stretched so thin that I could walk all the way to Paris and maybe not see another soul.

Despite the recent memory of the Malmedy Massacre, the guiding light of loyalty and belief in his brothers in arms caused him to choose to head east—as best he could tell it. He repacked his bag with a brown tarp—the remains of half of a pup-tent—pilfered some matches and crackers off a corpse, and headed out through the smoke and the cold.

Row after row of trees—many of them blackened, cracked, toppled altogether. He did what he could to avoid having to climb over the massive trunks across his makeshift path. He paid close attention to the sun, which was fading quickly, in order to avoid falling prey to the old adage that lost men wander in circles. After walking an hour or so, he began to see less and less wreckage, fewer and fewer dead men, and no tracks at all in the fresh snow. Knowing that he might have to spend some time on his own, he tried his best to find something useable on each cadaver he passed, but after repeatedly finding next to nothing of value, he slowly began to suspect that the unfortunate had already been picked over.

Somebody started a bonfire, somebody picked hundreds of bodies over, and yet they didn't notice me, practically right out in the open.

He shuddered with this thought. It was too improbable to be accidental.

But why would someone leave me there, gear and supplies intact?

He weighed the possibilities. If the Krauts had done it, they would have surely killed him or at the very least taken him prisoner—certainly they would have disarmed him. If the Americans had been successful in pushing them back, they were well enough supplied as to not need to plunder the dead—and why would they have left him there if they hadn't retreated? He thought about his choice in moving east. He stopped and turned to the west. He scratched back of his head and sighed. He had already trudged at least five miles and had seen nothing exceptionally different than when he left. No discernible clues whatsoever. With a grunt and a rough scrape of his throat, he spit and then turned back to the east. He had already made up his mind, and he had been taught not to second guess his gut. He trudged on.

Through an eerily open patch of forest he walked, then came upon a small gully and a frozen creek running through its center. Strands of dead grass and small saplings stuck through the snow, which was particularly ashy in this spot, and frozen mud rested in messy clumps at the bottom of the small valley. He slid down, left foot first, arms out to his sides for balance. He attempted to climb the steep incline on the other side, but lost his footing on a slick piece of ice and fell face-first against the exposed root of an ancient oak tree, splitting his bottom lip open. He sat up quickly as blood gushed through his hands and onto his coat. His spit covered the snow nearby with a spray of bright red. He held his sleeve to his mouth with the back of his hand and pushed against his bottom teeth with his tongue. One of his teeth felt very loose. The pain hadn't hit him as much as the warmth inside his mouth. The next time he spit, it was almost a whole mouthful of blood. It spilled from his lip and dripped off his chin in a steady flow. He thought he must have looked like an animal. He felt the wound with the thumb and forefinger on his right hand—the stinging gash was about half an inch deep. He opened his bag and ripped a small piece of gauze from its roll. He attempted to pack it in the wound as best he could. He knew he had to keep moving and find somewhere to settle before dark.

His second attempt up the sharp incline was immeasurably more successful than his first. Out of the gully, straight ahead sat an immense pile of boulders; gray, ancient bedrock blocking much of his view to the east. He readied himself and began to move around them with caution. On the other side of the rocks was a large clearing, leading up a steep hill and back into the brush. Several corpses were scattered about, mostly German—*this is a good sign,* he thought—twisted in cruel and unnatural poses, some of their eyes frozen open, pleading to the sky for help. He sat and listened for a few minutes, pressed the gauze back into position, and studied the edges of the clearing for signs of an ambush. While he was never comfortable with the idea of running across an open field in six inches of snow and in the middle of a war zone, he knew he must cross here or not cross at all. He gauged the distance at a hundred and twenty yards, took a deep breath, and sprinted.

The clean, cold oxygen set his lungs ablaze; his eyes did not deviate to the left or to the right. His feet crunched the fresh snow beneath him. Just as he reached the end of the clearing, his right foot caught on something—only by his toes—and he went sprawling awkwardly into the woods, landing hard on his left shoulder and rolling until he came to rest against a sturdy conifer. He quickly sprang to a kneeling position and looked back toward the clearing to see what had tripped him. About fifteen feet from the edge of the tree line, what looked like the sleeve of a coat stuck out slightly from under the snow. He moved quietly toward the boundary of his cover and looked closer. He could now make out the strap of a canvas bag and mulled over whether it was worth the risk to try to get hold of it. He crouched quietly and listened again. *Nothing.*

As quickly and adroitly as he could, he ran out to the bag, jerked the handle out of the snow, and darted back toward the relative safety of the wood. He slung his rifle back on his shoulder and began walking again, checking the bag for any contents. He found one D-ration, and while he was thankful for any sustenance he could count on, he was slightly disappointed that it was not a tin of something slightly more enjoyable. After ditching the bag, the thought then struck him that it had obviously been dropped by an American, and he took some comfort that he was headed in the right direction.

The terrain soon became steep, and he found it helpful to grab onto trees and limbs as he climbed. He put handfuls of snow in his mouth between his lip and bottom row of teeth to help prevent swelling. The dull sunlight was becoming more yellow and peaked through the brush at a steadily declining angle. A German soldier lay frozen and grisly, pinned to a tree by a piece of something invisible through his abdomen, eyes hauntingly open and black blood caked around his mouth and chin. Icicles dangled from his ears and his nose, and his femur jutted out, white and smooth, at an odd angle from his pant leg. Thierry drew close to see what kept the man pinned to the tree, but it looked like the wound had closed around whatever object was lodged inside him. He couldn't help but take more assurance and comfort in this sight, thinking again that he must have chosen correctly in choosing to move eastward.

His lip had ceased to bleed but continued to throb.

He went on in the hopes of encountering his unit until the clouds lowered, the wind picked up, and it began to snow again. He hoped it would snow heavily enough to cover his tracks. The sun was receding quickly, and he knew that he had to find somewhere to take cover for the night. He also knew that he would have to start a fire, and that it should be somewhere not easily seen.

After another quarter mile or so, the incline leveled out. Thierry stood and caught his breath, scanning the distance for either signs of humanity's presence or a safe place to camp. Off to his left, there was an entire grouping of felled trees in a pile. In the distance to his right, he could make out a somewhat steep decline and what looked like some boulders jutting, from the side of the hill. He moved in that direction and saw that there was enough room under the rocks to camp out of the elements and build a small fire which, critically, wouldn't be visible from above.

After laying his bag down in the small crevice, he readjusted his rifle on his shoulder and set about gathering tinder for a fire. He scooped another handful of snow in his mouth just as a gust of wind cut through his clothing and made his whole body shiver violently. Before descending back to his den, he crouched down to try to get out of the wind and listened to it howl. As long as he didn't hear anything else, he thought he might be safe.

With the fire glowing, he unpacked his canvas tarp and spread it over the frozen ground. He took from his bag his small wallet and one of his two D-rations. He sawed through a third of it with his knife and began chewing.

They can land an airplane on the deck of a ship in the middle of an ocean, but they still can't make one of these taste good.

The thick, chewy chocolate bar, distributed as an emergency nutritional supply made his entire mouth hurt. Suddenly, he felt something sharp and coarse grind against his molars and it almost made him gag. He spit the mouthful into his hand and saw his tooth lodged in the chocolate bar. He felt the space with his tongue and felt a rush of fresh blood build in his mouth.

That was easier than I thought it would be.

He put the tooth in his pocket without thinking about it and put the chocolate back in his mouth.

With a poke from a long stick, the fire stirred and grew, its warmth filling the small space under the rocks. From his wallet, he pulled out a small photo of Hope. His heart ached with the sight of her, and he immediately began to wonder again why she hadn't written him in the past several weeks. He thought he hadn't heard from her since Thanksgiving Day.

There's a problem with the mail service. They had to be overloaded with the holidays and all.

He couldn't think of any other explanation.

He ran his finger gently along her cheek and tried to remember the softness of her lips, the sound of her voice. He tried to harken the sensation of her small hand locked in his, the lightning that ran through his spine every time he kissed her lips. With a pang of guilt, he remembered her nude, the smoothness of her thighs, every perfectly feminine contour of her body, the warmth and heavenly comfort of her skin pressed tightly against his. He gazed in her eyes, those gorgeous green eyes—

Why did I do this?

—He kissed the photo and put it back in the wallet and put the wallet in the bag.

He crumpled the canvas bag and put it under his head and laid down.

His last thought before sleeping was, *I have got to make it home.*

He woke with a start and clutched his rifle.

The fire had smoldered down to just embers, barely giving any warmth off.

He laid still, listening intently for anything at all.

Two more inches of snow had fallen, and the wind was still.

It was dead quiet.

He rubbed his face with his icy hands and smacked his cheeks softly.

He felt his lip and, to his dismay, felt the gauze frozen solid to his bottom lip. He tried gently tugging it off by one corner but it wouldn't budge. He reached out from under the rock ledge and gathered a handful of snow which he then packed in his mouth to numb the dull pain. He curled his lip inside his mouth to expose the outside to the snow as well. He swallowed hard, gathering his nerves and then with one swift motion yanked the gauze from the wound. It took everything in him not to holler in agony, but he managed to stifle his cry for the sake of his safety. He flung the gauze angrily in what was left of the fire.

He checked his rifle and his bag and then crawled out of his hole. He rolled up the tarp and the bag he'd used as his pillow and put them both back in his knapsack. He stood slowly and peered around him. The clouds had given way to a sunny sky, cold as it might be. He didn't see anything in the woods around him that hadn't been seen the previous evening.

He looked up at the bright sky and thanked God that another night had passed without cause to use his weapon. He thanked God for his den, his fire, and his Hope. He prayed for her in the kindest terms—prayed for her safety, her comfort, and her happiness. He then prayed that there would be a letter waiting for him whenever he found his company.

Bag and rifle slung on his shoulder, he began to move east again. By the position of the sun, he thought it to be abut ten.

The forest was thicker than it had been the previous day, and he'd found it necessary to use his knife to clear the brush before his path. After he'd walked what seemed to be about five miles, he stopped to rest. He ate what was left of his D-ration from the previous night. He paused his laborious chewing when he thought he heard something in the distance. It wasn't a sound like a person or animal would make—it almost sounded like an engine. Slowly, the earth began to shake, and the dull moan began to roar. A B-25 Mitchell roared directly overhead from northwest to southeast, and he got just enough of a view to see the single white star painted on its side.

I am headed the right way after all.

He was relieved by the sight of the plane, although it passed out of the range of his hearing as quickly as it had entered. With new resolve, he set back to his path making through the brush.

Crossing small, frozen ravines and climbing through the densest woods he'd ever seen, he'd lost all track of all things human—not a single sign of man's existence on earth. He hacked his way through several nearly impassable thickets, trying desperately to keep an eye on which direction he was actually headed. Keeping a compass on the sun through the opaque awning of tree limbs became more difficult as he went.

Thierry stopped and sat after several hours, and, feeling at once lost and confident that his countrymen were in the vicinity, stopped to eat the last of his rations, save the D-ration he'd found. The canopy was so thick overhead that he had to squint to see what he was eating. It also felt like the temperature was dropping. The oxygen smoked from his lungs with every breath and his fingers were feeling numb. He tried his best to warm them under his armpits, but the outside of his coat was just as cold. The wind picked up and cut through the trees as it nipped through his clothes.

Columns of sunlight peered dimly through the low branches to his west, and he began to tremble furiously. He remembered taking off his coat with some effort, although he wasn't sure why. He slowly closed his eyes, and a warm rush flooded over him, like slipping into a warm bath. The harshness of his surroundings and his experiences began to dissolve into the comfort and contentment of a maternal embrace. His head rolled slowly on his shoulders, and he imbibed the ecstasy of all his earthly troubles fading and the cold, gray winter diffusing into the radiant, blissful glow of endless summer. He heard a soft whisper, in a strange accent, calling his name—a tender voice he hadn't heard since his childhood. His lips broke into an expectant smile and he opened his eyes. His mother stood over him, her soft fingers caressing his forehead, calling him to come home out of the cold. Suddenly, Hope sprang to his mind, and he tried to sit up. Nina urged him to stay calm and lie quietly.

What about Hope?

What about her? Came the soft reply.

Won't she miss me?

Yes, his mother replied.

Then I have to keep going.

No, my boy—your struggle is over.

But, mama, I love her.

And she loves you.

I can't leave her alone, Thierry answered.

She's not alone, son—it's you that is alone.

He began to be disoriented, and Nina's glow began to steadily fade.

I don't understand. I have to make it home to her.

Nina smiled tenderly. *Come with me, Thierry.*

Fear gripped him, and he began to flail about. He felt himself hit the cold ground, and it knocked the wind out of him. His mother stood high above him, reaching her silky white hands toward him. He heard a strange, foreign sound, which also reminded him of home, and he turned suddenly toward the west. Waves crashed against jagged rocks, and the snow fell steadily and quickly like rain. Out in the distance, just close enough to make out her shape, Hope stood among the waves—in her right hand an ancient feather pen, in her left a primitive scroll of papyrus. He called to her, but she did not answer, did not look up from her calm writing. He gasped for breath and felt his cheek against the frozen earth. His tongue rubbed against the deep gash in his lip, and she suddenly looked up. Her eyes brimmed with fear, and it wounded him. He cried out that he would comfort her, that he would be her savior, and at that moment, she turned the scroll toward him, but he couldn't get his eyes to focus on what she'd written. She was mouthing something that he could not hear and showing him words in calligraphy too practiced to be hers. *I can't read it,* he thought.

His eyes met hers.

Suddenly, a horribly violent screeching sound, like steel scraping.

Then, a loud snap, like a bone breaking.

His eyes shot open, and he lay still, trying to keep his breath paced and silent.

Someone was walking confidently through the dark. Maybe thirty feet from him. He adroitly felt for his rifle, careful with every subtle motion not to make a sound. The steps sounded at once like they were approaching and fading into the night. He listened intently until he could be sure that whatever—whoever—was walking was headed away from him. He pulled his jacket back over his shoulders quietly, slung his bag over his shoulder, and held the rifle at the ready.

It was at least thirty degrees colder than it had been that afternoon, and there were at least three more inches of snow fallen. From what he could tell, it still fell steadily. He realized that he had already been within seconds of death and became desperate. He began to follow the sound of the steps, determining by their gate that he followed another human, stumbling through the brush and slipping through the snow. He might be heard but he did not care—he had nothing to lose.

The wind howled. His senses heightened by adrenaline, he picked out the eery hoot of an owl in the trees above. The person he followed walked without struggle, as if he knew the layout of the woods—every bare bush, every fallen limb—from memory, even in the dark.

After ten or more minutes of struggle, through a clearing, the darkness was pierced by a small, yellow glow. It took him a moment to refocus his eyes, and then he saw the unmistakable shape of a tiny cabin. Wood smoke tickled his nose and finally brought him fully back to his senses.

He was alive. And this was real.

Down a small slope, and through the dell, he watched a man of maybe five feet, six inches carrying a neat bundle of wood under one arm, dressed in a dark fur coat, feet clad with heavy leather boots, open the door to the cabin, warm light flooding the snow in a long rectangle, and, shaking his feet in the threshold, disappear behind it. Thierry crouched down and tried to warm his hands with his breath. He concentrated on calming his breathing pattern and attempting to organize his thoughts.

He began to weigh his options. Should he wait for the man to reemerge? If he waited, how long should he wait? How long could he last in the elements? What kind of man was this? Were those military boots he wore?

Thierry sat for he knew not how long, thinking things over when the planked wood door to the shack creaked open again, and the same man, dressed in the same attire, this time carrying what appeared to be a hunting rifle, emerged. Thierry watched the man stop for a moment about ten feet from the door, adjust his fur hat with his left hand, and turn his eyes to the sky. The man studied the stars for a long minute, turning his head and pointing at the heavenly expanse. He then turned his back to Thierry's vantage point and headed off in the into the thicket.

If he would ever have an opportunity to steal a look into the cabin, this was it. Thierry shuffled out of the woods and as quietly as possible crossed the clearing, rifle at the ready. He crept up under the small window and crouched, listening intently. He heard the owl in the distance and that was all. Slowly, he stood with his back to the structure and peered into the window over his left shoulder. Nothing moved inside. There was a large, fire roaring in the hearth on the far side of the room, a small cot in the corner, and an absurdly large wood table with stools directly under the window. A small, leather wing chair sat caddy-cornered by the fire, across from the bed, and on the mantle sat numerous large pots and pans. Thierry's eyes focused in on the table directly below his view—several expensive-looking silver bowls and plates, saucers and teacups strewn about as if ten people had eaten there. A large bowl sat at the far end of the table, covered delicately by an oversized serving plate.

After checking his surroundings carefully, peering around the corners of the cabin—nothing moving or out of the ordinary, aside from a small shed in the rear—he went back to the door and opened it slowly. A burst of warm air hit him like he'd walked into a brick wall. He stuttered back for a moment and then snuck inside, closing the old door gently behind him. The first thing he did was to uncover the bowl on the table. A thick stew—still warm. He grabbed a spoon without thinking and began to eat ravenously. Potatoes, onions, and something that tasted akin to overcooked pork, and somewhat bitter. Thierry thought, judging by his surroundings, that it must have been venison or perhaps elk—definitely something he had never eaten before.

When he finally slowed to a stop, he began to feel nauseous, belched a couple times, and then slowly drew deep, warm breaths through his nose and exhaled through his mouth. The fire crackled softly and he took a quick peek out the window into the darkness. As far as he could tell, nothing outside stirred. He drifted over toward the bed and sat down gently, not sure initially that it could be trusted with his full weight. He listened cautiously for a moment, then leaned back and laid his head gently on the wood beams of the wall. His stomach was completely full and his body warm. He thought of Henrietta making Henry stoke the fire, and Henry complaining that he was sweating already. He thought about how he hadn't been able to take leave for her funeral because she wasn't his legal mother. Taking a deep breath, he realized that he would have to move out and knew that whatever he did, he couldn't fall asleep where he was. With this in mind, he allowed himself to close his eyes—only for a moment—and take in what small comfort he could. His mind wandered towards Hope as it always did, her lips, her gentle smile that he would have given the world to see for just a moment. He suddenly caught himself drifting off to sleep and opened his heavy eyelids without moving his head from its comfortable resting place. He glanced to his left and then to his right to make sure he was still alone, and thought that he would have to leave back into the woods and find a place to camp—in five minutes. Maybe ten. He closed his weary eyes again, but only for a moment.

Pressure—almost to the point of pain. He reached for his rifle and instinctively knew it wasn't there. When his eyes opened, he was staring into the wild black eyes of a gnome-like man, with a scruffy black beard and scraggly black hair. It was when he tried to sit up that Thierry felt the cold blade of the paring knife pressed to his flesh just under his chin.

"What do you want?" said the small, deceptively strong man in a French, maybe Belgian accent. He had pinned Thierry on the small bed and was holding the knife in his right hand and Thierry's right wrist down with his left.

"Nothing, nothing," came the nervous reply.

"Nothing? Then why are you eating my meat?" the man asked, leaning his face towards Thierry's. His rank breath went not unnoticed.

"I was so hungry, so cold, I meant no harm," Thierry replied.

"How many more of them are you?" the man said with a quick peek over his shoulder.

"None, none—it's just me."

"Just you? This is not possible," the man declared through rotting teeth, wagging his face in front of Thierry's nose.

"It's true—I was separated from my unit a couple days ago—I'm not even sure how."

"And you are British? American? Canada?"

"American—I'm here to help."

The man spat over his right shoulder.

"Help? You are here to steal," the man said, pressing the knife into Thierry's neck so that he was almost sure it was about to open the skin.

"No, no," Thierry pleaded. "Please, don't."

The man slightly alleviated the pressure on the knife.

"Where are you from in America?"

"New Jersey."

"New Jersey?" the man replied, almost with disbelief.

Thierry nodded quickly and carefully.

"I had a girlfriend from New Jersey once," the man said with a caustic chuckle.

"You did?" asked Thierry, interested only to know if this fact might save his life.

"She was bitch," the man said. "No class whatsoever—a real American."

"So it didn't work out?" Thierry asked, trying to get a wrap on where the situation was headed.

The man shook his head.

"I'm sorry," Thierry replied with as much sympathy as his current situation would allow.

The man shrugged nonchalantly.

"She wasn't even that pretty."

With that he relaxed the knife completely, let Thierry's wrist go, and sat up, although he still sat straddling his chest.

"So, you needed a place to get out of the cold, eh?"

Thierry nodded.

"You can stay here tonight," the man said. "I would offer you something to eat, but by the looks of my pot, you've already had your fill."

"I'm sorry," Thierry answered genuinely.

"It's ok," said the man, climbing off of Thierry and standing next to the bed. "I'll have more meat in the morning. Can I offer you something warm to drink?"

"That would be wonderful."

The man turned to the table and stretched to reach something underneath. Thierry could hear liquid being poured, and then the man turned back and handed Thierry a heavy square glass with caramel-colored liquid in it. Thierry sniffed and immediately recognized it as whisky.

"Warm," Thierry said with an ironic chuckle, holding the glass up to toast his host.

"My name is Clement," the man said. "And I am honored to have an American friend from New Jersey at my table."

"Thank you, Clement," Thierry replied. "My name—"

Clement waved his hand and shook his head.

"No, no," he said, still waving his hand. "It is ok—you are a soldier—and I don't want to know any names or ranks on either side. I don't want to know anything that can be used against me in any way—one side or the other."

Thierry thought this was curious, but just shrugged and took a sip of his drink. The alcohol burned the back of his throat and warmed his stomach.

"I'll just call you—New Jersey," Clement said with a chuckle.

Thierry laughed along out of courtesy.

"You still must want to sleep, eh?" Clement asked, kneeling down to put another log on the fire.

"I am very tired," Thierry replied.

Clement simply nodded his head, repositioning the logs with a metal poker. When he was satisfied with the blaze, he stood the metal rod against the stone, sharp side up.

"Well, New Jersey, you sleep then. I am a mostly nocturnal creature anyway, so I will be about my business in the woods and you rest."

"Thank you," Thierry said with a genuine smile and another sip of the alcohol. "Forgive me, but, I'm from the city… do you mind if I ask you what you do in the woods at night?"

Clement stared blankly at his fire and mumbled under his breath, "I will have more meat tomorrow," as if he hadn't heard the American's question at all. He looked back at Thierry, almost in embarrassment and said, "I'm sorry, did you say something, New Jersey?"

"Well, you said you had business in the woods, and I've never lived in the country like this so I just wonder, what is there to do in the woods at night—especially on a night so cold?"

"Tonight, I set the trap, and tomorrow, you'll see—I'll have new meat in the morning."

"How often do you get a kill?"

"Not often," Clement replied.

Thierry's stomach suddenly turned, and he thought he might be sick.

"How are you so sure you'll have fresh meat in the morning, then?"

"You rest, New Jersey," Clement answered, putting his warm palm against Thierry's forehead and helping him lie back in the small bed. "I am a very good hunter..."

The room began to swirl and the American thought the lights were dimming.

Just before he blacked out, Thierry thought he heard Clement say, "And sometimes, the prey comes to me."

He had violent dreams. He dreamed of Normandy, he dreamed of Dunkirk, he dreamed of battles he'd never seen and places he'd never been. He saw the eyes of men dying, heard grown men crying for their mothers as they slipped from one life to the next. The endless scraping of metal. Blood, thick and black as tar, pooled on filthy tiled floors. Limbs, piled in the corner like a heap of trash.

The sound of the metal grew louder and louder until he slowly opened his eyes. The thatched ceiling of the cabin, the sound of metal still scraping, but softer and more deliberate.

Out of the corner of his eye, he noticed Clement staring into the fire not five feet from him, sharpening a butcher's knife. The host turned toward him, eyes wild with bloodlust and malice. He raised the cleaver over his head slowly and with great anticipation.

In a flash of instinct, a combination of evolution and training as a human war machine, Thierry launched himself from the bed and collided with the smaller European. The two men slammed violently into the cabinet adjacent to the fireplace, and Thierry felt a sharp, intense pain just north of his right shoulder blade. Clement shrieked like the devil himself while he did his best to hack at his guest with the knife. The American did his best to parry the blows with his upper arm while seeking to inflict some kind of damage himself. The two struggled in primitive, animalistic warfare for what seemed like an eternity. Thierry choked on his host's grotesque body odor, their grip on each other not relinquished until out of desperation, the American sank his teeth into the devil's gaunt cheek. He felt warm blood squirt the roof of his mouth while his host's whiskers scraped roughly across his tongue.

"*Je ne peux jamais mourir!*" Clement began to scream.

With the force of a much larger man, he shoved Thierry backward. The American hit the back of his head on the mantel, and trying to keep from falling off his feet, reached downward to steady himself. As if by divine appointment, Thierry's hand fell against the metal fire poker. Clement wildly thrust himself at Thierry, his right cheekbone exposed to open air. Thierry had just enough time to acquire a firm grip on the poker, and with all the strength he could muster, he rammed the sharp metal upward and through his host's esophagus.

Clement crumpled slowly, eyes still blazing as he gurgled and gasped for air. Thierry watched him slide to his knees, black iron rod clanging onto the bloody floor.

The American quickly realized that he was barefoot and weaponless. He searched the room quickly and put on his boots, but his rifle was missing. He flung the old wooden door open and stumbled out into the snow, bleak daylight breaking softly. His feverish breath rising in a white plume toward the sky. It had snowed more overnight, and under a brooding grey sky, he trudged back behind the cabin toward the small wooden storage shed to see if his articles might be there. It took him a good minute to pry the rusty latch open. Light flooded into the small wooden shed and the first thing that caught Thierry's eye was the barrel of his rifle, protruding out from under a canvas blanket. He tossed the blanket aside and discovered the frozen remains of a human, eyeless sockets grotesque in the morning light. Obviously a male corpse, its skin peeled back in parts and flesh missing to the bone.

Thierry stepped back, put his hand against the side of the shack, and vomited violently.

He spit, and regaining his balance, began to sob, though his eyes remained tearless. He looked down at the corpse again, briefly, then with one strong tug his rifle was back in hand. He left the door to the shed ajar and headed east.

As the morning wore on, the clouds broke and warm sunlight split the trees, like rays from heaven sent to comfort him. His gait was slow and his mind weary. He began to believe he would not live through another night. As much as his training and his character pled with him to chase such thoughts, he began to resign to his fate. He checked his weapon and considered putting a bullet in his own brain, but kept traipsing on out of indifference to any other option. Tree after tree, landscape unaltered mile after mile. He was reconciled to the ending his life by cold, and the cold would be back in a few hours time. Thousands of men had suffered worse fates, including the man he had unwittingly eaten the night before.

From the position of the sun, he gauged it to be after fifteen hundred hours. He simply stopped in his tracks, turned and sat at the base of the nearest tree. Legs stretched comfortably in front of him, rifle nonchalantly across his lap, his thoughts became a disheveled melting pot of his mother's face blurring into that of Clement. Concentrated thoughts of his dear Hope were sullied by the horror inside the shed. A stiff breeze picked up out of the east, blowing drifts of snow over his legs. Clouds began to roll in, and it felt like a fresh snow would soon be upon him.

His heart began to ache. He suddenly began to mourn. He mourned the loss of his mother; he mourned his estrangement with his brother. He mourned his brothers in arms; he mourned the war. He mourned the man in the shed and he mourned his last mental image of Clement, thick blood squirting from his neck. He mourned for Hope when she would hear the news that he was dead and he mourned the beautiful children she would bear, as they would belong to another man.

Instinctively, he reached for her photo in his wallet, but his bag was not there. He had left Clement's shack without it, and now he was convinced she was gone from him forever. He mourned the suffocating sensation that his life had been robbed.

He awoke slowly, the feeling of his tongue flicking subconsciously between the numb flaps of skin on his lip amused him for some innocently childish reason. Was the sun rising or was it setting? The snow had ceased to fall.

He stood to his feet slowly and scratched his back against a tree like a brown bear waking from a winter's long hibernation. He felt oddly relaxed. He thought about her again and decided that if he was still living, she would be his reason to live. He continued walking east.

After what felt like two or three miles, the dense brush broke in two—a narrow, but well worn dirt path running north and south through it. He look both ways and waited cautiously before exposing himself by walking out to the road. He knelt beside it and noticed deep tire treads caked into the frozen mud.

There's gotta be some sort of civilization at the end of this road.

He started off south, with no particular logic behind the decision. He walked for another few miles as the road bent to the east before stopping to rest. He picked up a fistful of clean white snow with his bare hand and shoved it in his mouth. Only after swallowing the partially melted snow did he begin to realize how thirsty he'd become. After eating a few more mouthfuls of snow, he began his trek again.

Not five minutes later, his cautious ears picked up the distant hum of an engine. He knelt down on the side of the road, clutching his rifle in ready position. In another few seconds, he was able to discern that whatever the vehicle was, it was headed towards him, and quickly.

"Shit," he whispered as he scrambled to take up a better concealed position. He didn't want to be so far into the brush that he couldn't see the vehicle as it passed, in order to ascertain if it was German or American. He did his best to cover his tracks, swishing snow with his hands as he backed into the forest. He laid down on his side behind the trunk of a fallen tree and arranged some twigs and what leaves he could find over his body. The engine was coming closer, and from the sound of it, he thought it must be a fairly large truck. Shortly, down the road, over a small hill appeared an Opel Blitz transport truck bumping up and down violently over each crevice in the terrain. As it approached, he could see the driver and one passenger sitting next to him. The back of the truck was covered with a heavy green tarp. Suddenly, not ten feet from his position, the truck ground to a halt. Thierry instinctively reached for his rifle, as quietly as possible, but could not find it within his reach. Panic began to set in. The passenger's door opened, and out stepped a uniformed man, SS emblem patched on his shoulder. Thierry reached again, desperately for his gun, and then caught its faint glimmer ten feet ahead of him, lying in the snow next to the road. His heart sank. The SS soldier took a long, casual puff of his cigarette and then tossed it toward the front of the truck. He meandered directly across the dirt path, turned his back toward Thierry, unzipped his trousers, and began to relieve himself.

Thierry's mind raced, all the while keeping his eyes trained on the enemy solider before him. He considered his options: waiting it out, which might leave him entirely defenseless if discovered, or making a dash for his rifle. He knew he could take out the pisser and the driver before either could react to him, and decided on this desperate, and perhaps foolish, course of action. However, as his body tensed to launch itself over the log and down toward the road, a harsh voice cried out behind him, "*Stopp!*"

Thierry froze. His vision and mental energy had been so tunnel-focused on the truck's passenger that he neglected to notice four members of Sepp Deitrich's 6th SS Panzer Army had snuck up on his position.

"*Aufstehen!*"

Thierry extended his arms slowly to show that he was not armed and shook his head as if to signal that he did not understand the commands he was being given. The area around him began to crawl with armed soldiers, the man directly ahead of him calmly finishing his piss while smiling over his shoulder in Thierry's direction.

"*Aufstehen!*"

And with that, Thierry was roughly grabbed by both hands and stood up. He was shoved face first into a nearby tree and searched with both precision and harshness.

"*Woher kommst du?*" the soldier frisking him asked brusquely. Thierry shrugged his shoulders animatedly to show he didn't understand.

"*Baier, kommen hier!*"

A brown haired man of impressive stature appeared from behind the truck and came trotting over. He stood directly in front of Thierry and conversed with the other Germans for a few seconds, then he calmly leaned in towards Thierry's face and said, "What are you doing here?"

Although his German accent was heavy, his English was completely discernible to the American.

"I don't know… I got lost," replied Thierry.

"Lost?" the man cried with a quick laugh. "What do you mean lost?"

"Lost… like I don't know where I am."

The SS soldier slapped his knee and opened his mouth wide, although only a suppressed laugh came out. He began barking back and forth with the other soldiers, who soon began laughing heartily as well. He snorted and spit in the snow.

"Well, you picked quite a place to get lost," he replied. Thierry wasn't sure by the tone of voice if he was being granted sympathy or being mocked.

"I'm Klaus Baier, and you're lost in Panzer land," he said with another mysterious smile.

A few of the Germans snickered.

"American, correct?"

Thierry nodded. Baier nodded back and shrugged.

"I can't hold that against you, where a man was born," Baier said casually. "Well, don't cause any trouble, and in a few miles, you'll have some food and a place to sleep for the night."

They walked Thierry toward the back of the truck and lifted him in effortlessly. He was then jostled toward the front and seated with a shove on the edge of the narrow bench. Baier sat next to him.

"So, you don't speak no German?"

Thierry shook his head.

"What a shame! It's the language of the future, you know."

Thierry was not sure what to make of the statement and was not sure he even wanted to be engaged in conversation at all at this point—particularly conversation of the political genre.

"Ok, don't talk, American—although from the way you look, I'd say you haven't talked to anyone in quite some time, have you?"

Thierry looked at the floor silently and thought of his conversation with Clement for a brief moment before the truck lurched backward and began in a northward direction again.

"Are you hungry?"

He nodded, keeping his eyes toward the floor.

"Ah, food—the great wall-breaker among all peoples, huh? I swear to *Gott*, a Jewish mute would start reciting Emile Burnouf if he was hungry enough."

As the truck bumped erratically down the road, the conversation of the other soldiers picked up a bit and roused to quite a commotion at its zenith. Baier even laughed and shouted something back toward a soldier sitting near the gate.

In a few moments' time, the path seemed to smooth out, and after another minute or two, Thierry was sure he heard macadam under the enormous tires.

Baier lit up a cigarette and offered one to Thierry with a raise of his eyebrows. Thierry leaned forward to take it in his mouth, and the Nazi lit both cigarettes with the same match.

"So, what the fuck are you doing here?" Baier asked with a puff of his cigarette.

Thierry looked up at him with questioning eyes. "If I knew that, I wouldn't be lost in Panzer land, would I?"

Baier took Thierry's cigarette from his mouth, tapped the ash off the tip and put it back.

"I don't mean you in particular, I mean all of you Americans. Why the fuck are you in Europe—what business is this of yours?"

"I don't understand what you mean," Thierry replied out of one side of his mouth, holding the cigarette firmly in the other. The truck was picking up speed.

"Europe," Baier replied, as if the American should pick up on his meaning based on this alone. "What interest do you have in a fight between the Germans and English, or the Germans and the Belgians, or the Germans and the French?"

"Well, my parents were French."

Baier laughed heartily. "And if your grandma was a monkey, would you go fight some tribal war in the fucking Congo?"

The German took care of Thierry's smoke again and took a long puff of his own. Halfway through his exhale, he began again: "That's the problem with America—everyone is from everywhere and nobody belongs anywhere. If France was so bad that your parents left and moved halfway around the globe to some rat-infested city, why the fuck is their son risking his life for the sake of a few Parisians who can't sit at their favorite cafe and sip on God-knows-what while the rest of the world goes to hell? What the hell, the rest of the world is hell, isn't it?"

"Compared to what?"

"Compared to *Deutchland*," Baier replied with a proud smile. "Do you know who my two favorite Americans are? Ulysses S. Grant and Margaret Sanger."

Thierry found himself grotesquely curious. "Why?"

Baier smiled and snorted quickly before he spoke: "Ulysses S. Grant *hated* Jews—did you know that?"

Thierry shook his head.

"Well, you should learn your own damn history, then. 'General Order Number 11' was issued by Grant after the fall of Vicksburg and stated that Jews were not allowed to remain in the city, and could not, wherever they went, move southward. You see, those rats were up to the same thing back then—laundering money, black market trading in cotton. Grant didn't want them profiteering or getting their hooked noses into the business of the country any more than they already had. You didn't know that, did you? Did you go to school in America? What the hell do they teach you if they don't teach your own history?"

About half an hour passed in oddly polite chatter from Baier when shouting in German could be heard up ahead, and several of the men toward the back of the truck began to stand. The truck slowed to a halt, paused, and then continued, more slowly after making a right-hand turn. Thierry saw several soldiers on the ground closing a gate behind the truck.

"Welcome home—for the moment, anyway," Baier said, discarding Thierry's third cigarette and prompting him to his feet.

Once they came to a complete stop, several more troops appeared at the back, and they lifted Thierry down off the truck. Baier waved to him casually while lighting up another cigarette and beginning a conversation with another soldier. As the sun set slowly, Thierry was led down an alley between two metal buildings and escorted through a thick door at the rear of one of them. As soon as the door opened he could feel heat and his heart skipped a beat. The building was not warm like someone's home might be, but being out of the elements and in some sort of normal human temperature was fantastic. He was led down a narrow hallway and through another thick metal door. The dimly lit room looked like what might be a small office, but had no furniture aside from a short metal bench against one wall and a small bucket against the other. He was seated on the bench and one hand was then cuffed to it. The men who had escorted him into the room suddenly and, without a word turned, and left, locking the door behind them. Once the hollow echo of their footsteps faded, all was silent. Thierry shifted his weight towards the corner where he could lean his head, right hand stretched out and shackled. His situation began to catch up with him, and he drifted into a worried sleep.

Indistinct voices and shouting in German woke him. He opened his eyes without moving his head, and in the nearly dark room he couldn't tell if it was night or day. Footsteps were moving urgently up the hall. He heard the metallic clink of a key in the lock, and the door swung open. Into his cell rushed a blur of soldiers, too many and moving too closely together to count. One unshackled his hand and stood him up on his feet with a shove. Another grabbed him roughly by the shoulder and pushed him through the door and out into the hall. He was led toward an open door, blinding light shining through it. In a moment, he was inside the nicely apportioned room—something like a Persian rug at his feet, long, mahogany desk and several desk chairs scattered throughout. Behind the desk, a portrait of Adolf Hitler hung in a heavy wooden frame. A uniformed officer seated behind the desk eyed Thierry suspiciously. The guards that ushered him in handcuffed him to the chair in which he was seated and stood off to one side of the desk.

"What is your name?" the officer asked in courteous English.

"Thierry Laroque."

"Very well," came the soft reply. "My name is Amon Kuhn. And where are you from, Herr Laroque?"

"New Jersey."

"Huh," replied Kuhn with a knowing glance toward his subordinates. "I have a cousin in New York by the name of Kuhn, you might know him?"

"Never heard of him," Thierry replied. Previous experience had taught him to be cautious with anyone in this part of Europe who claimed to have anything in common with his home state.

"That's just as well," Kuhn replied softly. "So tell me, what are you doing in this part of the world?"

"Do you mean in this particular room, or are you referring to my country's interference in Europe?"

"You. Personally."

Thierry recounted the story of the last few days as quickly as he could—skipping the part about Clement altogether. Kuhn asked several clarifying questions and received courteous replies.

"...and so I'm here—wherever the hell here is," Thierry finished.

Kuhn nodded gently while scratching a few notes with a small pencil.

"Are you hungry?" Kuhn asked.

"Yes, I'm starving, and I don't mean that figuratively."

"You will eat soon enough," Kuhn said with a subtle nod of his head. "It is fortunate that you were unarmed when you were discovered. Because I would have had you taken outside and shot this moment. Do you have any idea where you are?"

Thierry shrugged, mostly out of pure bewilderment.

"You are behind German lines. Somehow, someway, you seem to have slipped through the cracks of the entire western front and behind our lines to sabotage us."

"I'm not a spy," Thierry began to plead. "I've been lost for days, trying to find my way back to my unit... or anything!"

Kuhn shushed Thierry and motioned gently with his hand for the American to calm down.

"You will not be shot," Kuhn said. "Baier believes your story and I trust his judgement. I assure you—every courtesy that is due you will be accorded, in due time."

The officer motioned to his men, who unlatched Thierry from the chair and stood him up.

"Thank you for your time, Herr Laroque, and best of luck to you," Kuhn said softy.

And with that, Thierry was gruffly led back to his cell and locked to the bench again. This time, rather than settling as comfortably as possible, he simply melted onto the concrete floor, right arm propped on top of the bench. He began to sob softly and then tried to compose himself. He could not let himself be discouraged or defeated—he was, after all, a prisoner of war, which meant he must be fed, clothed, and treated with dignity.

At that moment he felt the need to relieve himself, but his bucket was out of reach. He would just have to hold it, he surmised.

After probably fifteen minutes of the usual thoughts racing through his mind—his mother, his angel Hope, the demon Clement—he heard footsteps approaching his door slowly. A moment later, it opened, and Baier entered, carrying several bundles.

"Hello, there," Baier called jovially.

Without another word, Baier unchained Thierry, who stretched his shoulder gratefully.

"Now just remember, you must behave," he warned.

"No problem," answered the American.

"Take your boots off."

Thierry obliged him. Baier knelt down, removing a large green towel from the top of a bowl of water. He began inspecting Thierry's toes.

"Just like I thought," he mused. "But not as bad."

"What's not as bad?"

"Frostbite," Baier answered. "Just the beginning on a couple toes. Here, put your foot in the cold water and leave them there."

"Cold water?"

"*Ja,* cold. You have to gently rewarm the extremities to reverse its effects."

"Are you a doctor?"

"No," laughed Baier. "But my father is, and I used to assist him treating patients of all kinds of ailments from the time I was eight years old. And frostbite is a common ailment in the winters where I'm from."

"And where are you from?"

"A little town called Grainau in the Bavarian Alps, but I went to university in Munich and studied English, among other things."

"So, the frostbite…"

"*Ja?*"

"Should I be worried?"

"I wouldn't worry about a little frost bite on a little toe," Baier replied. "There are more better things to worry about than this."

"I don't know what that means," Thierry stated flatly.

"Was my English not good?"

"No, well—the English was ok, but I don't know what you mean—'there are more better things to worry about.'"

Baier nodded his understanding while he stood up to receive a tray of food being brought in by another soldier, intended for his captive. A small sausage and a boiled potato. Thierry began to eat ravenously. Baier watched him intently.

"The site of a hungry human being is quite moving, isn't it?" he asked rhetorically. "But there are many different levels of emotion, aren't there—just like there are many different levels of human beings? I've seen *Deutsch Kinder* starving on the streets and there was nothing I can do for them—but my heart is broken. I've seen the children of feeble races in the same position, reaching their grubby hands through a hole in the wire, and with bread in my hands, I walked past. I have no regrets—why should we allow the weak to bring down the strong?"

Thierry had finished his meal and was practically panting, and also trying to put together the pieces of what he'd heard and the pieces of what he knew.

"Are you talking about the Jews, again?"

Baier shrugged while he handed Thierry a wet washcloth to wipe his face down.

"*Juden, Slawen*, anyone but *Deutsche*. You see, there are many levels of people—based on many years of evolution. You Brits and Americans act as if all the races are equal, as if a human is a human no matter what. But you invented this shit! It's fucking Darwin and Davenport! 'Survival of the fittest!' Your own Supreme Court said we should let imbeciles starve rather than continuing on their race! 'Three generations of imbeciles are enough!' Do you have any idea who wrote that? Oliver Wendell Holmes—and he was right!"

"Where did you learn all this?" asked a perplexed Thierry.

"I read," Baier answered with a laugh. "You should try it sometime."

Baier unfolded a change of clothes and a blanket for Thierry.

"Go ahead and undress—let me look you over, and then you can change for the night."

Thierry stripped down completely. Baier motioned him to turn around.

"Ok, put these clothes on, they should be warm for the night."

"Thank you."

"Hmm," Baier paused, "let me see your lip—what happened there?"

"Had a bit of a fall," said Thierry.

"I can see that," Baier answered, feeling Thierry's bottom lip gently with this thumb. "We'll stitch it up after breakfast tomorrow and it will be good as new, okay?"

Thierry nodded his approval. "Why are you being so kind to me?"

"Because you're an American of French decent, and that justifies some sort of respectable treatment, does it not? Plus, you're not a Jew."

"How do you know that?" asked Thierry.

"I've seen you naked," replied Baier with a snicker. "Good night—I will see you in the morning."

The next morning, the lock opened and Baier entered to see Thierry sitting on the edge of the bench comfortably.

"Better without the handcuffs, right?" Baier asked. Thierry nodded enthusiastically. "Breakfast," the German said, handing the American a plate of brown meat and a boiled potato.

"Big on potatoes here, huh?" Thierry joked.

"Better than nothing, right?"

Thierry nodded again and began to eat. Baier placed the toilet bucket in the hallway after glancing quickly at its contents.

"So what's going to happen to me?" asked Thierry between bites.

Baier nodded sadly. "Well, today, my friend—my colleague—you will be leaving me. We will give you a shower and a new set of clothes and shoes, fix up your lip, and you will be put on a train to a prisoner camp somewhere I don't know."

"I still don't understand why you've been so kind to me, taken such an interest in me," Thierry remarked while licking some potato crumbs from his finger.

"What can I say—I like to practice my English?" Baier quipped. "And you don't get much practice as a member of the Waffen SS."

They both laughed softly for a moment.

"I bet you got about as much practice speaking Deutsch in the American army, huh? But that's it, I guess—in an odd way, you and I are brothers. I don't mean in a blood sense, but in a friendship sense, no? *Ja,* we fight the same war for different reasons—hell, sometimes we might not even know the reasons if we're honest, no?—but we're respectable—duty, honor, country. Those things are respectable."

Thierry watched him with a degree of incredulousness and nodded his head slowly.

After a brief moment of silence, Baier said, "Well, off to the showers now," and escorted an unrestrained Thierry down the hall. They passed through a metal door marked "*Dushen*," where Thierry stripped down and was handed a bar of soap by another soldier. The warm water coursing over him made him feel human again. He closed his eyes and wished to stay there forever, when after a few moments the soldier tapped something loudly against the wall and shouted, "*Sich beeilen!*"

Thierry turned the spouts off and began to towel dry. On a wooden stool nearby was a fresh set of clothing—baggy white pants, a loose wool shirt, and canvas shoes. He dressed and combed his fingers through his hair. The soldier pointed toward the door and nodded to Thierry to exit.

"*Danke,*" Thierry replied. The solider nodded again.

In the hall, Thierry saw Baier waiting for him. As he approached, Baier held up a pair of handcuffs. "For procedure," Baier stated. Thierry nodded and turned his back to the man, allowing himself to be cuffed. He was then taken to what appeared to be a small medical room where his lip was crudely stitched.

Thierry was then led outside and allowed to sit in the back seat of a covered Kubelwagen, a driver already in place. Baier plopped down in the passenger's seat. It didn't seem nearly as cold as it had been the previous day—although Thierry wasn't exactly sure how long he'd been in that building.

Looking around as the car began to accelerate, Thierry saw a small camp organized around those two metal buildings. Uniformed men were milling around, smoking and laughing as if a war wasn't raging just miles from their location.

Thierry and Baier were driven through the camp gates and down a smooth asphalt road for several miles in silence before pulling up near a small train station. Baier got out and helped the manacled American out as well.

"This is the end of the road for you and me, brother," Baier said, patting Thierry on the shoulders with both hands. "May *Gott* bless you wherever you are going, and may you see the other side of this war."

"Same to you," Thierry replied.

Another soldier came and took Thierry by the arm to lead him toward the train platform. A freight train was growing steadily louder as it rolled in from the west.

"One more thing," Thierry yelled over his shoulder as he was being led away. "Why is Margaret Sanger one of your favorite Americans?"

Baier stood by the Kubelwagen, lighting a fresh cigarette. With a huge puff of smoke and a brilliant smile, he shouted back, "Because she kills black babies!"

And with that, he ducked back into the truck and drove off.

Once his hand restraints were removed, Thierry was loaded, along with a couple more prisoners and a few civilians, into a train car. There were four bunks with a total of five mattresses screwed to the side walls, a small heater in the middle of the room, and one toilet bucket for eleven people. The other prisoners and civilians scrambled to lay their claim on a bed, while Thierry sat calmly on the lower level of one wooden bunk. The car had obviously been designed for freight, then crudely fashioned into a transport car. He heard the door being locked from the outside and felt the lurch of forward movement.

At first, no one spoke, everyone keeping to themselves. Thierry eyed the other prisoners—identifiable only because their dress was similar to his—to see if they might be American or at least spoke English. His one hope through this endeavor was to be delivered to a camp that housed prisoners who spoke his language, even if they were not from his country. The civilians were dressed shabbily as well—several skinny old men, a pair of blonde girls, who might well have been pretty in different circumstances, clung to each other as if they were sisters, and a boy who couldn't have been older than twelve. As the hours dragged on, several of the old men used the toilet bucket in plain view of the other passengers, as there was no other option. The car was unpleasant initially, but this made it even more so.

The two prisoners began to converse back and forth, speaking a language Thierry could not comprehend. At first, he thought it might be French, but quickly ruled that possibility out by the guttural harshness of some of the phrases. The two girls eyed the other passengers nervously and spoke to each other only in whispers. There were several different languages among the old men and the boy—none of which was English.

The only light in the box was granted through cracks in the wooden rails. Thierry stood and moved toward one of them, pressing one opened eye to get a view of the outside world as it passed. The train chugged along, black smoke trailing it, across pristine valleys and open fields. The passing landscape mesmerized Thierry, who watched mile after mile pass into even more unfamiliar territory. They were most surely traveling east, though from what he could tell, their route had a southernly slant as well.

As the day wore on, the light grew soft, and the temperatures began to drop. It was obvious that whatever the heater in the car was intended for, it was certainly not operational. Thierry sat back down on his bunk after what must have been three or four hours. No one else had stirred much aside from the old men using the reeking toilet bucket.

In the dusk, the inertia of the train began to slow and eventually came to a complete stop. After several minutes of standing still, the shouting of German commands could be deciphered, and in a few more minutes, the door of the car was unlocked. The brightness of a well-lit train station flooded the darkness of the car. Thierry noticed the two girls clinging to each other in fear. A soldier waved toward the boy and several of the old men, who rose and were allowed to exit the car. A few hunks of nearly stale bread were tossed into the box haphazardly—one of which landed in the toilet bucket. The prisoners and the remaining old men leapt down and began shoving and shouting over the bread, the girls lifted their legs off the floor as if to distance themselves from the fray below. Thierry locked eyes with one of the girls. Her soft, desperate blue eyes, pleading with him for some kind of help that they both knew he had no way to grant. In the light of the platform, he saw that she was indeed very pretty—wide eyes and soft, high cheeks. Her thin lips were tightly pursed in constant nervous agitation.

The next minute, more shouts were heard—most definitely in German—and what turned out to be something like twenty new prisoners were loaded brusquely into the small box. They pushed and shoved and shouted in foreign tongues. Someone knocked the toilet bucket over and its putrid contents splashed across the legs and feet of those seated and standing alike. Thierry was shoved this way and that until the whole group finally began to settle—several men standing as there was no room to sit any longer on any of the bunks. With that, the door was wheeled shut and locked again. Darkness fell over the cabin as they waited in anxious silence. With the addition of two dozen filthy prisoners and the dumping of the toilet bucket, the smell within the box became nearly unbearable. Thierry began to feel sick and few moments later began to hear one of the girls retching onto the floor in front of her, her sister following her seconds later. Several of the standing prisoners began to shout in disapproval, their legs being covered in fresh warm vomit—but what other option was there? A combination of whatever was left of Thierry's small breakfast and pure bile rose in this throat, and he leaned back and away from the prisoners towards the corner of the car and began to heave himself. No commotion was made this time, as he was able to miss the feet of his fellow travelers by puking against the wall of the car against which he was pressed.

Darkness fell further as the train began to move again. Thierry hung one arm around the wooden post of the bunk to his right and leaned his head against it. As the box was reduced to nearly complete darkness, Thierry felt numb and tired, and his head was pounding. He began to wish he'd frozen to death in the Ardennes as he drifted to an unsteady sleep.

He awoke to some commotion, not sure whether he'd had a nightmare or realizing he was in the midst of one. His eyes were well adjusted to the dark and he heard the sounds of heavy breathing and desperate whimpers. He leaned forward to see two prisoners, nude from the waste down, on top of the two girls. He stood to get closer and noticed that there were several onlookers. Over the shoulder of one man he saw the pretty girl on her back on the bunk, a hand pressed over her nose and mouth, her eyes more desperate than ever before, caught Thierry's, once more pleading for help. He pushed through the crowd of witnesses, some of whom were perhaps waiting their turn, to see the girl's sister being violated as well, though her face was already stiff and blue.

"Hey!" Thierry called loudly as he pushed toward the still living sister. A spark of hope flashed in her eyes, and she began to resist, biting the hand of the man on top of her. He let out a yelp as he removed his hand from her teeth, only to send it flying down in a brutal blow just as Thierry tackled him. Shouting ensued, and Thierry began to feel blows reign down on him from every direction. He was grabbed from behind around the neck and dragged away from the pile, being hit and kicked and choked from every direction. The loud voices and shouting in several tongues reached a fevered climax as he gasped desperately for air. The last thing he remembered was the face of the pretty girl, drenched in blood, her gentle eyes fading with a look of serenity and gratefulness. Then he blacked out.

When he awoke, it was late morning or perhaps midday already. He was curled on the putrid floor, caked in blood and vomit and human waste. His head pounded, and he felt sharp pain in his right side when he breathed. The car was quiet, other than a few hushed conversations. He slowly sat up, expecting to be hit or cursed, but no one seemed to notice. Next to him, in a filthy, crumpled ball, he could make out the clothing of the two girls in the transport. He leaned forward to see their nude bodies, bruised and mangled, in a heap near the door. The pretty one's neck was twisted at a most unnatural angle.

Of all the things he'd seen, this affected him the most. He dared not cry but felt his head swell and his eyes well with moisture. He leaned back and rested his head on the same wall he was sick on the night before. Without processing his thoughts quite so logically, he wondered indeed why he was here, fighting this war. If these prisoners—his supposed allies in this conflict—could behave so brutally, with such disregard for humanity, what was the point of freeing Europe? He'd been trained that the Nazis were barbaric and had no respect for human dignity, and perhaps this was true, but all he knew was that to this point he'd seen more humane treatment among them than he had among his so-called allies. He was part of the mission to free Europe from tyranny. *Was this what "freedom" looked like?* He wondered if monsters such as this were born or bred.

He began to wonder about the girl—where was she headed? Did she have a home? Who was her father, and would he ever learn what happened to her? Was she married, and if she wasn't, had she been a virgin? Was her veil of innocence ripped from her in such a savage way in order to satisfy the carnal lust of men who were supposed to be on the side of human dignity?

He thought about Hope again, and wished beyond anything in the world for her safety. Even if he did not survive this war, he prayed earnestly to whatever power there was to hold her safely and allow her a long life of peace and happiness.

As all these thoughts swirled in his mind, the train stopped. He rolled over to peer through a crack in the wall near the floor, and saw nothing but a vast, white valley. The bare trees stretched their feeble arms to the sky in either celebration or desperation. He knew not what the point of praying was anymore. He became filled with the vacuous notion that there was no God, no higher power working in the world on behalf of good. He came to grips with the idea that evil might run rampant, and that the last vestiges of goodness and kindness might vanish from the earth altogether. It was in this sense, not in any religious sense, that he became confident that he was living through Armageddon. The train sat for hours on end without moving, without a sound. The idea of the toilet bucket had become obsolete, and the remaining soldiers and old men relieved themselves where they stood. It was at this moment that Thierry noticed he had, at some point, soiled himself.

Suddenly he felt a blind, fierce rage bubbling up within him. He made up his mind that no matter the outcome, no matter his own state of degradation, no matter the inhumanity of his enemies or his allies, he would not allow his humanity to be robbed from him. In this way, one man could singlehandedly win the war.

In the early hours of the morning, snow began to melt on the top of the car, and drops of clean water leaked through the roof. Each man tried to quench his thirst by stretching his neck to catch falling drops. It was remarkably calm, mostly due to the fact that so much water dripped through that there was no need to fight over it. Hours later, as it grew dark, the train began to rumble forward again. The stiff, blue bodies of the young girls, congealed in filth of every kind, glistened with droplets of water beading on their skin.

The next morning, the train crept to a stop once more. Thierry peered out his peephole and saw across an open field in the distance what looked to be human figures standing in the open air. After what seemed like another eternity, the big doors flew open, and a dozen armed men, wearing SS patches, stood smiling in the bright sunlight.

"*Geh raus!*" one shouted loudly.

Several of the prisoners rose, and the rest followed their lead. Only the skinny old men were left on the train. As Thierry rose, he was shoved forward and nearly bumped into a soldier. The SS guard gave him a quick blow and muttered something under his breath. The prisoners were formed into a line and counted—once, twice, and then over again. As this was happening, Thierry noticed two soldiers hauling the bodies of the girls out of the car and hurling them down an embankment into the snowy underbrush. The nude bodies tumbled stiffly as the guards seemed to joke and laugh. One of the old men was removed from the car by his hair, kicked to his knees and shot in the head—all in a matter of seconds. The loud crack of the shot echoed for miles throughout the valley, and the spray of blood turned the snow crimson. Thierry looked away from the murder and noticed the prisoner standing next to him with a Star of David painted crudely over his heart. Thierry looked at his face and immediately recognized the man he'd tackled during his act of savage lust. The man gave him a look as if to ask, "What are you staring at?" Thierry turned his head and watched the rest of the train cars be unloaded. Once all the prisoners from the other cars were out and stood in an increasingly long line, several other passengers, including women and several young children, received the same treatment as the old man. Thierry watched one woman be dragged from the train, also by her hair—her dress ripped and her feet bare—clutching an infant to her chest. Two soldiers ripped the child from her arms and flung it down the embankment. It did not whimper or cry, and Thierry was sure it was already dead. The hysterical mother broke free of their grasp, or was allowed to break free, and chased her dead child into the cold ravine. An officer stood at the top of the embankment and fired a single shot from a semi-automatic weapon down towards her. Thierry could not see her to see if she'd been shot, but by the reaction of the others, he could tell that she, too, was dead.

When the train was empty, it rocked to a slow start and proceeded eastward until it was out of sight and out of earshot. Several soldiers walked down the long line of prisoners, pulling many forward to form a new line, but leaving many standing as they were. When it came the rapist's turn, the tall blonde German jeered something at him and then walked past. They looked Thierry up and down and pulled him by his filthy shirt to stand in the second line. As this process progressed, Thierry looked back over his right shoulder to see that every man standing in the first line had a Star of David painted on his shirt. The rapist's calloused eyes locked with Thierry's for just a moment before the soldiers shouted out some orders in German, and Thierry's line began to move across the tracks toward the group of men standing in the distance in the field. In the growing distance behind him, Thierry heard more gruff shouts in German. Then a volley of shots rang out which caused many of the men in the marching line to instinctively duck their heads. Two more volleys followed, and then more shouting and several individual shots, fired at will, most surely at those who took the chance to run. Thierry did not look back, because he did not need to.

He followed the man in front of him across the white field, all the while being barked at by the Germans. One took a disliking to one particular prisoner, several men up from Thierry. The captive didn't mutter a word, but the soldier who marched along side him was determined to flaunt his power over him and without a moment's warning shot him in the head, in stride, causing his body to lunge to the right and several steps forward before collapsing lifelessly in the snow. The soldier shouted something back to one of his comrades, then shoved the next prisoner forward to close the gap in the line.

As they approached their destination, Thierry could make out nothing more than a large, square fence, about eight feet tall, with barbed wire atop it, containing what was possibly hundreds of emaciated men, dressed much like he was. There was an impromptu guard shack set up near the entrance gate, but no other trace of human existence as far as the eye could see, apart from the railroad tracks. When they neared the gate, he began to notice the frostbitten noses and ears of the interred, skinny and huddling together for whatever warmth they could muster. He also noticed casual piles of frozen corpses scattered throughout the enclosure, and piles of snow stained with human waste. The prisoners inside the fence remained silent, but their eyes conveyed unimaginable suffering. One sentry opened the gate for the new arrivals, while another shot a prisoner inside, as if to warn them not to try to escape. He crumpled and then sprung forward and landed face first in the snow, blood pulsing rhythmically from the exit wound in the top of his skull. The new prisoners were herded into the enclosure, which was becoming quite a tight fit with their addition. Once Thierry was in, he was pressed firmly on all sides, several men having to be shoved violently in order to close the gate. Now completely enclosed, completely exposed, the soldiers began to yell loudly and fire rounds into the fence indiscriminately, those who were being shot unable to collapse but dying or suffering where they stood, mashed against the inside of the chain link fence. The guards laughed and called to one another before several of them walked off together into the brush at the far end of the field, while four stayed behind and huddled near the shack. Thierry felt a warm rush against his buttocks as the man behind him relieved himself and began to whimper in fear.

Low clouds rolled in as the sun faded from the sky, and the temperature began to drop rapidly yet again. Within what he perceived to be an hour or two after sunset, it began to snow as well—thick, fluffy, heavy snow. About an hour later, a rumble was heard in the distance, and quickly an armored train bearing swastikas all around it passed by headed east on the same tracks that brought Thierry to this frozen hell. The snow stopped eventually as Thierry shivered against the men next to him, some of whom he was sure were no longer alive. Later that evening, a troop transport thundered down the tracks headed west—reinforcements for the front. Thierry was determined not to sleep the entire night, as he was sure he would never wake if he did. Eventually, the first rays of day began to show over the mountains to the east, turning the sky from purple to orange and red through the broken clouds. Thierry thought he'd never seen a more beautiful sunrise in his entire life.

In the early morning light, Thierry craned his neck to see the man squeezed behind him, the man who had pissed on him the previous night—the man's head leaned awkwardly to his right side, pressed against the head of another prisoner. They were frozen together where they stood. Thierry thought he might be frozen to the corpse behind him but couldn't be sure because there was no room to move in any direction.

The guard changed as two soldiers exited the small shack and two went in. They chuckled something to each other as they passed. After the door to the shack closed, one of the prisoners in the second row muttered something under his breath, but apparently loud enough for the SS guards to hear. One of the guards, hair reddish blonde and a true brute of a man, approached the fence, glancing around, the face of a frozen corpse pressed against it.

"*Wer sagt das*?" the guard demanded. When no one responded, he asked again, his voice raised in anger. "*Wer sagt das?*"

The prisoner who had uttered whatever it was that he said raised his hand slowly. In a moment of blind rage, and to the shock of his shift mate, the guard unlocked and flung open the gate. The prisoners could not help pushing toward the opening, just to relieve some of the pressure that had been contained throughout the night. The guard began shuffling through the living and the dead alike, and grabbed the speaker by his neck, and led him out of the cage into the clearing. The other guard did his best to show control as the other prisoners watched the situation unfold. The brutish guard forced his captive to his knees and yelled something at him before proceeding to stomp the man in the back of the head. The force of the blow caused the prisoner's face to smack the snow, and for a brief moment, it looked like he would try to resist. However, before he had the opportunity, the guard slammed his heavy boot on the back of the man's neck, snapping it audibly. The guard kicked the lifeless body with all his might eight or ten times in a blind rage. His shift mate, along with the remaining prisoners, watched in shock and horror.

Panting, the murderous guard looked down at his victim and calmly said, "Nicht über meine Mama reden," and spit on him.

At that moment, all hell broke loose.

From behind him, Thierry felt a massive surge of humanity, and he was thrust forward, pushing over the man in front of him. He heard a snap like glass breaking, and he was freed from the corpse behind him, and the whole group of living prisoners dashed through the open gate. The first guard was overcome before he could even utter a word, while the second one, standing over the body, was able to pick off several prisoners with his rifle before he was overtaken, as well. Thierry did all he could to keep his balance, stepping over the limbs and torsos of the men who had fallen in front of him. As the stampede began to release into the open fields, the prisoners scattered in every direction, some falling dead just yards from the cage from out of sheer exhaustion. Once he was free from the mass of bodies, he spun on his heels and began sprinting back across the field toward the train tracks. Behind him, he heard the door of the shack fly open, shouting in German, and then shots ringing out. He glanced behind him to see runners dropping like flies with every crack. He ran as fast as his tired and aching legs would go in what was perhaps six or eight inches of snow. Then, he heard a shot whiz past his ear. He ducked low but kept running. Then another shot and another. He was only yards from the small hill on which the tracks were built when he saw another man passing him on his left side. The man was lean and young and certainly fast. As they climbed to the top stride for stride, another shot rang out—this one catching bone and flesh rather than whizzing past, and the young prisoner next to him stumbled and dove forward, down the embankment on the other side of the rails. Thierry heard one more shot whiz past him as he leapt in the same direction. The shots stopped, but the piercing pain in his right side almost knocked him unconscious. He held himself up on his elbows to see if he was being pursued anything further, only to witness the two remaining SS guards being bludgeoned to death by several prisoners, who, as soon as they were done, took the guns and boots off the soldiers and ran in the direction of the mountains.

He turned to see the prisoner who had been shot lying on his back and crawled over to him. The exit wound went right through the lower part of his rib cage; blood pulsed from it every time he exhaled. The stranger reached for Thierry's hand, and Thierry took it.

"*Ruslan,*" the prisoner said, pointing to his chest with his other hand. "*Ooo-kray-ina, Ooo-kray-ina,*" he repeated several times. Thierry shook his head to show he did not understand. "*Sov-yet, Sov-yet,*" the prisoner continued, pointing to his chest again.

"Soviet?" Thierry asked.

"*Da. Ruslan,*" he continued, pointing to himself.

"You're named Ruslan?"

He shook his head and then pointed to Thierry, who then said his own name out loud.

"*Ot-koo-da-vee?*" Ruslan asked desperately.

"I don't understand, I'm sorry," Thierry answered.

"*Ot-koo-da-vee?*" Ruslan asked again, then thought for a moment, while his breathing became more shallow. Thierry decided that Ruslan could not be more than eighteen years old, if that. "*Frantsia? Anglia?*"

"No, I'm American."

Ruslan's eyes lit up. "America?" he asked excitedly, and began clutching at Thierry's shirt with his left hand. "America?"

"Yes, yes, I'm from New Jersey."

Ruslan suddenly began coughing blood and shaking. The death rattle took over and the young man passed from life to death in Thierry's arms, a smile on his face and the word "America" on his lips. Thierry laid him down and closed his eyelids with his fingers, the tips of which were already beginning to show signs of frostbite. Thierry then sat down on the embankment, his elbows resting behind him when he noticed the girl from the train under a fresh coat of snow, not ten feet from him. He felt sad for her all over again and wished he could have done more to help her back in that train. Then his thoughts drifted back to Hope.

It was at this moment that he heard the distant hum of a diesel engine rounding the bend towards him. He immediately started into the thick underbrush, trying to conceal the open tracks behind him and proceeded to sneak off into the forest. He was positive that in the proximity of the prisoner of war "camp," there must be some kind of town. Something again told him to walk south, so he started in that direction through the woods.

He heard the train pass behind him without stopping, obviously oblivious to the carnage in the field. After a few miles of rugged terrain, he came to a clearing with a cottage on a hill and a small town directly across from it. His ribs were throbbing, and he was beyond exhausted. As he pondered whether or not to make a dash for the cabin in broad daylight, he heard steps shuffling quickly toward him and swung around to see who or what it was. He found himself on the wrong end of a rifle—an old fashioned hunting gun. Thierry threw his arms up, wondering when the nightmare would end. Holding the gun stood a man in his sixties and strongly built, with a reddish-grey beard that softened what might have otherwise been an imposing stature.

"*Wer bist du?*" the man asked gently.

Thierry shook his head and shrugged his shoulders.

"*Sprechen Sie Deutsch?*"

"I speak English," Thierry answered.

"English, *Ja,*" the man replied. "And who are you?"

"I'm an American soldier, lost for days or weeks, I don't know."

"If you are American, then you are most certainly lost, my friend," the man replied in nearly perfect English. Thierry nodded.

"I'm starving, and I'm hurt, and I would like to ask you to take pity on me," Thierry pled.

The man sniffed, and Thierry thought he saw his eyes moisten.

"If you behave," the man said, "you can come to my cabin there, and I will feed you and take care of your wounds."

The words, "Thank you," escaped Thierry's mouth before the man was even finished speaking. "May I ask your name?"

"We are friends, no?" the man replied. "So you may call me Jurgen. But most people in that village down there know me as Dr. Baier."

"What is the name of that village?"

"Grainau. Why do you ask?"

Thierry fell to his knees and burst out laughing uncontrollably, but then suddenly burst into tears.

"What is the matter?" Dr. Baier asked.

Thierry looked up at him, tears streaming down his face, "I know your son."

The doctor's eyebrows shot up. "Well, you have nothing to fear—you are safe with me. My son and I are two very different kinds of people."

With that, the doctor slung his gun over his shoulder and lifted Thierry under the arms. The soldier cried out in pain. Dr. Baier comforted him and helped him across the valley towards the cabin. Before reaching the door, Thierry lost consciousness.

FEBRUARY 1945

Thierry woke in Dr. Baier's cozy cottage in a warm bed, with clean white sheets—a fire raging in the hearth. He felt his lower lip with his tongue and noticed the stitches were gone. He tried to sit up but excruciating pain made him give up. Dr. Baier noticed this and spun around on his chair.

"No, no, don't move," he said calmingly. "You've got some broken ribs, and they will take some time to heal. You're fortunate that your lung did not collapse, or you'd have been dead long ago."

Thierry just nodded his head in agreement and appreciation.

"You've been here over a week now—did you know this?—and are making good progress in your recovery. Your fingers have been saved, as have your toes. I'd say in a couple weeks you'll be as good as new—maybe a few pounds lighter than at Christmas."

The doctor said all of this with such calm reassurance and kindness—such genuine concern.

"And don't be afraid," Dr. Baier continued, "nobody but me knows you're here. No one ever comes up to this cabin, as I treat my patients from an office in town."

The landscape outside was still blanketed in snow, the village to the south picturesque in its Bavarian beauty.

"Here," Dr. Baier said, setting a steaming bowl on the small table next to the bed. "Slowly, slowly, let me help you sit up."

With some effort, Thierry found himself propped by a couple goose feather pillows, holding a warm bowl of soup.

"Don't worry," Dr. Baier said, "if it tastes funny, it's only because you've never eaten grouse before—it's like quail."

Thierry looked at him suspiciously, spoon frozen between the bowl and his open mouth.

"It's ok," the doctor continued, "I've heard all about Herr Clement."

"From who?" Thierry asked nervously as he looked around the room.

"You raved for three days when I brought you in here. You told me all about Herr Clement—you even asked me not to try to eat you—and your mother, may God rest her soul, and your brother and your beautiful *Fräulein*, waiting for you at home."

Thierry sighed and took a sip of the soup. It was absolutely delicious. Dr. Baier tore a piece of bread from a loaf and put it down on the table.

"Eat this slowly," he said, pointing to the bread.

"Thank you for your kindness, Dr. Baier," Thierry said.

"It's nothing—and please, call me Jurgen—we are friends here."

"*Danke.*"

"So, you know my son Klaus?" Jurgen said as he sat in his chair across from the bed and folded his arms across his white sweater.

Thierry nodded and said, "Yes, just briefly—and, however long ago, I don't know, but he was in good health."

Jurgen nodded slowly. "And what was your impression of him?"

"Smart—he's very smart," Thierry answered. "I might call him a bit misguided in some things, but he is very smart. And he was very kind to me."

"I'm happy to hear he was kind to you," Jurgen replied introspectively. "I had some doubt that he still had it in him to be kind at all."

Thierry finished the soup and looked around the room while gnawing on a hunk of bread.

"I notice you don't have any pictures of the *Fürher* hanging here," Thierry said nonchalantly.

Jurgen slapped his knee. "Don't worry," he said, "It's hanging in my office in the village."

"Are you a Nazi?" Thierry asked. He wasn't quite sure if he was being courageous or idiotic to ask such a bold question.

"No, no," Jurgen said with a wave of his hand. "Far from it. I show respect as needed to the regime, they are the leaders of my people, as corrupt and evil as they may be, but mostly I do it to save my own skin."

"What do you mean?"

"To preserve my life so that I can continue to heal people. That is my life's calling, my life's work—to heal the sick. If I was thrown in prison or some camp, I would not be very capable of living out my calling, what do you think?"

"I see," Thierry answered. "So, you how did your son become an SS officer?"

"My wife Magda, God rest her soul, and I raised Klaus to be a respecter of all of humanity. We knew he would be very bright from an early age—he loved to read and discuss and argue from the time he could barely speak—which is why I would bring him to my office to assist me when he was not in school. I wanted him to see, first-hand, the suffering of the young and the old, the weak and the poor. I wanted him to learn that in healing a person, you restore hope in the common goodness of humanity. There is also—*there must be*—a great degree of humility in the practice of medicine. After all, the doctor did not create the person and the doctor did not cure them of his own power. He applies what has been granted to the creation, and in doing so comes face-to-face with the image of the Creator. I did not heal your frostbite or mend your wounded lip with some magical potion I concocted out of thin air—I used the knowledge of natural elements endowed to humanity over the years by the very Creator of those elements. And so, you see, a great deal of humility must accompany the work of a physician. I am a tool in the Maker's hands, not a god unto myself.

"It was this humility, or the requirement of it, that was distasteful to my son. He was always gifted—in school, in sports, in conversation, in looks—he had no need of humility and shunned it. He preferred to think of the world in black and white—them against me, me against them—and to think himself higher than his fellow man. He was influenced in school to believe that the Aryan race must stand above the rest in the evolutionary ladder. Now, don't get me wrong—I wish my country to succeed, to rise to the top—I served my nation for years as a medic during the first great war—but I do not wish my people to rise based on some insane theory of racial superiority, not on the backs of other men who have been coerced through brute force. This is the stuff of animals, after all, not a superior race. The signs of a superior race are not warfare, murder, and intimidation, but justice, freedom, and mercy above all.

"So, as it happened, Klaus went to Munich to expand his world, and it turns out that he narrowed it greatly. We didn't try to stop him, because every man must make his own way in the world.

"As for me, no, I am not a Nazi. I am a good German and will always be. As far as I'm concerned, those Fascist sons of bitches should be arrested and brought to justice for their crimes, including my son. But this must be done peacefully, under the order of laws, and not out of blind delusions of revenge. For if the victim lacks the moral fortitude to see justice done—and justice, not murder, not vengeance—then he is no better than his oppressor. This, my friend, is why I take such pleasure in healing you, in remaking you into the person you are—whole and healthy—because you simply are."

"You're telling me that if I was a Jew, you wouldn't treat me differently?" Thierry asked.

"And what, precisely, is the difference between a Jew and a Gentile?" Jurgen replied.

"Religious beliefs? Circumcision?"

"And so what is this? What are these differences that we should chase each other around the continent committing murder? If one man cuts his hair short and the other grows it long, does one cease to be a human being? If one man believes in one *Gott* and you another or no *Gott* at all, does that cut you off from your own species? It's absurdity—lunacy. To answer your question, no, I would not have treated you any different if you were a Jew or a German or a Japanese. You are a human being, and I am a doctor of human beings."

Suddenly, the doctor stood. He took the empty bowl from Thierry and placed it in the wash basin below the window.

"Well, my friend, I must be off to the office for a few hours. Would you like to recline and sleep again?"

"No, thank you," Thierry answered. "It's nice to be up for once."

"Yes, yes. Well, if you're feeling well enough—and I do encourage you to sleep as much as you can—I've got a book in English I can leave with you if you'd like."

"That would be wonderful," replied Thierry.

Jurgen walked to the bookshelf and pulled down an enormous book which, by the look of it, must have been bound many years earlier. It was *The Count of Monte Cristo.*

"I should have to stay here for quite some time if I'm going to finish this, Jurgen," Thierry joked.

"You can stay here as long as you'd like," said Jurgen with a sweet smile. "Or you can take it with you as a gift when you go."

"Thank you," Thierry said, holding the book up to express his gratitude.

"You are welcome," replied Jurgen. He then put on a coat, waved his hand, and walked down to the village.

March 1945

Thierry was well on the way to making a full recovery. He spent hours upon hours talking and eating with Jurgen. In many ways, the doctor felt like a kindred spirit. The snow melted rapidly over the course of a few days, and Thierry was even able to walk the garden and take in the warmth of the early spring sun. News about the war drizzled into the small town slowly at times, but it was clear that the allies were advancing rapidly; the word was that the Americans and the British had already crossed the Rhine at Oppenheim, and that the Red Army would soon invade Austria and eventually reach Berlin itself. The doctor and the patient took great pleasure in these reports and talked often about what would be the best time and the best procedure for Thierry to rejoin his countrymen. Jurgen was concerned that he might be seen as a deserter, and so he drew up documents and letters, explaining that he was a prisoner of war, being treated at a private medical institution.

One morning, the sun just peering through the trees and spreading its brilliant amber rays through the cottage, Thierry rolled over to see a man sitting in the doctor's chair. He immediately recognized Klaus Baier. Thierry shot up instinctively, but Klaus, dressed in a tattered and worn uniform, but still appearing dignified and stoic, waved his hand and laughed calmly.

"Don't fear, my old acquaintance," Klaus said. "I told you that if you behaved you would be taken care of."

"What are you doing here?" Thierry asked nervously.

Klaus shrugged and lit a cigarette. He offered one to Thierry, but he declined.

"The war is over, you see," Klaus said casually, with a wave of his hand, cigarette between his fingers. "Or at least it will be very soon. I came to say goodbye to my father, and you can imagine how shocked I was to see you lying there in that bed. Did you know that was my bed from my boyhood—the bed my father used to read to me in when I was young?"

"Why are you saying goodbye to your father?"

"Because I may not ever see him again. You see, word has gotten out about some of the things I've been part of."

"What kinds of things?"

"Things," Klaus answered coolly. "Things that were done for the benefit of my people and for no other reason. You see, before I was transferred to the western front, I was part of an *Einzatsgruppen* in the east, Ukraine to be particular. Do you know this word, *Einzatsgruppen?*"

Thierry shook his head.

"Read the history books in twenty years and you will. Have you given up smoking completely?"

"Yes, since I've been here."

"And how long have you been here, undoubtedly listening to my father's bullshit," he said mockingly.

"You're father is a very good man."

"This, I do not deny. But he makes assumptions that aren't based on science—draws conclusions that aren't based in reality—and this a doctor should not do."

"Give me an example."

"An example," Klaus mused. "There is a place in Ukraine called Babi Yar—ever heard of it? Don't worry, you will read about it in the history books, too. We killed many Jews there, shot in the back of the head like the vermin they are. We shot the young, we shot the old, we shot men and women alike. And every time I put a bullet through the brain of a Jewish child, I thanked the *Fürher* for the opportunity. And do you know why? Because some day, that Jewish brat would grow up to take the bread out of my child's mouth. There is your example of my father's bullshit. Do you not think that filthy Jew would put a bullet through my brain if it came down to bread for me or for his children?"

Thierry sat there in stunned silence.

"I simply… I simply can't believe you would do such a thing," he replied. "That you could do something so cruel to innocent people—and all because you think you're better than them?"

"I did not do it because I think I am better—I am better than them, and that is why I do it."

"And how has that ended for you, for your superior race?"

"This is the age-old problem we attempted to escape," Klaus said, flicking his cigarette into the wash basin. "The masses of weak, inferior animals, dragging the strong down into the mire with them."

"That's not what happened, and that's not how the world works," answered Thierry.

Klaus nodded thoughtfully. "If you believe that, you've missed the point of this fucking war completely."

"And what is the point of this fucking war?"

"The struggle," Klaus replied. "The struggle to succeed, the struggle to survive, the struggle to climb to the top of the ladder of evolution. The struggle against constantly being pulled down by the unworthy, degraded by the corruption of the inferior races—the struggle for freedom to make your own way in the world without those beneath you grabbing at your heels all your life. You see, you Americans think you're coming in to ride to the rescue of all the poor oppressed masses, but what you don't realize is that this isn't a new war—this is the same war our fathers fought thirty years ago. My people were disgraced, and the Jews in Paris and Moscow and London and New York have treated us with disdain, treated us with such disregard, that we had to fight back; we had to free our people. And if freeing our people cost the lives of a few Jews and Gypsies and other rats, then so be it."

"That's very sad," Thierry said after a moment.

"What isn't?" Klaus answered. "It's a sad world, a sad story. But hopefully we've done enough good on behalf of our people, of our blood—hopefully we've left enough of a legacy of courage in the face of oppression, that they will rise again—you'll see."

"I hope they rise again, too," Thierry answered. "But not on the backs of men who have been coerced through brute force."

Klaus laughed and slapped his knee.

"Now that sounds like some Dr. Baier bullshit right there, if I've ever heard it!"

At that moment, Dr. Baier appeared in the doorway. Klaus stood and walked to him. The two men embraced quickly and exchanged some words in German.

Then, Klaus turned to Thierry and said a quick goodbye. Suddenly, Jurgen grabbed Klaus in the desperate grip of a father knowing he would never see his son again, and through his tears, he said in English, "Klaus, no matter how you have shamed me, no matter what you have done, now matter what kind of man you've become, I am your papa, and I will always love you, no matter what."

Klaus embraced his father as well, and for what seemed like several minutes, the two men stood in the doorway, locked together. The father broke the embrace and kissed his son.

Without another word, Klaus left the cottage. Dr. Baier slumped into his chair, full of emotion and breathing heavily. Thierry stood and sat next to him, his arm around the doctor's shoulder.

After a few moments of silence, Jurgen looked Thierry in the eyes and said, "You could have been my son, you know."

In the early hours of the next morning, Klaus Baier was found on the stoop of the town's small church, dead of a self-inflicted gunshot.

May 8, 1945

Thierry Laroque bid his farewell to Dr. Jurgen Baier just hours after it was announced that Nazi Germany had surrendered to the western allies. The two men hugged tightly, much like Dr. Baier and his son had nearly six weeks before.

The American was given a ride to Munich in a Volkswagen by a personal friend of Dr. Baier and dropped off at the train station, letters from the doctor and *The Count of Monte Cristo* in hand. It was not difficult to find English speakers, as the streets teemed with American GI's. Before he knew it, he was standing before a Sergeant First Class and giving an account of his disappearance and his time as a prisoner of war. He was satisfactorily cleared of any suspicion of desertion, put on a train to Paris, and given two weeks of leave before reporting back to his regiment.

He received a bundle of mail, tied together, and sat down with a cup of espresso outside a quaint Parisian cafe. He untied the string and flipped through letter after letter—mostly addressed from Hope, although a couple from Henry were mixed in as well. It was odd, though, that the last letter she sent was postmarked the day before Christmas. The last and most recent letter was from his brother, postmarked in early January. He reasoned to himself that the post must be running behind with the offensive, or maybe some of the letters were returned to their senders.

He intended to take some time pouring over the letters from Hope in great and repetitive detail—inhaling whatever they might still possess of her scent, pressing his lips to the shape that hers left in lipstick at the bottom—so he decided to open Henry's letter first, out of sheer curiosity.

Thierry nearly fell out of his chair—the only thing he could comprehend from the letter was that his precious Hope was dead.

SIX

Give sorrow words;
the grief that does not speak knits up the o-er
wrought heart and bids it break.

WILLIAM SHAKESPEARE, MACBETH

DECEMBER 24, 1944

Dearest Thierry,

Merry Christmas, my darling. I can't tell you in words how much I miss you and wish you were here for Christmas. It's so cold out, and I miss those days when we would walk to town together and then come back and warm each other by the fire.

Nothing much has changed here since I wrote you last week. I try to stop by and see Henry as often as I can. He's getting along just fine, but is oh so sad these last couple months. It is very difficult to see, knowing how jovial and happy he normally is. Although, I am generally not as jovial and happy as I usually am, either. It seems that the loss, although temporary on my part, of a partner and a true love weighs heavier on the soul of a person than one can even imagine.

I worry about your safety day and night and pray diligently for your return to me in one piece. Although, truth be told, as long as I get you back at all, I will be exceedingly happy. I cannot wait to make a proper wife for you, and oh, I will be the best wife a man could ever ask for, for you are the best man a wife could ever ask for. I am so tempted to begin already signing my name Mrs. Thierry Laroque.

Is it strange that I dream about our children, the ones we will have one day? I think I would like to bear as many of your children as God will bless us with. Is it also strange that I have already thought of names for them? What do you think about William for a firstborn boy? Or would you prefer to name a son after yourself, or perhaps after Henry? I have also thought that Jacob is a fine name, and am partial to Elizabeth for a girl—what do you think?

Thierry, I wish you to know that you never escape my thoughts for a single moment, day or night. It seems that my whole life is consumed in longing either to live in the past or the future. I do not know how to bear the present, being separated by an ocean and a war from you. I close my eyes and wish so fervently that if only for a moment, I could be in your arms again, then my life, for that moment, would be complete. But then, I think that if that moment ended, I would have to wish for it again, as the hole in my heart that is you would open all over again, causing me this unquenchable longing to be yours for good.

Well, my dear, I must finish this and begin to prepare to go out. Your brother Marty invited to me a Christmas party all the way up in Deep Harbor and is picking me up in an hour. One of his professors and his wife are having the get-together. I'm nervous, because Marty made it seem like quite an upscale event, and I'm not sure a poor girl like me will fit in with all of those Yale professors and lawyers! And what am I supposed to wear? So many things to worry about! But, oh, darling, I always worry about you the most. I will write to you about the party in my next letter and tell you all the ways that I embarrassed myself.

Be safe, my love, and Merry Christmas,

—Hope

In what was her typical fashion, she then applied a heavy dose of lipstick and kissed the paper near her name. She spritzed the paper and the inside of the envelope in her favorite perfume, the kind that Thierry had saved up and bought for her birthday that year. Her heart ached as she sealed and addressed the envelope. She recalled those warm summer nights and days spent sunbathing by the sea with him, the warm sunlight on her bare shoulders, the softness of his lips against hers, and the desperation with which they kissed. On those days, she was sure that she was happiest woman alive. Her thoughts then turned toward that evening, although never completely from Thierry.

She dressed and prettied herself, all the while second-guessing why she had even agreed to go to this party with Marty, and to some degree, second-guessing why he had even asked her.

Once she was ready, she kissed her father, who had been drinking since morning, and walked to Henry's apartment. She had baked some cookies for him as a Christmas gift and delivered them by hand. His big eyes were moist with tears from the moment he opened the door, and she was sure the loss of his beloved wife was draining the very life from him. She did her best to try to cheer him up, and when it was a little after four o'clock, a car honked on the street, and she knew Marty was ready to pick her up. She hugged Henry like a daughter would a father. He sniffled softly on her shoulder and held her tight, then smiled and told her to have a good time that evening and, somewhat jokingly, to remember her manners.

She headed downstairs and put Thierry's letter in the mailbox with a long kiss.

December 27, 1944

Dear Thierry,

Hello my boy. I hope that this letter finds you healthy and alive. I have some news from home for you, and I have to say that I hate to be the one to tell you.

Hope was killed two nights ago. I cant imagine what reading that must feel like, but I had to tell you as soon as possible.

There is more bad news, too. Your brother Marty was arrested by the police and charged with her murder. I have not been able to see him yet, but I cannot believe he could have done such a bad thing. I'm so sorry for this. Please know that you are in my thoughts and prayers, and that I will do every thing that I can do to try to get to the bottom of this.

I will write again when I have more news. Be safe, I love you

—Henry

September 4, 1945

By this point, Thierry had read these letters a thousand times over. He had been honorably discharged in August and was ferried from Plymouth, England to New York City. The journey by sea took eight days—eight long days with nothing to do but let all the things he'd experienced and all of the things he was walking into fester.

In subsequent letters from Henry, some accompanied by newspaper clippings, it was explained that Hope was last seen with Marty leaving Dr. Winfield Aulgur's Christmas party in Deep Harbor, Connecticut, around ten in the evening. Hope did not come home that night, but was not missed by her father, who was passed out drunk on the living room floor. The following morning, Marty called the police from Dr. Aulgur's home and reported the location of her body. After some precursory investigation, the Newport Police Department arrived at Dr. Aulgur's home and took Marty into custody, charging him with Hope's murder.

The booking was based upon the evidence that Marty was the last person seen with Hope before she was found at the bottom of a forty-foot drop into the Long Island Sound, her body broken by the sharp rocks below. There were also footprints in the wet dirt, matching his and her shoes, in a roughly circular pattern, which then seemed to part, come back together, and then towards the car, where her footprints vanished. His footprints alone could be traced to the ledge, then back to the car, where its tire prints were followed back to the main road.

Fortunately for Marty, Dr. Aulgur happened to be one of Yale's finest law professors, having quite the track record as a criminal defense attorney in New York and Connecticut. His practice had successfully defended over eighty percent of clients who had actually gone to trial. In fact, in the last ten years or so, his presence alone on a case often deterred district attorneys from taking a case to trial if it was not in fact believed to be a slam dunk.

In one instance, Dr. Aulgur defended a man who was accused of raping and murdering a fifteen-year-old black girl in a back alley in Harlem. Cecil Nonis was seen by eight people zipping his pants and tucking in his blood-stained shirt as he walked away from the scene. His gold rolex had been torn off his wrist in the struggle and was found dangling from the right hand of the victim. The good news for Dr. Aulgur was that the parents of Cecil Nonis were up to their eyeballs in shipping industry cash, and a wonderful payday could be expected from taking the case, as bleak as it looked from the outside. At trial, the prosecution presented a damning account of the events of that evening, calling upon all eight witnesses who were barely cross-examined by the defense, as well as the arresting officers in regard to the arrogant and insolent demeanor of Mr. Nonis upon being taken into custody. Mr. Nonis had apparently boasted to the officers that, "She was the best lay I've ever had." The day after the prosecution rested its case, one of Dr. Aulgur's assistants somehow managed to get himself into a physical altercation in the courthouse men's room with the lead prosecutor himself, leaving the assistant with a broken jaw, and the prosecutor with a pending trial of his own. Judge Thomas Billings declared a mistrial, and, despite incessant pleas for justice from the victim's family, the district attorney never picked the case back up.

Cecil Nonis walked free and moved to Havana, Cuba after his father's retirement, where he lived on in luxury and debauchery.

Fortunately for Dr. Aulgur, Marty was one of his favorite students, and the two had formed a very close personal bond over the last sixteen months. The one thing Dr. Aulgur enjoyed most about teaching at Yale was seeing young people with unlimited potential rise to achieve greatness. Although a most comfortable living was certainly to be made in the practice of law, Dr. Aulgur saw in Marty something different, and perhaps foresaw the coming rebound of the American financial system. He encouraged Marty not to finish law school, but to pursue a career in finance. In fact, Dr. Aulgur had many close friends on Wall Street who would be happy to take a bright young man like Marty under their wing.

So, when Marty knocked on Dr. Aulgur's door at three-fifteen in the morning of December 25, seeking shelter and advice, Dr. Aulgur was more than happy to assist. After his arrest, Dr. Aulgur even offered his personal legal counsel to Marty *pro bono*. On December 27, at four fifty-six in the afternoon, Martin Laroque was released, and all charges against him were dropped. Later that evening, Hope's father stepped in front of a moving train that ended his life.

As Thierry stepped ashore, he was grateful to be back on American soil, but knew full well that this would not be a joyful homecoming. The first thing he would do would be to take a train to New Jersey to see Henry.

January 15, 1945

Little brother,

I know you've probably read or heard some things by now. I want to say first and foremost that I hope you're healthy and come back to us alive.

The last few weeks have been quite the ordeal for me, as you can imagine, and I'm only now finding the strength to write you a letter. I can't go into the details of everything that happened, nor do I want to, at least until I can see you face to face. But I want you to know that what happened was a terrible, terrible accident.

You see, Hope and I had gotten pretty close since you left—as friends, understand? And since my girl was in Chicago with her parents for Christmas, I asked Hope to come to a party with me at one of my professor's houses. I have to admit I was a little lonely and didn't want to show up to a holiday party as the only stiff without a date. We really had a great time and she seemed like she was enjoying herself. In fact, I don't think I'd seen her that happy since you left.

Well, on the way home, as we're driving up on the bluffs, she tells me she wants me to stop the car. So, I pull over and she gets out. We'd both been drinking a little bit, and so when she tells me she wants to dance, I don't think anything of it. I turned the radio up, and we danced to a couple slow songs, and even though it was cold and windy, all she wanted to do was dance. But then, I guess because it was so dark out, she loses her footing and I watch her slip over the edge and down onto the rocks below. I stared over the edge for what felt like an eternity—I was just paralyzed, I couldn't move—and I was sure she was dead, there was no way anyone could have survived that fall. Then, I just panicked. The first thing that popped into my mind was that the police were gonna be after me, they were gonna think I did it on purpose, so I got in the car and just sped off. I drove around for a couple hours, and then found myself back at Dr. Aulgur's house to ask his advice.

That morning, I called the police and let them know where she was and what happened, but they didn't believe me. You can't imagine what all that time in lockup feels like, your whole life, your whole future hanging in the balance. I couldn't keep but feeling like everything I've worked for my whole life was just going to disappear over one simple misunderstanding. I mean, I knew they didn't have any evidence against me—because it was an accident—but you can never be sure about the way things like this go. Anyway, thank God they dropped the charges and let me go.

Well, I just wanted to write to make sure you didn't think I'd done anything to hurt her. She was a good friend to me, and I know how much she cared about you. I want you and me to be straight when you get home.

Be safe, little brother,

—Marty

September 5, 1945

The reunion of stepson and stepfather the previous night couldn't have been more bittersweet than it was. Henry was overjoyed to have Thierry back safe and sound, and Thierry was overjoyed to be home at last. However, the old man couldn't help but be struck by the marked difference in Thierry's stature, as well as the thick scar on his lower lip. Thierry had left for bootcamp as his boy, but returned, just a year later, as a hardened man, a survivor.

Thierry, on the other hand, was saddened by how withered Henry appeared, and how skinny and weak he'd become. Henry had always been lean, but now he simply looked sick. The passing of Henrietta had certainly taken its toll on the old man. Thierry had thought of Henry often, but, to his shame, not nearly as often as he'd considered his own mother, Nina, and his darling Hope, while he'd been away.

And then there was the toll that Hope's sudden death and Marty's arrest had taken on both men, in different ways. Thierry was still not sure he had recovered from the shock of the news, even though he had poured through each letter hundreds of times. The first thing he asked Henry once they became situated was if it was really true, if she was actually gone. When Henry nodded his head, Thierry burst out crying, as if some burden of hope had suddenly been replaced with the burden of truth. For the first time, he actually began to mourn. Henry watched over the young man as he fell asleep in his childhood bed that he'd long outgrown and couldn't help but reflect on the first nights after Nina died. He then remembered his own recent loss, and what a comfort his own dear wife had been to the young boys during that time. He remembered the lullaby she used to sing to Thierry to calm his grieving heart and hummed it bar by bar, tears rising and falling over his wrinkled cheeks. After a long time of humming, mourning, and prayers for the future, he fell asleep where he sat.

Henry awoke that morning—with a stream of drool dripping from his chin and a stiff neck—to the sound of bacon frying. He rubbed his eyes and cleared his head—taking a moment just to remember where he was—and saw Thierry at the stove.

"Morning, pop," Thierry said with more cheer than Henry would have anticipated.

"Morning, son," Henry answered through a yawn.

"You still like your eggs over-easy?"

"I sure do."

Henry walked to the sink, rinsed his mouth and washed his face before putting his arm around Thierry's shoulders and squeezing.

"It's seems like you got taller, T. Did you get taller since you left?"

Thierry smiled and said, "No, you just must be shrinking."

"I wouldn't doubt it," Henry answered. "All this worrying I've been doing this last while is bound to take a man down a bit."

Thierry flipped the bacon, and then looked up as if he was struggling to manage his emotions and put on an appearance of strength.

"I hope you didn't worry too much about me."

"Why not? Was there nothing to worry about?"

"Not much," Thierry said with a shrug of his broad shoulders. "Just your regular solider stuff."

"Nothing out of the ordinary?" Henry asked as he took a seat at the same small table he used to share with his wife and Nina and her boys.

"Nah," Thierry replied.

"Look at me."

Thierry flipped the bacon again and slowly turned around, eyes focused on the floor in front of him.

"Your brother got a letter from the War Personnel Office or something official like that," Henry stated.

Thierry looked up and met the old man's eyes.

"It said you were missing in action, your whereabouts and status unknown."

"What?"

Henry nodded slowly. "The letter came here while Marty was back up at school, so it went unopened for more than a month. I kept looking at the return address and just thought it was something having to do with your pay or rations or something like that. I also wasn't sure if or when I'd ever see Marty to give it to him. And the mail was running haywire, anyway—we'd get a letter you wrote in October in November, and then three weeks later get one that you'd written in August. There was no telling how you were or where you were or anything like that. So when I finally opened the letter, it just didn't seem right—the timing, the wording. Then, sure enough, three days after Marty opened the MIA letter, we got the letter that you wrote all the way from some little town in Germany in March—the one where you said you had befriended a local doctor who was with the resistance."

Thierry looked back down at the floor again. Then the bacon snapped loudly behind him, so he spun back around to split the contents off the frying pan on a couple plates. He handed one to Henry and sat down with the other. Neither of them ate.

"I didn't know what was going on, T., but I knew something wasn't right. Getting that letter from the government—I guess I thought it could have just been a mistake—but your letters didn't sound right either."

Thierry looked up at the man who was the only father he'd ever had. He saw such genuine care, such devotion in his eyes, that it broke the young man's heart to hide from him, but he didn't think he had the ability to talk about his experiences that winter, especially in light of his current circumstances.

"What happened to you, son?" Henry asked gently.

Thierry bit his lip gently and just shook his head, trying to convince them both that what had transpired was no big deal.

"Son, let me tell you something," Henry said quietly, leaning in closer to Thierry's face. "Both my folks were slaves. I grew up in the deep south where twenty years after the war, some white folks still didn't consider me to be a proper person. I've seen my share of scars, I've seen a few lifetime's worth of suffering. Now I ain't gonna sit here and tell you that what you went through, whatever it was, was any more or less than what other people have gone through, but I am gonna tell you that those who survive are the ones who face it head on, the ones who look it in the eye and decide that they aren't going to cower, they aren't gong to let it beat them down. I'm not even saying you're ready yet—these are hard times, I know—but you can't keep running from it forever, and the sooner you come to grips with what cards have been dealt to you, the sooner you'll start to heal."

The two men's eyes were locked.

"Thierry," Henry said, putting his dark hand over his pale son's hand. "You can define your past and your circumstances, or you can let them define you. The choice is yours."

The young man nodded, looking back down at the cooling eggs and bacon on his plate. He took a deep breath and met Henry's eyes again.

"I saw things, pop," he said quietly, his voice trailing off. "But I can't right now. I just can't right now."

"No, that's good, my boy, that's good," Henry said, wiping his eyes with his sleeve.

"All the things that happened, some things that are so horrible that when I think about them, I feel like I was just caught in a nightmare that I couldn't wake up from… things that were so hellish, I don't think anyone would believe me even if I could tell them—they would think I was crazy… And still, none of that was as bad as finding out that I'd lost her."

With that, Thierry put his head in his hands and began to weep violently. Henry immediately moved his chair so that he could embrace his son. After a couple minutes, Thierry composed himself again and looked down at the table with red eyes.

"Your eggs got cold, pop."

Henry nodded.

That afternoon, Thierry set out to catch a train into the city to see his brother, who had just begun studying finance at Columbia University. Thierry was more nervous than a long-tailed cat in a room full of rocking chairs. He had missed his older brother deeply, the same as he always did when they were separated, but the circumstances of this meeting caused a knot the size of a cantaloupe in his gut. Donning his formal uniform, he received several kind greetings and humble gestures of thanks from elderly men passing him by on the platform, gazes of admiration and salutes from small children, and plenty of eye-batting and lip-pouting from eligible blondes, brunettes, and redheads alike. However polite he might have been in responding to this spectrum of attention, as he felt was his duty as a public servant, he felt eaten away inside and was unable to appreciate the sincerity with which these strangers admired him, as a victorious and handsome young man in uniform.

He sat silently as the train car rocked back and forth, his eyes drawn to a pair of pretty college-aged sisters seated facing him only a couple rows to his right, his mind drawn unintentionally into the dark past. He must have been staring for quite a while when he finally noticed the girls looking at him, then covering their faces and whispering frantically between themselves. He quickly glanced away and out the window, embarrassed. The upcoming meeting with Marty weighed heavily on his heart, as did the fact that some are gifted to live on in innocence and ignorance, while others are snuffed out before they've yet had a chance to shine.

He had planned to take the subway from Penn Station, but left early enough in the suspicion that he might feel like walking. He did.

It was a perfect day for walking in New York; late summer warmth with a hint of the autumn to come in the breeze. He passed a thousand shops, restaurants, and theaters, and everything seemed to be buzzing. With the war over in Europe that May and in Japan just three days earlier, New Yorkers had every reason to celebrate the end of that long and terrifying ordeal. America's sons were coming home, and they were greeted with every ounce of respect they had earned. Still, however, Thierry was distracted by his own loss and confusion, and felt in no mood to celebrate. It was a few minutes after six when, after nearly an hour and a half of walking, he arrived at his brother's new address on West 104th Street.

It was an impressive older building, columns and scrolls decorating its dark brick facade. Thierry double-checked the small paper on which he'd written down the address and then entered the small lobby inside through the revolving glass door. Marble floors and the fresh white walls, their condition betrayed by the overwhelming and unmistakable smell of wet paint. Thierry was sure that this wasn't a school issued dormitory, but rather an off-campus apartment building, and then began to wonder with what scholarship his brother could afford it. He took the stairs to the eighth story, and then searched the corridors until he found apartment 808 by the gold-colored numbers tacked on the forest green door, also smelling of fresh paint. He paused for a moment in front of that door, head bent and trying not to allow his mind to race as it so often did. He looked up at the gold 808, straightened his uniform, and then confidently knocked on the heavy green door. After what must have been more than a minute of silence, he knocked again, louder this time. While he waited he made his best efforts at regulating the pace of his breath and the rate of his thoughts. He again checked the scrap paper on which he'd written the address that morning to make sure he had the right number, but still, there was no answer.

Suddenly, a door swung open down the hall as a man spilled out into the corridor, hastily putting a tie around his neck. He was then followed halfway out the door by a tall young blonde in a night dress, her long arms reaching for his starched white shirt with a giggle.

"Baby, you know I'd love to stay, but I've got to get home tonight," he said while fidgeting with his neck tie.

"If you stay," she replied in a deep velvety voice, "I promise I'll make it worth any trouble you'd have at home."

"This weekend, Vivian, I promise," he pleaded as she drew him back towards the door. "We'll go out to my place in the Hamptons, and we won't have to worry about nothing—we'll have the whole world to ourselves."

She looked at him and pouted her lower lip. "You promise?" she asked slowly.

"I promise," he said hurriedly.

"Well then give me a kiss to seal the deal," she answered with a flirtatious smile.

She drew him in by his dress shirt until their lips met, his hands still around his tie. The wedding ring on his finger and the gold Rolex on his wrist glinted in the light of the glazed glass fixture above them. When their kiss broke, he turned suddenly in Thierry's direction, seeming to notice him for the very first time. Thierry quickly looked back at the 808 directly in front of him, embarrassed for feeling like he eavesdropped. He heard the man say something to the blonde in a low voice, and in his peripheral vision, saw him hand her what looked like a roll of cash, and then heard another quick smack of lips, and then footsteps hurried in his direction.

"Good day, sir," the man said as he passed near Thierry, who just responded by nodding and saying something nervously under his breath. He turned to see the man reach the stairs and turn down them, then looked back at the numbers on the door. He felt, however, that he was being watched. He slowly glanced to his left to see the scantily clad blonde still standing in her doorway, looking him over. He nodded to her politely.

"Aren't you just handsome?" she asked. "How long have you been back from the front?"

"Just yesterday," he replied softly.

"Just yesterday? Well congratulations on coming home safe and sound!"

"Thank you."

"Tell me," she said, leaning back against her doorframe while lighting a cigarette. "Who is the lucky lady you've come home to?" When he didn't answer, she blew out a puff of smoke and said, "It's okay, darling, I don't bite."

He cleared his throat and said, "I'm not coming home to anyone, miss."

"A handsome soldier like you and no girlfriend, no wife?" she said, placing a hand over her heart for dramatic effect. "I can't believe that's true!"

"It's true."

"Well, handsome, let me just say, if you're ever lonely and just want to have a little bit of fun, you know where I am, and you're more than welcome to knock on my door any time, day or night... except for this weekend of course!" her velvet words crescendoed into a velvet laugh.

He just bit his lip and nodded, then turned toward the stairs himself and started back down towards West 104th. When he got out onto the street, he pushed Vivian from his mind and began to ask himself where on earth his brother was. He guessed that maybe one of his classes had run late, so he decided to grab a bite to eat before checking back at apartment 808. He walked several blocks before he found a small, family run Jewish restaurant and ordered a pastrami on rye with a coke. The man behind the counter asked with a thick Eastern European accent whether he'd fought the Germans or the Japanese, and upon learning that Thierry was part of the offensive in Europe, refused to accept the young soldier's payment for the meal. Around eight o'clock, he finished his sandwich, grabbed a coffee to go and headed back to the building in which his brother was supposed to have lived. Within a few more minutes, he found himself again, straightening his uniform and relaxing his thoughts. This time, however, although he couldn't quite be sure, he thought he heard voices and music coming from inside number 808. He knocked, but again, no one answered. He waited for a few moments and then knocked again, nearly pounding on the door with the butt of his fist. Then, he was sure he heard some commotion inside, and then the big green door flew open.

Standing before him, with a look of shocked surprise on his face, was Marty. He was wearing a short sleeved cotton button-down, brown trousers, and had grown a small mustache in the style of Clark Gable. Marty looked Thierry up and down, his face breaking into a stupid smile.

"Hey, everybody!" he shouted over his shoulder, "Look who's here—my kid brother, the war hero!"

With that he turned back and squeezed Thierry in a bear hug. Looking into the apartment, Thierry saw a small crowd of people sitting across two sofas and around a small glass-top dining table. The room was large and comfortable and quite richly, for Thierry's tastes, decorated. Finally, Marty took Thierry firmly by the shoulders and looked into his face. In such close proximity, the younger brother couldn't help but notice the smell of alcohol on Marty's breath.

"Let me have a look at you, kid," Marty said gayly. "Goddammit, you look good!"

"Thanks. You, too."

Marty nodded, silly smiled plastered to his face again.

"I know, I know," he said with a laugh. "So, what the hell are you doing here?" he asked, smacking Thierry's arm with one hand.

"What are you talking about?" Thierry asked. "I was supposed to be here at six-thirty."

Marty shook his head, a blank look on his face.

"That was supposed to be today?"

"We talked about it this morning."

"Well, now that you're here," Marty said with a dismissive wave of his hand, "Let me introduce you to my friends!"

Thierry glanced across the room, his brother's arm proudly around his shoulder. Two scrawny, artistic-looking young men sat next to each other on the sofa. The one with the black wire-framed glasses was introduced as Chuck, while the one with the greased black hair was introduced as Kenneth. They both waved and smiled in a friendly manner, but then went back to flipping over records and pointing to various things on the covers.

Next was Barbara, a petite young brunette with a gold pin of an open book fastened to her white blouse. She was quite smart-looking, and she extended her small and bony hand for Thierry to gently shake. Sitting to her left was a tall, lanky man in an expensive and stylish wool sweater vest named Michael, whose prematurely graying hair might have been the only feature that remotely distinguished him from the masses of other bright, young men who swarmed the campus of Columbia University at that time. He shook Thierry's hand firmly and mumbled something about having not known that Marty had a brother.

"Well, let me get you a drink! What'll it be, brother?" Marty said with great enthusiasm.

Thierry shrugged. "I'll take a Scotch on the rocks."

"You got it!" Marty answered and slapped him on the back. He then turned and called into the kitchen, "Hey, baby, get my kid brother a drink, okay?" Then, turning back toward Thierry, he motioned him to a seat at the small dining table. "Sit, sit! Your drink's coming out!"

"Thanks," Thierry replied quietly.

"How long have you been back?" Barbara asked from the sofa while lighting a fresh cigarette.

"Just a day or so."

Barbara nodded and puffed on her smoke. "Are you happy to be home?"

Thierry nodded.

"Well, that's good," she said with a slightly pretentious smile.

Kenneth stood up from the opposite sofa, record in hand, and walked over to the table on which the player stood. He carefully set the vinyl disk down and lined up the needle. Before long, chords plunked across piano keys in no discernible order, which were then followed by a lone violin screeching seemingly out of place, a cello suddenly and slowly bowing unrelated notes, and then the clash of the piano again. It was all very chaotic-sounding, and Thierry was made even more nervous by it.

Marty walked into the kitchen with some mumble about what was taking so long, while Kenneth plopped back down on the couch next to Chuck, whose eyes were closed and head leaned back. Thierry glanced quickly towards Barbara after she let out an exasperated sigh.

"Would you turn that Nazi shit off?" she asked, or rather, demanded.

"What Nazi shit?" Kenneth answered as he slowly rocked back and forth to a beat Thierry couldn't pick out in the music.

"That Berg shit you put on."

"First of all, it's brilliant music, not shit, and secondly, it's Webern, not Berg," Kenneth said with an air of arrogance.

"It's not brilliant. In fact, it's not even music," she replied, leaning forward on the sofa and puffing her cigarette. "It's fascist horse shit."

"How can music be fascist?" Chuck blurted out, eyes still closed, head still resting on the back of the couch.

"When a bunch of nazis write it for the sake of attempting to create a parallel between music and mathematics and their insane racial theory."

"But Schoenberg was a Jew, how could his music be nazi?" Kenneth asked softly.

"Well, this isn't Schoenberg, is it?"

"It's not an attempt at anything other than the exploration of the universe," Chuck again opined. "It's an experiment on the human capacity for rational thought, and how that relates to the human capacity for emotion."

Thierry began to feel more and more out of place within this group and thought anxiously about leaving. Then, he heard some playful laughter from the kitchen and clinking of glasses and dishes.

"It's a way for the spirit to connect to all of the elements of the universe," began Chuck again, suddenly sitting up and staring through his spectacles dully at Barbara. "It's how the human heart can actually feel physics, experience chemistry and mathematics and every form of science in a completely rational, biological way. It's our key to opening the universe."

"It's atonal horse shit," Barbara answered firmly, furrowing her brow. "And I'm not staying if you continue to insist on listening to it."

"Fine," Kenneth blustered as he stood up and walked towards the record player. "I'll put on some Prokofiev for you."

Chuck snickered while closing his eyes and laying his head back again.

"Very funny," Barbara answered as she settled back on the sofa next to Michael, who had witnessed this entire exchange with a fascinated, wry smile curled on his lips.

Suddenly, Michael's smile cracked, and he began to chuckle and quickly nod his head. "It is horse shit," he said through his curt laughter.

"Dullard," Kenneth mumbled while rolling his eyes.

At that moment, Thierry noticed a drink being held before him by delicate, long fingers with painted pink nails. He cupped the glass with both hands and looked up to see the tall blonde from down the hall. He gave a quick start while she raised her eyebrows knowingly and smiled at him.

"T., I've been waiting for this pleasure for so long!" Marty burst in. "Let me introduce you to my best girl, Vivian."

Thierry set the glass on the table and stood to shake her hand, completely bewildered by this turn of events and unsure what to make of any of it.

"I believe we've already met, actually," she said slowly in her deep and velvety voice, shaking Thierry's hand gently.

"You have?" asked Marty incredulously. "Jesus, little brother, you've been back a day and you're already getting around, aren't you?"

Thierry shook his head and stammered nervously.

"We met earlier in the hall when he was waiting for you to come back from class—just briefly while I was coming in," she said calmly with a quick wink in Thierry's direction. "I thought he looked a little like someone I knew." She then walked to the arm of the sofa occupied by Chuck and Kenneth and sat down. Marty approached behind her and put his arm around her.

"Is she something or what, T.?" Marty asked, anxious for his brother's approval.

Thierry nodded and sat back down.

"She sure is," Marty exclaimed while planting a quick kiss on her cheek. Vivian arched her neck flirtatiously. "She's the most beautiful thing I've seen all week!"

"Oh, stop," she said, craning her neck towards him and shrugging her shoulder. Marty laughed like a simpleton. Thierry had never seen his brother act this way. Marty had always been so confident and, quite frankly, indifferent towards his girlfriends. Thierry wasn't sure, but he thought that this might truly be a time that his brother had come under the control of a woman. It was as if she had reduced him to a babbling adolescent.

The music started on the record player again, which Thierry immediately recognized as Benny Goodman, and began to feel a little more at ease. He took a swig of his drink and savored the warm comfort.

"I swear to God," Marty continued in a jovial manner, "if she would say 'yes,' I'd marry this girl tomorrow! What do you say to that, baby?"

"Maybe you should ask in the proper manner and I might consider it," she answered in a near whisper.

"Ask?" Marty seemed incredulous. "How many times do I need to ask you?"

"I said," she replied, seeming to grow slightly exasperated and nearly embarrassed, "you should ask in the proper manner, and I *might* consider it."

Marty looked up and grinned a stupid grin at Thierry, and then began to look nervously around the room at his other compatriots.

"Well," he stammered with a dimwitted laugh, "there you go."

An awkward moment-long silence was broken when Chuck said under his breath, "Some people aren't cut out for marriage."

When Marty heard this, his demeanor changed completely. His face began to twitch and his breathing began to quicken.

"And just what the fuck would the two of *you* know about getting married?" he asked through clenched teeth as he leaned forward in a nearly combative posture.

Chuck, eyes still closed, simply sipped his drink, and with a wave of his delicate hand, answered, "Like I said, marriage isn't for everyone."

Kenneth, who was sitting precariously between Chuck and Marty, looked nervous and his eyes darted around the room for help. Vivian put her hand on Marty's shoulder and began whispering to him in an attempt to calm his enraged temper.

Thierry remembered a time when he accidentally broke his older brother's favorite pencil. He went to school the next day with a black eye and swollen lip.

On second thought, while Marty had always shown the capacity for violence when he flew into a rage—and nearly anything could set him off—Thierry reflected that it was only on the rarest occasion that his brother, even when they were very young, had shown hostility toward him. As much as he might have felt neglected by his older brother, he had never felt completely unloved, and in that moment, he began to be overwhelmed with affection for his lost, self-centered sibling. As he finished his drink, it truly became difficult for him to believe, looking at Marty and the way he fawned over the tall, pretty blonde on the arm of the sofa, that his older brother would have had ill intentions towards his own life's single passion—Hope. Thoughts began to swirl in his head, and he became muddled by the events of the evening, the conversations, and the alcohol. He knew that he couldn't bring up the subject about which he had come all this way in front of Marty' guests, but, as it turned out, he wouldn't have to.

"So, Thierry," Vivian's dark voice began with remarkable kindness after another moment of verbal silence. "I was so sorry to hear about your girl—Hope, was it?"

His eyes locked with hers and he began to feel blood rush to his face. He simply tilted his head forward in recognition of her statement.

"Such a terrible accident," she continued, covering her heart with her right hand.

Marty began to grow visibly uncomfortable.

"What the hell, Viv?" he said, gesturing towards Thierry with his hand. "Don't upset the kid."

"I'm sorry," Vivian said as she leaned forward in Thierry's direction. "I didn't mean to upset you—it just seemed like the elephant in the room."

Thierry was slightly confused by the sincerity and honest kindness in her voice, as if she was truly concerned for him. In fact, he felt like she knew him already. He was even more confused by the sudden and strong rush of emotion he felt towards her. She was stunning, that was for sure, but, despite what had occurred in the hallway earlier that evening, he couldn't help but see a person of depth and a gracious spirit. He suddenly felt quite smitten with her, and this bothered him greatly.

"It's okay," Thierry answered, moist eyes locking with hers. Just then, the record ended, and the room fell into complete silence, aside from the rhythmic pulse of the vinyl spinning.

"Well, enough of all this," Marty blurted as he moved quickly towards his brother. "T., let me fill up your drink! Come on, everybody, we didn't come here to mourn and dig up the past—this is a celebration! The war's over, and my kid brother is home safe and sound!"

Marty dashed to the kitchen and called back through the silence, "Hey, Kenny, put something else on, like that Benny Goodman, that was nice!"

Kenneth put another record on, and Marty nearly shouted back that everyone should dance. Just a second later, he came back into the room with three glasses and handed one to Thierry, one to Vivian, and kept one for himself.

"We're actually going to head out," Barbara said, patting Michael's thigh to let him know to stand up.

"It's so early, still," Marty retorted.

"But Michael's got work early in the morning, and I have an early class," Barbara answered. "And come to think of it, you're in that class, too—7am comes awfully quick."

Chuck stood up as well, with the help of Kenny's outstretched hand. "We're going to hit the road, too."

"What kind of party is this?" Marty asked.

"It's not a party, Marty," Michael said. "You invited us up for a couple drinks. It's time to go."

"Jesus," Marty said, shaking his head. "Well, let me at least walk you down."

Marty's entourage collected their belongings, shook hands with Thierry, and headed toward the heavy door, which was painted white on the inside. Thierry downed his drink.

"Viv, can you watch my kid brother for a couple minutes?"

"He needs to be watched?" she asked sarcastically.

"And you," he continued, taking Thierry by the shoulder, "I'm coming right back, so don't you try anything." He slapped Thierry's face playfully and then added, "It's good to have you back, kid."

The rest of the guests left with Marty, and the door clicked quietly behind them.

"I'm really sorry," Vivian said quickly. "I didn't mean to upset you."

"No, it's okay. The whole thing's kinda crazy."

She smiled kindly, then went to the kitchen and brought the half-empty bottle of Scotch back with her. She poured Thierry's glass full and did the same with her own. Just then, a slow song came on, and he took a big swig.

"Do you want to dance?" she asked nervously.

His immediate instinct would have told him to decline politely, but he was mesmerized by the paradoxical innocence he saw in her. He downed the rest of the contents of his glass and stood up, albeit a little shakily. She smiled and put her arms over his shoulders. His hands fell to her hips and it surprised him, although it shouldn't have, that she was shaped differently than Hope. She was curvy and her hips were full. They also sat up much higher than Hope's. Her body moved against his in rhythm and her hair smelled like fresh cut flowers. He was intoxicated by her and felt an acute sense of guilt for more reasons than one.

"I want you to forget about my offer in the hallway," she said in her lush voice. "I didn't realize you were Marty's brother."

"I probably wouldn't have taken you up on it, anyway," Thierry answered slowly.

She seemed playfully offended and pouted her lips. "You don't think I'm pretty?"

"I think you're gorgeous," he blurted out in a near whisper.

She smiled affectionately. "Then what is it?"

"I don't… I don't think…" he struggled to get the words out, partially because of the alcohol, partially because of his bewilderment. "I think it's just too soon," he finally said.

"It is. Plus, you wouldn't want to get involved with a girl like me."

"And what kind of girl is that?"

She sighed and tilted her head. "Listen, you're a nice boy, and you deserve a nice girl."

"I think you're nice," he slurred.

"I might have been at one time, but I'm in over my head now, and I've obtained a little bit of a… reputation, you know?"

He thought for a moment, inhaling her essence and trying to collect himself.

"Does Marty know about the guy with the rolex?" he asked suddenly. Vivian did not seem at all surprised or embarrassed by the question.

"As much as he wants to know," she answered with a shrug. "And I know as much as I want to know about the revolving door of hussies that come through this apartment."

It can't be said that Thierry was surprised at this revelation, but he was disturbed by it. He leaned back and stopped dancing, although his hands rested still on her hips.

"And you two are okay with that?"

"Thierry, once you've been the places I've been, there's no going back. I'm a certain kind of girl that's good for a certain kind of thing and a certain kind of man, and that's all there is to it."

Thierry just shook his head in disbelief.

"Look," she continued, trying to convince herself as much as she was trying to convince him. "I'm not smart, I'm not talented—I've got a little bit of money and a pretty face. That's all that I have to my name."

"That's not true," he answered earnestly. "You are smart and talented, and above all, you've got a good heart. You've got much more than what you give yourself credit for."

For about five seconds, she looked him in the eyes and did her best to hold back her emotions, but they finally burst forth and she began to sob. She nestled her face in his neck, and he held her close and stroked her long, silky hair. After a minute or so, she sniffled and stared at him, her makeup streaking down her face.

"No one's ever told me that before," she said as she closed her eyes and kissed him. He resisted for a moment, and then the alcohol and his male instincts took over, and he kissed back.

"Vivian," he said, taking her arms in his hands and putting a little distance between them. "You're my brother's girl."

"I know," she answered with her kind smile, her mellow voice like a gentle kiss to his ears. "But that was for what might have been, in a different life, in different circumstances. You deserve a different type of girl, and I deserve whatever I have coming."

"That's not true," he said, nearly pleading with her to see in her the depths of beauty and innocence that he did.

"Thank you," she said in a whisper and added with a sweet smile, "but you're drunk. Anyway, make sure to wipe the lipstick off your face before your brother comes back."

He just nodded as she slipped from his hands and out the door, closing it gently behind her. Just at that moment, Marty came down the hall and saw her makeup.

"What the hell happened in there?" he asked.

She sniffled and answered, "Your brother is a good kid."

She kissed Marty gently on the cheek and went down the hall to her door. She dipped inside without looking back. The heavy green door clicked softly and Marty stood there for a moment in bewilderment. He then walked slowly to her door, a thousand questions running through his mind, and raised his hand to knock, but thought the better of it after a moment. He stood in front of her door and felt like something had changed, but he couldn't put his finger on it. When he reentered apartment 808, he saw Thierry spread across one of the sofas, finishing another glass of Scotch, the bottle standing on the floor beside him.

"You okay, kid?"

"Do you think I could stay here tonight?" Thierry slurred.

"Sure, sure," Marty replied. "But I've gotta be out early and probably won't be home until real late, okay?"

Thierry nodded and closed his eyes, letting the empty glass roll out of his hand onto the floor. Marty went to the bedroom and came back to cover his younger brother with a blanket. Thierry looked up at him sleepily.

"I'm glad you're home, kid," Marty said kindly.

Thierry smiled and drifted off into a heavy slumber.

After a moment of watching his brother, still in uniform, sleep soundly, Marty coughed and cleared his throat. He poured himself the last of the Scotch and walked to the telephone. He spoke briefly to the operator and was connected to a line in an apartment four blocks from where he stood. After several rings, a bright young voice answered.

"Hey, Ruth, you up?… You ready for me?… Okay, I'll see you in a couple minutes…"

He hung up the phone slowly, threw the drink down the hatch, and went to his bedroom to spritz himself with some cologne. He stood for another moment over his younger brother, who was by this time snoring heavily, and left the apartment. He paused outside the heavy green door and thought again about knocking on Vivian's door, but turned down the hall, down each flight of steps, and out into the late summer night's air. Within fifteen minutes, he was in Ruth's apartment, undressing her as quickly as his hands would let him.

September 6, 1945

As Thierry rolled on his side, a single ray of concentrated sunlight penetrated his eyelids, causing him to stir in annoyance. He rolled over, face buried in the sofa cushions, however, he was already awake. After a few moments of trying to gauge how bad his hangover was, he slowly sat up. He felt like his brain was resisting his neck's movement, and a dull pounding ensued as he wiped his eyes and yawned. He looked around the apartment, which looked curiously grayer than it had the night before. He called his brother's name softly and was answered, aside from the monotonous hum of engines on the street below and a pigeon cooing on the fire escape, by silence. He stretched and looked down in distress at his thoroughly wrinkled uniform. He checked his cheap watch and saw that it was already after noon. He rose cautiously, his brain fighting him every inch of the way, and found the bathroom. After washing up and shaving with Marty's razor, he found a pair of trousers and a shirt that would fit him in his brother's closet. He folded his uniform as neatly as he could and left it on the small table near the door. Finding a pen and paper in the top drawer of the writing desk in the corner, he left his brother a note that he would be back early that evening to collect his things and, hopefully, sit down and talk.

Upon closing the apartment door, he found himself wishing partially that he might run into Vivian, and partially that he would never have to see her again. A sharp pang of guilt hit his chest as his mind darted to thoughts about Hope. He closed his eyes for a moment and tried not to feel like he had betrayed her memory, betrayed her. In the flood of muddled emotions, he thought simultaneously that Hope would want him to let her go and set a new course in life, and that she was crying out for answers—or perhaps justice. He took a glance toward Vivian's unopened door, and then started down the hall and down the stairs toward the busy streets of Manhattan. The bright sunlight and noisy bustle did nothing for his headache. He bought a coffee in a shop on the corner and headed in the direction of the Bronx in possession of some money Henry had given him for his birthday the day before. He had missed the early Yankee's game, but would be just in time for the second game of the double header against the Detroit Tigers. His birthday gift would be spoiled as the Bronx Bombers followed up what was surely a rousing 14–5 victory with a 2–5 dud of a loss. Nevertheless, he hadn't seen the Yankees play in years, and his only regret was not having Hope by his side to enjoy America's greatest pastime. He thought if she'd been with him, they would have figured out how to get some autographs.

He grabbed a hotdog on the street and another coffee, and headed back towards Marty's apartment. The sun was gently setting, and the air was damp inside the building. He was becoming quite familiar with that lobby, those flights of stairs, and the gold numbers 808. He knocked, but to no avail. He rested his forehead against the thick green door and began, for the first time, to truly grow angry. He tried to give every human being the benefit of the doubt in any situation, but it was becoming harder and harder to believe that his brother was not trying to avoid him, and this nagging thought began to cause his gentle patience to wane. He looked at those gold digits and knocked again, this time more loudly and more urgently. The longer there was no answer, the harder he beat at the door until he was swinging at it viciously. He had become undone, and in a blind rage began shrieking with every punch of the green door:

"Goddamn motherfucking piece of shit! Open the door you piece of shit!"

Suddenly, he felt the unmistakably metaphysical sensation of eyes upon him. He turned in flushed embarrassment to see Vivian watching him, mouth gaping, in stunned silence.

"Thierry," she spoke softly. "What's the matter?"

He panted heavily and stood frozen momentarily before her.

"Oh my god," she said with shocked concern. "Your hand."

He looked down quickly to see blood seeping from his right hand, and glanced up to see red droplets streaming from the bottom of one eight and one zero. Almost immediately, sharp pain nearly brought him to his knees.

"I think it's broken," he said with a grimace as his senses flooded back to him.

"We need to get you to a hospital," she answered quickly. "Let me get a coat, and I'll walk with you."

She emerged a moment later from her door with a white towel which she gently wrapped around his hand. In the midst of the near-blinding pain and the endorphin rush, now quickly wearing off, he couldn't help but notice the enchanting smell of her hair again. She wiped his brother's door down quickly with another rag and helped the staggered war hero down the stairs. Darkness had fallen, and the city seemed warm and asleep.

Within a few moments, he was being seen by a doctor, who iced his hand and assured him that there was no structural damage. He received fourteen stitches, a couple of aspirin, and was sent on his way.

To his surprise, Vivian was still sitting patiently, her face curiously worried, in the waiting room.

"Hey," he said calmly.

"Hey," she answered with tense concern in her eyes. "Everything okay?"

"It's not broken."

"Well, that's good."

"Thanks for waiting for me. You didn't have to."

"I know," she said with her uniquely warm smile. "Let's get you back to Marty's place, okay?"

He nodded. "You're really kind, you know that?"

She gave a queasy smile and offered him her arm.

Standing in front of number 808 again, she asked if he might let her knock this time, which evoked an embarrassed laugh from him. But again, there was no answer.

"Why don't come into my place while we wait for Marty to get home?"

"Can I use your phone?" he asked.

"Of course."

She unlocked her door and he held it open for her with his left hand. The heavy green door, painted white on the inside, clicked slowly behind him. Her apartment had an airy and fresh ambience, and nearly everything in it—from the sofa to the table linens—was white.

"Phone's there," she said with a point of her finger.

"Thanks," he said, walking towards it and dialing the operator for Henry's number.

The phone rang and rang with no answer on the other side. He hung the white earpiece up gently.

She emerged from the bedroom in a white button-up shirt and tan shorts. The perfect shape of her long, sun-kissed legs nearly knocked him off of his. He instantly felt guilty and his thoughts reverted to

Hope and how his memories of her had helped him survive in the most dire times he had ever experienced. He looked toward his feet and when he looked up again, Vivian was handing him a glass of Scotch. He wasn't sure it was a good idea to start drinking, especially after the river of emotions and confusion he'd experienced the night before, but took the glass and downed it nonetheless. He hoped and prayed the alcohol would numb his feelings rather than muddle his mind. She motioned him to the sofa, refilled his drink, and asked if he wanted anything to eat. He courteously declined. She sat on the white sofa as well, separated from him by the middle cushion.

"How old are you?" he asked suddenly.

"Why?" she asked with suspicion.

"No reason."

"How old do you think I am?"

He knew better than to begin to attempt to estimate a lady's age.

"I'll turn twenty-two next month," she finally replied. "How old are you?"

"Nineteen," he answered. "Today."

"How come you didn't tell anybody it's your birthday?"

"There wasn't really anyone to tell," he answered with an uncomfortable laugh. His eyes fell to her slender, brown legs, tucked underneath her, then quickly looked away.

"Well, happy birthday!" she exclaimed. "I'm sorry I don't have any cake!"

"Oh, it's okay. I'm not so much in the mood for cake anyway."

"We should at least toast to it!"

She held her glass up and looked him dead in the eyes with playful seriousness.

"Here's to the nicest younger brother of any boyfriend I've ever had," her velvet voice crooned. "And here's to many, many more birthdays."

He smiled sincerely as they clinked their glasses together and drank.

"Do you mind if I try my pops again?" he asked, putting the empty glass on the table beside the sofa.

Thierry walked to the phone, forcing himself to concentrate on walking in a straight line. He let the line ring for more than a minute before placing it gently on the holder again. He checked his watch and began to wonder where Henry could possibly be past eight on a Thursday night. He plumped back down on the sofa in a bit of exasperation.

"Everything okay?" she asked.

"Yeah, I guess."

"No answer, huh?"

"It's just not like him to be out this late after work."

"I'm sure everything's fine," she said to reassure him.

"Yeah, me, too," he answered to reassure himself.

"How's your hand?"

"It's okay. Feels like it's throbbing," he answered while holding his bandaged appendage up and turning it over and back.

"You should really eat something."

"I don't think I can."

"Well then, at least have another drink," she responded. "It is your birthday, after all."

"Sure," he answered with a smile. "But just one more."

He watched her graceful form as she leaned and reached backwards for the bottle of Scotch on the table behind the sofa. His eyes followed her as she unscrewed the cap and extended her golden arm to fill his glass. Suddenly, cluttered by the beginnings of inebriation and the full effects of loneliness and lust, he grabbed her wrist with his left hand and pulled her close to him. He kissed her full, red lips and immediately felt her kiss back. The bottle clanked to the floor, its contents running unnoticed across the floor. He leaned forward, pushing her onto her back and laid on top of her. She wrapped her bronze legs around his waist, her heels digging frantically in the small of his back.

He slid his good hand under the fabric of her white shirt, feeling the warm and toned skin of her stomach.

"Thierry," she suddenly gasped, breaking from his kiss after allowing reason to get the better of her. "Stop, Thierry, please."

He initially ignored her until she became more adamant. She put her hands on his chest and gently pushed him pack.

"Please," she pleaded with him kindly.

He stared down at her, totally astonished for letting himself get so out of control, so blindly passionate. He sat up and put his head in his hands. She unwound her legs from him and shuffled back toward her own space on the sofa, wrapping her knees in her arms.

"I'm sorry," Thierry said, shaking his head in guilt and confusion. "I don't know what—"

"Please, don't," she interrupted.

He looked up and saw the deep kindness in her eyes.

"Thierry," she said softly. "Nobody has ever made me feel the way you have made me feel. And I don't... I don't want to ruin it."

He stood up quickly and walked toward the white door.

"Thierry?" she called.

He stopped before he reached it. Self-loathing washed over him, and he felt like he would drown in it. At the same time, the sheer cruelty of life hit him like a ton of bricks. He felt like he was meant for Hope, and she was taken from him. He couldn't deny that he felt like Vivian was meant for him, and she could not be his.

"I'm sorry," she said. "I don't know what to say."

"You don't have to say anything," he answered softly, turning back towards her. She smoothed her long hair with her hands.

"I wish it could be some other way," she nearly whimpered.

"Vivian," Thierry started softly. "I don't understand what's going on right now, but I know you're right—we can't be together, because of my brother. But please, for God's sake, if not for your own, try to see in yourself what I see in you."

She smiled sadly. "I think it's too late for that."

Just as he was about to respond, the phone rang. She rushed over to answer it.

"Hi, are you okay?" she asked. "God, what's the matter?... Why are you in Jersey?... Yes, he's right here—we've been waiting for you..."

She turned quickly towards Thierry, holding the phone's earpiece in his direction.

"It's Marty for you," she said worriedly.

"Hello?" Thierry said, taking the phone from her.

"Thierry?"

"Yeah, where the hell have you been all day?"

"I've been trying to get you on the phone at my place," Marty said. Thierry was alarmed by what sounded like near panic in his voice.

"What's the matter?"

"You gotta get over here."

"Over where?"

"St. Mary's in Hackensack," Marty answered quickly.

"St. Mary's? What's the matter? Are you okay?" Thierry asked nervously.

"No, no, it's not me," Marty replied hurriedly. "It's Henry, little brother."

"Henry? What happened—is he okay?"

"I don't know, I don't know. He was hurt at work—bad—and he's been in surgery for almost an hour already, and I've been trying to get a hold of you."

"Okay, okay," Thierry said in panic. "I'll see you as soon as I can get there."

He hung up the phone and spun towards Vivian.

"I've gotta run."

"I'm coming with you," she answered. She darted to her bedroom and came out in a skirt and her coat. "I'll pay for a cab to take us."

"Thank you," he said opening the door into the hallway.

They darted past 808 and down the stairs to the street.

Panic gripped him around the throat, and it wasn't until they were already in New Jersey that he realized he was holding Vivian's hand, squeezing it, in fact. He didn't remember if he had reached for hers or vice versa, but her slender fingers were now intertwined with his. This was the only amount of comfort his racing mind would be allowed. In the time it took to reach the hospital, his capable mind weaved through a distracted montage of painful memories. He tried to keep the worst fears from gripping his fragile state, but he couldn't scrub them completely from the movie screen of his mind. He told himself that Henry would be fine—he was so strong—while at the same moment, he thought that losing another loved one in such fashion would be a fitting event based on the course of his life to that point.

The cabby pulled up to the front door of the massive brick edifice—haunting and menacing in the dark. Thierry held the door for Vivian after she paid the driver, and they entered the foyer together.

They received directions down multiple hallways and met an anxiously pacing Marty in the waiting room. Vivian immediately ran to him and threw her arms around him. He held her close and took several deep breaths before opening his eyes and locking them with Thierry. For a split second, the younger brother thought he caught a mocking glance from his elder—a glint in the eyes and a curl of the lip that seemed to say, "Look what I have." The two lovers broke their embrace, and Marty's eyes seemed to soften. Maybe he'd imagined it. They sat down next to each other on cold metal chairs, and he waved Thierry over near them.

"What's the latest?" asked Thierry.

"Nothing," Marty said with a shrug. "I got here, and they told me he was already in surgery, and I haven't heard a damn thing since. Been almost three hours."

"Poor thing," Vivian said, stroking the side of Marty's face. He shrugged again and looked down toward the floor.

"What happened?" Thierry asked.

"He was helping to fix one of the presses or something and somehow got pulled into it or something—I don't know!" Marty answered, his own confusion brimming into anger. "They haven't been able to tell me a goddamn thing!"

"Calm down, sweetie," Vivian's velvet voice crooned, her hand resting on his shoulder. "I'm sure everything will be alright."

"How can you say that?" Marty asked, pulling away from her. "You don't know that—nobody knows that. Why would you say something as gospel truth when you know for a fact that you don't have the foggiest idea of what you're talking about?"

Her large brown eyes misted and she murmured some kind of apology.

Thierry couldn't help but wonder what kind of spell his older brother had cast over her. She was doing her best to be a comfort to him, and he treated her like garbage—and somehow, had subconsciously managed to convince her that she was the one who should apologize. The second hand on the clock on the wall behind the metal bars clicked, clicked, clicked. Thierry felt lonelier at that moment than he had ever been. It was cruel that Vivian had left his side so abruptly to tend to his asshole brother. It was cruel that Henry had lost his soulmate, and that he was now fighting for his own life. It was cruel that the one person he would have wanted to be by his side the most at this moment had been taken from him so suddenly.

At that moment, he almost thought he heard a bell ring inside his skull, and suddenly, everything became clear to him. He had no evidence, he had no clues; in fact, he didn't even have the luxury of conjecture, but at that moment, he became more convinced that his brother had killed Hope than he was that the sun would rise in the morning. He had kept an open mind to this point—certainly his brother was not capable of something akin to murder—but rage like he had never experienced in his life began to swell in his chest to the point where he felt it would explode. He trained his eyes on Marty and began to hate every last cell in his body. Suddenly, Marty looked up, and again their eyes locked, and again that cold glint and that murderous curl of the upper lip. Marty suddenly reached for Vivian's hand.

"What the fuck are you looking at?" Marty asked in steely tranquility.

"Baby!" Vivian admonished, squeezing his hand.

Thierry thought he would lose his mind if he sat there a moment longer. He popped out of his seat and practically sprinted back down the hallway toward the front door. He heard Vivian stir and say something and heard Marty tell her to stay put. Thierry was out the front door and into the darkness in a matter of minutes. His chest heaved as he tried to put together what he knew of what had happened to Hope, and why suddenly, in this place, at this time, he felt the way he did toward his brother. He bummed a cigarette off a passerby and smoked it frantically. He kept waiting for Vivian to come out to him, to try to comfort or set things right—even to apologize for his brother's outburst—*he's stressed, he's tired, he's overwhelmed.*

He's a piece of shit, that's what he is.

But she didn't come.

This served as further confirmation that his brother was a masterful manipulator, a psychopath capable of limitless coldness and deceit in the pursuit of his every whim.

He felt that he couldn't be in his presence, couldn't even be in the same building as him. He flicked the butt of the smoke into the street as a car flew by. He looked up at the single street light to see a large, dark bird perched atop it, standing erect in quiet contentment, like a looming harbinger of things to come. The glass door opened behind him, and Vivian quickly emerged. Her face was flushed and tears streamed down her cheeks. She stopped suddenly in front of him, and he searched her eyes for confirmation of what he already knew.

"I'm so sorry," she said quietly, taking his hand gently in hers. "He's gone."

He closed his eyes and tried to feel something other than anger. He tried to feel sorrow, he tried to feel pain, he even tried to feel numb, but it was as if the world was swirling down the black hole of his newly awakened fury.

"I have to get back inside to Marty," she said, words rolling from her dark voice like whisky into a glass. "He's a mess, Thierry."

"And what about me?" Thierry asked indignantly. "Am I not a mess?"

"Thierry, I'm sorry—"

"Sorry? You're sorry?" he cut her off abruptly.

"Yes, I am," she answered with conviction. "I'm sorry for him, I'm sorry for Henry, and I'm sorry for you."

She cut through the core of his rage, and it annoyed him that she'd done it so quickly. She had beaten him at his own game. He was sure that the words she said came not from the circumstances, not from some idea of societal procedure or politeness, but from the core of her being. She was real, just as Hope had been real.

"I'm sorry," he said quietly.

"Why don't you come back inside?"

"I don't—I can't—I don't think I can see my brother right now."

"Thierry," she said, ducking her head in an effort to catch his lowered gaze. "I can't even begin to tell you how sorry I am for your loss. I don't know what to say. But you haven't lost your brother, and you're all that he has in the world right now."

He felt deep sadness for her, being as deceived as she was by his brother. Marty wasn't alone—he had people everywhere—friends, lovers, mentors—and he had her. Rather than argue with her and try to convince her of anything at this moment, he decided, instead, to hide, to burrow himself inside his own mind.

"I can't, Viv," he said as he turned and began walking.

"Thierry," she called, pleading for him to return. "Thierry!"

As he walked under the street light, he was startled by the sound of the flutter of the massive bird's wings and looked up quickly, but saw nothing at all.

She continued to call his name as he walked away and disappeared into darkness.

September 7, 1945

His dreams were wretched—a terrifying swirl through macabre lands of the underworld and all that it owns. He weaved through pastures under gunfire and the screams of the dying, his footsteps crunching the ground, frozen with blood, beneath him. He heard his deceased loved ones calling his name, while Clement's defiant screams rang hollow in his ears. In one instance, Hope stood hauntingly pale atop the raging sea, her porcelain skin pricked with goosebumps as cold rain pelted her frail figure. She seemed to be saying something, but from his vantage point on the edge of a great precipice, he could not hear her. He couldn't hear her. In another place and time, he felt icy water filling his lungs. He heaved for oxygen, but with every desperate gasp, he choked on the rush of salt sea through his nose and mouth. At that moment of abject helplessness and despair, he saw her floating in the great, green deep, her chocolate hair soaked with blood, her body broken apart like a wood shack after a hurricane. He desperately swam to her, but she faded and faded into the deep. He could not reach her. His mind flashed from one dark place to the next without mercy, until he was awakened by a loud knock at the door.

He sat up, shorts and sheets drenched with sweat, and reached for his watch. It was nearly 11am. The door was pounded again and his head throbbed with each rhythmic bang. He immediately confessed to himself that stopping to buy those bottles of whisky on the way home was not the best decision he had recently made.

"Hold on, give me a minute," he called, shielding his eyes against the bright, mid-morning sun.

He stood and put on Marty's trousers, then noticed Henry's newspaper, folded neatly on the kitchen table resting next to his half–empty coffee mug and a small dish with crumbs left behind. He would have—he should have—come home after work, washed the dishes and finished the newspaper. He would have listened to his favorite radio show at 8pm, drank a cold glass of milk, and crawled into his lonely bed, only to do it all again the next day.

Thierry took a moment to compose himself before he answered the door.

"I'm sorry, kid," Marty said despondently, his own face tear soaked and red.

"What are you doing here?" Thierry asked impatiently, sleepily.

"Let me in, T.," Marty said as he brushed his way by his younger brother and into the apartment. He sat at the table and then asked if there was any coffee on.

"No, you woke me up. That's pop's from yesterday," he said with a pointed finger.

"This is awful, I just don't know what else to say," Marty remarked, glancing down at the cheap china.

"It's all awful," Thierry answered.

"I guess that's life, kid."

"No," Thierry replied, his hangover numbs quickly turning the corner into anger in his brother's presence. "There are some things that are not, 'life.'"

"What are you talkin' about? People have accidents, they get sick and old and die—it's gonna happen to all of us one day."

"Accidents?" the young one asked, running a hand quickly through his hair.

"Yeah, accidents," Marty answered nonchalantly.

"Accidents..." Thierry repeated, his breathing pattern quickening. "Davey Ferraro—who's folks still live over on Morgan Street—getting sawed in half by machine gun fire right in front of my eyes—that was an accident?"

"Oh, kid—"

"Or me, getting nearly eaten by a cannibal, getting captured by the fucking SS, and put in a pen like an animal to freeze to death—was that an accident, too?"

"You're misreading me, kid—"

"And what about Hope?" Thierry blurted out in an instant.

Marty bit his lip and leaned back against the table.

"Is that what this is all about, Thierry?" he asked.

Thierry stood silent in a near combative posture, like a tiger ready to pounce. Marty laughed incredulously and shook his head.

"Don't you fucking laugh at that," Thierry said.

"So what exactly is it that you're saying, kid? Help me get this straight in my own mind—is there something that you would like to accuse me of?"

"I'd like to know the truth."

"The truth?"

Thierry nodded his head urgently.

"Look—this is ridiculous. Pop just passed last night. Now is not the time or the place for accusations and slander—"

"The truth?"

"You're incredible," Marty answered, standing to his feet. "The only father we've ever known gets sucked into the gears of a two-ton metal shredder, and you can't even take a minute to get off your self-pity train and—"

"Self-pity?" Thierry asked, his eyes widening as far as they would. "That's what you think this is?"

"Yeah, I do," Marty answered coldly. "Your girlfriend, who you hadn't even seen in a year—"

"Excuse me, but I was in the middle of a world war, for God's sake."

"Yeah, and she's a red blooded, pretty young girl, and you never should have asked her to wait for you, not knowing if you'd even ever come back in one piece!"

"We were in love, you piece of shit!" he blurted out, his voice rising in tone for the first time.

"Yeah? And how would that have worked out if you came back a mangled mess, a vegetable or something—was she just supposed to put a ring on your finger and bid farewell to any kind of happiness she might have known?"

"You're out of your mind," Thierry replied, putting both hands on his head.

"So this girl, this puppy love of yours, you just expect her to go along with whatever happens, you can't see her, you can't even tell her you're coming home—and for all that she knows, you're shacked up with some French milkmaid outside Bordeaux."

"Shut your mouth."

"This dame of yours, she slips and has an accident—"

"With you—"

"—A *terrible* accident," Marty replied, raising his index finger. "And a year later, a full year later, and not twelve hours after pop dies, you wanna accuse me of—I'm just trying to get this straight—you wanna open the door to me, your big brother, who loves you, and accuse me to my face of murder—is that it?"

"I just want the truth," Thierry answered firmly.

"The truth?" Marty replied almost mockingly. "Well I want some truth, too."

"What are you talking about?"

"I wanna know what you've been up to with my girl."

Thierry stood in nervous silence.

"Yeah," Marty said with a knowing chuckle. "I want to hear from your own mouth that you didn't kiss her."

"I did kiss her, okay?" Thierry answered. "We had both been drinking—and for God's sake we were waiting for you to come back—and we stopped."

"You mutually stopped—or did she stop you?"

"Look, nothing would have happened—"

"You're my kid brother, and I love you, but you ever lay a hand on her again, a hug, a handshake—hell, if you even look at her in a way that I don't approve, I swear to God I will beat you to death."

"You're really somethin.'"

"You don't think I'm serious?"

"I think you're a piece of shit. Does Vivian know about Ruth?"

"That's between the two of us," Marty answered curtly.

"Vivian's too good for you."

"Listen, kid, she's got some baggage of her own—"

"She's still too good to be with you."

"And what—you think she'd be better off with you?"

"I didn't say that," Thierry answered, feeling a sudden twinge of guilt.

"It was kind of implied, don't you think?"

The two brothers breathed in unison.

"At least I'm headed somewhere," Marty broke back in. "At least I've got a big future ahead of me and some powerful people who are gonna help me get there. Who are you that women should just fawn and fall at your feet—an unemployed former soldier with no education, no money, no skills?"

"Is that how you see me?" Thierry answered quietly. He tried to let his anger shield him from the hurt these words caused, but to no avail. They sank in his soul like an anvil in the ocean.

"Look, T.," Marty said, feeling a little remorseful, a little embarrassed for his last choice of words. "You know I love you—"

"I just want the truth, Marty," Thierry said slowly, hand over his heart.

"I came over here today to tell you that I was sorry about last night, and that the funeral is tomorrow at church at nine," the older one answered, moving past his brother and opening the door to the hall. "If you want the truth, read the newspapers," he said dismissively, while cupping the younger one's head with one hand.

Marty looked his kid brother over, but they both avoided eye contact.

"I gotta go—Viv's waiting."

Thierry nodded silently, eyes glued to his father's coffee cup.

"Nice pants, by the way," said Marty.

With that, the door closed behind him.

SEVEN

No one feels another person's grief; no one understands another person's joy. People imagine that they can reach each other. In truth, they only pass each other by.

FRANZ SCHUBERT

September 15, 1945

Thierry did not attend Henry's funeral. This would prove to be one of the greatest regrets of his life.

He spent that week drowning in grief and cheap whisky. His nightmares were constant, and he would often wake up curled and sobbing. In the moments when he was most sober, he feared the terror that would be ushered in by sleep, but in much the same fashion he feared consciousness and the deep pain with which it burdened him.

Early in the week, the phone rang several times until he unplugged it. There were knocks at the door that went unanswered. He left the radio on continually, tuned to a frequency of that carried only static, just to not have to wallow in silence. He thought nothing of his life, nor of his future.

This particular morning, he awoke, head spinning and aching, cold in his own small bed. He was used to sweating through his sheets, but this was different. He reached his hand down and confirmed that he was lying in a pool of his own urine. It was dark and smelled like alcohol. He felt ashamed.

Slowly, he took the old bandage off his bad hand and stretched his fingers cautiously. He gathered some clean clothes, soap, and a towel and headed down to the community shower on the floor below where he bathed for the first time since Henry died. He began to feel human again and his week-long stupor began to feel like one big, foggy dream. He brushed his teeth and combed his hair, shaved, and put on a bit of Henry's bargain brand aftershave. He looked himself over in the mirror, dark bags under his bloodshot eyes. He snorted and cupped warm water in his hands to wash his shaved whiskers down the drain.

He cooked himself breakfast, after turning the radio off, and realized it was the first meal he remembered eating that week. He sat down at the small table in the apartment and left Henry's breakfast plate and coffee mug untouched. He couldn't bring himself, for some reason, to dispose of what he felt to be the last remaining proof of his adoptive father's life.

He took the sheets off his bed and did his best to clean his bodily fluid from his boyhood mattress. He remembered those nights he spent crying himself to sleep, pining for the comfort of his mother and the attention of his brother.

He sat at the table with a mug full of hot coffee and numb senses. He didn't want to talk to anyone; he didn't want to have to pretend anything, but at the same time, he was desperately lonely and needed some kind of human connection. He went down to the corner stand and picked up a newspaper, which he sat and read on a park bench until the schools let out and some teenagers began to play baseball at the diamond across the way. He walked over to the dilapidated wood fence from which Henry so often watched him play and stood vigil over the game. He smiled at the youthful innocence of the players, the youthful innocence of the game itself, and for the first time, his soul felt soothed. He cheered the runs that were scored, chuckled at the errors committed, and even caught a foul ball.

As the sun fell, the players began abandoning the field one by one, and a growing sense of dread fell over Thierry. He turned and began to walk home, but began to wander aimlessly, fearing being alone. As he paced through the center of town, he heard a voice call to him and had to turn to see from whence it came. The voice called again, and his eyes met a youngish girl standing in the alley between a run-down bar and the shoe repair shop.

"Handsome young chap like you headed home alone tonight?" she asked with a playful, albeit gap-toothed, smile. She wasn't particularly pretty, and her eyes were glazed over, though alert.

"How much?" he asked.

"A dollar," she replied slowly, twirling a strand of her lanky reddish hair around her finger.

"Have a couple drinks first?"

She nodded and turned the corner into the bar. He followed her, and they sat down at a table near the back. After two or three whiskies, a couple of cigarettes, and not much conversation, she told him she had a room they could use upstairs, but that he would have to pay up front. He fished three quarters, two dimes, and five pennies from his pocket and handed them over to her. She stood and handed the coins to the bartender, who put them in a jar under the counter.

She led Thierry up a dark staircase, their steps creaking loudly as they went, and down a narrow corridor with doors every few feet on either side, and into a room that wasn't much bigger than the twin-sized bed it housed. There were no windows, and the room smelled like must and body odor. She began to undress him and told him that he could call her Little Daisy, if he wished. He shrugged his shoulders.

When they were finished, he asked if he could hold her. She told him it would be an additional fifty cents for her time. He asked if she believed he was good for it, and when she replied that she didn't, he fished the appropriate change from his pants on the floor. She tucked the money under the mattress.

Thierry held Little Daisy's emaciated body close to his, being sure her slight weight did not fall on his bruised hand, and couldn't help but shiver. She sighed with boredom, but reflected on how easy this money was. After what seemed like ten or fifteen minutes, she sat up abruptly and told him that his time was up. It was the first time he noticed the bruise on her cheekbone and the cuts on her wrists.

"You've been a sweet boy," she said, pecking him the on lips. "Come and see me again sometime."

With that, she fished the change out from under the mattress, stood, and began to dress again. She fluffed her hair, applied some lipstick in the small, grimy mirror on the back of the door, and said, "Make sure you're outta here in five minutes, okay? Unless you want some trouble, that is."

And with that, she was gone.

He dressed quickly and quietly and headed straight home with only a stop at the liquor store.

He had nightmares again that night.

September 16, 1945

Thierry was wakened by a knock on the door. He thought by the light that it might be early morning, but his watch told him it was after noon.

"Who is it?" he asked groggily.

"It's your brother. Open the door."

He sat up and swung his legs over the bed slowly. He said, "Be there in a minute."

Thierry rinsed his mouth out in the sink, ran his hand through his hair, and opened the door. Had he not been hungover in such a bad way, had he been thinking in his own mind, he probably never would have opened the door to Marty.

"What do you want?" he asked impertinently.

Marty chuckled, "Glad to see you, too," and brushed himself into the small apartment. He placed Thierry's dress uniform, freshly laundered and folded, on the side table near the door. He took a quick look around and grimaced at the filth everywhere he looked. Empty glass bottles strewn about, vomit stains caked on the carpet near the bed, and Henry's coffee growing a thin coat of slimy mold on its surface.

"You got a science experiment going on here, or something?" he asked sarcastically.

Thierry replied with a shrug.

"Well," Marty continued. "Glad to see you're holding up so good."

"Why did you come here?"

"To check up on my little brother, that's why," Marty answered. "I stopped calling days ago after the phone wouldn't ring. I even sent Mabel from the church by here a few times, and you never came to the door. Once, she heard you snoring, so at least we knew you were alive."

"Well, I'm alive," Thierry answered, running his tongue subconsciously over his scarred lip.

"So, what are you gonna do?" Marty asked, brushing off a kitchen chair before sitting down.

"I suppose I've got to get that figured out."

"Yeah," Marty said, nodding his head and chewing the inside of his cheek.

The two brothers were silent for several moments.

"Hey, you mind if I put some coffee on?" Marty asked.

"Go ahead," Thierry replied, making his way back to his bed. He sat on the edge of it and worked his socks off from the day before.

"Hot out today," Marty remarked as he lit the stove.

"Is it?"

"Yeah, it is," the older brother answered. "I don't remember it being this warm in September when we were kids, you know?"

"Is that right?" Thierry answered as politely as he could. He wasn't so much angry with his brother at this moment as he was annoyed to be intruded upon in such a way.

"It always seemed to me like fall came early—like summer never lasted long enough."

"I never minded; I always liked autumn."

Marty shrugged. "I never liked the cold."

"I just liked the World Series coming around," Thierry answered. "Something special about that time of year."

"I guess. It just seems like you went from running around outside and having the time of your life to freezing your ass off as soon as school started."

"I don't remember it like that."

Marty shrugged and asked if Thierry wanted coffee.

"Look, I'm here for another reason, too," Marty said, handing Thierry a hot mug.

"Oh yeah?" came the curt reply.

"Yeah, on business."

"You gonna sell me a vacuum cleaner or something?"

Marty chuckled and took a thick envelope from his inside jacket pocket and tossed it on the bed next to his brother.

"Turns out pops had a little rainy day fund."

Thierry opened the envelope and sobriety hit him between the eyes.

"How much is this?" he asked incredulously.

"Five grand," Marty answered. "And some change."

Thierry felt the weight of the money in his hands. "This is ours?"

With a shake of his head Marty replied, "No, that's yours."

Thierry stared down at the money and could hardly hold back his emotions, though he wasn't quite sure what he was feeling.

"You can chase that down the bottom of a bottle a long way, if that's what you want," Marty said.

"Where did this come from?"

"From a magical reindeer who flew in my window last night—what do you mean, where did it come from? Henry had a bank account and apparently ever since Henrietta died, he's been putting money in every week from his check. No withdrawals; just deposits."

"I can't believe it," Marty answered, still staring down at the crisp, green bills. "I mean, I'm not surprised, I guess—but I still can't believe it."

"Believe it. There was close to twelve grand in the account. The will stated one thousand went to church, the rest split equally between you and me."

Thierry sat in stunned silence, leafing through the money with his thumb and thinking back on all the hard work Henry put in to earn it. He thought about how his pops hadn't thought for a minute about spending it on himself—buy a car or moving to a nicer apartment or anything—he just saved and saved. Henry had been content with his life. In a melancholy way, this made Thierry smile.

"Well," Marty broke the silence. "Aren't you gonna thank me?"

"What do I have to thank you for?"

Marty shrugged and looked about the room again.

"I dunno," he answered. "Bringing you your money?"

"This was pop's money."

"Okay, well then, maybe you could thank me for taking care of all the business that surrounded his death, then."

Thierry gnawed on the corner of his upper lip and stared his brother in the eyes.

"Oh, and nice of you to come to the funeral and all," Marty continued, his tone increasing in sarcasm. "You showed some real class, kid."

That one hurt. Thierry lowered his eyes and fought back tears. His head suddenly began to pound and he felt like he would be sick. He sniffled and cleared his throat.

"Did you go to Hope's funeral?" the young one asked quietly, looking back up at his brother's face.

Marty shook his head.

"No, I didn't," he answered.

Thierry nodded and began chewing his lip again. "I thought you two were such good friends and all—"

"We were," Marty said, and for the first time, Thierry sensed that his brother was being honest. It perplexed him greatly. "I wanted to go, believe me, but, my attorney didn't think it would be a good idea."

"Your attorney?" Thierry repeated, trying to wrap his head around his brother's logic.

"Yes, my attorney. He didn't think it would be good for the family for me to show up, since I'd been taken into custody and all—but I will remind you, by that point the police had already cleared me of any wrongdoing."

"The police cleared you?" Thierry repeated again. The older one nodded and cast a sidelong glance toward the stove. "Marty, I'm your brother—tell me what happened."

"I told you already, kid, read it in the papers."

"I don't believe what's in the papers!" Thierry blurted out.

"Why not? The police, the reporters—everyone's dug through that case a hundred times, and I've been cleared of any wrongdoing!"

"That's why I don't believe it," Thierry answered, his eyes filling again.

"What do you want from me?" Marty replied.

"I want you to tell me that you didn't do anything wrong—that you didn't… hurt my Hope."

Marty sat silently for a long moment, watching tears stream down his younger brother's face. He swallowed with some effort and then spoke slowly, "Hope was my friend—a good friend—and nothing more. I hate that she died. But I gotta tell you, little brother—I know you had a rough go of it growing up, and God only knows what you suffered during the war, but you are the only person alive in this world who thinks that I did something to hurt her, and life's not gonna get any easier for you if you don't let that go."

Thierry sat in stunned silence and suddenly the idea that he was losing his grip on reality flashed before his consciousness. His mind's eye raced through so many events that he couldn't see them all. He picked out a thought about losing his mother here, Clement's shack there, Hope's face, the nightmares, Henry's loss, the girls on the train, and feelings for Vivian that he couldn't quench, and began to think that something in his brain had snapped—he suddenly felt crazy. After all, who was he to question a police investigation? Who was he to question the integrity of the newspaper writers who wrote such detailed and matter-of-fact reports on the incident? The truth was, he didn't have any evidence, he didn't have proof of anything. He then felt a sharp stab of guilt for hating his brother the way he did—he looked at Marty's face and tried to read it for something real, something true, and then decided that even if he saw something there, how could it be relied upon as evidence to accuse him inwardly of murder?

"Hey kid, you don't look good," Marty said, getting up from his chair. He searched around for a glass but couldn't find one in the mess on the counter top, so he emptied his coffee mug and rinsed it out. "Drink some water or something, okay?"

He handed Thierry the mug, and he swigged it down fast.

"I don't feel good, Marty," he said, putting a hand to his forehead and letting the mug roll out of the other onto the floor.

"Yeah, it's okay, kid, lay down," the older one answered, helping his younger brother back onto the bed. "The way you've been living, it's no surprise," he said with a chuckle.

Thierry didn't see much humor in it and rolled on his side, facing the wall. Marty stood up and had another disgusted look around the room.

"Okay, well, you rest up. The money's on the table—hire a maid or something for gossake would ya?"

There was no answer from the young one.

"And by the way," Marty continued, moving toward the door. "Turns out the rent is paid through the end of year, so you've got some time to figure things out, okay?"

Thierry was relieved by the fact that things had been so taken care of for him. No pressure to move on, no pressure to do anything. He could just rot if he wanted to. And he wanted to.

Marty opened the door and stepped halfway into it. His mind took him back to his youth, to that little boy on the cot who would cry in his lap. He felt his own guilt for innumerable wrongs he had committed, several of which stood out hauntingly. He felt deep and true sorrow for his kid brother like he hadn't since he was a kid himself. He fought through his own tears as he said, "I love you, T. Never forget that, okay?" and closed the door behind him.

In the hallway, sitting idle and meek, Marty found a leather suitcase—edges worn and peeling, color faded, and cracked. He hadn't remembered bringing it up with him. He felt the stiff handle and ran his finger along the dull metal clasp. He opened it up on the floor, shielding his eyes from its contents, and stuffed his guilt, his shame, and his remorse down into it and locked it tight. He stood it back up, and the thumb of his right hand caressed the dry crimson leather. He left it in the hallway and moved quickly down the stairs, not looking back.

Pamela was in the car waiting for him, and the roll of Henry's money was burning a hole in his pocket.

December 14, 1945

The Yankees finished six and a half games behind the Detroit Tigers, who would go on to win their second World Series, both to that point over a certain team from Chicago. That World Series would see the Cubs cursed by a goat. Had the Yankees done better, it might have been enough to stir Thierry from his stupor, but as it was, the only baseball news that grabbed his attention, albeit for just a brief moment, was the signing of Jackie Robinson that month. The United Nations was established, the Cleveland Rams won the NFL championship, the Chinese civil war began, and civilian rationing of food and shoes came to an end. All of these momentous events went generally unnoticed by our young hero, who found no reason to rouse himself from his degenerate slumber. He drank more whisky than most people drink water and gambled more money away than most people made in an annum. He slept with a multitude of whores, mostly because he detested seeing the same one twice, and nearly always paid extra to lie next to them after the initial act was finished. He was wild, but never quite out of control—he might have had the inner fortitude to stop this lifestyle but couldn't ever think of a good excuse. Finally, in the midst of his downward spiral of self-loathing and self-injury, the whisky ceased to taste like it had and the women began to look the same. He had reached a point after months of debauchery where it no longer appealed to him. It did not repulse him, but it did not appeal to him either. That, and the legacy envelope Henry had left him was nearly two grand lighter, and he had nothing whatsoever to show for it. For this, he felt true guilt, and this was the morning of December 14, 1945.

He showered and shaved, pressed a clean shirt and trousers, and ate a quick breakfast. He caught a bus from the front of the courthouse to the library in Passaic, and then another one to a post office in Clifton, and from there, he walked over the line into Bloomfield and up to the auto repair shop on the corner of West Passaic and East Passaic Avenues that was owned by his late wartime friend, Robbie Fontaine's father, Pasquale. He peered into the open garage door, a mid-30's pickup truck jacked up in it, but saw no one. When he opened the door into the office, a bell jangled and a miserable old mutt with hip dysplasia sleepily craned his neck toward the visitor.

"Hello?" Thierry called.

Pasquale emerged from the small back room, wiping his grease–stained hand with a grease–stained rag.

"Can I helpa you?" he asked gruffly.

"Yes sir," Thierry replied, removing his hat. "My name is Thierry Laroque. I was a friend of Robbie's in Europe—I wrote to you about some work."

Pasquale looked him over intently. He was a man with a rough exterior, with dry, cracked hands, and dark, hairy skin, but his eyes betrayed his inner depth and even intelligence.

"I write-a you back two months ago," he stated, motioning passionately with his hands. "You no a-getta my letter?"

"I did, sir—"

"And you no need-a no work then?"

Thierry paused and nodded his head in acknowledgment. "I apologize, sir, but I was dealing with the loss of my fiancee and my father—"

"Is that the negro?" Pasquale interjected.

"Well," Thierry began with a bite of his lip. "I don't take too kindly to that expression—"

The short Italian waved his hand in apology. "I don't mean-a nothing by it. I'm a-sorry for your loss," and with that he crossed himself.

"Thank you," Thierry answered. "And I'm sorry for not replying to you in a timely manner. I understand if you don't need the help right now—"

"I need-a the help!" Pasquale nearly shouted. "I been a-needing the help for months now since that last *faccia di merda* left-a me high and dry!"

"Well, I would be glad to—"

"You start-a tomorrow. Be here a-five forty-five and a-you leave at three-thirty. I pay forty-cents an hour until I see what-a you can do."

"That would be excellent," Thierry answered with a smile that left his inner happiness at the arrangement undisguised.

The two men shook hands, and Pasquale mumbled something in Italian, then retreated again to the back room.

It took four buses for Thierry to get home. He passed the liquor store and ignored Little Daisy's cat calls from under the street lamp outside of the dingy bar where he'd flushed so much of his father's money away. He ate a sandwich and some dill pickles for dinner and got to bed early.

Another nightmare woke him up in a trembling sweat an hour before he needed to start the day, but he started the day anyway. He caught his first bus at four thirty-five, and arrived at Pasquale's at five thirty-five to see the squat old man already working on the same truck from the day before.

"You know how to change-a the oil?" Pasquale called, not looking up from underneath the truck.

"I do," Thierry answered.

"Then start on-a that one over-dere," he said, pointing his nubby finger at the late model Cadillac in the next bay. Thierry tossed his overcoat and hat on the rack in the office and got to work.

December 24, 1945

When Thierry left Pasquale's shop on Christmas Eve, he stopped at the liquor store and bought a fifth of nice Scotch. He spent the night with a middle-aged woman called Fiesty Frida and did not remember Christmas day at all. It turned out that Marty had tried calling him several times from Vivian's parent's house in Schaumburg, Illinois, to wish him a Merry Christmas, but no one answered the phone. Thierry was back at work at five thirty-five on the morning of December 26.

February 15, 1946

Thierry had worked hard enough and smart enough to earn Pasquale's good favor and a raise to fifty-five cents an hour. Though they never talked about Robbie, Pasquale couldn't help but feel a kinship to the young Franco–American, and was certainly happy to have a young and honest worker around the shop. Thierry was thrilled, himself, to have stable employment and a reason to wake up in the morning. The only thing that was already growing old on him, however, was the commute to work every morning, so he bought a paper on the way home and began searching the classifieds for apartments in Bloomfield. He would make calls in the morning.

He had been much more conscious of how much he drank, and was overly cautious on nights before a working day. Oddly, he thought less of Hope than he had in a long while and more of Vivian, though he had not seen her since the night Henry passed. Being clear-headed when he got home, Thierry sat down to write a letter to an old friend.

Dr. Baier,

I am sorry that it's been so long since I've written. I received your letter before Christmas and am glad to hear that you are in good health. I wish that I could say the same about my own self. It's impossible to fully explain, but if there is a soul on this planet who might understand how I feel and might be able to offer direction, I believe that it is you.

I found a job repairing cars with the father of a fallen soldier who was a friend of mine. I am thankful for the work as it keeps me motivated and helps to keep my mind occupied. The biggest problem I have, in fact, is my racing mind. I feel like I think more than normal people and sometimes am caught in a whirlpool of my own thoughts. I feel trapped by them at times, and I start to panic. I believe that I am a rational person, which is why I don't understand when my rational thoughts lead me to irrational conclusions, which leads bad behavior. After the bad behavior, I feel shame, which feeds the fire of depression and numbness that I feel.

I have been drinking far too much and, if I'm honest, have taken the company of many women, and for this I feel the worst. Before the war, when I was with Hope, all of my energy and all of my passion were directed at her—I couldn't comprehend the idea that there were other women in the world. I was all hers and she was all mine. Our love was tender, it was true, and it was real love—albeit mistimed by our youth and the lack of a marriage certificate. And I feel that when I go to sleep with another woman nowadays, I'm craving that connection I felt with her, but I feel more like an animal than anything else. On top of this, I have spent my father's hard-earned money on these vices and more, and for this, I again feel even more guilt.

In the spirit of true honesty, I also feel guilty that I think of my precious Hope less and less—in fact, some days I only think of her in my subconscious. I see her almost every night in my dreams—or in my nightmares. Sometimes this fosters fear rather than fondness of her memory. In her place, I find myself often thinking about Vivian with great tenderness, but as you know, she is my brother's girl, and I am sure they will be married soon. I cannot help but feel, though, that she and I were meant for each other, maybe in a different life or something, as the Hindus are fond of saying.

At the same time, my mind races from numbness to hatred for my own brother. I cannot stand the person he has become—arrogant and wholly selfish. He treats Vivian as a pet and not like she deserves to be treated. He sleeps with other women and flaunts it to the world. And again, I know that this is irrational, but I cannot for the life of me shake the feeling deep down that he had something to do with Hope's death, that he is responsible for it in some way—whether it was an accident or intentional, I don't know, but I feel very strongly that he is hiding something. I just don't know what that is.

Thank you, doctor, for allowing me to express these things to you. I don't have anyone else that I truly trust to share my feelings with. I hope and pray that this letter finds you well and that your beloved Deutschland is recovering to sanity. I am thankful every day that that damn war is over. Maybe the world can find some peace at last, even if its soldiers cannot.

Yours truly,

—Thierry

He sealed the letter and tossed it casually next to his keys on the table near the front door. He poured a glass of Scotch and downed it quickly. He stared at the bottle in his right hand and heard it call his name. Its voice was Vivian's. After several more drinks, he passed out on the floor next to his bed.

May 3, 1946

The rent was much higher in Bloomfield, but Thierry found a room that he could afford over the garage behind an older lady's house. Her name was Mrs. Parrish, and her husband had passed away the previous year. The room was very small, but had its own bathroom and shower, a luxury to which the young man was unaccustomed. In exchange for even cheaper rent than had been advertised, Thierry negotiated to help Mrs. Parrish take care of the lawn and perform basic home repairs when needed. She was a kind woman and would often have a hot meal ready for him when he got home from work.

He had been living comfortably and enjoying the spring weather. Baseball was back in season, and although he hadn't had the chance yet to see the Yankees play, he had taken the chance to see the Newark Eagles of the Negro League a couple times at Ruppert Stadium.

Pasquale had been teaching him more and more about cars and fixing them, and Thierry was starting to suspect that he was a natural. He loved the work, he loved his customers—most of them—and he loved his paychecks most of all.

His struggles with his vices continued, although he was able to continue to keep them from his employer and even his landlord. In the twilight of the day he felt a pressure on his chest that would not relent until he fell asleep—or passed out. He wondered if his letter had made its way safely to its intended recipient, and he wished for a response that might alleviate his mental suffering.

On this particular night, a Friday, he found himself coming out of the back of a seedy bar, inebriated and wobbly on his feet. He stumbled into the alley outside and was shoved roughly from the side. He tumbled over a rusty metal trash can and heard a crack in his wrist when he caught himself awkwardly on the pavement. He grimaced and rage welled within him. He flew to his feet to see a couple of young boys fleeing around the corner. He dashed after them and, though he was only able to catch one, beat him thoroughly and left him lying face down in the street. Panting, his wrist began to throb and shake uncontrollably.

He had sobered up by the time he reached the hospital. The good news was that his wrist was only sprained. The bad news was that he had contracted gonorrhea. He left with a tight bandage around his wrist and a bottle of antibiotics. He had a three-ounce pour of whisky to help dull the pain and was in bed at 3am.

May 5, 1946

Monday morning.

He was on time for work, but he looked rough. And his wrist was bandaged heavily.

Needless to say, Pasquale was not thrilled.

"How-a you expect me to have you-a in my shop looking like a *merda calda?* In front of my customers?"

"I'm sorry, I just—"

"No excuses! Today-a, you go home. And-a tomorrow, you come back, clean and nice looking—or you no work-a here-a-no more!"

Thierry nodded his head somberly and tried to voice an apology. Pasquale just waved his greasy hand and headed in towards the garage.

The young man was embarrassed. The weekend had hit him rough and had made him for the first time really look like the addict he was becoming. He went home and lay on his bed, work clothes still on. He decided again in his mind that his life would have to change. He couldn't go on like this, or he would find himself jobless and most likely homeless.

He slept until the mid-afternoon when the sound of the postman's truck awoke him. He splashed some water in his face and went down to get the mail. There was a letter from Dr. Baier which, after he dropped Mrs. Parrish's letters in the slot in the front door, he ran upstairs to read.

My dear boy,

Thank you for your letter. Thank you for your confidence in me. I hope you know that I look upon you as a son. My heart has been heavy ever since reading your letter. I wish I knew better how to help you think through some of the things that have been tormenting you.

The best thing that I can tell you is to forgive. There is nothing more destructive to the human spirit than holding on to an offense. I hope you don't take my words as hurtful, but I must try to speak the truth to you in the best way I know how.

Take my son, for instance. He grew to be a man who could not forgive, even a perceived slight. He held on to his rights and his demands over the rights of any other person, and look what he turned into—a monster. It pains me to say it to this day, and perhaps this is why I am so wary of what you've written to me. Of course, I don't believe you are a monster, but I believe that there is only one place where your pain and your shame can lead you. Let my son be an example of where that path ends.

You have not had an easy life, that is most true. But you are so young, you are so strong, and so gentle in spirit. You can make yourself into the man you wish to be, there is still time.

So, forgive my son for the way he hurt you. Forgive Clement for his violence against you. Forgive Hitler, and Himmler, and Goering, and Goebbels, and Heydrich. Forgive the soldiers who murdered your friends. Forgive your brother for whatever he is, and most importantly of all, you might just at the end of the day, find the strength and the peace of heart to forgive yourself.

There is a path to freedom, dear Thierry, but you must chose it.

I am in good health and pray for you constantly. Again, I wish I could do more to help. Please don't wait so long to write again, I look forward to hearing from you very soon.

Best wishes and love,

—Jurgen

Thierry held the letter in his right hand and wiped his tears with his sleeve. He began to sob, but he didn't quite know why—he read the letter over and over again but couldn't quite make sense of it. Even in the deluge of thoughts and emotions swirling round his mind, he was struck by these words somewhere deep in chest.

He had a hard time falling asleep that night, and when he did, he had nightmares.

The next morning, he was clean shaven and properly dressed and an extra ten minutes early for work. Pasquale showed up about five minutes after he got there and acted like nothing had happened the previous day. This was a relief for Thierry.

June 5, 1951

As the years went on, Thierry, like the nation after the war, began to heal. He enjoyed his work with Pasquale thoroughly and was now trusted to man the shop by himself while the old man took trips down the shore with his wife. The business had grown steadily as more and more people were able to afford to purchase cars, which, quite naturally, turned into more demand for automobile service. Pasquale refused, however, to put a gas pump on the lot, however, feeling it was beneath his dignity to pump gas for customers.

Thierry spoke with his brother from time to time—usually around holidays; although, Marty did make a point to call to let his brother know that Vivian had accepted his proposal of marriage. The ceremony was set for a Saturday in October in Chicago, and Marty sincerely hoped his kid brother could attend. Thierry didn't say much and certainly didn't promise to make the trip all the way to Chicago, but he did read and reread Dr. Baier's letter from years before once he hung up the telephone. He closed his eyes and repeated in his mind that he had forgiven his brother—for what trespass he did not name, because, quite frankly, he couldn't. He had one small drink and lay back down on his bed. He had been doing a lot better with his alcohol habit, allowing himself only a single drink only a couple nights per week, and he had steered clear of the brothels and bad parts of town altogether. He had been completely celibate for over a year now. He did cry himself to sleep that night, however, confused about what he thought over Vivian marrying his brother. Even if she couldn't be with him, why was she making such a bold and intentional mistake by tying her life to Marty?

During the time that elapsed since receiving Dr. Baier's "forgiveness" letter, he had done everything he could to mold himself into the person he wished to be—he went above and beyond the call of duty in helping Mrs. Parrish with chores and maintenance around the house, he began to volunteer at a soup kitchen which served the homeless in Newark, and saved every penny he possibly could.

He met several truly nice girls along the way, too. He sometimes went out of his way to avoid them in public places, because even though he had long been clear of the clap, he didn't trust himself to be completely proper and well-intentioned with a young lady just yet. The longer he went, however, without female company, the more he found himself dwelling on Hope. He began to dream of her almost every night. He would often wake in the morning feeling so somber that he couldn't stay in that dream world with her that he had the hardest time finding the motivation to get out of bed. Usually, however, after a couple cups of coffee, he felt better and began to greet the world with expectation again.

About an hour after he got home from work that evening, and after he finished changing the oil in Mrs. Parrish's '47 Chrysler Town & Country, he received a phone call from Marty.

"Hey bro, how you doing?"

"I'm hanging in there, how bout you?"

He's forgiven, he's forgiven, he's forgiven…

"Doing okay—hey I was wondering, the old piece of shit's been making a really bad noise when I get up to speed—like a real bad clanking noise."

"Okay, well—do you want to bring it by and I can take a look at it?"

"Yeah, yeah—how's Saturday look for you?"

"Nothing on the schedule—bring it by."

"Sounds good, I'll see you around noon on Saturday."

"Wait, is Vivian coming?"

Thierry thought he detected the slightest hesitation.

"Maybe later on, why?"

"Oh, I was just wondering—I haven't seen you two since the engagement, and I wanted to congratulate her—and clean up my place if you were both coming."

I'm such a bad liar.

"Yeah, well, if I've got to leave the car with you or something, she might come pick me up and take me back to the city."

"Okay, well, sounds good—I'll see you Saturday."

"See you Saturday."

June 9, 1951

Thierry awoke early and restless. Before the sun rose, he was out walking the streets around his neighborhood. There were several rows of houses under construction; he paused by them and wondered briefly if he would ever own a home of his own, fill it with a charming and good–natured wife and curly–haired, rambunctious children. Maybe even a dog. He'd never owned a pet. He wouldn't even know what to do with a dog. But he was sure the children of his future dreams would adore it.

There was something gnawing at him on the inside, but oddly enough, he didn't even feel like it was the impending visit from his brother. In some strange way, he believed it would be just like old times, although he wasn't sure what he was basing his hopes on, or even what memories of good times past he might be reminiscing for.

As the sun rose, he started back towards his home, past the small grammar school his future children might someday attend. The air was warm and much more humid than it had been. He wiped his damp forehead with his sleeve and stared for a moment down at the sweat stain it left behind.

That morning, he mowed the lawn and fixed one of Mrs. Parrish's kitchen drawers that had come loose. He went back to his small apartment above the garage and showered. It was only ten. The next two hours of waiting felt like a week. The next four felt like a decade. Finally, at exactly six minutes to four, Marty pulled up in his 1942 Buick Super sedan, royal blue with tan interior. The chrome grill shined, and the white wall tires stood out in sharp contrast with the dark paint on the car's exterior. It was a thing of beauty.

It was also the last car Hope had ever been in.

"Hey, kid," Marty called from the window as he peeled rather recklessly up the narrow driveway.

"Where you been?"

"What are you talking about?" Marty called, taking off his sunglasses and stepping out of the car gracefully.

"You said noon."

"Did I?"

"Yeah," Thierry answered.

"Well, here I am!" Marty cried, pulling his younger brother close to him and embracing him roughly. "You look good, kid!"

"Do I?"

"Yeah, you do. You look like you gained some weight—in a good way. You were looking kinda thin and pale for a while there—but look at you now!—my kid brother, grease on his hands like a real working man!"

"I am a real working man," Thierry replied.

"I know! And I'm proud of you."

The brothers stood for a moment in silence.

"Well, you wanna show me your place?" Marty finally asked.

"Sure thing," Thierry answered and motioned his brother toward the garage.

After a cursory tour of the small apartment and lots of shallow compliments from Marty, the two walked back outside to the yard.

"So, you wanna tell me about the car?" Thierry asked.

"Yeah, sure. You see, every time I get up over forty or so, the thing starts making a clanging noise and it sounds real bad."

"Does it happen when you shift gears?"

"Not particularly. Seems like it's more related to the speed than the shifts."

At that moment, a shiny red Cadillac pulled up the driveway cautiously. When Vivian came into view, Thierry felt as though he'd been struck by a thunderbolt.

"Hey, sweet cheeks," Marty called with a wave.

Vivian smiled back, her bright white teeth piecing through her deep crimson lipstick.

"Hi, boys," she called melodically.

She stepped out of the car, and Thierry had to purposely look away, suddenly feeling flushed and, for some reason, embarrassed.

"You figure it out yet?" she asked casually.

"Oh, no, not yet," Marty answered. "We really hadn't been working on it too long."

"Hi, Thierry," she said sweetly.

"Hi, Viv," he replied sheepishly.

She hugged him quickly and then looked towards Marty.

"So, do you two need some more time?"

"No, I don't think so," Marty said, turning towards his brother. "Hey, kid, it's really okay for me to leave it with you for a bit? I don't want to cause you any trouble."

"Oh, it's no trouble."

"Ok good—cause we're gonna get running. We're heading down to Atlantic City for a couple nights. Do you think I could pick it up on the way back?"

"Sure. I might have to take it down to the shop depending on what's going on with it, but I should have it fixed up at least by tomorrow."

"Thanks, T.!" he said with a pat on Thierry's shoulder. "And if you get it fixed up early, feel free to take it out wherever you want, okay?"

"Thanks."

"Okay, gorgeous—you ready?"

Vivian smiled and nodded and flipped her keys over to Marty.

"Bye, Thierry," she said sweetly and hugged him again.

He couldn't help but notice the freckles on her bare and sun–kissed shoulders. *How the hell does a girl who lives in the city get so goddamn tan,* he wondered.

She moved with an effortless grace to the passenger's side of the car. Both brothers watched her as she went.

"Is that not the finest piece of ass you've ever seen in your life?" Marty asked after she closed the door.

Thierry just stared at him blankly. He was offended on so many levels. It was also the first time he noticed that he was a good two inches taller than his older brother.

"You're such an asshole, Marty," he said flatly.

The older one suddenly bent in two, hands on his knees. Thierry wasn't sure if his brother was suddenly having a heart attack or if he'd really been hurt by those words until Marty reared upright, hands on his chest, trying to breathe through a fit of uncontrollable laughter. Thierry couldn't put a finger on his emotions at the moment, but he thought it was somewhere in the area of disgust. After a good moment, Marty finally caught his breath and put his hand on his younger brother's shoulder.

"I think you might be right, kid," he said with a fat smile.

He embraced his younger brother quickly and then jumped in the red Cadillac and started it up.

"Thanks again for the car," he shouted before closing the door.

Thierry just waved as Marty peeled backwards down the driveway. Vivian waved and directed something like a sympathetic smile towards the young mechanic from the passenger's seat. In a moment, they were gone.

Alone again, he turned back towards Marty's Buick and popped the hood. He looked over the engine quickly, scanning for obvious problems. He checked the fluids and found that there was practically no oil.

How long has it been since he's changed the oil in this thing?

He started the car up and listened with a careful ear. It sounded great. He drove it the short distance to the shop and pulled it into the bay. After changing the oil, he decided it was time to try to get it up to speed and see if he could hear the horrible noise his brother had noticed. He pulled it out onto Route 3, headed east, and merged into the fast–moving traffic. Forty, fifty, sixty miles an hour and no noise. He passed a car in the right lane and gassed it up to seventy—still no noise. *What the hell was he talking about?*

He merged onto Route 21 in Rutherford going south towards Newark and gassed it again. Nothing. *Well,* he thought, *I guess I'm just going to have some fun this weekend.*

He decided he'd spend the rest of day in the sunshine and found his way to Route 9 with Point Pleasant on his mind. He reminisced for a moment about Hope and the times they had spent there, and then the guilt came. He thought he should go anyway—that she would want him to enjoy such a beautiful day, such a beautiful car, and such a beautiful drive. He asked her forgiveness for the thoughts he had about Vivian and then decided he would turn the car around and head home. It was already almost seven—what was he going to do—watch the sunset by himself?

At that moment, the car swerved violently in direct correlation with a loud popping sound. For a brief moment his mind flashed to the sound of gunfire and he instinctively ducked his head. He was able to retain control of the car, but he could hear the undeniable sound of a flat. He cursed and pulled off on the shoulder.

Other drivers whizzed past as he exited the car and opened the trunk. He pulled the donut out and was slightly surprised to see only a single tire iron beneath it. He searched in disbelief through some of the trash and random books and newspapers in the trunk to no avail. *You gotta be kidding me, Marty.* He couldn't believe that his older brother treated his car with such disrespect—not changing the oil, no lug wrench, missing tire irons. *God, it must be nice to have to care so little,* he thought with a swell of bitterness.

The sound of air brakes made him turn around. A Herman semitruck was pulling onto the shoulder behind him. Out of the cockpit jumped a well–built man who looked to be about thirty, with wavy dark hair and hands like bear paws.

"Hey, buddy, you need some help?" the truck driver asked.

"I do, but I'd hate to trouble you, sir."

"You a military man?"

"Yessir."

"What branch?"

"Army, sir."

"Europe or Japan?"

"Europe."

"I was in the Pacific," the brawny driver answered casually. "Navy." Thierry nodded his head. "You see much action?"

Thierry nodded silently. "You?"

The driver nodded silently.

Then, the good Samaritan extended his bear paw and said, "My name's Pete, and I'm already done with my runs, just headed towards home, so, whatever you'd be needing's no trouble at all."

"Thank you, sir," Thierry answered. "I'm Thierry."

"Thierry?" Pete answered, pronouncing the name remarkably well, considering the nearly deafening sound of the truck engine. "It's nice to meet you. What seems to be the problem?"

"Got a flat on my brother's car here, and the big dummy doesn't have tire irons or even a lug wrench back here."

"Well, I know I don't have anything that'll help you get that tire on in the truck, but I do know of a shop a few miles up the road. Hop in and I'll take you."

"Thank you very much," Thierry replied as he climbed into the cab.

"So," Pete started, checking his mirrors and merging back onto the road. "What kind of name is Thierry?"

"French."

"Are you first generation or were you born over there?"

"My parents came a few years before I was born."

Pete nodded. "How do they like it here?"

"Oh, well," Thierry started. "I never really knew my dad, but my mom seemed to really like it once she got on her feet, but—I really couldn't tell you for sure—she passed when I was pretty young."

"That's terrible! I'm sorry to hear it."

"Well, thanks."

"I'm first generation, too."

"Is that right? Where'd your folks come from?"

"Russia—after the revolution."

"Smart move," Thierry said with a chuckle.

"Sure was."

"I met a Ukrainian in Europe once—is that kind of like Russian?"

"Yeah, I guess you'd say they're like cousins, the Ukrainians and the Russians," Pete answered. "My wife's Ukrainian. She's first generation, too."

Thierry nodded.

"What about you—you married or anything?" Pete asked.

"I was engaged before I left for the war."

"She call it off or something?"

"Um, not exactly," Thierry answered, searching his thoughts for a way out of explaining what had happened to Hope.

"Oh," Pete just said, not wanting to press the matter further.

For some reason, though, Thierry felt like this complete and total stranger could be trusted. As big and burly as Pete was, Thierry sensed an uncommon softness lying under the surface.

"She passed while I was there," Thierry said slowly.

"Oh no! That's terrible!" Pete exclaimed. "How on earth did that happen?"

Thierry squinted in the dying sunlight and thought for a moment about how candid he wanted to be in the moment.

"To tell you the truth, I'm not completely sure."

Pete cast him a quizzical, sidelong glance.

"The police and the newspapers said it was an accident. She fell from some heights."

"That's terrible," Pete replied. "So why do you say you don't know what happened?"

"Well," Thierry said with a shrug. "My older brother was with her at the time, and for some reason, I've had a lot of trouble with the idea that there wasn't some kind of foul play."

Pete just whistled and shook his head.

The two men drove on in silence for a minute or so before Pete asked, "What does your brother have to say about it?"

"I don't know," Thierry answered with a shrug. "I really can't get him to talk about it. He wrote me a letter before I got home from Europe, but it really didn't explain much. Sounded like he was giving me the *official* story and not the *true* story."

"Well, do you have any evidence that makes you think he might have had something to do with it? I mean, surely the police would have done something if they'd come across anything fishy, don't you think?"

"In normal circumstances, I would say so—but my brother has some powerful friends and I don't doubt that they could make something disappear—"

"If there was something, you mean?"

"I suppose I do," Thierry replied reluctantly.

"Hmm," Pete said. "Is your brother a good person? I mean, are you two close?"

"We were as kids, but you know how it goes. As far as being a good person—I think he's got a good heart down there somewhere, but I honestly wouldn't put anything past him."

"Even *murder*?"

Hearing the word out loud made Thierry feel ashamed at the persistence of his feelings toward his older brother. He had always thought of it in terms of foul play or some missing element to the story, but Marty wasn't capable of *murder*—was he?

"I don't know," answered Thierry. "I hadn't really thought about it like that."

Pete shrugged and made a sweeping right turn. They pulled into the auto shop parking lot a couple blocks later, and, sure enough, it was closed.

"Great," Thierry muttered. "Now what am I supposed to do?"

Pete looked at the frustrated young man sympathetically and thought for a moment.

"Well, look, it's getting late. I've got a spare room and my wife is making dinner—why don't you spend the night with us and then tomorrow we'll get your tire fixed up?"

"No, I couldn't—"

"Why not? I'm offering—from one military man to another. I've got a friend who owns a car shop downtown, and I can get a tube and tools from him tomorrow afternoon. Then, I can drive you back, and we'll get you fixed up. As long as you don't mind coming to church with us in the morning?"

"No, I don't mind, but I really don't want to put you out."

"It's no big deal, I mean it," Pete assured him. "We've got plenty of food and an extra room in the attic."

"Well, sounds great, then," Thierry answered.

"Good!"

Pete spun the big rig around and pulled back out onto the main road. The sun was starting to set.

"Oh, I did forget to mention, though, the church service will be mostly in Russian. I hope you don't mind."

"No, not at all—it'll be an experience," Thierry replied. "But I'm sorry to say I don't have any church clothes with me."

"I'll loan you a shirt and tie, and you'll be all set."

Thierry chuckled at both the generosity of his host and the idea that any of Pete's shirts might fit him remotely. They were both tall, but Pete was built more like a linebacker and Thierry more like a telephone pole.

"You're sure your wife won't mind?"

"Of course not—I mean, I'm sure she'll be surprised when I bring you home, but it's really no trouble. My folks live with us, and my wife is expecting our first child in a couple months, so if we're not used to a full house now, we better get used to it soon!"

They dropped Pete's big rig off at the truck depot, and Pete ran inside to clock out. They jumped in his blue Oldsmobile and headed off toward his comfortable house on Main Street in a small town. Thierry met Pete's wife, a pretty girl who appeared to be several years Pete's junior, and his parents—neither of whom spoke much English. They had a warm roast beef dinner with potatoes and carrots and Coke, and pieces of homemade chocolate cake for dessert.

There seemed to be a glow around this family, and maybe, more specifically, this family life. Thierry thought about how much he wished for a small house somewhere, warm meals every night, and a good girl to sleep next to.

Pete showed him to his room on the third floor. He settled into his surroundings and undressed to his shorts before slipping into the small bed. The window was open next to him and a nice breeze fluttered in and out, like the waves of the ocean he'd planned on seeing that day. As he closed his eyes, his heart ached with longing as he pondered the life that had been ripped from him—whether intentionally or not, he felt he'd never know. He thought of Vivian and the life his brother was ripping from her. She had no idea what she was getting into, did she? Maybe she did, and maybe that was the point. Maybe she had herself to blame as much as Marty for the disaster that was most certainly looming just over the horizon of their lives. As much as he assured himself that if he kept on the right path, if he stayed sober and made the choice to forgive, everything would end up alright, he was hardly convinced. He drifted to an unsteady sleep, wondering if he would ever achieve happiness, if he would ever be blessed with the kind of marital comfort Pete had found.

June 10, 1951

He was embarrassed to have to be woken up in the morning, and nearly jumped out of his skin upon hearing the knocks at his door.

"Hey buddy," Pete called. "We've got to leave in about a half hour, just wanted to make sure you were up."

"Oh yeah, yeah," Thierry answered. "Uh, I'm up."

"Great—you know where the bathroom is, right? I left you some clothes in there. There's coffee and some bagels downstairs whenever you're ready."

"Okay, great—thank you."

Thierry washed his face and put on Pete's clothes in the bathroom on the second floor. He chuckled at how much the white dress shirt hung off his shoulders. He walked with the family through the back yard and down Hillside Avenue to the small church building. There were a couple English speakers among the congregants who greeted him warmly, and several who had apparently been misinformed that they were English speakers.

The service was long and the room was hot. Thierry recognized the tunes of some popular hymns and gospel songs and marveled at how different and nearly forced they sounded with Russian words. There were also some songs in minor keys that seemed to be more native to the culture. The pastor preached for what seemed like an eternity, the congregants laughing at times and saying "*Ah-meen*," at other times—Thierry had no idea why in either case.

After the service, they walked back home and had sandwiches for lunch. At the table, Pete's father, a sprightly man who appeared to be in his early sixties, began to speak in Russian quite fervently to Pete, while motioning his hand toward Thierry.

"He wants to know," Pete began with a small chuckle, "if you are a believer."

"Believer?"

"Do you believe in Jesus?" Pete clarified.

"Oh," Thierry stuttered. "I guess so—although, maybe I'm not so sure."

"You should," said Pete casually. "It's a big deal, you know? What a man believes."

"Yes, it is," Thierry replied. "I suppose that's why I'm taking my time figuring it out."

Pete's father spoke to him in Russian again and smiled.

"Pop says that a man who doesn't know what he believes is like a sailor without charts—or a mechanic without tire tools."

Thierry laughed.

"Well, I can't deny that I've felt a little more lost lately than I've felt in a long time," he answered.

"You should think about it more," Pete said. "We've all done bad things, things that God's not happy with—we've all fallen short of his glory—and he wants to forgive us and make things right, but we have to want to be forgiven, you see?"

"Yeah, I see," Thierry answered politely.

Pete said something back to his father in Russian, and the two went back and forth for a minute.

"Anyway, I think we've heard enough preaching today, don't you think?"

"Yeah, I think so."

"If you're ready to get started, let's get a move on."

"Yes, and thank you so much for lunch—and for everything," Thierry said, addressing the whole family.

After another minute or two of thanks, handshakes, and gathering themselves, the two men were in Pete's Oldsmobile and on the way to his friend's shop, where they picked up a couple tubes and a new set of tire tools at an obviously discounted price. From there, they were on their way to his brother's car, where they had left it on the side of Route 9 in Old Bridge.

"What are you going to do about your brother?" Pete asked over the gospel quartets on the radio.

"Well," Thierry hesitated. "I feel like I'm making progress toward getting over the whole thing. I was in a real bad spot about it for a while, but I'm starting to believe that I can forgive Marty. Which sounds crazy, right? Forgive my brother for something that, in all probability, he didn't even do."

"If you put it that way," Pete chuckled. "It does sound a little loony. But, I'll tell you, the part that doesn't sound loony to me is the fact that you're hurt because you don't feel like your brother cares."

Thierry looked up at him quizzically.

"You told me yesterday that he won't talk to you about it. I would be hurt over that, too. I would want to hear from his own lips what happened and how he felt. Even assuming it was an accident, and even if there was nothing at all he could have done to prevent it, I would want to hear my brother tell me that he was sorry. I think that's just natural."

Thierry subconsciously nodded his head, wrapping his mind around the sudden illumination of some of his deepest feelings.

"To me, it just seems like you want to know that he's sorry it happened—that he cares about the loss that you've endured."

"I think you've hit the nail on the head, Pete."

Pete just shrugged and nodded.

They drove the rest of the way to Marty's Buick in silence, listening, oddly enough, to Hank Williams singing "I Saw the Light."

The two men changed the tire, got the new tools, settled in the trunk, and stood, looking down at the car for a few minutes.

"Beautiful car," Pete said.

Thierry nodded his agreement.

"Well, my friend," Pete started. "I'd say you're good to go, and I better get running, too. I've been working a lot of overtime trying to save some money up for when this baby comes, and I haven't hardly seen my wife at all this week."

"You're a good man, Pete," Thierry said. "I can't tell you how much this has meant to me—from the help on the road to the meals and church and the whole thing. Even your pop's preaching."

Pete smiled and put a bear paw through his hair.

"Well, it was our pleasure to have you."

The two friends shook hands and parted back to their cars.

"I'll be praying for you, okay?" Pete yelled over his shoulder. "Feel free to keep in touch!"

"I will!" Thierry hollered back. "Thanks again for everything!"

Pete waved his hand and was off in a moment.

Thierry sat in his brother's car for a long time with the windows down. Eyes closed and hands in his lap, he allowed the rush of passing cars to be felt in his soul.

June 11, 1951

When Thierry got home from work, he was surprised to see the Buick still parked in front of Mrs. Parrish's garage. He had fully expected his brother to swing by and pick it up without having to exchange the usual pleasantries. *Maybe they're still on the way.*

He sat up and waited until he could hardly keep his eyes open, and got into bed a little after eleven. He still thought he'd hear the sound of the engine revving in the middle of the night at some point, but his brother never came.

June 12, 1951

The first thing he did when he sprang out of bed was to check the window looking out over the driveway. To his surprise, the car was still there. As he started getting ready for work, a life of past tragedies and accidents began to get the better of his emotional state. His thoughts became erratic geysers of worst-case scenarios bursting through his consciousness. *What if something happened to them? Could they have been robbed? What if they got in an accident or drowned or something? Maybe I should call the hotel.*

He picked up the phone and then thought to himself that he didn't even know at which hotel they had planned to stay. He swigged some coffee, splashed some cold water in his face, and decided that he was going to have to be calm, rational, and adult about this. It was quite possible, after all, that they had simply decided to stay an extra night and hadn't thought to call him.

It would be a lie to tell you that his brother's safety and wellbeing, and that of Vivian, wasn't on his mind the entire day at work. At one point, the thought even popped into his mind that maybe they'd had some sort of argument, and Marty had somehow hurt Vivian. He quickly chased such thoughts and forced himself to concentrate on his work. However, even Pasquale noticed something was amiss and asked him if he was okay several times throughout the day. Business was a little slow that day, so the old Italian finally told him to go home a couple hours before closing time. Thierry simply thanked him and rushed out the door.

When he got to his humble apartment, he called his brother's apartment in the city. The phone rang as he waited anxiously. No one answered. He paced around and tried to calm his nerves. He threw back some whisky and that seemed to help. Four attempts later, still no one answered his brother's phone. He then decided to try Vivian's, but again—no luck. He sat down on his bed and tossed down another drink.

I feel like I'm losing my mind.

Just then, he heard a car slow on the street and he leapt up to peer out the window. Sure enough, Vivian's shiny, red Cadillac was pulling up the driveway, his brother behind the wheel. Marty popped out, and Vivian gracefully walked around to get in the driver's seat. Before she did, he grabbed her roughly—playfully, but roughly—and grabbed her backside with both hands and lifted her onto the hood of the car. Thierry thought she squealed in surprise and delight, but he couldn't be sure. His brother pawed at her like a schoolboy as she laughed and playfully pushed him away. After a moment or so, they kissed quickly and she drove away, not so much as a glance or a thought in Thierry's direction. He felt slighted and he felt sick.

As Thierry nearly stumbled out the door of the garage, his brother was walking around the car, inspecting it.

"Hey, kid!" Marty called when he saw Thierry.

"Hey," Thierry answered.

"Well, you got it running?" he asked with a queer smile.

"There's nothing wrong with the car—other than the fact that you probably hadn't changed the oil in a year."

"Has it been that long? Hmm. I'll have to get that done."

"I already did it."

"I figured you would."

The two stood in silence for a moment—Thierry in wonder and Marty in mysterious anticipation.

"Well, if you don't mind, next time you're gonna grope your fiancee, please don't do it in full view of my eighty-something year old landlady."

"Oh, that?" Marty asked jovially, pointing towards where Vivian's car had been. "Were you watching that? What are you, a pervert or something?"

Thierry didn't think it was a very funny joke.

"What's this all about, Marty?"

"What are you talking about?" he asked playfully.

"This whole thing with the car," Thierry answered, his frustration starting to build. "You told me about some sort of terrible noise, but I drove the thing thirty, forty miles and never heard a goddamn thing."

"It runs nice?"

"Yeah, it runs nice. It runs like a fuckin' dream."

Marty smiled and stuck his tongue out slightly. Thierry hadn't seen him do that in fifteen years.

"Thierry, tell me, tell me—and be honest—when we were growing up, did you ever think there would come a day that you'd own a car like this?"

"Marty, right now, I don't think I'll ever own a car like that."

Marty laughed and pointed at the blue sedan. "You do now."

"What are you talking about?" he asked impatiently.

"The car, stupid," Marty answered playfully. "I'm giving it to you."

The words hardly registered in Thierry's cluttered mind. The young one just stood there with a dazed expression on his face; the old one just stood there with his silly tongue-out smile.

"It's yours, kid!" Marty finally exclaimed.

"Marty, wait, wait—"

"No, no—it's yours. It's a gift from your older brother to show you how much I still love you. And you deserve it, kid."

"Marty," Thierry answered slowly. "I don't know what to say."

"You don't have to say anything. But you do have to give me a ride to Weehawken so I can catch a ferry back to the city."

Thierry laughed, eyes gazing at the majestic car as if he'd never seen it before.

"But why the whole charade about the weekend in A.C. and everything?"

"It's wasn't a charade," Marty answered with a chuckle. "We did go down there and had a few nights of fine dining and exquisite love-making. But I didn't just want to come out and tell you—I wanted to get you to test drive it first and make sure you liked it."

"Of course I like it—I love it," Thierry replied, running his hand along the lines of the trunk. "But how are you gonna get around now without a car?"

"Viv's dad just bought her that Cadillac, and since we're gettin' married and all, I just didn't figure we needed two cars—especially in the city."

"Not that I mind driving you to the ferry, but why didn't you get a ride back with her?"

"Ah, she's on her way to see a *friend* of hers in West New York," Marty answered with a ting of melancholy. "I didn't want to hang out there."

Thierry wondered about the man with the gold watch.

"Plus," Marty continued, his tone brightening suddenly. "I figured I could buy you a hot dog or some pizza on the way. It's been forever since we've just been together, you and me."

"Yeah, it has."

"Welp, start up your car, kid! Let's ride!"

The two brothers raced down Route 3 toward the skyline of the greatest city in the world in that blue dream machine, warm air whipping in through open windows, Les Paul and Mary Ford's "Mockin'bird Hill" shrill and divine over the radio. They were young, they were free, and all seemed right with the world.

EIGHT

We forge the chains we wear in life.

CHARLES DICKENS

June 12, 1951

The two brothers, for the first time in many, many years, enjoyed a meal in each other's company. They sat for nearly two hours at a little diner in Hoboken and told stories about conquests in love and war; they laughed, and they talked about the future. Thierry couldn't believe that he had convinced himself that the sweet, caring older brother he had known in childhood was gone. He began to feel empathy for Marty for the first time, realizing that the two of them were, through blood and shared experience, brothers in a very real and tangible sense. Their lives were inextricably connected and, for the first time, it felt good.

Marty had grand plans of a career in finance. He was apparently gifted enough—and Thierry did not believe for a minute that his brother was exaggerating—that several of his professors had already attempted to secure positions for him at various financial institutions, pending his graduate degree. He was, in fact, receiving stipends from several corporations in hopes that the money would convince him to join their firms.

They even had a remarkably honest conversation about Marty's relationship with Vivian.

"Look, kid, things have been complicated for a long, long time, I'll just tell you that. I guess you could say that neither one of us has been the person we'd like to be, and I think that's why maybe it works for us—we feel like when we're together, we're looking in the mirror, and I don't mean at all the bad things, although those are there for sure. What I mean is, when I look at Vivian, I see who she really is deep down and it makes me want to be a better person just for her, you know?"

Thierry sipped his coffee and searched his brothers face. He couldn't shake the notion that his brother was truly speaking from the heart and it warmed him.

"She's a swell girl, Marty."

"I know she is. And as much as I joke around or whatever… I love her, bro. I really do."

"That's great Marty. You just make sure and treat her right. She deserves a good husband."

"I know," Marty replied seriously. "And for the first time in my life, I think, I'm ready to be a good husband. The last ten years, I've been running around, hell, practically living on the streets and doing whatever I wanted. I'm done with the escapades, the chasing skirts, and all that. I want to get a good job, go to work, and come home to a nice house and a nice wife."

"And some nice kids?" Thierry posed playfully.

"Oh, I dunno about that," Marty said with a sigh. "I think I'm ready to be a good husband, but I don't know if I'd ever make a good father."

"Sure you would."

Marty shrugged and smiled coyly.

They got some coffee to go, Marty paid the tab, and they hopped back in the Buick.

"So what about you, kid? What's the future look like?"

"I don't exactly know," Thierry answered, weaving through the city blocks toward the ferry. "I'm happy to be holding down a job at this point. Pasquale pays me good and I like the work. Maybe someday I'll have my own shop."

"Cheers," Marty said, raising his paper coffee cup. "That's the American dream right there."

"Well, I figure the more people buy cars and can't take care of 'em, the better business will get."

"Three thousand miles goes pretty quick, you know," Marty said with a self-deprecating chuckle.

"Yeah, driving around in the city, I'm sure it does," Thierry joked.

Thierry carefully pulled the car to a stop in a parking spot in front of the ferry gate entrance.

"Oh yeah," he said with a laugh. "I meant to tell you I got a flat on Saturday night, and there were no goddamn tire tools in the back, you klutz."

Marty's face suddenly went cold as stone. He stared at the skyline and dark blue water and Thierry was almost sure his eyes widened into—was it panic? Marty blinked hard twice, more like twitched, and suddenly the passenger's side door was open and Marty was halfway out of the car.

"Jesus, Marty, I'm just busting your balls."

"Oh yeah, yeah, you know, I just can't, you know, I'm just bad at keeping up with stuff like that," he stammered nervously. "Well yeah, kid, I'll see you around, thanks, uh, thanks for the ride and all—"

"Well thanks for the car, Marty—" the younger one said as the door was slammed quickly.

He sat there and watched Marty through the gate. He was walking so awkwardly fast that it was obvious he wanted to run, but was trying to hold himself back. He disappeared around the corner, and Thierry sat there for a minute, perplexed, giant buildings looming across the river.

As he pulled out of the parking lot, he, oddly enough, flipped the radio to the country station he'd heard in Pete's truck. The Tennessee Plowboy was crooning "That's How Much I Love You," as he revved back onto Route 3, heading west. He just shook his head and chalked the last two minutes of his time with his brother as yet another example of how little he understood him. He decided not to let it rob him of the good feeling he had from finally connecting with Marty again, and actually laughed about how typical it was of his brother to pull some stunt like that after such a nice time together.

Once he'd parked the car in the driveway outside his humble apartment, he turned off the ignition and just sat there in the dark, a dumb smile glued across his face. He ran his hands along the dashboard and his fingers over the buttons and knobs on the radio. He laid his head back on the plush headrest and thought that car was so wonderful that he might want to just live in it. How much he would have loved to drive his dear Hope around in a car like that, her tender frame pressed snuggly against him on the bench seat while her hair fluttered in the wind. He thought about her smile and her sparkling eyes.

The thought dawned on him that she had, indeed, been in this very car. He glanced down at the far end of the seat, where his brother had been not thirty minutes earlier. She had sat there. That was the last place she sat before she was gone. And then, almost as if someone had said it out loud, his mind suddenly settled on the missing tire tools. His eyes raced in pace with his thoughts.

Was that the missing piece?

His brain, in a matter of a second, recalled the empty feeling of discovering that the tools were gone and the look of panic—*it was panic, wasn't it?*—on his brother's face when he mentioned them.

That son of a bitch. He was just trying to buy me off with this damn car, trying to get me to stop asking questions. Or was he just trying to stop feeling guilty? What a sick, twisted son of a bitch. He gave me this car because it was the car Hope was in when he—

Thierry burst out of the Buick as if it was radioactive. He backed up from it in horror and turned and ran. He sprinted down the driveway and out onto the street. He ran as fast as he possibly could, as if his primal biological instincts were trying to outrun his own thoughts, until he was puking up hotdog, coke, and coffee onto the curb on Broughton Avenue. He stood there, hands on his knees, heaving and spitting and sucking wind. A sharp pain pierced his side and his abdomen felt like it had been put through a shredder. He suddenly lost his balance and found himself stumbling backwards and onto his bottom on the grass outside a stranger's home. He started to sob and covered his face with his hands. At that moment, there could have been no god, there could have been no afterlife; in fact, he wasn't even convinced that the sun would rise the next morning. Of one thing and one thing only was he certain: he had just had dinner with the devil.

June 13, 1951

Early the next morning, he phoned Pasquale to tell him that he wouldn't be in to work because he had an urgent family matter to attend to. The old mechanic seemed worried and asked if everything was alright. Thierry told him that, to be honest, he wasn't completely sure, but that he would call him later that night.

He hadn't slept at all, and now at ten after six, he paced around the Buick, his left arm folded across his body, his right elbow resting on it as his right hand covered his nose and mouth. He drank enough to take the edge off, but didn't want to be drunk—he wanted to have the mental clarity to try to piece things together. His final decision was to drive up to Connecticut that day and try to do some digging, and maybe discover something, some shred of evidence, that the police had overlooked. And if not, he would simply murder his brother. He had killed men before, but had never taken pleasure in it. This killing, however, he would enjoy. He would plan it with meticulous attention to detail—not so that he wouldn't get caught, but so that his brother would suffer. He took a swig of whisky and then tossed the flask onto the seat beside him.

The whole way, he drove with the radio off and the windows rolled up. He had looked at the map ahead of time and committed the route to memory. He drove with calculated urgency. He parked in the lot outside Deep Harbor's city hall and police department and watched police officers, attorneys, and other civilians come and go. He took another swig of whisky and gathered the strength to go inside.

He walked up the oversized stone steps leading up to the door and opened it for a petite, middle aged woman in a button-front blue dress. She thanked him quickly and he nodded silently, then entered the open lobby area himself. The floors were marble, and the woman's high heels echoed as she clicked towards her destination. He scanned the various doors and hallways until he saw a brown sign with gold metal letters indicating the direction of the police department. Down a hall and through a heavy oak door, he found himself standing face to face with a rather overweight and unhappy-looking officer with thinning hair and a black mustache seated at a desk. Papers, coffee mugs, and various awards and plaques, and a name plate that read "Sgt. Bellamy" were strewn about the metal office desk in what was obviously no particular order. Thierry stood in front of him in silence for what seemed like a laughably long time. Finally, the officer looked up and was immediately annoyed at Thierry's very presence.

"Can I help you?" he asked gruffly and with much irritation.

"Yes, sir, I'm looking to obtain a copy of a police report," Thierry answered politely.

"Records," the officer said bluntly.

Thierry just nodded his head, not sure if he was being asked a question or if the officer was making a simple statement.

"You need *records*," Sergeant Bellamy belted.

"Yes, sir," Thierry answered.

Sergeant Bellamy rolled his eyes and huffed as if much effort was required. "Turn left out this door—second door on your right."

"That's swell. Thank you for your time."

The officer dismissed the young man with a discourteous wave of his hand. *Public servants,* Thierry thought, nearly out loud.

Sitting behind a much neater desk in the small reception area of the records department was the woman in the blue dress, identifiable as Mrs. Eleanor Fantoni by the polished nameplate facing the door.

"Hello," she said in a flat, New York sounding accent. "How can I help you?"

"Hi, I'm trying to obtain a copy of a police report."

"Date?"

"December twenty-six—nineteen forty-forty," he answered, almost forgetting to include the year.

"Do you have a case number?" she asked, her tone pierced with boredom.

"I'm sorry, I don't," he replied.

"Names of parties involved?"

"Either Martin Laroque—"

"Spell that for me please?"

"M-A-R—"

"No, the last name, sweetheart."

"Oh, oh, ok. L-A-R-O-Q-U-E," he answered as she wrote on a legal pad. She then tilted her head curiously toward the name and stared at it for a moment.

"Any other names?"

"Uh, yes. Hope Blackburn."

She looked up at him, a look of recognition of the given names in her eyes.

"What do you want a police report for, young man?"

He shrugged. "She was my fiancee, and I would just like to read anything pertinent to her passing."

"Why did you wait all this time?" she asked, squinting suspiciously at him.

He thought for a moment, then lied. "I couldn't bring myself to face it before now."

She leaned back in her chair and folded her arms. He had no idea what was going on in her mind.

"Is it not a matter of public record?" he asked.

She frowned and sat upright. "That'll be ten cents. You can pick it up tomorrow after four."

"Tomorrow?"

"Yes, tomorrow and only after four."

"Look, I came all the way up from Jersey, and I've got to work tomorrow. There's no way I could pick it up this afternoon?"

She looked at him with exasperated disdain. "If it would be available this afternoon, I would have told you to come pick it up this afternoon, not tomorrow, after four."

"Could you mail it to me?"

"We don't mail police reports."

"Ok," he said with a frustrated sigh. "I'll see what I can do to be here tomorrow."

He put two nickels on the desk and she wrote him a receipt on a piece of carbon paper, including the names and case number associated with the report. He thanked her briefly and her eyes followed him out the door.

Upon exiting the building, he realized that he hadn't eaten since the previous night and began to feel light-headed. He saw a small, family owned diner on the corner across the street and was seated by a teenager with Greek features and black hair. He tossed his keys on the table and unfolded the receipt from the records office. He stared at it for a while, thinking about how he couldn't miss work the next day, or it would put Pasquale in a truly foul mood—foul enough that he might actually lose his job. When his bacon and eggs arrived from the kitchen, he put the receipt on the table and ate. He didn't even notice the fifty-something year old man in the brown suit sitting across from him and staring his way. Abruptly, the man stood up and caught Thierry's eye.

"Do you mind if I have a seat for a minute?" the man in the double breasted suit asked.

Thierry just shrugged.

"I'm Julius Mayhall, and I hope you'll pardon the interruption, but your face looks awfully familiar to me. Do we know each other?"

"Well," Thierry started, wiping his mouth with a paper napkin. "I don't think so, but your name sounds awfully familiar to me. I'm Thierry Laroque."

"Did you say 'Laroque'?" he asked, extending his hand.

"Yeah, why?"

Julius Mayhall glanced down at the pink paper next to the bottle of Heinz ketchup and back up at Thierry.

"What do you need a police report for?"

"Why does everybody want to know why I want a damn police report? Is it not a matter of public record?"

"Hey, hey," Julius replied, hands open in a calming gesture. "I'm just interested to know, because I reported on a possible homicide involving a Martin Laroque a few years back."

"You're a reporter," Thierry said, recognizing the man's name from newspaper clippings he had read and reread.

"Yeah, for the *Deep Harbor Express*. Our office is just upstairs," he said, pointing to the ceiling.

"Well, nice to meet you."

"You, too," Julius replied. "How are you related to the suspect?"

"Well, he's not a suspect, because it was ruled an accident—"

Julius gave the young man a quizzical glance.

"He's my brother."

"I see. And did you know the young lady who lost her life that night?"

"We were engaged."

The reporter's eyebrows shot up and his mouth curved into an open "o" shape.

"Have you read the report yet?" Julius asked.

"No. And it doesn't look like I'll get to. They told me to come back tomorrow after four, but I've got to get back to work in Jersey tomorrow."

Julius snickered. "Bunch of pricks in there, huh?"

Thierry shrugged his shoulders in agreement.

"Well, I tell you what, I've got a copy of that old thing locked in my safe upstairs—would you like me to bring it down?"

Thierry sat straight up in the booth. "Would you?"

"Sure thing."

A couple minutes later, the reporter was back with a stack of what looked to be between twenty and thirty pieces of paper.

"Now, look," Julius said. "This is pretty valuable to me, so let me have this little pink piece of paper as collateral, in case you decided to race off with my copy of the report."

"Sure," Thierry replied, handing over his receipt.

"You gonna hang out here for a little bit?"

"Yeah, I figured I'd go through it here and drink some more coffee."

"Ok, I've got a run out for a bit, but I'll be back around lunch. There's a couple interesting things that don't appear in that report. Maybe we can talk about it?"

The two men shook hands before Julius donned his round brim hat and headed out onto the street.

Greedy for knowledge, Thierry pushed what remained of his breakfast toward the opposite side of the table and began scouring the report. Notes taken by the officers responding, including one Field Officer Wallace Bellamy, notes on the position and location of the body, notes on Martin's statement, and then three pages, all blank except for the hand written letters "A.E." and the name and signature of Captain Roger Devlin.

A, E, A, E. Thierry let those letters roll around in his mind but couldn't make heads or tails of them.

The last four pages were the coroners report. As Thierry began reading he pictured his sweet Hope's delicate face and had to choke back tears.

Sternum broken. Both lungs punctured. Right femur shattered. Left ankle broken. Both kneecaps broken. Both arms, wrists broken. Cervical spine C4-C6 broken. T3-T6, T9-11 suspected broken. Lumbar 1-4 severed. Victim's left orbital socket broken. Nose broken. Jaw broken. Sever laceration to left ear, severe damage to temporal bone. Several ribs broken, hip broken, and on and on and on.

Thierry closed his eyes and fought back the carnal desire to cause his brother's autopsy report to match Hope's.

The official cause of death was listed as "Blunt cardiac trauma caused by fatal fall from heights."

He was able to calm himself after another cup of coffee and then poured over the report several more times, including the blank sheets designated "A.E." He began to write on a clean napkin all of the questions he had for Julius and then sat in dejected boredom, unable to cause himself to dig any deeper. He turned toward the window and people-watched. He then noticed five or six police officers exit the building and clop unceremoniously down the wide stone steps, among them Sergeant Bellamy. The group of gregarious cops, ages ranging from early twenties to mid-fifties, crossed the street, thumbs stuck in belt loops or pockets or waving about jokingly, and entered the restaurant. Thierry tried to slink down into the booth and slowly turned the police report facedown, hoping not to be seen or recognized. The officers sat down at a booth across the aisle, Sergeant Bellamy with his back toward the young man. It was just after eleven and the restaurant was mainly empty, pre-lunch. The voices of the police officers guffawed and bellowed as if they owned the place. Their conversation ranged from the Yankees to summer vacations down the shore to lewd remarks about the pretty, young waitress, some of them Thierry was sure she heard.

"So you'll never guess what happened this morning," Sergeant Bellamy bellied. "Kid comes in wantin' a report, so I send him over to records. Eleanor tells me later on that kid wants records on that accidental fall happened on Christmas all them years ago. What is he, writin' a book or somethin'?"

"Jeez," another officer answered. "People don't know when to leave well enough alone, do they?"

"I know!" Bellamy answered loudly. "It's bad enough we've got to deal with that Julius 'Mayhem' digging up our asses all the time!"

"That piece of shit wouldn't know a news story if it bit him in the ass," someone else bellowed.

"Well," Bellamy started with a laugh. "Whatever can-o-worms that kid is trying to open up is gonna get brick walled when it comes to the old 'A.E.' "

"All I can say, is Aulgur ain't gonna be too happy to have all this brought up again. I wouldn't sleep too heavy at night if I was them two."

They bellowed and laughed and changed subjects. Thierry was beginning to believe he might not be safe sitting there for long, especially if it appeared that he had been eavesdropping on their conversation, so he quietly gathered the police report, stood, and paid his tab. He went outside and turned the corner and found the entrance for the newspaper office and headed upstairs. He was greeted by a redheaded receptionist and shown to Mr. Mayhall's desk, where he waited patiently. The office, one large room holding maybe six or seven desks, and, from what Thierry could gather, a conference room and a couple executive offices, was nearly empty at lunch time. At about twelve-thirty five, however, the reporter strode into the office, caught a glimpse of Thierry and seemed to breathe a sigh of relief.

"I really thought you might have taken off," he said, putting his briefcase down on his desk and shaking Thierry's hand again.

"Nope, just didn't want to sit in that restaurant with all those cops."

"I wouldn't blame you, especially if they know who you are."

"It seems like there's something going on that I don't have the foggiest idea about."

Julius nodded and pulled at both pant legs before sitting down.

"There's a lot that I don't think anybody knows about," Julius said sternly.

"What does A.E. mean?"

"That's a good place to start. A.E. stands for 'Administrative Error.'"

Thierry looked at him blankly. "So what does that mean?"

"Officially, it means that some pages were inadvertently left blank in the typing or filing of the original reports. Unofficially, it means there are some pages containing information that somebody in charge didn't want to end up in the final record."

"So what happened to them?"

"The missing pages?" Julius asked. "Poof. Vanished into thin air."

"How is that possible?" Thierry asked, bewildered. "How do official records just disappear? Isn't there some kind of accountability?"

"Sure there is. If a senior officer, or the chief, or even the mayor himself wants something to disappear, everyone below him from field officers to typists are held accountable for making such information non-existent."

"But that's got to be illegal or something, isn't it?"

Julius shrugged. "Only if you get caught—and who's going to catch the police chief?"

Thierry just shook his head in disbelief.

"What do you think might have been in the missing pages?"

"The best guess I can venture," Julius answered, "is something that would make Dr. Winfield Aulgur's client look bad."

"Wait, so you're saying the police didn't want anything incriminating to come down against a defense attorney's client? The suspect in a murder?"

"You have to understand, Dr. Aulgur might be a big name in New York, but he's practically a deity around here."

"I don't understand," Thierry confessed.

"Dr. Aulgur is a millionaire, several times over, ok? This is a small town, relatively speaking. Every year, Dr. Aulgur donates tens of thousands of dollars to the police benevolence society here in town, and every year, they give him an award for outstanding community service. If, for instance, Dr. Aulgur were to be made to look bad in the public eye by the police department, or hell, even if one of them looked at him the wrong way, all that money would poof—just the way those pages marked 'A.E.' go poof. In fact, there's only one police officer that I suspect isn't on Dr. Aulgur's payroll in one form or another, and that's only because he's just been on the force a couple of weeks."

"Can I ask you something personal?"

"Sure, kid. Go ahead."

"The articles that you wrote," Thierry started, "they were basically verbatim from the police reports. If you had suspicions or any kind of other information, why didn't you report it?"

The reporter nodded and leaned forward toward Thierry. "Because there's *accountability* around here, too. I did find a couple things that perked my interest and to this day have made me want to break that case open somehow, but the powers that be—" his open palm showing the direction of the executive offices.

"What kind of a world do we live in?"

"We live in the only one we got, kid."

"You said you had some other information?" Thierry asked, nearly pleading.

Julius nodded his head and unlocked the bottom drawer in his desk. He pulled out a manilla envelope and from inside it, a white legal pad emerged. The pages, from what Thierry could see, were covered in sloppy handwriting—black and blue ink, maybe pencil, too. The reporter licked his thumb and pointer finger and began flipping through the pages quickly, until he settled on one about halfway through the pad.

"Here's the first discrepancy—of many," he began. "I spoke with Field Officer Bellamy—that lowlife piece of shit—early on the morning of the twenty-sixth. He specifically told me that Martin Laroque—your brother—was pleading the fifth and hadn't said a word during his interrogation."

"But the police report has Marty's whole side of the story—the part about them dancing and her slipping and all."

"You're starting to catch my drift. If your brother didn't say a word—and he was smart not to—than that story had to come from somewhere. And my guess is it came word for word from the mouth of the much esteemed Dr. Aulgur."

"What you're saying, in essence, then, is that the police took a story from a defense attorney as a direct statement from a suspect during interrogation?"

Julius nodded. "And we're just getting started."

Thierry shook his head and rubbed his eyes. "Ok, what else have you got?"

"The corpse, and I saw the corpse that night, up close—pardon me," Julius said, reading the discomfort in Thierry's face. "The coroner told me she'd been found face down on her right side, but there were some pretty horrific wounds to the left side of her face. He said he couldn't be sure, but there was a possibility that wounds on the left side were inflicted before the fall. But again, zero mention in the final report."

Thierry closed his eyes and took a deep breath to try to compose himself.

"Are you ready for more? Do you need some coffee or something?"

"I need a stiff drink," Thierry answered.

"I gotcha covered," the reported replied, reaching into his top desk drawer and pulling out a small bottle of Scotch. "Help yourself."

"Thanks," Thierry said, taking a solid swig from the bottle.

"Then there's Mr. Terence Coates of"—he looked down toward his notes and flipped a couple pages over—"335 Bluffs Avenue, which is less than three quarters of a mile from where your brother's car was parked and the incident took place. Mr. Coates had fallen asleep in his chair and was awakened by what he thought was shouting—like a man and a woman shouting. He got up and looked out his front window to see a blue Buick in the distance. He kept an eye on it for a minute, but couldn't see anything and, sure enough, the shouting had died down. Now, he was an old man, and as he'd been quite merry that Christmas evening, felt the need to lay down and went to sleep."

"Did the police interview him?"

"No—but when he heard about what had happened out there, he thought he should call in and let them know what he'd seen and heard that night. According to him, however, Field Officer Bellamy was dispatched to his house to get a statement. Somehow, as you know, that statement is not in the police report."

"Oh my god," Thierry said, taking another swig of drink. "Does he still live there? I'd like to maybe talk with him."

"Unfortunately, about a year ago, Mr. Coates died of a stroke."

Thierry thought about his bad luck for a minute. "Do you have anything else?"

"Mhmm," the reporter answered, flipping through pages of notes with purpose. "Does anything in particular that might be missing from the report you read strike you as odd?"

After a long minute, Thierry couldn't think of anything. "Nothing I can think of—but I'm not a police investigator."

"Well, as I see it, there are two real elements to this incident—the cliffs and the car."

"The car?"

"Did you read anything in that report about the blue sedan?"

Thierry shook his head again.

"Don't you think, if investigating a murder, you might want to peek inside the car that was there the night of the alleged crime? Don't you think you might want to check out the car that was driven by the alleged suspect, in case, perhaps there are signs of a struggle, droplets of blood, or any other kind of evidence?"

"Of course," Thierry said, thinking again about the beautiful car his brother had given him. "I have the car here—that's the car I drove to get here! Should we search through it?"

Julius quickly shook his head. "Your brother and Dr. Aulgur are too smart to let any evidence of a struggle stick around for very long. Any blood would have been cleaned, or the upholstery replaced altogether, dents in the car fixed, tire tools washed or replaced altogether."

"Damn it," Thierry said quietly under his breath, feeling his case slipping away from him. Then, the synapses in his muddled brain fired in rapid order and he asked, dumbfounded, "Wait—did you say tire tools?"

"I did," replied the reporter.

"Oh my God!" Thierry nearly shouted. The receptionist, who was returning from lunch at this point, looked up suddenly in alarm. Julius simply raised his right hand to assure her that everything was in order.

"What is it?"

"Tire tools," Thierry repeated, burying his face in his hands. "How could I have missed that?"

"What about the tire tools?" Julius asked, leaning in closely.

"I had a flat on Saturday—in that car—and the wrench and a couple of the irons were missing."

Julius leaned back in his chair, a look of contented enlightenment on his face. Then, he started to laugh gently.

"I cannot believe it," he said.

"What is it?" Thierry asked.

"Those missing pages, the dropped charges, as you can see, none of it ever sat well with me. So, around New Years I went down to the bluffs, and climbed down to where the cor—the victim—was found. I'm not exactly a spring chicken anymore, and it was wet and cold, so it took me a while to get down there. Sure enough, my shoes and my pants got soaked through completely by the waves and I nearly came down with pneumonia later that week—but it was worth it. It was worth every damn minute because I was about to give up—what the hell was I gonna find down there that wouldn't have been washed out in the sound—but then—then, a glimmer caught my eye. It was something completely out of place among the gray rocks and those black cliffs. It was metallic and shiny and I knew I'd found something. It took me a few more minutes to navigate my steps in that direction, and sure enough, wedged between two massive crags was a chrome tire wrench."

"So, what are you saying?" Thierry asked in disbelief at this new revelation.

"I'm saying we've got a murder weapon, kid," Julius said sternly.

Thierry closed his eyes and took a big gulp of Scotch.

"I just," he stammered. "I just can't believe it. I mean, I always had suspicions—even before I had any evidence. But this… this proves it, doesn't it?"

"I don't know about proves it," Julius answered with a shrug. "But it certainly does make a circumstantial case, don't you think?"

"Do you still have it?"

"The wrench? Of course. It's somewhere very safe. But, I don't know that it would ever do any good—after all, if there was any blood on it or anything of that nature, it was washed pretty clean in the salt water. It doesn't look any different than any other tire wrench at this point."

"Damn it," Thierry said under his breath. "So what do we do?"

"Well, kid," Julius said with remorse. "I'm sorry to tell you this, but I don't think there's a goddamn thing we can do."

Thierry leaned forward and held his head in his hands. The reporter put a hand on his shoulder. By this point, nearly the whole office was returned from lunch, several of them, however, were too hammered to notice the scene at the desk of Julius Mayhall.

"Listen, this has been a tough day for you. My best advice is to get home, have a few drinks, and go to sleep. Don't do anything out of emotion or haste. Take my card—it's got my office number on it—and I'll write my home number, too. We'll keep working on it. I wasn't engaged to her, but I can't get past the idea that the poor girl deserves justice, and I won't stop digging until either I kick the can or I put every one of those sons-a-bitches away."

"Thank you," Thierry said through his sniffles. He dried his red eyes with his sleeves and shook the reporter's hand firmly. "Really, thank you for everything."

"You're welcome. I wish I could do more, I really do."

Thierry sat outside the police station in the Buick for quite a while, sipping at the bottle of Scotch Julius had let him take. He was certainly tipsy, but not quite drunk when he left. He drove around the town and eventually found the spot where the incident had taken place. He sat for a while on the hood of the car and overlooked the sound. The sun warm on his back, the gentle breeze, and the smell of saltwater were so paradoxically pleasant compared with the inner anguish he felt. He looked around, took some dust in his hand, and walked to the edge of the land. He looked down and was suddenly dizzy at the sheer distance to the jagged rocks below. He swigged the last of the Scotch and seriously contemplated throwing himself down to join his beloved in the depths. He thought about his mother, he thought about Henry and Henrietta, he thought about Dr. Baier and Pasquale, and he thought about Hope. That's not what they would want for him. They would want him to figure it out, and even if he couldn't, they would want him to live a long life and do something—create something of himself. He threw the empty glass bottle and followed its trajectory into the sound and then sat down, feet over the cliff, and waited there as the sun began to set. He told Hope how much he missed her and how much he wished he'd been there to protect her.

In the twilight and soberness of mind, he climbed back into his brother's car and decided to drive home. Unfortunately, he had gotten rather crossed in his directions and was lost in the small town, not sure how to get back to Route 15 toward New Jersey. He thought about pulling over and asking for help, but wasn't in the mood to talk to anyone at the moment. He drove down tree-lined street after tree-lined street and was only then amazed at how affluent this small coastal town was, each house made of brick and landscaped neatly, Cadillacs and Mercedes and Jaguars shining like trophies in each driveway. The uniformity and bland pomp of them made him somewhere between nauseous and angry. He turned down Pine Street and the houses got even bigger and more ostentatious. He thought about the men at work in their glass high-rise offices, screwing their secretaries while their wives screwed the instructor at the equestrian center where she took riding lessons every week. He thought that his brother would fit perfectly into that world. He decided to show his disapproval at his mental image of wealth and lack of moral character by gunning it and flying down the lane. The engine revved and roared, and he gripped the wheel with determination until something—and he couldn't be positive—caught the corner of his eye. The brakes squealed as the Buick went from sixty to zero. He put the car in reverse and backed up slowly in front of the biggest house in the neighborhood and perhaps the biggest house he had ever seen in his life. It could have been Thomas Jefferson's Monticello. White columns stood mighty and proud, a rotunda, a fountain in the middle of a lawn so green and lush it made him want to walk barefoot through it. He saw a couple lights on in the massive house and backed up further. On the black mailbox on the curb were printed in gold the letters, "A-U-L-G-U-R."

After not a moment's hesitation, he knocked loudly on the front door. As he waited for an answer, the thought did briefly cross his mind that he had no idea what he was doing there. He knocked again loudly and the twelve foot high oak door was suddenly opened. He wasn't sure what he'd expected—a butler or footman or some other servant in a tuxedo, but standing there before him was a portly and bald man, perhaps sixty years old, in a red velvet robe and Norwegian house slippers. The man looked Thierry over for a moment, sternly but cautiously.

"Can I help you, young man?"

"Are you Dr. Aulgur?"

"I am," came the calm reply.

After a long moment's pause, Thierry introduced himself. "I am Martin Laroque's younger brother."

"I can see that," the man replied. "Well, I'm sorry to tell you that your brother is not here, if you are in search of him."

"I'm not."

The lawyer pursed his lips and nodded. "Well then, may I ask the reason you've knocked on the door of my personal residence at ten-thirty in the evening?"

"I'm sorry for the hour," Thierry answered, suddenly feeling embarrassed. "I didn't realize it was so late."

"You've been drinking? But you're not drunk, are you?"

Thierry shook his head.

"Well, I suppose it's rude of me to leave you standing on my doorstep without inviting you in."

With a wave of his hand, Dr. Aulgur showed Thierry inside the house, closed the massive door gently behind him, and led him into a front room—obviously, his home library, complete with twenty-foot ceilings, rich dark wood shelves stuffed with gold-lettered law books, a desk bigger than any Thierry had ever conceived, and a fireplace that must have been ten feet wide. The host offered his guest a Cognac, poured the drinks, and then motioned Thierry to sit in one of two massive leather chairs.

"So," Dr. Aulgur said, sitting across from the young man in the opposite and matching chair. "What is it you'd like to talk to me about?"

"Honestly," Thierry began to stammer. "I'm not sure, sir. I was just driving around town and saw your name on the mailbox and—"

"You thought you might stop in for a Cognac and a chit-chat."

"Well, no, sir—"

"How did you fancy Mr. Mayhall?"

"Excuse me?" Thierry asked in surprise.

"Young man, I may make my living in New York, but I make my home in this small town, and it behooves a man in my position to know the goings-on in said small town."

"I see," answered Thierry nervously.

"I know that Mr. Mayhall would have you, and everyone else, for that matter, believe that I am some kind of bogey-man, and I'm sure he made mention of my numerous donations to this towns police benevolence society?"

Thierry nodded slowly.

"I am also positive that he did not happen to mention the particular fund to which my donations are applied?"

"No, sir."

"Of course not," Dr. Aulgur continued. "Because that would not fit within the 'bogey-man' narrative. Every year, I donate a percentage of my income to the Winslet Family Educational Fund, which is overseen by the police benevolence society. Do you know why a police benevolence society might oversee an educational fund? Of course you don't—how could you? You see, about ten years ago, a break-in was reported down at McMillan's furniture store on the square—I'm sure you passed it at some point today. The responding officer was a thirty-seven-year-old man named, coincidentally, Martin Winslet. Officer Winslet observed the suspect exiting the shattered front window of the shop holding a cash drawer under one arm and a Tiffany lamp under the other. When confronted, the suspect dropped both items and ran. Officer Winslet pursued him for several blocks, until the man turned and fired a revolver five times in the officer's direction, hitting him but once. However, that one bullet pierced Officer Winslet though the esophagus and severed his carotid artery. He lay there in the street, in a pool of his own blood, gasping for air and all alone, until his wife, who heard the shots in their home just two doors down, looked out the front window and saw her husband, prone and bleeding in the street. Mrs. Winslet's husband died in her arms, a week before Christmas, over the theft of perhaps a few hundred dollars.

"The police benevolence society established the Winslet Family Educational Fund to pay for the education of Officer Winslet's five children, all of whom, at the time of his murder, were under nine years old. His eldest, a daughter named Maureen, just finished her freshman year at Standford University—she's a bright girl. His next eldest, a son named Martin, Jr., graduated high school this year and will go on to attend Rutgers University in the fall. We have equally high hopes for Marsha, Milton, and June.

"Do you know why I tell you this story, young man?"

Thierry just shook his head in trauma.

"Of course you don't," Dr. Aulgur continued calmly. "Because you don't know the *facts*. I'm sure that even if Mr. Mayhall had found it in his heart to tell you the truth about my financial donations to such a worthy cause, he most certainly would have neglected to inform you that Officer Winslet's murderer was a man by the name of Howard *Mayhall*—the younger brother of Mr. Julius Mayhall himself.

"Now, how did I come to deserve the scorn of Mr. Julius Mayhall, you may wonder. Simple enough. As an attorney, I believe that every man accused of a crime deserves the finest legal representation. However, not every man can *afford* the finest legal representation. I would have been happy to represent Mr. Howard Mayhall, but unfortunately, you cannot buy fine wine on a cheap beer budget. Old Julius did his damnedest in repeated attempts to convince me to take his brother's case on a pro bono basis. However, I did my damnedest to make clear to Mr. Julius Mayhall that my pro bono work goes to benefit widows and orphans, not men who cause wives and children to become widows and orphans. I suppose, being that Mr. Howard Mayhall was put to death by the electric chair in 1946, that his brother has never since forgiven me the crime of declining to represent his brother, the murderer."

Thierry was shocked so thoroughly that even if he'd thought of something intelligent to say, at this moment, his body would have utterly failed him in its deliverance.

"So, there you have it," Dr. Aulgur said, puffing smoke from a freshly lit cigar. "You can't believe everything you hear."

"I'm sorry," Thierry blurted, pushing himself halfway out of his armchair. "I shouldn't have ever—"

"Of course you should have," Dr. Aulgur interrupted with a polite wave of his hand. "Please, sit down."

Thierry obeyed.

"There is something else I'd like you to know about me. You see, I have been blessed with great fortune, as you have no doubt ascertained. I find that it is, therefore, my duty as a citizen of this great nation, and as a citizen of the kingdom of God, to be a blessing to others who may be less fortunate. Take your brother, for an example. He was a street kid, a parasite, when he was brought to my attention. But it was also abundantly clear to me that he had a genuinely robust intelligence that would most likely go to waste if someone capable did not intervene. You see, I would rather your brother, Marty, go on to fulfill his God-given potential and serve society. So, I put a plan in motion through my foundation to take this troubled, but talented young man under my wing, provide for his living and educational expenses, and show him the way. In a sense, Marty has become like the son I never had, and I have become like the father he never had."

Thierry felt the hair on his neck bristle at these last words.

"You may call it foolish, and certainly it is," the lawyer said, laughing through a puff of acrid smoke and a dark smile. "Because had I not rescued your brother, he would have certainly gone on to be a fine client."

Thierry chewed at his upper lip and tried to find something appropriate to do with his hands.

"Young man, my life's work has been dedicated to the betterment of society through the rule of justice, and there is something certainly unjust about bright young minds going to waste due to poor upbringing, bad luck, or any number of other factors. I sponsor dozens of bright young scholars, like your brother, who would have become a drain on society rather than a healing balm on it. There are former beneficiaries who are congressmen now, attorneys, doctors, company directors, and even an olympic athlete. The current class which I sponsor, including your brother, may be the brightest yet. Take George Ridgemont, for example. His family was so poor that he would pick through dumpsters for his dinner after school each day. Now, his professors tell me that he may be the soul that one day cures cancer. Or young Steven Yates. His miserable parents abandoned him because they thought him an oddball, mentally retarded. Well, I'm told that he may be the man who figures out how to put an American on the moon.

"So, tell me now," Dr. Aulgur said, leaning back and crossing one fat leg over the other. "Do you still think I'm some kind of monster?"

Thierry thought for a moment—his head and his gut at odds—before finally managing a, "No, sir."

"Well, good!" the lawyer said with a grin and a slap of his meaty thigh. "Now, if you will pardon me, I do have an early deposition in the city in the morning, and would like to perhaps manage a couple hours of sleep before then."

"Of course," Thierry replied as he stood, unable to conceal the defeat in his voice.

"Well, good night then. Allow me to show you to the door."

Thierry found himself standing on the outside of that massive door and turned to shake Dr. Aulgur's fleshy hand.

"One more thing, young man—a piece of advice, if I might," the lawyer said. "Whatever you think happened on that night, all those years ago, between your fiancee and your brother, whatever suspicions you have or dark thoughts you might harbor, remember what you learned here tonight—don't form a judgement of a man when you might not be privy to all of the *facts*."

With that, the fat lawyer shut the door. Thierry heard it latch on the inside.

Bewildered and beaten, he found himself wanting desperately to get out of that town. He was, however, still lost in terms of his whereabouts and the proper route home. He drove for a few miles and found himself in the downtown area again. He was able to get his bearings and did his best not to think while he methodically headed toward Route 15. A couple miles from the highway, he heard a siren and suddenly saw red lights racing up behind him and thought for a moment that he was about to get pulled over. He checked his speed and tapped his breaks. The police car, however, flew past him. Not a minute later he was passed furiously by a fire engine.

When he reached the intersection of South Maple Street and Route 15, he saw across the way the unmistakable orange glow of a house on fire and a pillar of smoke billowing from its roof. There were half a dozen police cars and two fire engines, lights still whirling on the roofs, parked in all directions outside it. He thought a quick prayer for the family involved and then turned left onto the highway and back toward New Jersey.

June 14–15, 1951

Morning came way too quickly.

Thierry made it to work, on time, however. Pasquale was nervously happy to see him.

At about three that afternoon, a report came over the shop radio that a journalist for a hometown newspaper in Connecticut was killed in a house fire overnight, along with his wife. The report mentioned that it was suspected that a lit cigarette was dropped into the bed accidentally when the couple fell asleep. No names were given, but Thierry already knew.

That night, he called the home phone number on the back of Julius Mayhall's business card. The number had been disconnected. The following day's Jersey Record, however, featured a full page article, picture included, along with an obituary of Julius Mayhall and his wife Murtie. Their house had been razed to the ground. Their names had not been released to the media the previous day because their adult children had yet to be notified.

Thierry felt sick to his stomach. Despite his conversation with Dr. Aulgur and the "advice" he'd been given that night, he couldn't help but believe the newspaper man's death—and the death of his wife—was truly something other than an accident. What were the chances? He felt deep in his being, much the same way he had felt that his brother was responsible for the death of Hope, that Dr. Aulgur was in some way responsible for the deaths of Julius and Murtie Mayhall. He also felt that in a horrible twist of blind fate, his digging into the past was the spark that led to the fire. The only problem now was that he was back to where he started, and he had lost his only ally in the process.

July 4, 1951

Marty had tried to reach Thierry plenty of times. Once, he called, and Thierry had answered, then feigned a bad connection and hung up. Plenty of other times, the phone just rang and rang. He had tried to contact his younger brother at the shop, but was informed by Pasquale that he held a strict policy of "no personal phone-a calls" for all of his employees. When Marty asked how many employees the mechanic employed, he was curtly disconnected.

He had heard from his attorney friend about his younger brother's trip to Deep Harbor and the late night confrontation at Dr. Aulgur's home, and had decided that he needed to at least try to smooth things over. He also felt the need to persuade his brother to travel to Chicago for his wedding. He hadn't planned on it before, but he got the idea that Thierry would be his best man, and that this would pacify any lingering doubts as to the state of their relationship. When he mentioned this to Vivian, she went on for a good ten minutes about what a wonderful idea it was. He thought he would talk to his brother on the phone and say something like, "Hey kid, you know that I love you, and that I've always considered you to be my best friend. I'd like to ask you to stand as best man when I marry Vivian," and imagined his brother saying something like, "Marty, are you for real? First, you give me a car, and then you ask me to be best man at your wedding? I'm honored—of course I will!" The fact that he hadn't been able to get a hold of his brother bothered him, and the idea that Thierry was avoiding his calls bothered him more.

At about eleven in the morning, Thierry was just finished cutting Mrs. Parrish's lawn, sitting in an outdoor chair by the garage with a cold beer, when Vivian's red Cadillac turned in and crept up the driveway. Thierry's eyes caught his brother's as Marty parked the car behind the blue Buick and got out slowly.

"Hey, kid," Marty said sprightly.

"Hey," Thierry answered without emotion.

"I've been trying to get a hold of you for weeks."

"Have you?"

"Yeah, I have. What, you don't pick up your phone anymore?"

"Not unless I'm expecting a call."

"Well, you should. What if it had been an emergency or something?"

"Emergency?"

"Yeah, an emergency. Like what if I'd been killed in a car accident or something like that?"

"Killed?"

"Yeah, killed."

"Well, I guess I would have read about it in the papers, then, huh? And plus, I don't think accidents happen to people like you."

"What are you talkin' about, 'people like me'?"

"People with protection. People on the right side of the the right people. It seems to me that accidents only happen to people with nothing to lose—people like pop and people like Julius Mayhall and his wife."

Marty shook his head. "Why are you being like this, T?"

"Because I think you're a fucking liar, and if I'm honest, I actually think much worse of you."

"Wow," Marty answered, scratching the top of his tilted head. "And to think, I came out here to ask you to stand as best man in my wedding."

Thierry bust out laughing, nearly spitting out a mouthful of beer.

"Glad to see you think it's funny."

"Funny? Marty—are you that thick?"

"You're my kid brother, and I've always considered you to be my best friend."

"Your best friend? When have we ever been best friends, Marty? I can't remember a time. You know what I do remember, though? I remember when mom died, you ran away. I remember crying myself to sleep as a kid because I felt like I'd lost my mother and my brother at the same time. I remember you coming around only because Henry made you. I remember you coming to my baseball games and having the look on your face that you'd rather be anywhere else on the planet. I remember you being the last person who saw the love of my life alive, and I remember you going pale as a sheet when I mentioned missing tire tools from the trunk of your car."

"You look like you hate me or something," Marty said slowly, unable to hide his genuine hurt at his brother's remarks.

"I think I do hate you."

"I see."

After a minute of silence, Thierry continued, "Marty, your whole life, you've been smart enough and talented enough and good-looking enough or whatever to skirt every responsibility you've ever had, and get away with it. You've never had to work for anything—it's just handed to you. And if there was ever something that you couldn't have, you just took it. And God only knows what you would do if there was something that you couldn't take—something that you wanted that was beyond your grasp. Like my Hope."

Marty looked his younger brother over for a minute. "Is there something you'd like to accuse me of, kid?"

"I think you killed her."

Those words hung in the thick, humid air.

"I think you wanted her, and you couldn't have her, because she was mine, and I don't think you could handle that. I think you killed her because if you couldn't have her, you damned sure weren't going to let me have her. And I think you gave me this car to buy me off. And I think you were going to ask me to stand as best man at your wedding out of guilt."

"Have you lost your mind, kid?"

"No—no, I've haven't lost my mind. I've finally put the pieces together and have drawn my conclusion—you're the most evil person I've ever know, and I knew a cannibal once."

Marty winced at that declaration. "Well, I guess I ought to go then."

"I think you should."

"You're really breaking my heart, though, kid. I want you to know that."

"You're a piece of shit, Marty."

"Well," Marty said sadly. "Whatever you might think of me, I love you."

Thierry took a gulp of beer and averted his eyes.

"Ok, then," Marty said, jingling his keys in his right hand. "I guess I'm out of here."

Thierry raised his near-empty beer can, and in a moment, Marty was gone.

July 5, 1951

Shortly after 1am, Vivian sat suddenly up in her bed. She listened quietly, and sure enough, the gentle knocking that had awakened her occurred again. After wrapping herself in her robe, she went to her door and cautiously peered through the peephole.

"Thierry!" she said, swinging the door open. "What are you doing here?"

"Can I come in?"

"Yes, but is everything, ok?" she asked, moving aside so he could enter. "It's after one in the morning!"

"I know," he said as he brushed past her. "Terrible timing, I'm sorry."

She closed the door and spun on her heels to face him.

"You look beautiful," he said.

"Are you drunk?"

"Not a bit," he answered. He spoke slowly and confidently. "I had my last drink at noon. I'm stone-cold sober."

"What are you doing here? Did you come to see Marty or something?"

"Nope. I came to see you."

"I don't understand," she said, nervously attempting to straighten her bed-worn hair.

"I came here to ask you to marry me."

"You must be kidding."

"I'm completely serious. And for the first time, I feel like I'm in my right mind. I want you to be my bride."

"I'm marrying your brother in three months. Don't you have any shame?"

"Not about this," he answered calmly. "You deserve better than him, and I deserve some happiness in my life."

"Of course you deserve happiness, but I'm sure I'm not the person to give it to you."

"We would be great together, Viv. Think about the beautiful children we could make, the life we could build together."

"Thierry, you're talking crazy, and you're making me upset."

"Marry me," he pleaded.

"No," she answered with a gentle shake of her head.

"Ok," he said, gathering himself. He reached in his pocket and pulled out a thick wad of bills. "Then how much would you charge to sleep with me tonight?"

"What?" she said incredulously.

"I've got two thousand here," he replied. "Come on, you're a businesswoman, aren't you?"

He would never forget the look on her face at that moment. She bit her lips, but he could see that they were trembling. Her eyes glistened, and she simultaneously managed to look like she might vomit. It was the worst thing he'd ever done, and he knew it.

"You need to go," she blurted.

"Look, Viv, I'm—"

"Get out now," she turned and abruptly opened the door.

"I'm sorry," he murmured as he slunk into the hall.

She let her head out the door and said, "As one final act of kindness, I promise that I won't tell Marty about this. But I do want you to know that I think you're a piece of shit, just like everybody else in this rotten world."

With that, the heavy green door with the gold numbers, 813, closed in his face.

July 6–28, 1951

Pasquale had closed the shop and traveled with his wife to a small village in southern Italy to visit family for the entire month of July. Thierry found himself a man freed from any kind of attachments whatsoever, so he packed up nearly all of his earthly belongings in the Buick and told Mrs. Parrish he would be gone until the beginning of August.

He took Route 1 South to Washington, D.C., where he spent a day visiting the sites. He next stopped in Atlanta, and from there was on to Miami. He spent a few days in the sun and a few nights with a black-eyed Cuban girl, whose wavy, raven-colored hair fell to the small of her back. From there, it was up the west coast along the gulf and through Dothan, Alabama towards Nashville. He spent a week listening to country music in tiny honky-tonks and even visited the Ryman Auditorium to take in to some of the best gospel music he'd ever heard. He decided it was time to head home from there and left on Highway 70 in an easterly direction. About thirty miles out, he came through a small town and remembered that he needed to have the oil changed. Upon driving through the bustling town square, he saw J.C.'s Auto Repair and Tire Shop and decided that as a final luxury on this vacation, he would pay someone else to change the oil for him.

"Anybody here?" he asked once inside the shop.

"Be wit' you in a second," called a gruff voice from the back.

A moment later a sixty-something year old man in a greasy jumpsuit emerged, blue letters "JC" embroidered across a white patch, wiping sweat from his forehead with an old rag.

"Can I help you?" the old man asked.

"Yeah, I need an oil change, please."

"You don't sound like you're from around here, are ya?"

"No, sir. You don't exactly sound like you're from around here either," Thierry answered.

"Nah, I'm from the East Coast—spent a lotta time up in Ohio, though."

"I'm from the East Coast, too. New Jersey."

"No kiddin'. What part of Jersey?"

"Northeast. Right outside the city."

"That's where I grew up!" the old man exclaimed. "Jasper Carrington," he said, extending his oil-stained hand.

Thierry shook his hand firmly, and at the same time, his mind raced for where he might have heard that name before.

"Wait a second—are you related to Beth Carrington, by any chance?"

"Yeah," answered the old man in disbelief. "That's my mother, God rest her."

"You gotta be kidding me," Thierry answered. "My mom was Nina Laroque, she worked for your mother before she passed—back in the thirties!"

"No shit!" Jasper nearly yelled.

"I'm Thierry Laroque."

"Pleased to meet you, Thierry."

"You, too, Mr. Carrington."

"Call me Jasper—we're old friends, after all! And I remember your mom! I can't tell you how much she meant to my mother."

"Well, that's nice to hear," Thierry answered.

"So how is your mom doing?"

"Oh, well, she actually passed back in the thirties, too."

"Oh, god, I'm sorry to hear that. She must have been pretty young, then, huh?"

"She was."

"Oh, Jesus," Jasper said. "That's terrible. You must have been pretty young, yourself."

"Yeah, I was just a boy."

"Life can be pretty rough like that," Jasper said slowly. "Well, do you live out this way now?"

"No, sir. I've actually been driving around the south pretty aimlessly and just by chance happened to stop in here."

"What are the chances of that?"

"I know. And how about you—how did you end up here?"

"Land," the old man answered. "My wife passed about six years ago, and with the kids all grown up and living all over the place—Philly, Detroit, Omaha, San Francisco—I figured it was time to get some land to myself and live a nice, quiet life. And, I'll tell you, land is cheap as dirt down here."

"No kiddin'," Thierry replied thoughtfully.

"Yeah, it's real different down here, as I'm sure you've found out, but I like it. Life has a slower pace, and the people might be simple, but they're kind."

"Any chance you're looking for some help around here?" Thierry asked.

"Desperately," Jasper answered. "My last two helpers quit to move north, and the one before that I had to fire because he kept showing up drunk off his ass. You know anything about fixing cars?"

Thierry left the next morning and arrived back at Mrs. Parrish's home to collect the rest of his belongings and leave her an extra month's rent as notice that he was moving out. He mailed a letter to his brother informing him that he had moved to Tennessee and wished him well in his marriage. He even made an international call to tell Pasquale, who tried desperately to dissuade him, and even cried.

This was what he needed, he thought. He would forget his pain and rise like a phoenix from the ashes.

NINE

It is not violence that best overcomes hate—
nor vengeance that most certainly heals injury.

CHARLOTTE BRONTË, *JANE EYRE*

September 7, 1990

"Aren't you going to wish me a happy birthday?" Thierry asked as his old truck merged with traffic on I-40 West.

"That was yesterday, wasn't it?" Marty answered, staring straight ahead.

"Sure was," Thierry replied. "But I don't think you've wished me a happy birthday in probably fifty years, so it's not like I was expecting it. Hell, I wasn't expecting to see you at all yesterday, was I?"

"I suppose you weren't. But, happy birthday, anyway."

Thierry nodded his head.

Eddy Arnold was crooning on the radio as the brothers rode in silence.

They got off on Donelson Pike in Nashville and turned in toward the small airport. Thierry parked outside the main terminal and turned to look at his sad, old brother. Marty clutched his garment bag like a lost child clutches a knapsack. The truck idled, and Marty stared at the floor. After a long minute, he turned, his eyes full of something Thierry had never seen in them before—fear.

"Is there nothing that will change your mind?" he asked nervously.

Thierry thought for a long moment. Memories he had replayed so many times that he wasn't even sure if they had actually happened raced violently through his mind. Hope, the cliffs, Dr. Aulgur, the blue Buick, Vivian. The pain of all those years lived without closure.

"I don't think so, Marty," he finally replied.

The older one's mouth twitched, and the fear in his eyes collapsed into panic.

"Well, don't drop me off here, then," Marty said quickly.

"Why not?"

"Because, I told you, I can get on an airplane, but I don't have anywhere to go! Is there a homeless shelter or a hospital or something downtown where you can take me? Nashville is as good a place to die as any, I guess."

Thierry nearly rolled his eyes as he threw the truck back into drive. He got onto the interstate heading east.

"The sign says Nashville that way," Marty nearly shrieked.

"Yeah, I know."

"So where are you taking me?"

"To my house."

"Oh," Marty said, the panic suddenly subsiding. He sighed heavily in relief and then coughed spastically. "Why?"

"I don't exactly know," Thierry replied.

"Thank you," Marty answered quietly. He suddenly wiped his eyes with his sleeve and then clutched his bag again.

That afternoon, Thierry put fresh sheets on the bed in the guest room and set out towels and soap for his brother. Marty took a long shower—so long that Thierry thought of checking in on him to make sure he was alright. The brothers ate pork chops from the grill along with a couple beers and then sat on the back porch along with Useless and Duke and watched the sun set in near perfect silence.

September 24, 1990

Marty had a massive supply of morphine pills. Thierry asked about them, and his brother simply indicated that he expected to be in some amount of pain in the coming weeks and that the source of his medication was a strictly private matter. The young one did not push the issue any further.

They talked minimally, though most of their conversations were a series of complaints and rebukes.

"It's too damned hot in here."

"Welcome to Tennessee in the summer."

"This television is too small."

"Get a better pair of glasses."

"Why does your house have so many stairs?"

"Because I never installed the up button on the elevator."

And so on.

Eventually, however, Thierry's hostility towards his brother warmed to mere complacency, and if he was honest, he might tell you that after so many years living in an empty house—Useless the dog, aside—he enjoyed the company… in a general sense of the word.

As his brother's health declined in front of his eyes—Marty's weight loss over the course of just a couple weeks was alarming, as were his fits of coughing, mostly at night—Thierry had much trouble reconciling the hate he had harbored for so many years with the compassion he felt for his older brother's suffering.

One night as rain whispered on the back porch's tin roof, Marty displayed for the first time an interest in Thierry's personal life.

"How come you never got married?" he asked while Duke purred on his lap.

Thierry shrugged. "I got close—a few times."

"And what happened?"

"Well, there was Hope, as you know," Thierry said mildly. The muscles around Marty's eyes recoiled as if he'd been stung by a bee. "And then there were a couple of nice girls down here."

"Tell me about them."

"A couple years after I moved down south, I met a girl named Mary Sue at a friend's house. She was young and bright-eyed and full of wonder at the world. On one hand, she was the type of person that you could feed off of her energy, and I think that's what I liked so much about her. At the same time, she could be moody and—oh, I don't know if unpredictable is the word—more like spontaneous, but almost to a fault. She couldn't keep plans, she couldn't settle down at all. And I think that's why I hesitated like I did."

"Hesitated about what?"

"See, that's exactly what I had always wanted—to settle down. To have a nice wife and some nice kids and spend my nights sitting on the porch in peace. But that wasn't her—that wasn't what she wanted. We went steady for a few years, and things were good for the most part—like I said, she was so invigorating to be around. But in the end, she got bored. Bored with the routine, bored with this little town, bored with me. And I think she got caught up in the times, too. The late fifties, early sixties—they were exciting times—you remember. She packed up and moved to California, and that was the last I ever heard from her."

"That's a shame."

"Well, it was for the best. For both of us."

Duke flipped over in Marty's lap in order to have his belly rubbed.

"Was there anyone else?"

Thierry nodded and thought for a moment. "There was Priscilla, too. And we were actually engaged for three months before it ended."

"Who broke it off?"

"I did, actually," Thierry answered with a note of remorse in his voice. "Broke the poor girl's heart, too."

"Why didn't you go through with it?"

"She was a wonderful girl—really wonderful. Innocent and faithful and beautiful—really beautiful. She had everything a man could want. She was young and pure and brimming with optimism, perhaps even naivety," Thierry paused and sighed. "And I was broken."

"What do you mean—broken?"

"The things I had seen, the loss I had endured—I was a broken man. I was sober enough and honest enough to realize that there was a dark cloud hanging over me. Priscilla was made for sunny skies."

The two men sat in ponderous silence for a few minutes.

"Anyway, it worked out best for both of us. About nine months after I called the wedding off, she married a bank manager in Nashville. They were very happy together and had, I don't know, six, seven children. They live in a big house in Brentwood now. I've seen her a couple times though the years—just bumping in to her around town. She's always been very nice and very eager to show me how happy she is, and never in a malicious way. And I'm happy for her—she deserves it."

"Was that it?"

"Just about," Thierry replied. "I had a few more flings here and there, but I eventually got to the point, oh, I don't know, where I just felt like it was better for me to be alone."

"That makes me sad," Marty said slowly, eyes fixed mournfully on the cat in his lap.

"Why's that?"

"Because you're a good man, little brother, and you would have made a wonderful husband to someone and a wonderful father—and you deserved that."

Thierry nodded, and Hope flashed in his mind.

"Can I be frank with you, Marty?"

The older brother looked up and their eyes locked.

"I never was able to get over Hope."

A sudden coughing fit began, and Duke jumped instinctively off the old man and onto the floor, drawing the ire of Useless the dog. Thierry watched his older brother wipe spots of blood from his lips onto his handkerchief and stuff it self-consciously back into his pocket.

"Can I get you some tea, or something?" Thierry asked kindly.

"Which kind?" Marty answered with a chuckle.

"The hot kind."

"Sure, that would be great. A little bit of extra—"

"Honey—sure thing. I know how you like it by now," Thierry said with a smile, heading back into the house to boil the water.

When he returned with the mug, the first thing Marty did was pop a morphine capsule in his mouth.

"Pain?"

Marty nodded and took a gulp of the hot liquid. "Yeah, pretty bad."

"I'm sorry."

"It's not your fault."

The rain stopped, and a fresh breeze began to blow from the north.

"Got chilly quick, didn't it?" he asked, pulling his coat tightly around his shoulders.

Thierry was going to make a comment about how nice it felt, but realized that it might be taken wrong, giving his brother's illness.

"I have to tell you something about Hope," Marty said after a moment or two of quietness between them.

"Go ahead," Thierry said with a nervous gulp of saliva.

"I never quite got over her either—or at least the whole situation."

Marty looked up to see his younger brother's eyes intensely fixed on him.

"I can only imagine what kind of suffering you've dealt with because of her loss, but what I've had to bear through the years because of it hasn't been easy, either. You might have lost a fiancee, but you see, I lost a brother because of it—my own flesh and blood—and there was no amount of pleading or begging or proving that could have changed that. I feel like whatever pain you went through, whatever bad decisions you made or whatever unhappiness you felt, you blamed on me. So the fact that you didn't get married—Marty's fault. The fact that you never had the children you wanted—Marty's fault. The fact that you holed yourself up in the wilderness with hardly a penny to your name—Marty's fault. Have you ever thought about that? Have you ever thought about what kind of psychological burden that has been for me to bear?"

"A burden for you to bear?" Thierry asked incredulously.

"Yes, and a heavy burden at that."

Thierry shook his head in disbelief and his tongue ran along his scarred bottom lip.

"I'm just curious, though, to know what gives you the impression that I have hardly a penny to my name?"

"Are you kidding me? Look at that old, beat up truck you drive! And this old rickety house you live in!"

"This house is my home."

"And that's how I know you don't have any money! I mean, for god's sake, Thierry, you were a mechanic!"

"Do you have any idea how much the land you're comfortably squatting on is worth? Do you have any idea about that?"

"Come on, Thierry—" Marty dismissed the question with a wave of his hand.

"Do you want the conservative estimate or the top of the market price?"

"It's wilderness, Thierry—it's not Fifth Avenue—"

The younger one abruptly got up and went back in the house. Marty's eyes followed him nervously. A moment later, Thierry emerged with a stack of letters in his hand.

"Which one do you want to start with—Liggett Property Development, Hanson and Joseph Real Estate Brokers, Groves Investment Realty?"

"What are you talking about?" Marty asked dismissively.

Thierry flipped the letters over to his brother nonchalantly.

"Shit, Thierry," Marty blurted, leafing through the letters one by one. "Hanson and Joseph offered you two point three? How long ago was that?"

"Last week," Thierry answered coldly. "I haven't even typed my rejection letter yet."

"Well, shows you how much I'm out of touch with the real estate market in Tennessee."

"You're out of touch with a lot of things, Marty. And the fact of the matter is, Middle Tennessee is going to explode in the next ten or twenty years and this property will probably triple in value."

"I stand corrected, little brother."

"And let me tell you what else I've got going on, just so you don't worry that the two of us might be turned out onto the street any time soon on account of *my* financial state," Thierry continued with indignation. "Every last thing I own is paid for in full, land and house included. I've got the approximate value of fifty-four thousand dollars in gold bars sitting in a safe in the basement, snuggled up with roughly forty-five thousand dollars in cash. One million, four-hundred thousand dollars in highly diversified, growth stock mutual funds, five rental properties in this very town with a combined value of roughly four-hundred and ten thousand dollars, four oil wells outside of Odessa, Texas—all paid for, I'll remind you—and a house on the beach in Destin where I vacation a few weeks a year. Again, paid in full."

"Little brother," Marty stammered. "I have to say, I'm impressed."

"You damn well should be."

Marty just shrugged hands in defeat.

"And do you want to know how I got rich quick?"

"Sure."

"I got rich slow—real slow. I worked my ass off and I saved every penny I could. I bought everything in cash—I didn't borrow, I didn't gamble, I didn't blow it on women and wine and new cars and whatever else you can blow money on."

"Well, you did great—that's for sure."

"I did—and do you know what, on top of it?"

"What's that?"

"You're the only person who knows the full extent of it. I don't brag about it, I don't flaunt it, and I sure as hell make sure it isn't front page news."

Marty coughed and pulled at his coat sleeves, absorbing this last bit of venom directed at his formerly lavish and fully public lifestyle.

"So you can take whatever little self-pity party you're throwing," Thierry continued. "And shove it up your ass."

"Jesus, Thierry," Marty began apologetically. "You win, ok? You did great for yourself, and I'm very proud of you."

Thierry suddenly felt ashamed of himself, making such a thorough point of his collection of wealth at the expense of his destitute and dying brother. "Well, don't mention it," he finally said.

"So what are you going to do with all of it?" Marty asked.

"With all of what?"

"The money, the money? I mean, you can't take it with you to the great unknown. Aren't you going to at least enjoy it?"

"I am enjoying it, and I may enjoy a little more of it as time goes on," Thierry explained calmly. "But I want to see it grow and leave it intact so that some day, I can right some wrongs with it."

"I see," Marty replied. "A philanthropist."

"I guess you could call it that."

The two men sat and listened to the crickets and frogs and the droplets of water from the roof hitting the ground. Thierry sipped his coffee; Marty sipped his tea. After a long time, the older one said, "I am proud of you, T."

"Thanks," came the calm reply.

"Welp," Marty said, pushing himself out of his chair with some effort. "I'll be headed upstairs."

"Good night, Marty."

"Good night, Thierry. And thanks for letting me sleep indoors again tonight."

Thierry chuckled and squeezed his brother's hand as he passed.

"Let me know if you need anything, ok?"

"Sure will."

Due to the tandem of Marty's terrible coughing and his own terrible dreams, Thierry had trouble sleeping that night.

October 7, 1990

Mesmerized by the rhythmic pulse of the ceiling fan, Thierry thought he might not get out of bed that day. The last few weeks had been tough on him, physically, despite a renewed sense of relationship and purpose with his brother. Useless had even stopped growling at him. Marty's health, however, had deteriorated quickly, and he refused to see a doctor of any kind. Since arriving on Thierry's doorstep a month earlier, Marty had lost nearly thirty pounds. He maintained a decent appetite for a man in his condition, but began vomiting more and more after meals, which left him completely fatigued. He managed his pain with the pills he'd brought from New York.

When Thierry pressed him to see a doctor or go to the hospital, usually after a particularly bad vomiting spell, he would say, "If I'm going to die—and I am—I intend to die in peace. That's why I'm here and nowhere else." When he had the strength and the breath, he would usually continue along the lines of, "Who needs to be poked and prodded all day and night when there's no good it'll do you anyway. You got the time that you got and that's it. There's no use in trying to change that."

Thierry turned to the old, analog clock radio on the old, wood nightstand beside the bed: it was 7:14am. And he couldn't move.

He laid there for another twenty minutes or so, until he thought he heard some sort of commotion in the kitchen—like the banging of pots. He sat up and tried to listen more closely to make out the sounds. Putting on his jeans from the night before and holstering his handgun, while instinctively praying that the day would again pass without cause to use it, he moved cautiously into the hallway. He peeked into the guest room where his brother stayed to find it empty. He paced down the stairs and when he turned the corner into the kitchen, there was Marty, fumbling over some eggs and peppers and country sausage in a pan.

"What are you doing, Marty?"

"Making breakfast, why?" he answered without turning around.

"Are you feeling ok?"

"I'm feeling great! Better than I have since I got here, in fact!"

"Did you sleep ok? I didn't hear you cough that much."

"Slept great, in fact."

The pan sizzled as Marty cracked a few eggs in it.

"That makes one of us," Thierry said, rubbing his eyes and pouring a cup of coffee. "I am glad you're feeling so good, though."

"Yeah, I can't make heads or tails of it," Marty answered, busy flipping eggs. "Woke up this morning—and early, too—sprung out of bed like a man in his twenties! I even made coffee and sat on the porch to watch the sun come up with the animals!"

"And no pain?"

"Not so far, today!"

"That's wonderful."

"Say, since the weather is so nice and I've got a spring in my step, why don't we go do something today?"

"Like what?"

"I don't know, what is there to do around here?"

"We could take the boat out on the lake, if you'd like."

"What kind of boat?"

"Oh, it's not much more than a rowboat, unfortunately. Definitely not like the catamarans you're used to. For starters, there's no champagne."

"Fah," Marty barked with a wave of his hand. "I think I would love that."

After breakfast, the brothers dressed, packed the boat with fishing tackle, a thermos of coffee, and some extra blankets, and hitched it to the truck. Within twenty minutes, they were on the lake, a cool breeze wafting against their cheeks. They didn't catch but a couple small crappie, but Thierry thought he could see his brother taking it all in—the gentle rocking of the boat, the trees and the birds, the sunshine. He thought that Marty looked utterly refreshed by it all.

"You know, this country living isn't so bad, T."

"I'm glad you can finally appreciate it."

"All those years, cooped up in apartments and lofts—the honking horns, the angry people, all the pressure, and all the wives—I'm starting to see that maybe I was so afraid of being poor, so afraid of being simple, that I never enjoyed the money while I had it."

Thierry just listened calmly.

"Thierry," Marty said after a moments pause. "Do you think I'm a good person?"

He hesitated, not for lack of answer but for lack of vocabulary.

"Yes, I do," the young one finally answered. "I think you had your priorities mixed up for a long time, but I know you. I know you've got a good heart and that you didn't have an easy life, an easy time growing up, and that sometimes doesn't help."

Marty thought for a minute. "You know, I have a really strange memory that's been popping up in my mind the last few months—and I can't shake it. I don't exactly know if it actually happened, either. Maybe it did, maybe I just saw it in a movie or something."

"Tell me about it."

"I feel like I was very young," Marty began with a wrinkle of his nose. "I couldn't have been more than two or three, maybe, but you were there, too, in diapers, I remember. And I remember sitting with you on the floor, on a nice rug—oriental pattern or something like that—God I, don't even know where this took place—and I was making some kind of funny face, and you were squealing with laughter, and I kept hugging you and hugging you, and you had this little wisp of hair that kept sticking out from the side of your head, and I kept tucking it behind your ear with my two little fingers. God, I loved you."

Thierry did his best not to tear up, but it was no use. Marty continued, staring off into the distance, as if the tree line was a portal into the past.

"Then I remember being suddenly alarmed by shouting, and I remember you looked scared. And at that moment I would have done anything in the world to ease your fear. But the shouting got louder and louder, and then there was a crashing sound and, oh, I don't know… I remember a man yelling—a big man—and hitting mama, he hit her so hard. I can only guess, but I believe that this man was our father. I remember thinking that I could somehow make it stop, mostly because you looked so scared. I remember being out in the hallway and there was blood, a lot of blood, and—and I don't really remember anything after that."

Thierry sniffled and wiped his eyes with his sleeve.

"I wasn't scared, little brother. I don't know why, but I wasn't scared."

A much bigger boat passed them and its occupants waved. The brothers waved back.

"Marty," Thierry said, once they were alone again.

"Yeah."

"Are you scared now?"

Marty's eyes told Thierry everything he needed to know.

"Don't be."

Marty nodded stoically.

"Are you hungry?" Thierry asked.

"Yeah."

Thierry fired up the engine and they headed back towards the cove where they'd launched the boat.

"Any place I can get a good pastrami sandwich?" Marty asked.

"This is Tennessee," answered his brother with a laugh. "But I do know a place that makes a great patty melt."

"Sounds good."

When they arrived at the boat ramp, Thierry was surprised to see Nate Hendricks, the young man infatuated with Nicole Burns, sitting on the back of the old pickup truck. After being introduced to Marty, Nate helped Thierry trailer the boat.

"What brings you out to these parts?" Thierry asked.

"I was walking—again, and I saw your truck parked here and figured I'd wait for you," Nate answered nervously.

"Well, what can I do for you?"

"I need to ask your advice on something."

"Shoot, Nate."

"Well," he hesitated. "I think I might be… in a little bit of trouble."

"What kind of trouble?"

He squinted and look out on the lake. "Legal trouble."

Thierry's eyebrows popped up in surprise. "Nate, what happened?"

"I was at a party last night after the football game, and I heard Billy Alderman and Josh Pace talking about Nicole—well, Nicole and Kevin. They were saying all sorts of nasty things and I started getting upset. They said that she did this to Kevin's this and this he did that to her that and… I don't know, I just lost my mind."

"So what did you do?"

"I drove to Kevin's house, but he wasn't there. So I waited for him to come home. It was three hours I just sat outside his house in the dark, just stewing and brewing and gettin' madder and madder. I knew those things weren't true. I know that Nicole ain't that kind of girl. So I just wanted to find out if it was him that started them rumors or if it was his stupid jock friends."

"I see," Thierry said slowly.

"He finally came home about two and I came up to him as he was getting out of his car. There was another girl with him, too. She was straightening her shirt and her bra like they'd been moved around—you know what I mean?"

Thierry nodded.

"So I straight up asked him—'Did you and Nicole Burns sleep together?' And he kind of laughed and said, 'Why—are you jealous?' And I said, 'No, I just need to know if it's true or if it's some of your bullshit.' And he said he didn't think it would matter to me because I was a queer—which I'm not. And then he just started runnin' his mouth about the way she looked without her clothes off and everything and I just snapped."

"You hit him?"

Nate just lifted his right hand. It was twice the size of his left and his knuckles were red as crimson.

"Damn, son," Thierry answered. "You really did."

"The first time, he acted like he didn't even feel it. He just kind of smiled at me. But the second time—"

"He felt it?"

"I think I felt it more than him. I could feel like, bones crushing and stuff. It was horrible. That blonde girl he had with him started screaming, and he just crumpled like dead weight, and all I knew to do was get in my truck and hoof it. So I parked over by the state park and just been walking ever since. I was actually thinking about heading to your house. For all I know, I killed the man, Mr. Terry."

"I have to say, it doesn't sound good, Nate."

"What do I do?"

"Why don't you hop in with us, and I'll take you back to my place," Thierry said calmly. "I'll phone the judge and see if he can meet me and my brother for lunch and we'll see what he says. I get the feeling you're going to have to turn yourself in, son."

Nate nodded knowingly.

"Is your hand ok?"

"Yeah, it's not broke or nothin'."

Thierry smiled. "I nearly broke my hand real bad once."

"Did the guy live?"

"Oh yeah, he lived," Thierry laughed and pointed. "He's sitting in the truck."

The young man's eyes bulged nearly out of their sockets.

"Don't worry, I didn't break it on his face—I was stupid enough to break it on his front door." Nate smiled nervously as Thierry put his arm around him.

They parked the boat in Thierry's garage and phoned the judge. Nate kept a bag of ice on his knuckles and his left hand on the top of the dog's head. He watched the Dallas Cowboys win a close one over the Tampa Bay Buccaneers while the brothers left for lunch.

The judge was already seated with a sweet tea when Thierry and Marty entered Warren's Restaurant. There were a few other church crowders in, but no sight of Nicole. Warren's nephew Caleb was taking orders. The two brothers sat down and the elder was introduced to the judge.

"Now, let's get down to business," the judge said sternly. "Do you know where the boy's at?"

"I do," Thierry answered.

"You *gawn* turn him over, right?"

"As soon as we talk, judge. I won't be accused of harboring a fugitive from the law."

"Ok, glad we've got that out of the way," the Georgian remarked, sitting back in his chair more comfortably.

"Have you heard anything on Kevin's condition?" Thierry asked.

The judge shrugged. "He's hurt pretty bad, I'm not *gawn* lie. He's over at University Hospital—broken orbital bones, jaw, you name it. He'll live, and he'll recover, but he'll be drinking his meals through a straw for the foreseeable future."

"I'm very sorry to hear that—and I'm positive Nate will be, too."

"Sure enough."

"Will he be in considerable trouble?"

"That's not my call, Terry, and you know that."

"Well, of course," Thierry answered. "I'm asking more for your legal assessment of the situation."

"There's good news and bad news," replied the judge. "The bad news is that Kevin's *deddy* wants to press charges to the hilt and beyond."

"And the good news?"

"The good news is that when the sheriff's deputies arrived on the scene, they noticed a peculiar smell emanating from the young victim's car. Turns out old Kevin had enough marijuana in the trunk to get a grizzly bear higher'n Cheech and Chong."

"How would that be good news to Nate?"

"Look," the judge began with a wave of his hand. "All I'm sayin' is that you know Sheriff O'Hara as well as anybody in this county, and I'm sure if you took the boy down there to get processed and interviewed and all that, and if you personally vouched for him that he wouldn't ever get into anything like this again, they might just seize Kevin's pot and let bygones be bygones. It might just go that way, is a I'm saying."

"I think that would be a result we could all hope for."

"Now that's not to say that Kevin's *deddy*, that ole redneck *son'v'a'bitch* don't try to take him to civil court, but he'd be dumb enough to settle for a couple hundred bucks."

"Well, I suppose that's good news, too," Thierry answered.

"Take the boy down there, and tell O'Hara we had lunch," the judge said reassuringly.

"Thank you, judge."

"Nate's a good kid," the judge said with a shrug. "And from what I heard, the whole thing was over him stickin' up for little Nicole."

"I heard that, too," Thierry answered.

"So, you must be the famous stock broker from New York," the judge said gregariously, turning his attention toward Marty.

The three men sat in conversation and ate for about an hour before the brothers returned home. Nate hadn't hardly moved an inch since they left. The young man agreed to go down to the sheriff's office with Thierry, but was visibly nervous. Thierry reminded him that although he may have acted out of good intentions, his actions were irresponsible, and that real men took responsibility for their actions.

At the police station, Nate was handcuffed, mirandized, and processed. He was embarrassed and jittery, but compliant and resolute. Thierry noticed that Marty was jittery as well and thought his brother might be feeling worse than he had that morning, but in truth, the police station—the smell, the hazy lights, the long, cold corridors—were bringing back a flood of memories he had tried for years to repress. The young man was placed in a holding cell and the two older men were escorted with much courtesy to a small waiting room that smelled of burnt tobacco and old coffee. After about thirty minutes, Sheriff O'Hara sauntered through the thick oak door and waved the two men back towards his office.

"Can I get you two coffee or anything?" he asked as he motioned them to sit in two maroon upholstered chairs in front of his desk.

"No, thank you, sir," Thierry answered.

"Mr. Terry, how well do you know the boy?"

"Fairly well—we've shared some deep conversations in the past."

"He a good kid?"

"Yessir, I believe he is."

"His daddy's good people," O'Hara said calmly.

"Yessir, he is."

The sheriff nodded his head.

"By the way, the judge wanted me to tell you that we spoke about this early this afternoon. He was the one who suggested I come with the boy."

"Figured that," O'Hara answered. "Did he tell you the worst part about it all?"

"I'm not sure," Thierry replied cautiously.

"That Kevin kid—mister drugs, mister football player, mister tough guy?—shit his pants at the scene. The son of a bitch shit his pants like a toddler."

"I can't say I like to hear that," Thierry said.

The sheriff spit tobacco into a cup. "Welp, with the amount of narcotics we found in that boy's car, and seein' as how our boy Nate seems truly remorseful, I don't really see any problem in letting this one be a lesson learned to all parties involved, what do you think?"

"They're a couple of foolhardy kids, is what I think."

"You're about right," O'Hara answered. "Good to see you again, Mr. Terry, and nice to meet you, Marty."

"Thank you, sir. And good to see you again, too."

The two brothers got up and headed toward the door before they were stopped by the sheriff's deep voice. "One more thing, Terry—you happen to talk to Nate's daddy, you let him know I'm gonna need some work done on my truck here in a few weeks. I'm gonna need a good price."

"Sure thing," Thierry answered with a meek smile.

Once they were back in the waiting room, Marty said, "I simply can't believe it."

"What's that?"

"It's like the wild west down here—cuttin' deals with the sheriff to get sonny out of jail time and all. That would never happen up north!"

"You don't think so?" Thierry answered.

"Hell, no!"

"I think that's rather naive, don't you?"

Marty suddenly turned red and silent, and it seemed to Thierry that his head tried to disappear between his shoulders as if he had a turtle shell to hide in.

"You know that deals get cut all the time. You know that damned well. It's just usually not for a couple people with a combined net worth under a thousand dollars or rich lawyer friends, is it?"

The two sat in silence, save for the ticking of the caged clock on the wall, until the oak door swung open again, and Nate emerged. The young man practically flew into Thierry arms.

"Thank you, thank you, Mr. Terry," he repeated profusely.

"It's ok, Nate—I'm glad you're free."

They drove Nate back to his truck, and he headed home from there. He'd had enough sense to call his parents from Thierry's earlier in the day so that they wouldn't worry about him. When he arrived home, they were stern, but thankful that he'd been released. The next day, they did send him up to the University Hospital to apologize to Kevin. Nate was not allowed into his room.

It was nearly seven o'clock when the brothers Laroque pulled down the long driveway leading to the old house. When they passed through the clearing in the woods, Thierry immediately noticed Nicole's car parked next to his garage. She was sitting on the front steps of the house, holding Duke in her lap.

"Hey there," he shouted after parking and exiting his truck. "What are you doing here?"

She waited for the distance between them to close before she let him see that she was emotionally distraught.

"What's the matter, sweetie?" he asked tenderly. He tossed his brother the house keys and Marty let himself in—and Useless bounding out.

"Oh, Mr. Terry," she nearly squealed, pushing herself up from the step and into his arms. The force of her hug nearly knocked him off his feet. She started sobbing and blurted, "What's gonna to happen to Nate?"

"Nothing, sweetheart," Thierry answered kindly, holding her at arms length.

"Nothing?"

"Not a thing. I just left the sheriff's office and so did Nate."

"But how can you say that—you don't know Kevin, he would never let him get away with embarrassing him like that."

"I don't think he has a choice in the matter, dear."

"Oh, thank god," she exhaled, brushing her auburn hair back from her eyes.

"Have you been to see your boyfriend?" Thierry asked.

"Kevin?" she replied, shaking her head.

"Oh, no?" Thierry asked in surprise.

"I broke up with him—or maybe he broke up with me."

"How did that come about?"

"Well," she hesitated. "He wasn't a gentleman, let's just say that."

"Tell me more," he said, waving her towards the porch. "Have a seat. Can I get you anything—coffee or a coke or something?"

"I'd love a coke," she answered, then said with a giggle, "Funny—you've never waited on me before."

"I just hope you're a good tipper," he chuckled, letting himself, and his dog, into the house. A couple minutes later the man emerged with a tall glass for her and a warm mug for himself. He sat in a rocker beside her.

"So Kevin wasn't all that he was cracked up to be?"

"I dunno," she said, sipping her drink. "I mean, I've never dated the *quarterback* before—I've practically never dated anybody before—so that part of it felt good—being on his arm after games and having all the attention and excitement around him. I felt, I dunno, important."

"I can understand that."

"But, I guess along with all of that there were certain… expectations, if you catch my drift. Kevin is used to getting what he wants from girls, and as much as I might have liked the attention, I've never done that kind of stuff. It's not that I'm a prude or anything, but I'm just not ready to be that serious with somebody."

"That's good. You're still very young. You have plenty of time to be serious."

"Well, I was at a party with Kevin last weekend, and he was drinking and stuff and flirting with some of the cheerleaders and I got to the point where I was really uncomfortable and asked him to take me home. He seemed annoyed at first, but then agreed, and so we left. But then, he wasn't driving towards my house, and I started asking him what he was doing, and he just got this stupid smile on his face. He finally pulled in over by the state park and turned the lights off. He told me that if I'd kiss him he'd take me home, so I kissed him. And one kiss led into another and then we were—oh, I'm embarrassed telling you this."

She suddenly covered her face with her hand.

"You don't have to tell me anything."

"Well," she said, looking back up at him. "He started really pawing at me, and I started pushing his hands away, but he was really getting aggressive and was practically climbing on top of me. I started saying, 'stop, Kevin, stop,' but he just wouldn't listen. He told me that I should be a good girlfriend and let him have what he needed. I tried pushing him away, but he was so strong. He grabbed my wrists and squeezed them so hard, I thought they were gonna break. Then, out of nowhere, a pair of headlights turned into the park entrance and shined directly into the car. I pushed again and, I guess cause he was afraid it might be the police or something, he got off of me and back into his seat. The other car made a quick U-turn out of the lot, but I took the chance to get out as quick as I could and just started running towards the road. I heard Kevin's car start and heard him throw it into gear. I thought he was going to try to run me over for sure. I had never been so scared in my life. I was crying and running along the gravel and thinking that this was how I was going to die—and what a stupid way to go—what would my daddy think of me? What would you think of me?"

Thierry looked at her with understanding eyes.

"As you can see, he didn't run me over. He just sped past me and yelled, 'bitch,' out the window. He left me all alone, in the dark. I got out on the main road and just started walking back toward town. After about a mile or so, I came to that general store with the old tractor parked out front, and got into the payphone booth. I was going to call my daddy, but I was afraid to tell him what happened. I thought about calling you, but I didn't want to bother you because of everything you have going on, well, with your brother and all."

"You could have called me," Thierry answered, assuringly. "You can call me any time you ever need anything."

"I know, I know," she replied. "But it was the strangest thing—the only person in the world I wanted to call at that moment was Nate."

"And did he come get you?"

"Yes," she said, smiling girlishly. "He came and opened the door for me and didn't ask me a single question. He just drove me home. He didn't even say anything when I thanked him. He just looked me in the eyes and nodded."

"Interesting," Thierry remarked. "He didn't mention a word to me about your little late night adventure last week."

"He's not really a talker, is he? He is more a man of action than anything else."

Thierry thought about himself as a young man.

"All last week, I couldn't get him out of my mind—and I'd never really thought about Nate like that before. But all of the sudden, I realized that ever since I've known him, he's always been there for me when I needed him, and never asked a single thing in return."

"I think he really cares about you—as a friend, I mean," Thierry added.

"I feel a little weird saying this, but… I think he loves me."

"You might be on to something, there."

She smiled in satisfaction, her brown eyes welling with life. "You want to hear the craziest thing that I'm just starting to realize?"

"What's that?"

"I think I love him, too."

Thierry grinned and sipped his coffee.

The two sat and talked on the porch until the sun went down, then embraced warmly before Nicole left. Thierry sat with Duke in his lap for a while longer before going back inside. He was startled to find Marty sitting, hunched over, at the kitchen table, back to the door.

"Hey," he called. "Is everything ok?"

Marty's shoulders just rose and fell for a moment, and then he shook his head.

"I'm not feeling very well, T.," he said slowly, lifting his head out of his hands.

Thierry was surprised to see his brother's eyes sunken and tear-stained. Marty was pale and gaunt—he looked like he had aged a decade in the span of just a couple hours.

"Pain?" Thierry asked. "Did you take something?"

Marty nodded. "Would you help me get up the stairs to bed?"

"Sure, sure thing."

The older one put his arm around his younger brother's shoulders, but could barely find the strength to stand. The two men labored up the stairs and into the spare bedroom, where Thierry undressed Marty, helped him into pajamas, and then into bed.

"Can I get you anything?"

"No, I don't think so," Marty said slowly. His breath was wet and labored.

"Ok, well, just call if you need me," Thierry said as he turned toward the door.

"Thierry?" Marty said.

"Yeah?" his brother said, turning on his heels.

"I don't deserve this—to have you taking care of me like you do."

Thierry shrugged and hesitated. "It's not a question of deserved or undeserved, Marty—"

"I just meant to say… thank you. That's all."

"Don't mention it."

Thierry grabbed a bottle of Scoth from the cabinet in his study and sat at the kitchen table sipping it. He let the liquid fill his empty stomach—warm and tingly. Between his brother's sickness, the incident with Nate, and his conversation with Nicole, he felt like he couldn't settle his racing mind on any one thought in particular. Marty coughed loudly a couple times and Thierry went upstairs to see him sleeping soundly. As the night went on he continued to drink, but was careful not to get drunk. After a few glasses thoughts and memories from the years of his life—seemingly disconnected and foggy—sped through his mind and then disappeared like smoke. He checked his watch—it was 1:34. He swigged the last of his Scotch, checked the locks on the doors and headed up the stairs to bed.

October 8, 1990

At the top of the stairs, he peeked into Marty's room and thought he saw movement.

"Marty?" he whispered.

"Yes," came the hollow reply.

"You ok?"

There was silence for a long moment before a small voice in the dark said, "Can you pull up a chair?"

"Sure," Thierry said. There was a writing desk in the room, so Thierry moved the chair next to the bed. "What's up, Marty?"

"I heard," the older one began slowly. "I heard what you were talking to that girl about through the screen."

"Did you?"

"Yes, I did."

"What about it?"

"Life hangs on a thread, doesn't it? Have you ever felt powerful, Thierry?"

"Powerful? How do you mean?"

"*Powerful*—like you could turn the earth on its axis, like you could change the course of history with a snap of your fingers."

"I suppose," Thierry replied to the darkness. "Perhaps when I was younger—I think many young people feel that way, like they can't die, like—"

"That's invincibility," Marty interrupted with a slight gasp. "That's different from power."

"Then, I guess I don't know, brother."

"Most people don't. Most people feel small and insignificant and alone. But what they don't realize is that… they have a tool so simple, so pure, that can forever alter the course of their lives and the lives of countless others at any moment."

"And what's that?"

"Choice."

Marty's breathing was shallow, and Thierry was becoming concerned.

"Can I call the doctor?"

"No, no," Marty answered fervently. "We need to talk."

"Ok."

"Have you been drinking?"

"Yes."

"Good," Marty said, taking a moment to catch his breath.

"The night I took Hope to the Christmas party at Aulgur's house… I can't tell you how miserable I had been up to that night. I had Vivian, but I knew what she was—nothing more than a call girl. There was something deep in me that was very lonely, you see, very troubled and afraid. I had been speaking with Hope and we had seen each other on more than one occasion—on friendly terms, mind you. But that night, that night at Christmas… she made me so happy. I caught a glimpse of what my life could be like—normal, settled… happy. I caught a glimpse of what life was supposed to be like, with her on my arm."

Thierry forced himself to sit silent. After pining for answers all these years, he suddenly found that he wanted to run out of the room and down the stairs and out the door and into his truck and onto the interstate heading west.

She was perfect, Thierry—that night, she was perfect. Everyone was happy, everyone was jolly and the party just went on and on—as if we had all forgotten, or wanted to forget, that there was a fucking war going on—that our fathers and sons and brothers were dying and missing and suffering. But it was Christmas, and to us, on that night, all seemed right with the world. My friends loved her, she was charming and warm and beautiful. Several of them remarked that we looked like a wonderful couple. She didn't even correct them—she just let me have my moment of glory.

When we finally left, it was late and we'd had a lot to drink—both of us. It was so cold and the car was taking forever to warm up. I could hear her teeth chattering, so I asked her if she wanted me to put my arm around her. She hesitated for a minute and then scooted across the old bench seat and got right next to me. I can't tell you I was thinking about right or wrong or even you—all I can say is that it felt right at that moment… she felt right. We were over by the cliffs and she saw the lights of some ships out in the sound. She practically forced me to pull over to see the ships. The radio was on, and she said she wanted to dance—she was drunk, or so I thought. We got out and left the radio on, and she motioned to me like she wanted to dance, so I did. Both of us had had enough that we were stepping on each other's toes and a couple times, I almost lost my balance altogether. The stars were out, and the moon was bright, and the lights in the distance were… they were just beautiful.

After a while, we got tired of dancing, and she said she didn't want to leave yet, that she wanted to enjoy the night as long as possible. She said it felt good to be dressed up and to rub shoulders with rich and important people. She said she felt important, and she had hardly ever felt that way.

I got a blanket out of the trunk and the two of us sat, just steps from the cliff, wrapped in it for a long time. In those moments, I convinced myself that I was in love with her. I thought about how I would call things off with Viv, how I would explain things to you, how she and I would make a happy family together. She stared out at the expanse before us; I stared at her. She was a goddess—beautiful, yes—but more than that. She was other worldly. Holding her in my arms felt like holding god herself, holding life and existence in its primal form in my arms. I knew that I would never be able to give that up. I leaned in to kiss her and our lips touched. For a moment, it felt like she would kiss back, but then she stiffened up.

"What's wrong?" I asked.

"Marty, I'm sorry," she said. "I am so sorry if I gave you the wrong impression."

I'm thinking to myself, "Wrong impression, my ass." I wasn't a rookie—you know. I'd been around the block before, and this was how it was supposed to go. Only, this time was supposed to be the real thing—that's how it felt.

"Don't you want to kiss me?" I asked.

"Oh, Marty, can't we just leave it at this?"

"How do you mean?"

"Marty, we can't—you know that."

"Why not?" I asked. "I think I love you," I just blurted out.

"I'm sorry, Marty. This has been a lovely night, but you and I both know—"

"Know what? That we're supposed to be happy—aren't we?"

"'But Marty, I'm your brother's girl—his fiancee.'

I was so dead set on having her—I didn't want to hear about why it was wrong.

"You wanted to kiss me back," I said.

"I did Marty, but only because I'm lonely and scared. And… I know I shouldn't say this, but you holding me, you kissing me—it reminded me of Thierry."

More than anything I didn't want to hear your name at that moment.

"Marty—I miss him. God, I miss him so much."

"How do you know you picked the right brother, huh?' I asked, just searching for a way to get to her. 'How do you know you're not supposed to be with me instead of him?"

"Marty!" she nearly shouted, pulling away from me. "Your brother is my one and only, and nothing will ever, ever change that."

"But why?" I shrieked. "Why does my kid brother get all the happiness, and I get nothing but heartache and loneliness. Why does he get you and I don't?"

"What about Vivian?"

"She's just a whore! She's nothing like you!"

She was shocked by what I'd said. "Again, I'm sorry if I gave you the wrong impression, but I'd like you to take me home now."

"'Wrong impression?' I turned on her. 'You were using me, weren't you? You were using me to feel close to my brother in some sick way.'

"That's terrible, Marty. But if you feel that way, I'm sorry."

"You're crazy, that's all there is to it. I'm giving you the chance to get out of the situation you're in—I'm going places, you know. All those important people you met at the party tonight, they're *my* friends, not my kid brother's. You could have it all—clothes, cars, whatever you want—you wouldn't have to worry about money ever again."

"Please take me home, Marty."

"You could have a first class life, but instead, you want my uneducated, unconnected brother who, chances are, won't even live through this damn war anyway."

That hurt her. And she got angry.

"You son of a bitch," she said with venom, standing up suddenly and moving back towards the car. "You're a son of a bitch, Marty."

"Get in the car," I said, picking up the blanket as I stood. She followed me to the back of car while I put it back.

"You selfish bastard," she nearly shouted. I had never seen her like that before—she was livid. "You don't have the character, the talent, or the brains in your whole body that your little brother has in his pinky finger."

"Shut up!" I shouted, trying to fold the blanket and stuff it in the trunk quickly.

"You're a liar, you're a cheater, and most of all, Marty," and she said this slowly: "You're unimpressive."

At just the moment, those words were searing a hole in me, the tips of my fingers glanced the lug wrench. I don't know what I thought would happen. I guess I just meant to scare her into shutting up. I grabbed the tire iron and spun and swung it wildly... But she'd move closer behind me than I thought she was... The whole left side of her face looked like it had melted—there was a huge chunk of her hair missing. Then... I can't even tell you how many times this has haunted my dreams—all this blood suddenly rushed to the surface and started pulsing out of her skin. It was thick like molasses... and black in the moonlight. It was black... She put her hand up to her face to touch it but didn't. Her hand was shaking. She kind of collapsed to one knee and looked up at me, that black blood oozing from her cheek and her jaw and her nose. I expected her eyes to be filled with hate or disgust or something like that—but they were simply pleading... for an explanation, for mercy—for what? I couldn't stand that look in her eyes, like she'd been right the whole time, and that I had just proved that I really was the person she said I was. So I swung again. There was this horrible popping sound and then she just crumpled into a ball on the ground. She started moaning and I suddenly realized what I had done. I saw my whole life going down the drain—I was supposed to become something, someone. I couldn't spend my life in prison, I couldn't waste away behind some metals bars and gray walls—I was destined for something far better than that. My mind raced, and I knew that I would have to make it look like an accident, so I picked her up—her face... oh, her face was horrible, there were little bones sticking out and—she was limp in my arms and I just carried her to the edge. Then I dropped her over and watched her fall. She bounced around on the rocks like a rag doll before she finally settled. I was sure she was dead. I saw some lights come on in a house a ways down and just panicked—was there a witness? So I just threw the tire wrench over and tried to get rid of all the tire irons, too—thinking I could claim I bought the car without any—and my coat with her blood on it, and drove back to Aulgur's house.

Thierry sat paralyzed, feeling the urge to scream and cry and run, but he was glued to his seat in shock.

"Thierry, I'm telling you this," Marty said after a long pause. "Because, for all these years, I couldn't live if you knew the kind of monster I was, but now, I couldn't die unless you did."

The younger brother felt sick. He felt like he would suffocate in that room or anywhere else.

"I would tell you that I'm sorry," Marty started after a brief coughing fit. "But it wouldn't matter, would it?"

Thierry watched his brother's barely perceptible face in the dark.

"You wouldn't forgive me, and there's no way in hell I'd expect you to. But I've done what I can to set it right on my account."

Suddenly finding himself outside, Thierry bent at the waist, clutching his hands over his ears. The woods sounded as they always did at night, but all Thierry could hear was pounding in his head. His feet were unsteady, and the moonlight was hazy through clouds. He stumbled and found himself on his backside, one elbow propping him up while his hands clutched his heaving chest. *What did a heart attack feel like?*

A light rain began to mist around him, and he forced himself up to his feet again, spitting phlegm into the grass as he climbed back onto the porch. As he plopped into the chair in which his brother had spent a wet night, he suddenly would have given anything to un-hear what he had grieved to hear for nearly fifty years. But those words, those terrible words, had been spoken, and there was no unspeaking them.

He gazed out numbly over all he owned, and for not the first time, thought that his life meant nothing at all.

Joy is an illusion; suffering is all there is.

After that moment, a rather large bird landed with effortless finesse on the hood of his pickup truck, not fifty feet from him. The winged creature was as elegant as it was menacing, and Thierry was caught between admiration and dread. He had seen plenty of hawks and vultures around his land, but this bird was so large that it was out of place—otherworldly. It sat there until out of the grass Duke launched himself onto the hood. With one powerful burst, the bird was airborne and gone. It was such a foolish attempt on the cat's part that it couldn't have been taken seriously—the bird was at least ten times his size. Duke, slightly dejected after having lost his impossible prey, scurried back under the tree line and out of the rain.

And that was it. Like a firework illuminates the night sky, his perspective fell into place. In so many ways throughout his life, he had beat the odds. He had conquered the loss of his mother, he had conquered poverty, he had conquered Europe, for god's sake, and he knew now that he must do the impossible—he must conquer the suffering of his own heart.

The sun did not rise that morning as much as the night dissolved into day. It was still dark beneath the heavy grey clouds, and Thierry was still seated on the front porch. He watched his cat race through the falling drops of water toward the back of the house. A minute or two later, he heard a scratch on the storm door and peered in to see his dog waiting to be let out. He was exhausted physically, but couldn't help feeling that he had experienced his very own Bodhi Awakening. He felt like he must have been glowing and couldn't help but smile at the beautiful mess that was the life of Thierry Laroque.

He let Useless out and then walked upstairs to Marty's room. He stood in the doorway for a moment, observing. His brother had faded even more drastically during the night, and Thierry saw several empty bottles of pills splayed about—on the floor, on the bed, on the night table. Marty's eyes opened slowly and laboriously, his breathing was wet and shallow. Thierry walked slowly and sat in the chair next to his brother. Marty's eyes followed him. Thierry placed his hand on his brother's forehead—he was burning hot. He took his brother's hand and looked intently into his weary eyes.

"Marty," Thierry began slowly, with cosmic confidence. "I want you to know, I do forgive you."

The dying one's face twitched, and he squeezed his brother's hand with all of the frail strength he could muster.

"Did you hear me, Marty? With all of my heart—I forgive you."

The older brother's eyes closed, and he began to shake. Thierry squeezed his hand tightly and tears began to stream from between Marty's eyelids. He began to rock and sob and cough. Thierry got down on his knees and embraced his brother.

After a few moments, Marty's emotions were overtaken by his physical sickness again, and he began to cough blood. Thierry cared for his brother in silence the best he could—with cool washcloths on his fiery head and warm blankets on his shivering frame.

He thought that he would call an ambulance—but what purpose would that serve? He sat with Marty, holding his hand, kissing his forehead from time to time. The coughing stopped, and the breathing grew heavier and heavier as the morning went on. Marty seemed comfortable, and Thierry knew that nothing else could be done. He felt a warmth and a freedom he wasn't sure he'd ever felt before, and he hoped in his heart that his brother felt the same way.

TEN

As for you, Morrel, there is neither happiness nor misery in this world; there is only the comparison of one state to another, that's all. Only a man who has experienced the most extreme misfortune is able to feel the most extreme happiness. He must have known what it is to want to die, Maximillien, to know how good it is to live.

EDMOND DANTES, IN *THE COUNT OF MONTE CRISTO*

December 22, 1990

He flipped his collar over his neck and tucked his scarf into his jacket and zipped it. The dusting of snow made him think of his childhood and even Bastogne. Without even thinking about it, he ran his tongue over the scar on his lip. Years of mild southern winters had thinned his blood. He shivered while he bobbed and weaved through the mass of humanity that moved as a singular organism with a singular mind—a flock of birds dashing to and fro in a boundless dance of freedom and connectedness.

Glancing down at his watch, he realized he still had some time. He popped into a bustling coffee shop and ordered an extra cup to sleeve the scalding liquid gold against his skin. Outside again, he checked the cross streets and headed south. Two blocks down, the human traffic seemed to thin a bit as people flocked into the warmth and gaiety of department stores and electronics stores and toy stores with mechanized Santa's and shiny new compact disc players and Teenage Mutant Ninja Turtles in scenes of fluffy cotton snow. He noticed a man sitting at the edge of an alley, his sooty face and ragged coat standing out in the din of holiday cheer.

"Man, I'd kill for some coffee right about now," the man said.

"Would you really?" Thierry asked sternly.

"No, man—it's just an expression—"

"I know that," the old man answered with a hearty laugh. "I hope you take it black."

"I take it any way it comes."

With that, Thierry unsleeved his second cup, poured half his coffee into it, and handed it to the man.

"Careful, it's hot."

"Thank you, sir," the man said, taking a moment to absorb the smell. "You're a saint."

"You either give me too much credit or yourself not enough."

"I don't know about that," the man replied. "But Merry Christmas to you."

"Merry Christmas to you, too."

Minutes later, he was on a train bound for Schaumburg. In the paper, he noticed the next day was a Blackhawks home game and he thought about getting tickets if he was still in town. Surely he would be. Over the years, he had developed an affinity for ice hockey, having watched many games during the Eastern Hockey League's tenure with the Nashville Dixie Flyers, which ended in 1971. His mind began to jog, and he thought that the last time he'd seen a hockey game must have in St. Louis and might have been against those very same Blackhawks. His mind then drifted toward the spring and how he could make another trip up to see the Yankees play the White Sox or even the Brewers. The train shook and lurched from side to side in a bend, and out of nowhere, he thought of the girls on the train when he was young. He looked down at his wrinkled hands and then closed his eyes. He slowly breathed in their suffering as well as his own, and breathed out forgiveness and renewal into the world. Moments later he had arrived at his stop. He thought it was remarkable that he wasn't in the least bit nervous, though he certainly should have been.

White, fluffy flakes cascaded in slow motion as he stepped onto the platform. He zipped his coat up again and looked to the left and the right. He checked his watch and walked to the end of the concrete and onto the sidewalk toward the parking lot. Several cars were parked there and running in the dusky light. He scanned the rows until his eyes landed on a red Cadillac Coupe de Ville, motor running and lights on. He smiled. The driver's door opened, and Vivian emerged. He had forgotten how tall she was. She wasn't twenty-two anymore but didn't look anywhere near her current age either. She was as stunning to him as she'd ever been. He quickly approached the vehicle, but stopped short of her.

"Hi, Viv," he said calmly.

"Hi, Thierry," she answered breathlessly.

"You look great."

"So do you."

He chuckled, thinking of his old hands.

"Can I give you a hug?" he asked.

She just nodded.

They embraced and the world felt as it should be. She began to cry gently, then kissed him warmly on the cheek.

"It is so good to see you."

"Should we get out of the cold?"

"Yes, let's go. I hope you like Italian food."

"More than almost anything."

October 13, 1990

"So what happened between you, two?"

"I'm not sure which part you're talking about."

"The estrangement."

"Ah, I see. How much do you know?"

"Only that he said it was about a girl."

"It was."

"Wait, so—was this before Vivian was in the picture?"

"No, it was during."

"That doesn't make any sense, though. If dad was with her already—who was the other woman?"

"She was my fiancée."

"So… what—he tried to steal your fiancée? And then you didn't get married?"

"That's right."

"It was so bad that the first time I ever meet my own uncle, who seems, by the way, to be such a normal human being, is when I'm twenty-six years old and at my father's funeral?"

"That's a very good question. It's a tragedy, in fact."

"Then how is it that suddenly the two of you are reunited and best pals moments before he dies?"

"Look, Michael. I received some advice years and years ago from a trusted friend, someone saved my life once, that I chose to ignore. I was too proud and too hurt to allow your father—my brother—off the hook for the things he had done that had hurt me. I'll give you the truth without going through the more petty details—I lost my fiancée because of him. And I couldn't let that go for many, many years. I was so traumatized and focused on my own pain that I fed it. Every single day I fed it. I was able to move on with my life in so many ways, but when it came to my brother, the only thing that would suit me was to be angrier and angrier with him—and it affected the other parts of my life—like the fact that I never once married or had children. And what's at the end of this road?"

Michael stared at his uncle.

"Two old men who are both alone."

The nephew nodded quietly.

"It's a cycle, a violent cycle that chokes the very life out of you, Michael. You think that as long as you hold onto your hatred, you've got the upper hand. You feel like you're holding them accountable for how they hurt you, but what you're really doing is chaining yourself to the consequences. The only way to break the cycle—and I discovered this in my heart very recently—is to absorb the blow, and freely forgive."

"I don't think I can forgive, though. Not for what he did to my mom, not for what he did to me. I mean, he wasn't even a father to me."

"I understand how you feel."

"I just—for all the expensive Christmas gifts and trips he'd take me on with whatever girl he was with at the moment—he was always trying to impress me with all this… all this stuff. And I started to get the feeling that it was because he didn't think I would be impressed with him and the more I got older, the less I was. I mean… I can't think of anything—anything—good about him."

"I felt that way about him for a long time, myself."

"I don't want to hate him, though."

"You don't have to."

Michael looked up at Thierry's eyes from the very chair his father had slept in on the porch.

"How?"

"It helps to realize the common humanity in each person. No matter how bad a person appears—no matter how selfish or how hurtful—we must ask ourselves whether we are inherently good or inherently evil. If we're all evil, then I don't think it's possible. But, if the good in me can see the good in you—however far it might be buried under the weight of your own pain and suffering—then forgiveness is possible. You know, your father had a very hard life, a very hard childhood. And as hard as you might find it to believe, he had a gentle heart—an amazingly human heart—buried and packed away under all the other stuff. If you can imagine that he was looking for love and affirmation and reconciliation just like we all are, I think that's your starting place."

"It's hard to see it that way."

"I know it is. It takes a purposeful awakening to it. But if you are awake to it—the power and the freedom are awe inspiring. When you realize that you have the power to forgive any purpose, any deed, your life becomes your own for the first time. It's the most paradoxical thing I've ever experienced. What feels like strength is brokenness, and what feels like weakness is true freedom. It's not easy, but when you allow your claims on bitterness and revenge to die, you become the best that humanity has to offer."

"I don't think I understand."

"It's okay. It took me many, many years to understand something that was so simply put and right in front of my eyes. I would ask you, just don't close yourself off to the possibility."

"I won't."

"I'm glad to hear it, Michael."

May 4, 1992

"Baby, did you grab the mail on the way in?"

He answered with a guttural sound that clearly indicated the idea hadn't even crossed his mind.

"I'll run back out in a minute."

He kissed her on the mouth, then kissed the crying infant on the head, before he went to the kitchen sink and washed his greasy hands.

"Don't wash in the sink—you're gonna get the dishes all dirty."

"They're already dirty," he answered with a chuckle. "I'll wash them anyway after dinner."

He dried his hands with a rag and went back outside in the rain to collect the mail from the box across the street. The usual—circulars and junk and sales ads, all soaked through. He turned back to the tiny house, headed straight to the trash can by the driveway. As he flipped the mail into the bin piece by piece he came across a letter he hadn't seen previously. He shook it off and wiped his feet on the porch rug before going back inside.

"You pay the rent yet?"

"No, not yet."

"It's due."

"I know, but we just paid the pediatrician bill and we ain't got the money for rent."

"But it's due."

"Baby, I can't pay rent with money I don't got."

"What are we gonna do?"

"I'll go talk to Mr. Andrews tomorrow on lunch. I got a check coming Friday that'll cover it."

"Okay. I'm sorry—I just get nervous about that kind of stuff."

"Nikki, you know somebody in Illinois?"

"Illinois?"

"Yeah—Schaumburg?"

She shook her head. "Maybe it got delivered to the wrong house."

"It's got your name on it."

Nate handed her the damp envelope, and she handed him Nate, Jr.

"Baby, this is from Mr. Terry," she said.

"Mailed from Illinois?"

"That's really odd."

"How long's it been since you've seen him, anyway?"

"I'm not sure—probably since right before I had the baby."

"He's four months old. It's not like Terry to disappear for such a long time."

She shrugged and turned her back to him to read the letter. Nicole suddenly cupped her hand over her mouth and plopped down at the kitchen table.

"What is it, baby?"

"He's moved—to Illinois."

"What?"

"And he's giving us his place."

"Come again?"

"He's giving us his place—he says he don't care if we live there or sell it, but he wanted to set us up nice. He says it's paid in full, and all we gotta do is go down to see the judge and sign some papers… and it's ours."

"I always knew that old man was crazier'n'hell," Nate slurred in disbelief.

"He loves us," Nicole said, smile brimming from ear to ear.

"He loves you," Nate answered.

"Well, who wouldn't?"

"You're right about that."

She jumped out of her chair and practically knocked the two Nates over with a hug. The young couple danced around the galley kitchen on the rusty linoleum floor so hard that she had to remind him through her giddy laughter not to shake the baby.

July 12, 1992

There is almost nothing better than a fresh BLT on toast on a summer afternoon by the pool. He crunched through the layers—warm on the outside, cold on the inside—with much aplomb. He sipped an iced tea—unsweet, naturally—and gazed out over the water. Gracefully drifting by in an inflatable float—he had always marveled at how quickly her skin bronzed—she waved a dainty hand in his direction. He had learned that she was part Cherokee, and he thought this explained her ability to tan so well. It was funny, he thought, that her ancestry hadn't come up until so recently. Maybe it wasn't.

"What do you want to do tonight?" she asked.

"Are the Cubbies playing?"

"Atlanta but I think it's an afternoon game."

"Ok, well then I've got no plans."

"I think we should go downtown anyway."

"Sounds great."

"Maybe we could eat at Sal's? It's been a while since we've been there."

"That would be wonderful. I've missed proper Italian food for so long, you know."

"Yes, I know you have. I bet you'll start missing pulled pork sometime, too."

"Say, I've been thinking—would you like to go to Italy sometime?"

"That would be incredible! It's been years since I've been!"

"I've never been there."

"What part are you thinking about—Rome, Naples?"

"All of it."

"I'll call Maria first thing tomorrow morning!"

"Who is Maria?"

"Our travel agent."

"Oh. Well, yes, that'd be grand."

He took another hearty bite of his sandwich and relished the warm sun on his face as he chewed.

"Viv, would you mind another stop in Europe, since we'll be there already?"

"Of course I don't mind! Where do you want to go?"

"See if Maria can book us a flight to Munich."

"Munich?"

"Or maybe the rail would be easier, depending on where we're coming from."

"Why Munich? We can ski in the Italian alps."

"No, no—I don't want to go there when it's cold. But there is a little Bavarian town I'd like to revisit. I have some final respect to pay."

"You know somebody in Germany?"

"Knew—he saved my life, in fact. But he passed many years ago. I always thought that if I had the chance, I would visit his grave, bring some flowers or something."

"That sounds wonderful."

She gracefully climbed the pool steps, grabbed a towel, and leaned in to kiss Thierry. Useless was vexed by the droplets of water that fell on him as he sat under the man's chair. The dog, however, did not stir.

"Maybe while we're there, we can try to look up some of your family in France—wouldn't that be interesting?"

"Perhaps. I've never really thought about it."

"That would be amazing—think about it, you've got cousins and maybe even nieces and nephews you've never met—people who don't even know you're alive!"

"I'm not opposed to it, necessarily."

"But you don't seem excited about the idea."

"Maybe not," he said, taking her hand in his. "The way I see it, I've got all I could ever ask for right here."

FIN

ABOUT THE AUTHOR

Brandon Dragan grew up in northeastern New Jersey and attended Belmont University in Nashville, Tennessee.

He is currently a 2L Juris Doctor candidate at Belmont University College of Law.

Brandon enjoys road cycling, cigars, Irish whisky, and is an avid supporter of the Arsenal Football Club.

He and his wife Jami live in the Nashville area with their two daughters.

For more information, visit:

BrandonDragan.com

CPSIA information can be obtained
at www.ICGtesting.com
Printed in the USA
BVHW071241051120
592525BV00002B/42

9 781938 480713